BEAUTY IN THE BROKEN

A DIAMOND MAGNATE NOVEL

CHARMAINE PAULS

Published by Charmaine Pauls

Montpellier, 34090, France

www.charmainepauls.com

Published in France

Cover design by Simply Defined Art

(www.simplydefinedart.com)

ISBN: 978-2956103189 (eBook)

ISBN-13: 978-1095763919 (Print)

❀ Created with Vellum

CHAPTER 1

Johannesburg, South Africa

Damian

*H*arold Dalton shoots up from behind his oversized desk so fast he almost stumbles over the wheel of his equally oversized chair. "What do you want?"

The coward is afraid. He should be. After all, he framed me and stole my diamond mine. He's the reason I spent six innocent years in jail.

His fat chin quivers. He doesn't take his eyes off me as I cross the floor. Taking my time to inspect the room, I make him sweat it out. The home office hasn't changed, except for three more deer heads staring miserably from the wall.

"What do you want?" he repeats when I reach his desk.

"Ah. Whatever could I want?"

His fingers tremble as he splays them out on the desktop. The cocksucker is so arrogant he either forgot I got out yesterday or believed I left prison a defeated man. Any less of a self-assuming bastard would've put a dozen guards in front of his door today. His mistake.

A liver-spotted hand glides toward the drawer where he no doubt keeps a gun, but I'm faster and stronger. My grip on his wrist makes him whimper. I can almost smell the fear in the sweat that stains the armpits of his shirt. I'm not the twenty-two-year-old man who walked through this door in a threadbare shirt. I'm a man in an eighty-thousand-rand suit, a man with a vendetta.

Six years is a long time, long enough to soak in the juices of your vengeance until your heart is cooked in all that bitter acid. Six years of cruelty and torture make beasts out of men. Six years in the company of the hardest criminals and most notorious mobsters also make the right connections and a fortune.

"What do you want, Damian Hart?"

This time, there's acceptance in the question, the kind only people with money can muster. Bribe money.

Letting go of his wrist, I take two pieces of paper from my inside jacket pocket and slide them over the desk. He unfolds the first, the proof of what he's stolen, and pales as he reads. The second is an affidavit the corrupt judge signed right after I'd cut off his finger.

The papers flutter in his hands. "Name your price. Most of my money is tied up in investments, but I have property. My house in Camps Bay is worth ninety million. I can sign over the deed in less than twenty-four hours."

Laughable. "Ninety million isn't going to cut it. I'd say one thousand four hundred and fifty-five days and a diamond mine worth billions deserve a little more, don't you think?"

"The mine belongs to investors. Only thirty percent is mine, and I can't simply give it away. The board has to vote on a change of ownership."

As if I wouldn't know. "I'm not after your small change, Dalton. I want your biggest asset."

The pastry layers of his face crease into a frown.

Turning the gilded photo frame strategically facing the visitor's chair around, I push it slowly toward him.

His eyes widen as comprehension sets in. Not even the threat of my presence is enough to prevent the anger from erupting on his features.

"You must be bloody kidding me," he hisses, crumpling the incriminating pieces of evidence in his fists.

Angelina Dalton-Clarke.

Daughter of Harold Dalton. Widow of Jack Clarke. She inherited her late husband's fortune. Worth billions, she's the wealthiest widow in the country, and also the craziest. Her suicidal and self-harming tendencies had Clarke declare her incompetent and mentally unstable before he put a gun to his head and blew his brains out. Lina Dalton-Clarke isn't allowed to touch a cent of her riches. Her father manages her finances. He has all the signing power. As her husband, that *chore* will fall to me.

"She's mentally ill," Dalton splutters.

"I read the reports." It wasn't difficult for a cellmate to hack into the medical files.

Dalton looks as if he's about to have a heart attack. I wait until his face is purple, giving him time to live the beginning of his end, before I continue with my instructions.

"Send her to the library. I'd like to see my *asset* in person. Oh, and not a word about our discussion. I'd like to break the happy news to her myself."

He stands frozen, staring at me with whatever sentiment is festering in his rotten chest. It's only when I'm on the other side of the room that he jumps back to life, coming around the desk.

I hold up a hand. "I'll show myself to the library." Mockingly, I add, "I know the way."

The helpless indignation on his face as I shut the door fills me with more joy than I've experienced in all those years his family stole from me.

I'm from a poor upbringing, but I'm not a complete commoner. I know the rules of the gentry, which is why I give it some time before going to the library. Who knows what state Ms. Dalton-Clarke is in? She may be lounging around in sloppy attire or sunbathing naked.

Her hair may be a mess and her face scrubbed clean of make-up. She may need a few minutes to make herself presentable. I'm guessing most women, when faced with an enemy, would amass whatever power they can, even if said power is derived from six-inch heels and red lipstick. Any lesser appearance than the show she puts up for the world will put her at an unfair disadvantage for the surprise visit, and although I don't give a shit about playing fair, I do believe in treating a woman like a lady when it matters. Telling her she's going to become my wife definitely matters.

At my order, Mrs. Benedict, the same old housekeeper from before, grudgingly serves me a cup of Earl Grey on the terrace. It's not by coincidence I've wandered out here. It's the spot where I'd been sitting when Angelina Dalton came to me on the infamous night that sealed my fate. What will it be like to finally face her again? The onslaught of emotions at the thought is a familiar cocktail of apprehension, excitement, and a bloodthirsty need for justice. I'd lie if I say lust isn't running thick under the surface of it all. Who can blame me? She's been the focus of my fantasies, both the vengeful and lustful kind, for the past six years.

Earlier in her father's study, I barely glanced at her photo. I didn't have to. Her features are imprinted on my mind, even if we only met that once, an angelic face with outer space blue eyes and a golden cascade of hair. I see her in my dreams and with my eyes wide open. When I close them, I see her walking to me through the French patio doors with a beautiful display of innocence and vulnerability. It's a night I can never forget. It's a night when the best and worst moment of my life collided. Whilst Dalton wins the grand prize for fucking me over, she takes the trophy for snatching my heart in a few seconds flat only to throw it back in my face. She's my best, and my worst. She had no right to be pretty and nice to me when she had no intention of falling as hard for me as she made me fall for her.

The memory is always fresh, always new. Poor as fuck but armed with youth and ambition, I'd donned my only button-down shirt and set out to meet her father not at his office, but at his house. It was an idiotic idea. Any man with a little experience of high society could've told me I'd be out of my depth with the formal dinner, from the four forks and knives lined up next to the gold-rimmed plates to the hand-rolled cigars that concluded the five hour-long ordeal. Between the other guests in their tuxedos, I stood out like a mongrel dog among racehorses. I stepped outside for air and sat down on this very terrace wall. I was freezing my butt off without a jacket in the middle of June when she exited in that pretty white dress, her curls pinned in some fancy up-do, with a fucking green granny shawl sporting a couple of holes wrapped around her shoulders.

"Aren't you cold?" she asked in a voice that rang as beautiful as their fancy dinner bell.

The ignorance of a rich girl. What the fuck did she think? My teeth were chattering and my knees knocking together. I wanted to go inside where it was warm, but I needed another minute to get my shit together. I wasn't going to let the older men with their expensive clothes and knowledge of cutlery intimidate me. I carried my future in my pocket, a discovery that was going to put me on the map, but I was yet to speak to Dalton, the man who was going to help me make it happen. I was nothing but a poor bastard, and I didn't want to answer her, not really, because admitting to being cold would've been admitting to things I didn't want the exquisite young woman staring at me to know.

Before I could think of anything appropriate to say, she unwrapped that ugly shawl from her frail shoulders, exposing the thin straps of her impractical evening dress, and draped the moth-eaten wool around me.

"There." She didn't quite smile, but she looked pleased. "It was my grandmother's. It makes me feel safe."

I stared at her like a fool, dumbstruck by the beautiful, wealthy girl who'd given me her warmth and safety. That's how her father found us when he stepped through the doors. The minute his gaze fell on us, his eyes turned colder than the winter night. He walked over with an empty tumbler in his hand, his steps unhurried but urgent.

Putting an arm around his daughter, he said, "Go inside, Lina. You'll catch your death in this cold with no coat."

The silk of her dress accentuated the tightness of her ass and the shift of her globes as she turned and obeyed.

Dalton's breath fanned my face, reeking of whisky. His words were soft-spoken but loaded enough to lash like thunder. "She'll never be yours. She's destined for someone worthy of her."

I couldn't answer, not because I didn't have a quick comeback. I grew up rough. I knew how to throw back subtle insults, but he'd punched me in the gut with the truth. It had nothing to do with me not being worthy of her. It was that I *did* want her to be mine. I just didn't know it until he'd said it, but it was suddenly out in the open, the truth set free by his words, my worst nightmare of a fantasy set in motion. That fantasy haunted me for every long, lonely night I fucked my fist in jail.

"Come on in." Dalton tilted his head toward the house. "I'm ready to see you about that business proposal." At the doors, he turned, his figure a stark outline in the light. "Do take off that shawl. You look ridiculous."

Inside, I sought Lina out despite Dalton's warning, telling myself it was to return her shawl. I blatantly trespassed in corridors that weren't leading to Dalton's office or the dining room until I found her. She stood in front of the guest bathroom with Mrs. Benedict shoving a fur drape at her and mumbling something about her mother turning in her grave. I never did give her back her shawl. I didn't want Mrs. Benedict to take it away. I draped it over a chair back, hoping she'd find it. Then I'd gone to her father's study and she'd married Clarke, the man who'd granted Dalton the excavation rights for the mine he'd stolen from me.

Pushing the bitter memory aside, I leave the Royal Albert teacup on the garden table—a perversely careless act for such pricy crockery —and go back inside. Dalton is nowhere to be seen. He's probably planning my murder for stealing his princess, the one I'm not worthy of. Isn't karma a funny thing? If Lina turned as self-destructive and batshit crazy as her medical reports claim, our situation is ironically reversed.

She stands in the middle of the library when I enter, not in front of or behind the desk, but right in the middle, between nothing and the fireplace. I take a few seconds. The moment is huge. I'm not going to rush it. It's not what I expected. It's not my memory reincarnated. Nothing is left of the angelic girl from that evening in June. She doesn't come to me with kindness. Her back is stiff and her posture regal. The tip of her nose is tilted to the ceiling, her chin high.

What does a crazy person look like? Not like her. Maybe. It's hard to say. Take me, for example. You'd never say how warped I am just from looking at me. Does wearing a green granny shawl to a fancy dinner qualify as crazy? Does self-sabotage count as insane? I close the door quietly, like one would close a church door. I'm not sure why, only that I feel like I did when I held my mother's hand, and she led me down the aisle toward the portrait of Mary carrying the baby Jesus in her arms.

At the sound of the click, Lina's back turns even more rigid. Her ribcage expands and contracts too quickly, as if she's battling to breathe. Taking more time, longer than any *normal* person would find comfortable, I study her. With her hair like spun gold and her skin like bone china, she could easily be a fairytale princess, but that's not what I see when my gaze drops to her lips. They're a darker shade of pearl, full and shimmery. Lip balm. It's not lipstick or gloss. There's no mascara on her golden lashes or blush on her cheeks. No cosmetic courage. No high-heeled power. What she resembles is an ice queen— cold, untouchable, unobtainable. From head to toe, she's dressed in black. A polo-neck top with long sleeves covers her from her neck to her wrists. A wide skirt brushes her ankles. Black boots peek out from underneath. The top is tight fitting and the waistband of her skirt broad, accentuating her slim shape and small waist.

She stands quietly until I've done my evaluation. When I finally approach, she meets my eyes with a hint of loathing. The gold and green specs seem to light up the darkest of blues as her gaze flashes with distaste.

I smile. Good. I'm glad she looks at me like that, or I may have gotten lost in the strange unworldliness of her eyes, a dark galaxy dotted with green and gold stars.

"Mrs. Clarke."

"Mr. Hart."

She speaks. For six years I passed the sleepless hours of my nights trying to recall the exact sound of that voice, wondering if—hoping that—it has changed. It's not what I'd hoped for. It's not harsh or cracked or flawed. It's still like a bell, clear and resonating strongly.

"I see I've been announced."

Her level stare defies my assumption. "I remember you."

Just because of that angelic voice, I start counting her shortcomings. She locked herself in a room for over two years. She refused to see anyone, sometimes even her husband. "How can you blame him for killing himself?" people ask. "With a wife like her..." and they leave the sentence hanging.

She tried to commit suicide by throwing herself out of a second story window of their home. That was before the husband shot himself, so it couldn't be blamed on the tragedy of his death. Speculation has it mostly as the other way around. He shot himself after her suicide attempt.

She spent a year after his funeral in an institution with a fancy name, which is just another term for an asylum. For that year, she was nursed back to health from her alternating disorders of bulimia and anorexia. Doesn't look like they've achieved much. She can do with another few kilos.

The worst is in her eyes. It's in her silence as she stands there, letting me weigh her and find her too light. Too damn much. The coldness and craziness appeal to me. I'm a man intimately acquainted with broken things, enough to know what stands in front of me is ruined, not broken. I still want her, as much as—no, more—than when she was eighteen and sweet and a princess. A memory of Dalton bringing her into the dining room, dressed in that white frock that showed the cleavage of her small breasts and tight buttocks, flashes

8

through my mind. I knew what he was doing. He was parading her, showing off his bargaining chip.

She waits patiently. Maybe locking yourself up does that to you. It ruins your mind but teaches you virtues.

"It's been a year," I say.

She doesn't ask.

It makes me want to shake a reaction from her, but instead I lash out with my words. I lash out with my eyes, filling them with disapproval. "Do you still have to wear black?"

Her voice is collected, indifferent. "I'm mourning."

"He's been dead for a year."

"I didn't say who I'm mourning."

Gripping my hands behind my back, I walk around her. Her head turns as her gaze follows me, but she stops at three o'clock, allowing me to look at places she can't see, like her sculptured back. It's too bony, the way her vertebrae show through her top, and somehow there's perfection in even that. Frailty. Vulnerability. Femininity. I've never found skinny women attractive, but Lina is a first for me in everything. It's a fact that no longer surprises me.

I stop in front of her, drawing her gaze back to me. "Is it true?"

She waits.

I caress the lines of her face with my gaze. "Are you crazy?"

"Aren't we all to a greater or lesser degree?"

That damn, musical voice. There's no judgment there, just a factual statement. Clever. It wins her this round. There's nothing to argue.

"I suppose you'd like to know the reason for my visit."

She looks straight into my black, soiled soul. "I know why you're here."

"Is that so?" I give her a smile that's meant to be intimidating. "Tell me."

"For the same reason they all are."

They all are. I fucking hate the sound of that. "What reason is that?"

"To marry me for my money."

My vision goes blurry. My anger ignites and unjustly escalates. She makes me see things I don't want to, images of many rivals on one knee, asking for her hand. That's where they went wrong. I won't be asking.

"Yet," I drop my gaze to her naked ring finger, "you rejected everyone."

"For the same reason I'll be rejecting you."

I smother a laugh. On second thought, I let it out, cold and soft. I round her again, like a buyer evaluating livestock. I lean into her, like an owner staking a claim. She smells of an exotic perfume, something musky and oriental, alluring and deadly, like a pretty, poisonous flower. She's toxic to me. God knows I've suffered every classifiable, slow-killing symptom, but I can't resist.

"If you think I only want you for your money," I whisper against the shell of her ear, "you're sadly mistaken."

A shiver runs over her body. It starts at her nape and ends at the base of her spine. I feel it where our bodies are touching, separated by two layers of black clothes. This time, my laugh is silent, unnoticed at the back of her head. I don't need to win a round over her with a mocking smile. This round is mine.

She steps away, putting space between us. Her head is turned to the side, but she's not looking at me. "You can't make me."

"Think again."

She twirls around, eyes a bit wider and nostrils barely flaring. There's the tiniest crack in her veneer, and there she is, the crazy woman behind the curtain of ice. The jugular vein in her neck flutters like a trapped butterfly. There's fire in her, yet.

She places soft emphasis on every word. "I said no."

"You're making the mistake of assuming it was a request."

The frost is back in her eyes, her chin tilted haughtily. "Leave before I call a guard."

"You don't want Daddy Dearest to die, do you?"

The little color left in her cheeks vanishes. She's a wax doll, unnatural and startling beautiful.

"Bribery. Tsk-tsk. A High Court judge, no less." Taking a photocopy of the signed affidavit from my pocket, I hold it up for her to see. "When this goes public, your daddy ends up in prison. He won't make it out alive. I've made enough friends in six years to make sure of it. A phone call, a message via a guard is all it'll take."

She's big enough to drop her bravado and read the text. When her eyes meet mine again, there's something else. Fear. More than fear. She's terrified. "How did you get this?"

Not the question I've been expecting. "Does it matter?" I have blood on my hands for the piece of paper I'm clutching, and I'd spill it again.

"Is it fake?"

"If there's one thing you should know about me, it's that I never bluff."

"Does he...?" She swallows. "Does Harold know?"

"I assume he's having your bags packed as we speak."

Her chest rises and falls. Clasping her hands together, she drops her gaze to the floor. A few seconds pass. I let her have them to process what's happening.

When she lifts her unworldly eyes back to me, they're composed. Serene, if not sad. She's already accepted what she can't change. Some may see her lack of fighting as weak. I see it for what it is, a trait of a survivor. She's doing what she must to get through this. It doesn't strike me as the kind of behavior of someone with self-destructive tendencies. The ease with which she does it tells me it's a practiced skill.

"The ceremony will take place on Saturday at the Anglican church in Emmarentia. Four o'clock. Don't be late. You won't like the consequences."

Gripping her fingers, I press a kiss to her hand. Her skin is cold, but her palm is clammy. Inclining my head, I bid my fiancée goodbye.

There's nothing more to say.

Now we wait.

Until Saturday.

Lina

RUNNING TO THE TOILET, I empty my guts for the second time. My body heaves, not getting the message from my stomach that there's nothing left. When the wave finally passes, I slide to the floor, clutching the toilet with both arms and resting my forehead on the rim. I'm hot and cold, shaking all over. I'm frightened.

When I can't put off getting dressed any longer, I force my legs to stand. Bent-over, I make it to the basin. In the overhead cabinet is a bottle of pills, but there's no pill for what I'm suffering from. There's no medicine that will help. Shaking two tablets against nausea from the brown bottle, I swallow them dry. It takes a few breaths for my stomach to settle and a while before my strength returns.

This bathroom, I hate it. I hate the beehive tiles and the spa tub. It's been mine since I can remember, but I never wanted it. I've never been happy here. I always wanted to leave, and now that I have to, again, I'm afraid. There's no way out of this, though. I can't let Harold die. If he does, what I want most in the world is gone with him.

After splashing cold water on my face, I go to my bedroom. My wedding dress is laid out on the bed. It's a simple cut with lace over-laying a silk lining. The pillbox hat with net veil lies next to it. It feels like I'm dressing for my own funeral, tying a bond with another cruel man. I sensed Damian's desire to hurt me in Harold's library. I suppose I've become good at reading that underlying darkness some men crave.

Moving behind the screen, I strip naked in front of the full-length mirror. I always do. I do so I can look, so I can remember who I am. Turning sideways, I study the scars that line my arms, first the left, then the right. I count every unsightly, embossed line, unevenly spaced from my shoulders to my wrists. Sixteen on the left, twelve on the right. Each one represents the loss of a part of my soul at the price of my life. The parts of me I can't see in a mirror are too ugly even for me to face. When I can't stomach more, I pull on a random set of underwear from the drawer before stepping into the dress. I fix my hair into a tight bun and secure the hat with pins. There's no one to go through this with me. I'm alone. I long for my mother with a fierce-ness that cripples my heart. It's her pearl earrings I fasten on my ears, and my grandmother's necklace I clasp around my neck. It makes me feel close to them, as if I'll draw strength from their spirits.

"The driver is ready," one of Harold's bodyguards says from the open door.

I glance at him in the mirror. It's Bobby, one of the kinder ones. He's not looking into the room, but straight ahead. By now, the guards are used to the fact that I never close a door. Respectfully, they don't stare. That's what crazy women do. They get dressed with an open door in a house full of men. Closed doors give them anxiety attacks. That's the real reason the men don't look. They're afraid of insulting Harold by admitting with their curious staring just how crazy I am.

"Harold?" I ask cautiously.

"He already left."

Getting to my feet, I grab a clutch bag in which I've stuffed my phone, anti-nausea pills, tampons, and tissues. I never go anywhere without tampons and tissues. My period is irregular, often arriving when I'm under more duress than normal.

"Do you have everything?" he asks.

I nod. My single suitcase has been taken to Damian's house earlier. He sent a driver to collect it.

"Let's go then," he says. "Mr. Dalton will skin me alive if we're late."

I don't show Bobby my fear. Fear makes you vulnerable. It makes you an easy victim. I hand him my bag while I fit my shoes.

"I'm ready," I announce.

I don't have a choice.

Damian

THE BELLS TOLL in the stone church tower. It's a haunting and beautiful sound. Rare. They only use the bells for special occasions because they're old and fragile. The fact that they're using them for me tells the witnesses in the church I'm a man to be reckoned with. There's not a face turned to me without fear. It's there, in their fake smiles and plastered-on expressions of goodwill. They're only here to witness the beginning of the fall of the Dalton empire.

One, two, three. The last dong falls like a verdict on four. The sound reverberates through the acoustic interior, carrying on the dubious silence that follows. When the sound dies down, the guests stand, and the organist starts playing. The first notes of The Wedding March fill the space. It's dramatic and theatrical. I picked it specifically, just like the cascades of white roses and the thick candles burning in golden candelabras on both sides of the aisle. Facing the entrance, I await my bride.

Despite the flamboyance, there's something in my chest, a tightness that borders on nerves when the doors don't open immediately. My posture is straight and my face stoic, but my hands ball involuntarily into fists. I only relax slightly when the double doors start swinging inward. A fan of light falls into the shadowed church, letting sun into the somber, cool interior. The beams burst through everywhere, up toward the gallery where the organ is playing and down over the stone floor. They keep on stretching, reaching, until the doors are fully open. It's blinding. After the darkness inside, I have to blink for my eyes to adjust. Like a revelation, a figure stands in the midst of all that pure white. I almost breathe easier, but not yet. It's a long walk down the aisle, and an even longer way to saying yes.

Dalton stands next to the door. As the music goes into the second sonata, he offers his arm, but Lina steps past him, as if she doesn't see him, and then she stops. I don't have time to ponder the observation, because the sonata is in full swing, and she's still not moving. My heart beats faster. My breathing speeds up. She's a silhouette of a shadow, obscured by the light. I can't make out her face or expression, just that she's not fucking moving. Dalton goes forward. She trips slightly as he nudges her. I'm about to shoot to the end of the aisle and drag her to the altar by her arm when she finally puts one foot in front of the other.

Something in me lifts, making me feel weightless, but it only lasts a second. The same someone who opened the doors closes them. The daylight is expelled, and the interior is once more basked in a gloomy light. It's then that I make out her face, her figure, her dress. Her fucking dress. God help me. I fist my hands so hard my knuckles crack. From her fashionable little hat to her elegant shoes, she's dressed for a funeral. In front of all these people, she makes a mockery of me, coming to me in black.

CHAPTER 2

Lina

Gasps fill the space. Shocked gazes follow my slow progress, turning sympathetic as they fall on the groom who waits stoically at the altar. They gauge Damian's reaction. Whispers rise above the organ. Words like *lunatic, out of her mind,* and *sacrilege* reach my ears. The stiff notes of the Wedding March, the flowers, the candles, everything befitting of a white dress suddenly seems exactly what it is—a show, and a kitsch one at that.

I try to walk with unfaltering steps, each one bringing me closer to an uncertain and dreaded future. Damian watches me with the intensity of a panther. The calmness with which he studies me is the quiet before his storm. His dark eyes promise retribution, but I don't think about it. For now, I rejoice in my small victory. It's the small victories that keep my spirit alive.

A hush falls over the church when I reach the man to whom I'm about to make unthinkable promises. Dressed in a black suit, white shirt, and silver cravat secured with a diamond pin, he looks like a man who belongs in Harold's world. He's nothing like the boy I remember. The boy I met had thick hair that needed a cut. The ends brushed the strong column of his neck. The rich, ebony stands made me itch to thread my fingers through them. The neat way in which it's brushed back now, not a hair out of place, looks stiff. If he was distant on the night I first met him, he now looks unreachable.

The fire in his brown eyes is no less fierce, but it's burning colder. Those eyes are the color of chocolate, not the sweet kind, but dark and bitter. The stark lines of his face are harder. High cheekbones, sharp nose, and square jaw, there's nothing compassionate about his features. His handsomeness is unconventional, and the cruelty of that beauty lies shallow under his skin. It's there in the storm that brews in his eyes, letting anyone brave enough to look deep know disobedience isn't an option. He's a man who gets his way, and who'll do unspeakable things to make it happen. What makes grown men's stomachs turn won't elicit as much as a blink from him. He's too used to getting his hands dirty. He's fought too hard to survive.

Only the way his thick eyebrows lift marginally in an expression of self-assured arrogance gives away his vulnerability. In our world, people who don't come from money hide behind arrogance. This is his only weakness. The rest of him screams danger. Dominance. This is the man who takes my hand with possessive ownership, placing it on his arm as if it belongs there even before I've promised to become his in law and faith in front of God and our audience. Covering my fingers with his palm, he locks it in place on the flexing muscles of his forearm. The fabric of his jacket sleeve is scratchy—expensive wool. He gives me a smile, one that heats me from the inside out. While it promises nothing good, he disarms me with his masculine power and fake charm, letting me know he'll come at me in ways that will leave me utterly defenseless. Our gazes remain locked for another second, knowledge and understanding passing between us in the primitive way of hunter and prey, and then the priest speaks. I'm mercifully released from the draining hold of his eyes as we both face forward while the charade begins.

I hear the priest's voice, but nothing he says. Even if he doesn't look at me, Damian's presence is overwhelming. A head taller than every other male in the church, his physique screams virility and strength. He's broader and more muscled than when I first met him, a change that can only be contributed to long hours in the gym. He smells of winter, of a citrus forest against a stark sky. The scent is subtle, but the haunting perfume of trees stripped of their leaves and a sky missing a sun invades my senses until it's all I smell. He shifts his weight, and our arms touch. It's as if his very male, very bossy energy wraps around me and squeezes until I can't breathe.

It's a summer's day, but it's too cold inside. Goosebumps break out over my arms despite the long sleeves of my dress. I feel the effect of no food in my stomach, my head starting to spin as my blood sugar level drops. A warm, strong hand presses firmly on my lower back, supporting my weight when I sway on my feet. I'm tempted to give in to its comfort, until I tune back into the moment and register to who it belongs. My body grows stiff. My legs turn wooden.

I regain my composure just as the priest starts with, "Do you, Angelina Clarke, promise…"

The rest is white noise. There's a ringing in my ears. The warmth leaves my back and settles on my shoulder. I'm turned to face the man blackmailing me into this. My captor stares down at me, urging me on with a smile that doesn't warm his eyes or fit the situation. His fingers dig into my flesh when I don't answer. I can do this. I've done it before.

I open my mouth, forcing the words from my parched lips. "I do."

His hold on me loosens, but he doesn't let me go. He keeps my eyes prisoner, his dark gaze drilling into mine as he says, "I most certainly do."

He slips a simple, platinum band onto my finger. When his right-hand man hands me a similar band for Damian, my hand shakes so much Damian has to steady it with his strong grip to aid my action. I stare at our hands clasped together, the matching rings symbolizing our union.

It's done.

We're husband and wife.

Now comes the worst.

. . .

THE REST PASSES IN A BLUR. We sign the register. Our witnesses are men I don't know. Harold comes up to congratulate us. He makes a big show of shaking Damian's hand and even manages to wipe away a tear as he, for a second time, literally gives me away. Bobby hands me my clutch bag. People queue outside with wishes of long lives and blissful happiness. Most of them I recognize from Harold's business dealings. All the influential players in the diamond industry are here.

A crowd of journalists wait on the outskirts of the church lawn, held back by men in black suits who must be Damian's security detail. There's no bouquet to throw, not that I expect anyone would've wanted to catch cursed flowers, so we make our way to Damian's waiting car fairly quickly. Thank God there's no reception.

My husband's hand is on my elbow as he guides me into the back of the car. The windows are tinted, and I sag in the seat, not having to keep vigilant under the scrutiny of the curious eyes and the unforgiving flashes of the cameras. When Damian tells his driver to take us to an upmarket restaurant in Sandton, my spirits sink. All I want is to escape to the luxury of privacy, but I won't be so lucky. Pulling out the pins digging into my scalp, I remove the hat.

We don't speak on the way to the restaurant or during the elevator ride to the top floor of the Sandton Center. Our reservation is at Nelsons where a meal is worth the equivalent of the average worker's monthly wage. I refrain from pointing out it makes more sense to eat at Buccaneers downstairs for a tenth of the price and donate the saving he'd make to the starving beggars on the street corner. I doubt Damian is a charitable man.

A hostess seats us and spreads my napkin. Not three seconds later, the sommelier arrives with a bottle of Krug and an ice bucket. While he uncorks the bottle and pours two glasses, a waiter serves hors d'oeuvres.

When the staff is gone, Damian lifts his glass. "Congratulations, Mrs. Hart." Then he says it again, "Mrs. Hart," not as in testing the sound, but rubbing it in.

His smile is tight, but it's the darkness of his expression that makes me not test him on this. As he presses the glass to his lips, holding my gaze, I take a sip. He looks at me with the same intensity from the church, except there's an undercurrent of something darker, something more dangerous. I wait for the blow, but the fact that he says nothing about the dress only makes me tenser. He's not going to just let it go.

He motions at the food on my plate. "Eat."

My gaze flitters to the pastry topped with pink caviar mousse. Although I need to feed my body, I'm scared I'll be sick again.

"Lina."

My eyes snap back to his face at the way he says my name.

"I'll feed you if I have to."

Taking another sip of champagne, I swallow away the dryness in my mouth before putting the pastry on my tongue. Under normal circumstances, I wouldn't waste such a delectable treat, but my stomach turns at the taste of the salty mousse. I chew and swallow, washing it down with some water.

"Don't you like it?"

I dab the napkin to the corner of my mouth. "Just nerves."

He nods, as if he understands, and it's not entirely unkind.

The rest of the courses follow in a steady, well-paced flow, our menu pre-ordered, all the dishes extravagant.

I can't stop myself from commenting on the arrogance of ordering on my behalf. "I suppose it's a good thing I'm not allergic to shellfish."

He fixes me with a knowing smile. "I know everything I need to know, including that you have no allergies and lobster is your favorite."

The statement takes me aback, but I'm not going to ask how he obtained such knowledge.

Throughout the meal, he watches me, focusing on every bite I take and swallow, until I'm a self-conscious mess. He insists I clean everything off my plate. Thankfully, the portions are small, but by the end of the meal I feel like I'll burst out of my dress. I decline his offer for coffee, and when I excuse myself to visit the ladies' room, he's on his feet before I am. Coming around the table, he extends a hand.

I stare at his proffered hand. "I'm sure I'll find the way."

"I'll accompany you."

Not in a position to argue, I accept his hand, letting him lead me to the ladies' room. He doesn't stop at the door as I expected but pushes it open and enters like he owns the place, pulling me behind him.

"What are you doing?" I exclaim.

A woman applying lipstick at the vanity gives us a startled look.

He shrugs at her. "Newlyweds."

She flushes a little and then wilts under his stare before gathering her make-up and leaving us to it.

He opens the door of the first stall and steps aside. I wait for him to leave, but instead of budging he gets comfortable.

Crossing his arms and ankles, he leans his shoulder against the wall. "I suggest you get started, unless you want me to pull down your panties."

"You can't be serious. You're going to stand here while I...?"

He gives me a half-smile. "Pee? Yes, I am."

What the...? Oh, my God. Angry heat warms my cheeks. The old shame creeps up on me. My face burns with humiliation. He's standing guard, making sure I don't barf my expensive meal. Pushing past him, I fling back the door to shut it, but he catches it with a palm.

"The door stays open."

I'm so angry I'm shaking. Facing him squarely, I let all the bitter loathing show on my face as I wiggle my panties down under the tight skirt of my dress. It's my turn to watch him as I relieve myself, balancing gingerly in the air, but he's immune to intimidation. He hands me a wad of paper from the dispenser when I'm done, which I yank from his hand. The smirk on his face stays intact as I adjust my clothes and wash my hands. Two women come in while I'm busy. Their smiles turn knowing as their eyes roam appreciatively over Damian where he stands waiting for me. The vexation he ignites overrides every other emotion, so much so that I forget to be nervous until we arrive at Damian's home.

It's already dark, but the neighborhood is well lit. I swallow a gasp when we pull up to a large property. Where did Damian get the money to afford a place like this? He went to prison with the same thin shirt he'd worn to Harold's dinner party. How does a man make money from behind bars? His house is an imposing Victorian structure on a hill in Erasmuskloof, an upmarket suburb of Pretoria. Hidden behind high walls and an electronic gate, it's three stories high with a tower hugging each end. A porch runs right around. The front windows are wide and high, light shining from every one of them.

A guard waits on the steps. When the driver parks, the guard opens my door and helps me from the car. Knowing what's to come, my nerves shatter. I clutch my bag so hard it feels as if my fingers may snap. Damian puts a hand on my lower back, guiding me up the stairs and through the front door. A redwood staircase frames either side of the entrance. In the middle of the floor, under a skylight, stands a table with a huge bouquet of flowers. With wooden wall panels and oriental carpets, the interior is either gloomy or cozy, depending on which side of Damian you are on. As he nods at the guard who followed us inside, I assume I'm not on his good side. The guard takes my clutch bag, clips it open, and turns it upside-down on the table. The content clatters onto the top, the tampons rolling off the edge. I stand stoically, as if it's normal for any groom to search his bride's bag, but the heat under my skin tells me I'm turning pink.

Damian stands equally motionless, waiting patiently as the guard checks my phone, pills, and even the travel-size packet of tissues. The guard pockets my phone and bends to retrieve the tampons. When he's packed everything back, he hands me my bag.

Under my cutting look, he lowers his eyes. Without a word exchanged, he takes up a position by the door.

"Come." Damian makes his way to the stairs.

For a second, I hesitate. I don't want to be here. I don't want to go through with what's going to happen. For a crazy, heart-racing moment, I consider making a run for the door on the left, but where will I run? I'm trapped in Damian's house—my new home—with his guard blocking the front door.

Damian stops and turns. He regards me with a disturbing light in those bitter chocolate colored eyes, an expression I can't decipher. If I've learned anything, it's that it hurts worse when you resist. Forcing my feet to obey, I walk to my husband, coming to a stop in front of him. I'm not rewarded for my obedience. No approving light or victorious smile transforms his features. Then I really get scared, because all I see in his dark eyes are disapproval and suppressed anger. It pierces me like an arrow through the ribs. Damian is furious. He controls it well, and that frightens me more.

My fear escalates with every stair we mount, my heels sinking into the plush carpet. On the landing, we turn left. He opens the first door and steps aside for me to enter. I walk into the room as if there's nothing to be frightened of, keeping my back straight and my shoulders square while my insides shake. The walls are lined with shelves and filled with books. Two armchairs face a fireplace, and a desk stands in the far corner. It's not where I expected him to bring me.

Leaving me to stand in the middle of the room, he walks to a liquor tray and pours a whisky. He surprises me again by carrying it to me and putting the glass in my hand.

"You look like you need it."

"Thank you," I say, because it's more mercy than I've ever been granted.

I down it in one go. The liquor burns down my throat and heats my stomach. My eyes water. He's right. I do need it. I need it for what I have to do, and I'll be damned if I let him see how much it scares me. Feigning courage, I leave the tumbler and my clutch on the table and walk to the desk. I lean on it, facing him. I resent him so much, this beautiful man staring at me. Fear-filled expectation is worse torture than the physical kind. I just want it to be done.

"What are you waiting for?" I taunt, lifting my skirt and spreading my legs as far as the dress allows. "Get it over with."

CHAPTER 3

Damian

*I*t's not going to happen like this. Anyway, I'm so angry with Lina for the dress stunt, I feel more like strangling than fucking her.

Her lush, usually pink lips are a shade paler. The lip balm makes them shimmer like mother-of-pearl. "Are you a man or not?"

Provocation. This is what it is, but I fall for it all the same, being in the state I am. In three long strides, I've crossed the floor. Her eyes grow large, betraying her brave performance. My hands are on her before she has time to blink. Twisting her around, I bend her body over the desk and pull up the skirt of her dress, the ugly black fucking dress. I lean my weight over her, crushing her chest to the wood. No doubt she can feel my dick growing hard between her ass cheeks. Her breath catches when I drag my hand up the inside of her thigh.

"Is this what you want?" I whisper with my nose pressed against her ear.

She shivers. "Does it matter what I want?"

I squeeze her thigh, applying the slightest of pressure. "Answer me."

She jerks. I guess that shiver wasn't the good kind. Repulsion, maybe.

Her voice is small. "No."

Slowly, I straighten and let her go. The minute my hold lifts, she flings around.

Her face is ashen. "Why don't you just get it over with?"

"I'm not in the habit of forcing women into my bed."

"Just into marriage?"

Yeah, I'm not in the habit of forcing women—never had to—but I do force a smile that must look as stiff as it feels. "When it suits my objective."

"Ultimately, sex is part of your objective. This is what you want, isn't it?"

Her question is a challenge, a hopeful one that begs for denial, but I've already admitted as much in her father's library. I'm not going to lie to her. It doesn't matter that she's unstable and certified crazy. I still want her. For that, I hate her almost more than for destroying my life.

Besides, it's not an easy question to answer. I want more than sex. I want to punish her for the part she played in her family's sins. I want to destroy her for making me want her when she damn well knew she wouldn't be mine. I want her to know what it's like to desire someone so intensely you physically ache. I want her to know what it's like to masturbate with one person's face in your mind for six never-ending years. When I'm done with her, I want her to never want another. I want her to covet me and pine away into a ghost of herself when I'm gone. I want her to imagine my face when she comes on her fingers and cry out my name in her sleep. I want her to go down on her knees and beg me to fill her with my cock, because that's the force with which I want her, and I'm not in the habit of nurturing unrequited passion, either. I want to ruin her for all other men. *That's* what I want.

I settle for the simple answer. "I'll take what I want when you're offering."

Her delicate nostrils flare. "Never."

Chuckling, I trace the line of her jaw. Her flawless skin is soft under my calloused pad. Her smooth and my rough rub together like good girls and savages disguised as gentlemen. Beasts like me, our clothes fit us well because brand names and tailored cuts cover the flaws of an unrefined education and less than honorable heart. The dishonorable beast in me likes the way we rub—her vulnerability and my power. He likes it very much.

"You know what they say about never, angel."

She jerks her head away and escapes with a sideways step. The rapid movement of her chest draws my eyes to her breasts. They're firm and pert. Beautiful, unobtainable, out-of-my-league Lina is mine. She may not want me—yet—but that doesn't change a thing. As of today, I'm her legal guardian. I'm responsible for her. She can't make a single decision without my approval, and I'm still high on the knowledge.

"We need to lay down the rules."

Silence.

"Russell, the bodyguard you met downstairs, is at your disposal. You won't leave the grounds without him." As much for her protection as to ensure she doesn't try to run away. "My housekeeper will show you around. If you need anything while I'm gone, Zane will take care of it."

"You're leaving?" she asks with a tinge of hope she hides too late.

"Not by choice. I have to take care of urgent business, but Zane will play host until I'm back."

"Zane?"

"Yes, my housekeeper is a man. Is that a problem?"

Something akin to panic sparks in her eyes. "You're leaving me alone with him?"

"You have nothing to fear. He's a good friend, and he also happens to be gay." Which is the only reason I trust him with her. I take the new phone from my pocket and hand it to her. "This is yours. My number is programmed."

She hesitates but takes the phone after a moment.

"Play by the rules, and it'll be smooth sailing." More or less. "Any questions?"

She licks her lips. "No."

"I'll be home tomorrow night. I suggest you get some rest. It's been a taxing day."

I grip her slender fingers and press them to my lips. The touch is to remind both of us to who she belongs. Like her, I have patience. It's only a matter of time. I would've preferred to not leave straight away, but the business I'm about to conduct can't wait. Maybe this trip is the best thing that could've happened. I haven't had sex in six years. I shouldn't trust myself around her, especially not when my lust is tainted with anger. With a squeeze, I drop her hand and take my leave.

At the door, I turn. "One more thing. Your father isn't welcome in my house. He won't visit whether I'm here or away, and neither will you visit him. Are we clear?"

"Yes."

"Good."

I trail my gaze over her one last time, imprinting the dishonor she bestowed on me to memory before calling my driver and ordering Zane to the study.

Lina

HAS DAMIAN REALLY GONE, letting me off the hook? With the new phone clutched in one hand, I grip the edge of the desk behind me with the other, unable to believe my luck. He hasn't taken me like I thought he would. He hasn't punished me, although I'm sure it'll come. For now, I'm all right, and I've become good at living in the moment. Letting my shoulders drop under the strain of the day, I alternate between dragging in breaths and puffing them out. My act slips and my bravado falls away, leaving my knees weak in the aftermath of all that could've been. I'm still gasping like a fish on shore when the door opens, and a man enters.

I give a start but am incapable of adopting my earlier proud posture. I simply don't have enough strength left.

The glint is his eyes is sardonic. "Did I give you a fright?"

Dressed in a black T-shirt, dark jeans, and white sneakers, he's not the stereotyped butler in a stiff waistcoat and bowtie I expected. He's young—early twenties with a bronze complexion and brown hair. He's not attractive by general standards, but he has an open face, the kind that would elicit trust if he's not scowling, like now.

Crossing the floor, he does a visual inventory. His perceptive gaze misses little.

"It was a beautiful ceremony." The compliment sounds sarcastic. "I brought some of the flowers from the church home to put in the entrance."

"You were there?" I don't remember his face from the crowd, not that I'd been taking in much of what was going on around me.

"For the whole fiasco." He looks me up and down. Satisfaction laces his tone when he says, "Not exactly a wedding dress." He's happy I look nothing like a bride. "I can't imagine Dami liking it. He hates black."

"For a man who hates black, he sure owns enough black suits." Given, I've only seen him twice, not counting our first meeting, but he chose black for both occasions. Or maybe it was just for me.

"I meant on a woman." He smirks. "Although, I can't say I'm surprised that black's your choice of wedding gown color after unpacking your bags."

If I don't own any other color than black, it's none of his business. "I didn't expect you to unpack my bags but thank you."

He shrugs like it's nothing, but the tense set of his shoulders gives away his resentment. "It comes with the job." Seeming to consider me for a moment, he continues, "I'll be honest with you, no one here is pleased about the turn of events, so do yourself a favor and do as I tell you. Otherwise, try to stay out of my way."

I smile. "Glad we're on the same page."

"Come." He turns for the door, knowing I'll obey because I don't have a choice.

I collect my clutch and follow him down the hallway, not surprised to see Russell still guarding the front door. He's not as tall as Damian, but meatier. His presence would've been scary if I weren't used to the bodyguards in Harold's house.

At end of the hallway, Zane opens a door to a bedroom.

"This is you," he says, entering ahead of me.

I step inside cautiously. Burgundy wallpaper covers the walls, and the windows are draped with heavy curtains. A four-poster bed stands against the far wall. Two stuffy armchairs face a fireplace. The decoration is somber and masculine. I don't need the faint remnants of Damian's cologne to tell me this is his room. The scent is earthy like a misty day and tangy like citrus. Cold like winter. It's both disturbingly male and refreshingly clean. I can't stay in this room that bears Damian's stamp on all sensory levels. I don't want to share a room with a man who's a stranger.

Oblivious to my consternation or simply not caring, Zane takes my clutch and phone and leaves them on the table by the cold fireplace.

I'm curious as to this man's friendship with Damian. For someone who doesn't know me, his hostility is fierce. "How do you and Damian know each other?"

"From jail."

"Oh. What were you in for, if I may ask?"

"Same as Dami."

"Theft?"

"Come," he says again.

I follow him awkwardly to an adjoining dressing room. The closets don't have doors and the shelves are open cubbyholes with smaller ones for belts and ties. There are a few shirts, one spare jacket, and a pair of pants. Damian only got out a week ago. I suppose he hasn't had time to fill his sadly lacking dressing room. Those lonely shirts in all that vast space look forlorn. The sight elicits an involuntary and unexpected pang of sympathy for a man who, not so long ago, didn't even own a jacket. Zane pulls my nightdress from a drawer and shoves it into my hand before pulling me by the arm to an en suite bathroom.

"You have five minutes to shower."

The door slams in my face. It takes me two seconds to register the dull ache his fingers have left on my arm and another for panic to set in. Dropping the nightdress, I fling myself at the sealed exit. I grip the doorknob, twisting it in my clammy palm while jerking on the door. I'm about to yell for someone to let me out when the knob turns, and the door opens. I'm not locked in. Resting my forehead against the wood, I drag in deep breaths. When my heartbeat calms, I open the door wider and peer around the frame. I'm alone. The bedroom door stands open. I leave the bathroom door open a crack and rush through a shower, finding my shampoo on the shower shelf.

When I'm done with my shower, I take a little time to familiarize myself with the bathroom. My cosmetic bag is set on the vanity and my robe hangs on a hook behind the door, next to a robe I assume to be Damian's. Half of the cabinets are stocked with male toiletries—shaving cream, razors, hairbrushes, and deodorant—and the other half is empty. The arrangement screams at me like a taunting message. Refusing to give it too much thought, I brush my teeth. Instead of using the space left for me, I pack everything back into my cosmetic bag. If I don't put my toothbrush next to Damian's, I can pretend it's just temporary. I can pretend I still have a choice in something.

Pulling on my robe, I go back into the bedroom, but stop in my tracks. Zane sits on a chair next to the door, filing his nails.

"Feeling better?" he asks with a mocking smile.

I prefer to ignore him, but it's hard to do when he grabs my arm and manhandles me to the bed.

"Take off the robe," he says.

When I've done so, he drapes the robe over a chair, pushes me down on the left side of the bed, and pulls the covers up to my chest. With my long-sleeved nightdress, it's too hot, but I lie stiffly while he arranges my arms on top.

"I'm sorry, honey," he says, not sounding apologetic at all.

"What for?"

He yanks my arm above my head.

"What are you doing?"

I'm wrestling with a renewed bout of fear when he takes a pair of handcuffs from his back pocket and cuffs my wrist to the bedframe.

"Dami's orders. In case you feel like jumping out of a window." He grabs my face in one hand, his fingers digging into my cheeks. "Do you know what Dami is capable of? Do you know what he'll do to you if you try anything stupid?"

I have an idea, but I say nothing as we stare at each other. Refusing to avert my gaze from the hatred that burns in his green eyes, I take a good, long look. I let the emotion settle in and lock it away in my heart where I keep stock of my enemies.

Lips curling, he pushes my head into the pillow. "Try to get some sleep."

When he moves away, hysteria sets in. I'm trapped. I can't breathe. "Unlock me."

He keeps on walking, not sparing me a glance.

"Please, don't lock me in. Don't close the door." I'm blabbering, but I can't stop. "Don't lock me in. Please."

At the door, his patience snaps. Before I can blink, he's back at the bed, his backhand connecting so hard with my cheek my ears ring.

"Shut the fuck up, you crazy bitch."

"You don't understand." I can't breathe if I'm constrained.

"I said quiet," he yells. "It's bad enough I'm saddled with being your babysitter. I don't want to listen to your wailing all night." Mumbling *lunatic* under his breath, he marches back to the door.

I buck and yank on my constraints, saying please and promising to be good, but my pleas fall on deaf ears. The door shuts with a bang.

"It's fine," I whisper. "It's fine. I'm fine."

I'm not.

Panic gets the better of me. I start to struggle in all earnest, jerking and pulling on the metal around my wrist like a mad person. It feels as if I'm drowning. I can't breathe. Shit, I can't breathe. I can't breathe! Twisting and kicking at the sheets trapping my feet only makes it worse. I can't think. It's mind over matter, but I'm not a cognizant human being. I'm an animal, trapped and pushed into a corner. I behave like an animal, the sounds coming from my throat scaring even me. I'm vaguely aware of the burning of my skin where I'm fighting the cuffs like a feral cat. My tears and silent wails degrade me further, lower than an animal and closer to a pathetic, wild creature at the most basic form of existence, fighting for every breath.

Breathe. Breathe.

I can't give in to this. I can't.

With enormous effort, I still. It takes inhumane willpower to calm myself enough to drag in air. When I finally manage, I choke on oxygen. I cough and choke, and choke and cry. It's no big deal. It's just a panic attack. I'm breathing. It's going to be all right. The door is just closed. It's not locked.

I repeat the mantra until I'm calm enough to breathe normally, and it doesn't feel like my lungs are collapsing. I'm not fighting any longer, but I'm far from relaxed. Every muscle in my body is taut. Every conscious moment is a battle to hold onto the calm and not slip back into panic mode. I need to distract my mind. I mustn't think about the fact that I can't get up and move freely. I grasp for straws, sifting through my brain for a buoy that will keep me afloat, and the first thing that drifts within reach is hope. The thought I grab onto is the one thing I'm set on finding. It's the evidence Damian holds over my head, the scraps of paper that threaten Harold's life and affect mine in ways no one can understand. It's where in this house he keeps it, and how quickly I'll find it.

Damian

THE CHARTERED Cessna lands on an airstrip outside the heavily secured area south of Sanddrift in the Richtersveld, a stone-throw from the Namibian border. It was only a three hour-long flight, but the minute I step off the plane, I power up my phone and look for an update from Zane. His text message says Lina is in bed and all is well.

All is well.

Nothing can be further from the truth. All hasn't been well since the day I set foot in her father's house. It will only be well again when I see the look on his face as he realizes I've put him out of business.

Shielding my eyes against a dust storm, I send a quick reply to Zane, telling him to keep me updated, and shake the hand of the nervous Dalton Diamond Corporation mining representative waiting next to a car. My reputation exceeds me, no doubt, but that very reputation prevented the Senior Operations Manager, Fouché Ellis, from declining my request. I may also have hinted at wanting to make a big investment. It's an unorthodox visit Dalton is unaware of, but one he'll learn about soon enough.

"Welcome, Mr. Hart. I'm here to drive you to your accommodation."

"I know why you're here," I say, buttoning up my jacket.

The evenings in the semi-desert are cool. The familiarity of something as simple as a weather pattern strikes a chord of homecoming in me, as well as the perverse thrill a hunter feels when his prey is within grabbing distance.

The representative shoots me a wary look. I'm ruder than intended, irritated that the meeting had been scheduled for this evening when I only got married in the afternoon. Given, Ellis had arranged the date before my wedding plans were made.

"May I congratulate you, sir?" the man asks as he runs next to me to keep up. "On the wedding."

At my look, he clears his throat.

Wisely, he keeps his mouth shut for the rest of the drive, only handing me the reports I've requested. After we've cleared the security checkpoint, we follow the dust road to the mining office and accommodation area. We pass the excavation site, visible from beyond the barbwire fences in the floodlights. The last time I saw this part, it was virgin ground. Now it's scarred by Dalton's bulldozers and the black metal construction of the screening plant. Heaps of sand lie like rejected mountains on the south side of the riverbed. Muddy puddles reflect in the yellow spotlights that shine from the guard towers.

The accommodation doesn't look much better. It's a hostel built from pressed wood that has to get as hot as hell in the high day temperatures. Ellis meets me at the canteen. We order two beers and take them to a private meeting room at the back.

It's no industry secret that Ellis and Dalton disagree on everything from operating procedures to environmental conservation and safety controls, which is why I've chosen him. Plus, he holds thirty percent of the shares. They were given to him as part of his remuneration package when Dalton employed him, and he knows as well as I do those shares will soon be worthless.

"I'll play open cards with you," he says once we're seated on opposite sides of a small table. "I don't like going behind Harold's back. He's still the CEO."

"I'm sure you've guessed there's a good reason for meeting off the grid."

"Yeah. Harold won't approve of whatever you're proposing."

Adjusting my tie, I smile as kindly as I can manage. "I wouldn't use *approve* to describe Dalton's reaction to this meeting."

"There's not a lot Harold and I agree upon. Still, it's a hell of a far way to come for a meeting. We could've talked on the phone."

"This is a meeting I prefer to conduct in person." You can't read someone's non-verbal language over a phone. I need to know if I can rely on Ellis. "I also wanted to see the mine. I assume a visit has been arranged for tomorrow before I leave?"

"You said you wanted to invest. What do you want to know?"

I like a man who cuts straight to the chase. "I need the geology reports of the initial exploration."

He motions at the file in my hand the representative has given me. "You have them."

"The ones *before* these."

"What makes you think there are earlier ones?"

"The fact that I requested them when I applied for the reconnaissance permission."

He braces his meaty hands on the table. "Are you saying what I think you're saying?"

"I'm saying I want the reports."

"Wait a minute. The application for prospecting rights was filed by Harold."

"Who granted them?"

"Jack Clarke from the Department of Mineral Resources."

"Convenient that Clarke, who I may point out was the same age as Dalton, then became Dalton's son-in-law."

"You're saying Harold's daughter married Jack for mining rights?"

"Why else would a pretty eighteen-year-old girl marry a man old enough to be her father?"

He moves to the edge of his seat. "Are you trying to prove you have a stake on Dalton Diamonds?"

"I already have the proof. I'm not here to dwell on the past. I prefer to focus on the future. What I'm offering is pumping new money into the project."

"You'll be wasting your money. We've depleted the gravel bed. There's nothing left to bulldoze."

"You have to go down to the bedrock."

"We'll need a vacuveyer. Too costly."

"Money isn't an issue."

"The kimberlite we tested yielded lower quality diamonds. It won't be worth the investment."

"Not if those diamonds are colored."

"The colored diamond market has been existing for as long as the natural diamond market. It's never been in as high demand."

"Not black."

He rubs his chin. "Black diamonds? Who the hell wants black diamonds? Yeah, there's a new fashion thing going on, but they're still well below the natural diamond value, and it's nothing but a phase. It'll fall out of fashion as quickly as it became a rebel slash gothic craze."

"In a few months' time, it'll be all the rage."

"How can you be so certain?"

"I believe in making the waves, Mr. Ellis, not in surfing them."

"You're going to create a new trend? May I ask how?"

"Let's just say I have the resources and contacts to make it happen."

"Why aren't you presenting this directly to the board? Why tell me?"

"I'm going to take over this mine, and when I do, I'll need a skilled Operations Manager. The mess Dalton Diamonds made of this site is going to be cleaned up. I want to turn this place around and give the miners better working conditions." I wave the report in my hand at him. "The records you made public prove if you don't change your prospecting program, you've reached your excavation limit. My initial geology report proves there's more to this mine. If this mine remains with Dalton Diamonds, it'll be dead before the end of the year. I'm offering to give it a facelift and a lifespan of at least twenty years longer, if not more. Are you with me, or not?"

"It'll be one hell of an output. How much money are we talking about?"

"Ten billion."

"Not easy to come by."

"I've got the means."

He regards me from under his bushy eyebrows. "Yeah, I heard you got married yesterday. Lina is a sweet woman. If what you say about her is true, then you and your wife are cut from the same cloth."

He has no idea. "Oh, we are."

"Don't you think if going down to the bedrock was worth a shot, Harold would've made the investment?"

"Like I said, Dalton stole my prospecting work. I spent two years of my life searching this soil. This land is in my blood. Dalton did nothing but ruin it. He depleted the riverbed and destroyed the environment. I know you disagree with his methods. No doubt he's paying the right people at the Department of Mineral Resources to turn a blind eye. Dalton couldn't make this mine a success even if he wanted. He might've stolen my plans, but he couldn't steal my vision. My vision has never been to yield high quality diamonds. There are too little of them in the gravel bed. My vision has always been to extract the lower quality diamonds of which there is a much higher yield in the bedrock. My vision is to color them and build a new brand of diamonds that will become the next most sought-after gemstone."

"I'm going to be frank with you. This sounds a lot like revenge."

"Dalton fucked me over, and I'm about to return the favor in so many ways he'll never see them coming. Yes, it's about revenge, but it's also about realizing this mine's true potential."

"Excuse me for pointing this out, but as an ex-convict, you're not exactly great management material, especially not in the diamond industry."

"Don't be naïve. This whole industry is made up of crooks."

He's quiet for some time. After a while, he says, "Let's say hypothetically I'm on board. What do you want from me?"

"Your vote."

"What for?"

"For me taking over Dalton's shares."

"Taking over? He's going to give them to you, just like that?"

"Call it a wedding gift to his new son-in-law."

He rubs a hand over his head. "I don't know which one of you is more corrupt."

"We may both be corrupt, but there's only one of us who can save this mine."

"What about Warren and Stone? They each hold twenty percent."

"Let me worry about them."

"Warren might consider, but Max Stone is as loyal to Harold as a puppy to the hand that feeds it meat."

"Max Stone and Bell Warren will sell out to me. If you vote for it, it'll be a done deal." That'll make seventy percent of the shares mine.

"How can you be so certain they'll sell out?"

"Trust me."

"You've got dirt on them." His eyes bulge. "You're going to blackmail them? You're joking, right?"

"Life's too short for jokes." It's a lesson six years in jail has taught me. "Whatever the case, I give the mine another twelve months, eighteen at the most, before it's depleted. Dalton knows this. It's in these reports." I wave the file at him again. "In another few months, he would've sold his shares and bailed on you when the mine closed down and the workers got paid off, leaving you with a pocket full of worthless shares. I'm offering you a chance to grow with a mine that's going to triple its profits in a year. You can walk away unemployed next year—let's not forget how hard it is for a man of your age to find employment in South Africa—or retire in twenty years with a nice pension fund and flourishing shares. What's there to lose?"

Folding his hands over his big stomach, he regards me solemnly. "I don't know. My honor? My conscience? You tell me."

"Knowingly or unknowingly, you were part of the scam when Dalton stole my mine." I get to my feet. "I'll wait for your call. You have until tomorrow noon to make your decision. I'm meeting Warren and Stone at three. Just know that if you're out, you're part of the enemy, and I won't rest until my enemy goes down. Every single last one of them. Good night, Ellis."

"Yeah." He wipes a hand over his mouth. "Night, Damian. I hope you can sleep at night."

I chuckle. I haven't been sleeping for years. "It's Mr. Hart to you."

The expression on his face as he watches me leave is one I'm well familiar with. It's a mixture of hate and fear.

Lina

WHEN MORNING COMES, my eyes burn and my muscles ache. My body is stiff. The worst is my desperate need for the bathroom. Just when I think I can't hold it any longer, Zane enters dressed in his black attire. Does he get the irony of chastising me for my choice of color? I say nothing while he uncuffs me. He takes one look at the raw skin around my wrist before he blows up our silent ceasefire with another backhand that hurts my jaw.

"I warned you," he snarls, shaking my wrist in front of my face. "Dami won't like this."

"Will he like you hitting me?"

"Oh, he may. He may even enjoy watching."

The statement hits a nerve, memories from a previous life I can't face.

He must've mistaken the reason for the grimace on my face, because he continues with a smirk. "You really don't know what Dami is capable of, do you? Don't worry. You'll find out soon enough."

When he lifts his hand again, I steel myself for the blow, but it's only to yank the covers down. "A word about any of this to Dami, and I'll make your life so miserable you'll wish you never set foot over this threshold." He pulls me to my feet by my arm. "Get dressed and remember what I said about staying out of my way."

When he's gone, I dash to the bathroom. My arm is coming to life with pins and needles. After massaging the muscles to get the circulation going, I do my grooming and get dressed.

Despite last night's big meal, I'm hungry. Do I need permission for food? Damian said he'd be gone until tonight, and Zane asked me to stay out of his way. I'll optimistically assume that means I can help myself to whatever there is to eat in the house, provided the kitchen is stocked. I don't have a cent of money on me, and no access to my bank account. Unless Damian withdraws the money for me, my hands are tied. I can't take a measly rand of my inherited wealth, not that I want to. It's Jack's money, which makes it dirty.

The feeling of helplessness isn't new. I've lived with it for all of my life. I've been treated like a minor into adulthood. My independence has been stripped. It's not easy to be a certified mental patient. It's even harder to get back a status of normalcy. Once you're on the list of crazies, you're branded. You have to pass many tests and convince a jury of psychologists that their torture has healed you, a pointless exercise when your legal guardian testifies against you. Being marked as mentally incapable left me vulnerable and alone. Even if I had access to money, I have no one to ask to drive me to a supermarket. Not having a driver's license or a car, I can't drive myself. When I got home from the institution, Harold refused to let me learn how to drive. He limited my freedom in all regards. He's been in charge of my decisions. Now, those decisions are in Damian's hands, which doesn't stop me from testing my boundaries. I'm famished enough to risk it downstairs in search of the kitchen.

Russell is at the door. I presume he got some sleep, because he gives me a cheery, bright-eyed greeting. Thankfully, Zane is nowhere to be seen. I pass a living and dining room before I find what I'm looking for. The kitchen is spacious and old-fashioned with a corner fireplace. The house must be old. The double-door fridge pulls my attention. Hurrying to it, I pull on the doors. It's not locked, and it's stocked to the brim with cheese, eggs, meat, and milk. I can have scrambled eggs or French toast. No, wait. Scones with cream and strawberry jam. Or scones and bacon. Or bacon with pork sausages and baked beans. Except that I don't know how to prepare any of it. I was a prisoner in Jack's house, locked up in my bedroom. Harold always had a cook. When I returned to Harold's house a widow, my meals were rationed, and the kitchen was off-limits.

"Good morning," a female voice says behind me.

Giving a little start, I bump my head before extracting it from the fridge. A young woman with red hair and freckles faces me. She has a pretty face, made even prettier by the smile she wears. It comes easily, that smile, and it makes me warm to her.

"Hungry?" She winks.

It takes me a moment to catch her implied meaning. "Oh. No. He left. I mean, it's not what you think."

She crosses the floor with an extended hand. "There's no need to explain. I'm Jana. Nice to meet you, Mrs. Hart."

We shake hands. "Please, call me Lina. Are you a guest here?"

Her brow pleats. "Mr. Hart didn't tell you?"

"Um, we didn't have much time to talk. He left for business last night."

"On your wedding night?" Flushing, she adds hastily, "I'm sorry. That's none of my business. It was an inappropriate remark."

"Don't worry about it. I know it must seem strange, but we haven't..." How do I explain it? She's obviously not aware of the dynamic of our forced relationship. "He hasn't told me much about the running of the household."

"He hasn't?"

"We haven't exactly been dating. Not long, I mean. We haven't been dating for long."

Her frown deepens, but she's polite enough not to pose questions. "I'm doing the catering as required. It's still early days, so I suppose we'll iron out the schedule as we go. Mr. Hart wasn't sure how often my services would be needed."

"I thought Zane is the housekeeper."

"He can't fry an egg. If he tries to make toast, he'll probably burn it."

"Oh." I fold my hands in front of me, not saying that I won't fare much better.

Her gaze flickers to my wrist, finding purchase there. It takes a moment to realize what she's staring at. Moving my hands to my back, I bury them in the folds of my skirt.

She recovers quickly. "Don't let that stop you from whatever you were going to make."

Self-consciously, I shut the fridge doors. "Do you have any recipe books?" On second thought, I should just go get my new phone to Google something.

She takes an apron from a hook and ties it around her waist. Her eyes trail over my ribcage. "How about I prepare you some bacon and eggs?"

I wrap my uninjured arm around my waist, trying to hide as much of my thinness as I can. "You don't have to."

"It's my job." She gives me another sweet smile. "Grab a seat at the table. I'll have it ready in no time."

I'm pathetically grateful to this woman who isn't mean.

In no time, as promised, I have a full English breakfast with fresh bread rolls and coffee in front of me. I don't know where to start. Ignoring the eggs, I go for the bacon first. Mm. Oh, my God. So good. It's crispy and salty. I butter a roll and bite into the fresh bread. It melts on my tongue. I've had more boiled eggs than what I care for, but the fried ones are soft, the yellow runny enough to scoop up with the bread. I hum my approval with every bite while Jana whistles as she tidies the kitchen. The fact that she knows where everything goes tells me it's not her first day on the job.

"Have you been working here for long?"

"Four years."

"For who?"

"The previous owners. You can say I came with the furniture when your husband bought the house."

"He bought it, furniture and all?"

If my lack of knowledge about how my husband acquired the house shocks her, she doesn't show it. After her initial surprise about how little Damian has shared with me, she's schooled her features. "He just walked in here and made the owners an offer to take over everything."

That explains how he managed to set up a house with staff so quickly after coming out of jail only last week.

"It must've been a good offer for them to have just packed up and left like that."

"They're an elderly couple who've been contemplating retiring at their holiday home on the coast for some time." She looks up from wiping down a counter. "I guess the offer came at the right time."

How ever did Damian make so much money, and in prison, no less? The obvious answer is disconcerting.

Saving the best for last, I bring the mug to my lips and inhale the heavenly aroma. Reverently, I take a sip. It's strong but smooth. My first coffee in two years.

"I'm going to do the shopping for lunch," Jana says. "Any special requests?"

I shake my head, the simple decision suddenly overwhelming.

"With this hot weather," she says, "I recommend a melon and Parma ham salad. Will that do?"

"Perfect, thank you."

"The menu is my responsibility," a hostile voice says from the door. Jana and I turn in unison. Zane stands in the frame, his face tight.

"You'll run it past *me*," he tells Jana.

She gives him a startled look.

"I'll be in the lounge when you're ready," he continues.

A strained silence remains as he leaves.

Jana is the first to come to her senses. "Right." She unties the apron, and adds uncomfortably, "I'll see you later."

As I get up to take the dirty dishes to the sink, she says, "You can leave that. The cleaning staff is coming in today." She adds, most probably for my ignorant benefit, "They come in twice a week."

When she's gone, I nick two of the rolls, slipping one in each skirt pocket. You never know. It's good to be prepared for rainy days, and rainy days are plentiful in my world.

I QUICKLY FAMILIARIZE myself with the layout of the mansion. The study and bedrooms are upstairs, and the rest of the living quarters downstairs. There's always a guard at the front door, and the back door is locked. The keys are not in the door. When I ask Russell about it, he tells me Zane keeps the keys. None of the interior doors in the house is locked, which will make my search for the evidence easier. Russell says Damian has an office in the city, but also works from home. I pray the evidence is somewhere in the house and not at his office.

I'm not the only one with that piece of evidence on my mind. Just after lunch, Russell finds me where I'm carefully placing my stolen bread rolls on the windowsill of an unoccupied bedroom to inform me Harold has arrived at the gate and refuses to leave.

I follow Russell on the long walk to the gate. Situated on the outskirts of town, the grounds are huge. Harold's Bentley is parked at the gate, and he's standing in front of it like a sulking child, his hands fisted on the iron bars.

"Tell them to open the gate," he calls when I'm still a distance away.

I only reply when I stop in front of him. "You're not allowed inside."

"Tell them," he insists. "You're my daughter. It's my right to visit you."

The automatic rifle hanging from the shoulder of the guard

manning the guardhouse makes me nervous. Harold must really be pompous not to be bothered by such a threat.

"They won't listen to me." For the first time in his life, Harold isn't getting something he wants. The ugly part of me feels satisfaction at his red-faced frustration. "They're following Damian's orders."

"We need to talk."

"As I said—"

"I'll tell Damian about your arms."

I go rigid. I quickly look toward the guard outside the gate, but he drags on a cigarette and blows smoke into the air, appearing unfazed by our conversation. Luckily, Russell is out of earshot, standing a few paces behind.

I lower my voice. "You have to leave."

"Come out here, then, if I'm not allowed inside." His eyes narrow menacingly. "Unless you want everyone to know your secret."

I've been living with my scars alone, and that's the way I intend to keep it. The world doesn't need to be a witness to how much I've been degraded.

"Let me out," I say to the guard on the other side.

The guard exchanges a look with Russell.

"I'm not a prisoner," I say to the man stumping out his cigarette under the heel of his boot. "And please pick up that butt and put it in the trash."

The man clenches his jaw and grips the rifle tighter.

Russell smirks. "You heard her."

Eyes locked on mine, the guard bends to retrieve the butt. He doesn't look away when he chucks it into the trashcan next to the guardhouse.

"Now," I say sweetly, "open the gate."

"I have instructions—"

"Our instructions are not to let Mr. Dalton onto the property," Russell says. "Mrs. Hart is free to leave whenever she wishes."

The guard takes a wide stance. "I don't answer to you, Roux. I only answer to Mr. Hart, and to Zane in his absence."

"Call Zane," Russell says. When the guard doesn't move, he takes his smartphone from his pocket. "Do you want me to call him for you?"

With a scoff, the guard enters the guardhouse and types a number into the intercom phone.

A few ringtones later, Zane's voice booms over the line. After listening to the guard, he tells him to let me out. Harold gives the man a victorious grin as I step through the gates. The minute I'm out, he grabs my arm and pushes me toward his car, but Russell blocks his way.

"She's not leaving the premises," he says. "You have five minutes."

Uttering a string of expletives that shames me to be connected to him, Harold leads me down the road that cuts through an empty plot and exits onto the highway.

"You have to find the evidence," he tells me when we're out of earshot. "That blackmailing bastard must be keeping it in the house."

"I figured."

He stops at the end of the road. "You know what will happen to me if the evidence falls into the wrong hands, don't you?"

"You'll go to jail and get killed."

"That's right. What will happen if I'm dead?"

I purse my lips and look toward the distance.

"You'll never know," he answers on my behalf.

A physical ache blooms in my chest, twisting itself like thorny ivy around my heart. "You said you'd tell me as soon as Jack's estate was yours to manage."

His fingers dig into my muscles. "Now it's Hart's to manage, isn't it?"

"It's not my fault. If you didn't steal his discovery and frame him for theft, this wouldn't have happened."

"Doesn't matter why or how it happened. Bring me what I want, and I'll tell you what you want to know. Don't bring it, and I'll tell the world the truth."

"What truth?" There are so many, I've lost count.

"That you committed a murder in cold blood."

I'm backed into a corner again, a feral cat in a cage. I feel like shredding his face and scratching his eyes out of their sockets, but I don't move a finger. I force myself to detach from the moment, like years of practice taught me. If I can get the evidence, I can blackmail Harold myself, but as always, he's one step ahead of me, demanding the proof of his crimes in exchange for his silence about mine. Where does that leave me? My only hope is an exchange—the evidence for my baby.

CHAPTER 4

Damian

The men around the table stare at me, their expressions varying from angry to downright murderous. I'm offering to buy them out, the price well below the current value of their shares. They'll accept. I have dirt on both of the fat bastards who'd sat at Dalton's table the night he condemned me.

"Stone." I push a stack of photos of him with his cock in a stripper's mouth across the table.

Women are his weakness. His marriage won't survive this particular weakness, and his wife owns the wealth. The very investment in Dalton Diamonds, the money that helped bring this corporation off the ground, came from Mrs. Max Stone. She'll strip him naked and throw him to the wolves.

He glares at me, rebelliously refusing to look at the photos my industrious private investigator provided.

Warren's turn is next. His weakness is getting high while having his ass pummeled by his masseur during his weekly appointment. Said massages he claims back from his medical aid fund for health reasons. The high-res images are a colorful array of him on his hands and knees, butt naked with his stomach hanging on the floor. It only gets more colorful as oily dicks join the picture.

"Jesus." He flicks the images over and puts a hand on his forehead. His face has gone from white to red.

"You son of a bitch," Stone says.

"Careful with the insults, Stone." I distribute the files. "Your contracts, gentlemen."

They both sign, agreeing not only to sell out to me, but also giving me their votes for acquiring my portion of the shares.

"Nice doing business with you," I say as I collect the signed contracts. "Keep the photos. Consider it my parting gift."

"Fuck you," Warren says.

"I don't think so. From where I'm standing, you're the one who's fucked."

"You don't know it yet, buddy," Stone says, spit flying over the table, "but that mine is dead. If you think you've struck the jackpot, think again. You're going under."

I clip my satchel closed. "We'll see."

Fuck, yes. It feels good to stand on the other side of the table. If I'm playing dirty, Dalton only has himself to blame. He set that wheel turning.

Lina

THE NIGHTMARES ARE LESS frequent now, but I have a particularly bad one that night. It's so terrifying, I wake not only myself, but also Zane who comes charging into the room in pajama bottoms, looking like a bull fuming from the nose. Handcuffed to the bed, I'm unable to escape his fury.

He shakes me until my teeth chatters. "Shut the fuck up. You're waking the whole damn house."

Meaning him. Jana doesn't stay on site.

I refuse to apologize. I can't help my dreams, and even if I could, I'll never say sorry to him.

"You're high maintenance, you know that?" Mumbling, "Stupid, rich bitch," under his breath, he walks from the room to return with a glass of water and a pill, which he holds out at me.

"Take this."

I turn my face sideways. "No. What is it?"

"If you don't drink it, I'll shove a suppository up your ass. You choose."

He grips my face and turns it back, applying enough pressure to force my jaw open. When my lips part, he pushes the pill onto my tongue with his thumb, making me gag. I have no choice but to dry swallow. The pill gets stuck in my throat, the bitterness lingering, but he doesn't offer me the water.

"What did you give me?"

"A sleeping pill."

"I don't take sleeping pills."

"You do now."

"I could be allergic."

"I know you're not allergic to food or medicine and that you get a rash from cheap brands of sun cream. I know you don't have STDs and that your period is irregular. I know all of this because Dami left me with a medical file the size of an encyclopedia."

Oh, God. He read the file. I feel the blood drain from my face, because it's hard to act tough when your enemy knows your worst humiliations.

"Yes, Lina. I know about your eating disorders and suicide attempt. I know about your exhibitionist tendencies and persecution syndrome. I know you married your ex-husband for money and kept it all to yourself after driving him to suicide. I know everything there is to know about you, so don't you forget that."

"You know nothing about me." It's a cliché, and it sounds flat, but it's the truth.

"Dami deserves better than you."

"I'm not the one who forced him to marry me."

49

"He didn't have a choice. He needed the money to get back his mine, and the only way was marrying you."

Damian didn't tell him money isn't the only reason. Sex is apparently also high on his list. "Are you justifying what he did?"

"He's a good man, the best I know. You don't know how lucky you are."

I snort.

His face contorts with fresh anger. "No one knows Dami like I do. Now put a cork in it, or I'll gag you."

There's nothing more to say. I keep quiet as he leaves the room. I'm left with only my will not to succumb to claustrophobic panic, and my newly discovered insight.

I could never have guessed the depth of Zane's hatred for me, which reflects the intensity of his feelings for Damian. Unknowingly, he gave away his secret when he showed me how much he cares. The caring goes deeper than friendship or loyalty.

He's in love with Damian.

~

Damian

ZANE'S MESSAGE JARS ME. In the back of the car on the way home from the airport, I read it again. Lina has met with her father. She's already disobeyed me. I'm furious, but I'm not surprised. I can't say I didn't expect it. I stare at the dark factories on the side of the highway as we approach Pretoria, contemplating an appropriate punishment, but my body and mind are tired, refusing to cling to the anger and tipping toward excitement at the thought of finally spending time with my disobedient little wife.

I rub my burning eyes. It's close to midnight. Ellis agreed to my terms. The meeting to sort out the logistics took forever. Despite my fatigue, my chest buzzes with a warm sense of contentedness. I'm high on my accomplishment.

Zane greets me at the door. At least he takes my jacket and asks about the trip before rubbing in Lina's defiance.

"I told you marrying her was a bad idea. She's already undermining your authority. They did you in once. They'll do it again. She did it on purpose, humiliating you by marrying you in a funeral dress, which the whole city is talking about, oh, and don't read the tabloids because it's all over the gossip pages, and she ignored a direct order, in front of the guards. You can't let this go, Dami."

I roll up my shirtsleeves, accepting the drink he pours. "You shouldn't have waited up."

"Are you kidding?"

"It's late." I go toward the stairs, eager to see my wife.

"Dami."

Irritation at his persistence simmers under my skin, but Zane is like a brother. We had each other's backs in jail, and I swore I'd never let him down, which is why I squash the annoyance and pause to look at him.

"Tell me about the meeting. Tell me how they took it. I wish I could've seen their fucking faces when you dropped the bomb."

"Tomorrow."

His face falls, but he knows when to stop pushing me. I leave the drink on the table with the ridiculously oversized bunch of flowers and make my way up the stairs. On the threshold of my room, I stop to look at Lina. My wife. In the light that comes from the bathroom, I can make out her features. She looks peaceful in her sleep. One arm is raised above her head, cuffed to the bedpost. The other lies over her stomach. The sheets are a knotted mess at her feet, almost as messy as the crow's nest of hair spread over my pillow. She must've tossed quite a bit to work that golden mass into such a tangle. Her plump lips are slightly parted, and her chest rises and falls with an even rhythm that's soothing to watch.

Quietly, I walk to the edge of the bed. The long nightdress would normally cover everything from her neckline to her ankles, but the silk has hitched up around her legs, exposing a slender calf. Her feet are narrow and small, her toes perfectly proportioned from the big toe that's the longest to the little toe that's the shortest. Who the hell has perfect toes? Who in fuck's name has sexy little toenails with moon-shaped cuticles and baby-pink nails?

The neckline of the hideous, black nightdress sits askew. The upper curve of her right breast shows. I own her, but not in a way that permits touching her in her sleep. Not yet. I do it, anyway, brushing my knuckles over that curve. Underneath the fabric, her bare nipple tightens. Fuck, I can't stop myself. I drag my index finger over that hard, little tip. It pebbles further. She doesn't stir. Testing my willpower, pushing my luck, I feel the full weight of her tit in my palm. She fits my hand like she was made for me. I move lower, smoothing my palm over her abdomen. Gently, I place her free arm next to her body. Like a doll. In her sleep, she lets me arrange her. It's in her sleep, goddamn, but I tell myself she lets me, because I can drag my hand lower over her sex and between her thighs. She sighs. Her lashes flutter, but she doesn't wake. I take my exploration farther, the silk gliding under my greedy palm like the slickness of cum over a sweaty skin, and all I can think about is ejaculating everywhere on that skin.

Wake up, Lina. Tell me the fuck to stop.

But she sleeps, and I reverse the direction of my hand, pushing the inky blackness up her pale legs until there's a balloon of fabric around her waist. I torture myself with playing a guessing game of how slick her slit is underneath the matching black silk.

After years of fantasizing about touching her, it's as much as I can take. I pride myself on being strong when it matters, but when it comes to her, I'm weak. I've always been weak for her. It's my weakness that's put us in this fucked-up situation, but as long as I have her in my bed, messy in my sheets, I can't make myself care. I can't even summon guilt. I've lost my conscience a long time ago in a cold cell behind bars. The only thing I can focus on is the hardness of my cock and the need to get off.

Pulling off my clothes, I get down on the bed beside her. I press my side against her breast and hipbone. Gently, I run my fingers over her arm, down and up, over her breasts. Her nipple turns hard for me, every time. *Good girl.* There are plenty more games we're going to play where she'll give me her body, and I'll learn how to read it. I'll learn how to please her until she screams. My hand moves over her stomach and between her legs where her skin is warmer, damper. Fuck. Down her thigh and knee to her ankle. With every stroke my cock thickens more. Christ, does she know what she does to me?

The high of having her here, like this, of doing to her whatever my heart desires, is like a drug. I could punish her because she conspired with her father and gave her virginity to my enemy. I should punish her for defying the most important rule I laid down when I brought her to my house. Most of all, I want to punish her because she turns me into a weak man for wanting her. Or, I can admit the truth, that I'm a broken man who doesn't need a reason. I want to punish her because it makes me hard. I'm a bastard and a devil, because I'm going to use her.

Grabbing my cock in my fist, I drag the head over her naked hip. The contact with her skin makes me hiss. In one of the most defining moments of my life, she sleeps soundly, unconscious to the madness of my lust. It's been six years since I laid my hands on a woman's body, six years since I buried my cock in the velvet fist of a pussy. My load is about to blow, and still, she doesn't move. I'm a shipwrecking storm, and she's the welcoming quiet of the ignorant beach.

It takes everything I've got and some more to pull away from her unconscious body and pump into my fist. I groan, none too softly. If she's going to wake up it's now, but she sighs again. I thrust faster, squeezing the base until the pain becomes a trigger for the pleasure. I fuck her black-clad body so hard with my eyes, I shoot within seconds like a horny teenager watching his first porn. My breathing is heavy. Her panties are soaked with my cum, the slickness wasted on silk instead of skin. The sheets are soiled too, and it's not enough, not by far, but I fucking promised myself it wouldn't be like this. All I can do is pull her against my softening cock and close my eyes.

If I didn't touch her, it doesn't matter.

It's a lie, because in my head, it's the same.

Still, on a demented level, I'm happy. She's here, and she's mine. I love her in silk, but I prefer her naked. If she has to be dressed, I'll take any color over black. She's my wife, not a widow. I keep on telling myself that until my body slows down enough for my lust to take a secondary place to filling my lungs with oxygen, to simply living. Slowly, our breathing falls into sync as if it has always been one.

THE TIME on my wristwatch shows it's past five in the morning. I have to get up for my work out and run. I've been out cold for over four hours, the longest stretch of uninterrupted sleep I've had in six years. I take a moment to enjoy the warmth of Lina's body. I've fucked a lot of women before I laid eyes on her, but I've never slept next to one. It's a first, and I like it. I like that it's her. I like the way we fit. My hand seems to find its way all by itself to the delicate column of her neck, always drawn to her body, always needing to touch. Pushing the nightdress off her shoulder, I press my lips against the exposed skin.

"Lina."

Goddamn, I want to fuck her so badly. Need is both a physical and mental torture. My dick is so hard it hurts, but the images in my head are worse. The things I imagine doing to her are the ultimate sins.

Letting my lips barely touch her skin, I drag them over her neck up to her ear. I can't bear to leave without saying good morning. It pains me to disturb her sleep, but it pains me more not to see her pretty eyes, so I start waking her gently.

"Lina."

Nothing. Well, hell. She's a deep sleeper. Nipping her earlobe, I repeat her name, this time giving her shoulder a soft shake. Not a stir. An alarm goes off in my mind, shrill and fearful. Bolting upright, I shake her harder.

My voice comes out angry, like a cold command. "Angelina, wake up."

She's still the ragdoll I used from last night, beautiful but unconscious of my actions.

Fuck. Shit. Fear is cold and hot and every temperature in between.

I just married her. I couldn't have fucked it up already. I'm in my pants before I've finished yelling for Zane. I've just covered her body with the sheet when he storms into the room, wearing boxer shorts and rubbing sleep from his eyes.

"What in God's name, Dami?"

"Keys." I flick my fingers at him. "Handcuffs."

He looks between confused and grumpy. "On the nightstand."

"Do it."

My instructions are cryptic, but I'm too frantic to think, let alone speak. She has suicidal tendencies, and I allowed Zane to leave her alone.

Straddling Lina, I slap her cheeks. "Wake up, angel."

She groans in protest, and something inside me gives, something I didn't know I had. It's a needle at the bottom of a haystack of emotions, but I don't pause to dissect it. I'm too busy pulling Lina to consciousness.

Zane fiddles with the key, at last managing to free her arm. She whimpers as he lowers it.

"That's it," I coo, not only nursing this small, too frail woman, but also my nerves. "Open your eyes."

Her lashes flutter as she fights to obey. I know the feeling. I fought my way back to pain from the mercy of unconsciousness on a concrete floor more times than I care to recall. Finally, she breaks through. Her eyelids lift and her freaky blue eyes stare at me. There's incomprehension as she tries to focus and remember where she is. Prying first the left then the right eye open, I study the blood vessels in the white of her eyes and the size of her pupils.

"What did she take?" I ask Zane who stands by quietly.

"A sleeping pill."

I want to knock his head into the bedpost for being so careless, but I tamp down my anger. Information first. "Only one?"

"As far as I know."

"Bring me the bottle."

"I took it away. I'll have to go get it in my room."

First clever thing he did. "Get it."

He jumps at my barked command, almost running for the door.

Her voice is hoarse. "Damian?"

"I'm here."

Her body tenses as she fully surfaces from her chemically induced sleep. Her eyes settle on my face. She takes in our positions. "What are you doing?"

"What did you take?"

She pushes at my shoulders, the grogginess gone and the fight back. "Get off me."

I probably should. My belt is hanging open, the button of my pants undone, and even under the circumstances, I'm hard for her. Zane returns as I get off the bed. He pushes a bottle of pills into my hand. I read the label. I'm not a medical expert, but the brand is a household name. The dose is way too strong for her weight. I fix my gaze on Zane. I don't have to speak for him to know I'm fucking furious.

Flustering, he blabbers, "She said she needs it to sleep. She begged me. How was I supposed to know?"

God knows I owe Zane, but I'm in his face. "Fucking common sense." I shake the bottle. Pills rattle. Zane flinches. "This is too strong for her."

"Am I supposed to contradict her doctor?"

"If this happens again…" I can't finish the sentence, because I'll have to give the one man who has my back a threat. Instead, I let it hang, let him get where I'm going, and he does.

He hangs his head. "I'm sorry."

"Get me a glass of water."

He rushes to the bathroom. The faucet turns on. It's only then that I turn my attention back to Lina. She's not only watching me, she's looking into my soul with the keenness of a practiced observer. My worry over her leaves me wide open, but I can't make myself care. I'm too relieved she's here, present, in her scrunched-up nightdress and cum-crusted panties.

Zane returns with the water. I don't thank him. He doesn't deserve my gratitude. When I support her head and bring the glass to her lips with a command to drink, he's still standing at the bedside with his hands clasped together.

I turn my head and catch him watching me feed Lina the water.

"Leave us."

His green puppy eyes plead with me. "Let me help. Tell me what you want me to do. I can take care of her. You go for your run."

I don't answer. I don't need to. My silence, quietly explosive, says it all. His shoulders slouch as he turns and leaves. It's irrational, but I don't like him seeing Lina with her sleep-tussled hair and eye-fucked body. This feels too private. She feels private. It's crazy. Zane isn't a threat. Still, my cum is on her underwear, and I feel her warmth in all the places I am cold.

Lina regards me warily as she pushes up against the headboard. "What happened?"

There's no easy way of explaining, so I walk to the bathroom and ransack her cosmetic bag. I take out every bottle of pills. There's stuff for headaches and nausea and menstrual cramps, but it's over-the-counter medicine. Satisfied that there's nothing life-threateningly dangerous, something she can overdose on, I pack everything into the overhead cabinet.

"Happy?" she snipes when I walk back into the room.

There's something in her eyes, something like hurt, as if I'm at fault for not trusting her when she can't be trusted. Even then, even if trust isn't something I can give her, I want her. I have a feeling I'll want her forever. No, I know with the kind of clarity that comes once in a scary lifetime. Lina is my obsession, now that I have her even more than before, if such a thing is possible. Nothing can ever happen to her.

I cross my arms. "You'll take no more medication without my approval."

No answer. I only get her defiant look, an expression that's going to cost her later, turn me hard, and make us both come.

"I didn't ask for the pill," she says. "Zane forced me to take it."

Zane is many things, certainly not a good person, at least not in the traditional sense, but I trust him with my life.

"Lina."

"You don't believe me." She utters a wry laugh. "Of course you don't."

I don't believe Lina is lunatic crazy like her old man implies, but I do think she's a danger to herself. Sometimes, that is. She's not always on a hunger strike, a hermit, or suicidal. I do believe she has issues, as her history shows, and I don't believe lying is beneath her.

My little wife doesn't like my silence. She doesn't like what it implies. Throwing back the sheets with an angry movement, she prolongs her act of defiance as if it's going to make a difference. She's in the process of swinging her legs from the bed when she freezes. She looks down at her bare thighs, and then her crotch. Her face pales at the same time as her cheeks redden, creating a stunning contrast of shock and embarrassment. My gaze follows hers. We're both looking at the dried cum on her black silk panties. She inhales and exhales once, twice. She wrestles with her anger. I see the battle in the rigid set of her shoulders and the stormy blue hue of her eyes when she lifts them to me.

Her voice is chilled. It doesn't ring like bells, but like ice cubes. "What happened?"

We're back to the same question, and I still don't have an easy explanation.

Her volume rises in panic. "What happened?"

"Don't worry." I lean against the doorframe, trying to sound dry when I'm hard, harder than earlier. "I didn't fuck you." Only with my eyes.

Jumping up, she yanks the underwear from her legs. She can't free her feet fast enough. It stings, but I let it slide. Sooner than she realizes, I'll make her sleep with her pussy full of my cum all night.

"You ejaculated on me, you sick pervert."

Can't deny it. That I did, and that I am. "I jacked off in bed. Don't you?"

She flushes, not the angry, blotchy red, but a full-on face red. Guilty.

"Maybe I'll make you show me," I say.

Bundling the panties in her fist, she marches to where I stand, coming to a stop with her breasts inches from my chest. She waits. I'm blocking the door to the bathroom, and I don't move. She waits. I'm not going to apologize for something I don't regret. It's a stare-off. She breaks first, like I knew she would.

"Do I need permission for the bathroom, too?" She throws the permission part in like a jab, getting back at me for what I said about the pills.

I step aside. "The bathroom is free."

Her eyes slice me up in ten different ways. When she pushes past me, I grab her wrist. It's partly to touch her, and partly to let her know I'll let her get away this time, but the decision is ultimately mine. When my fingers close around the circumference of her delicate bones, she sucks air through her teeth and winces. I didn't grab her hard. I'm mindful of my strength and her much smaller body. I slacken my hold and look down. Like firecrackers, my anger ignites. It's not the volcanic eruption of earlier but rather an ongoing chaos of sparklers.

"What's this?" I ask.

She pulls on my hold. "It's nothing."

I lift her wrist for closer inspection. The skin is chaffed. A raw riff marks her flesh. It must hurt like a bitch. I'm angry with her for injuring herself and livid with Zane all over again for allowing it.

"It's not nothing."

She finally keeps still, succumbing to my examination.

I brush a thumb above the aggravated line. "Why did you struggle?"

She shrugs like it doesn't matter, but the gesture shows the opposite of what it's supposed to mean. There's more than what she's admitting.

"Lina."

"I get claustrophobic."

"You weren't closed in a small space."

"Being constrained does the same."

I rub my thumb over her skin. Left. Right. Left. "Will you jump through a window or run away if I don't cuff you to the bed?"

The ice melts in her eyes, and a bit of fire kicks in. "I guess you'll just have to wait and see."

I can't help the smile that creeps over my face. "Then I guess you'll just have overcome your fear of being constrained."

This round is mine, and she doesn't lose gracefully. She yanks on my hold again. "Let go."

"Get your ass into the bathroom." I all but shove her ahead of me.

At the sink, I wash her skin before drenching it with disinfectant and applying a bandage from my medical supplies. She sucks in a breath whenever my fingers make contact with the wound, but she doesn't complain.

"Better?" I ask when I'm done, planting a kiss on the bandage.

She doesn't thank me, not that she should. It's my fault she got injured, another mistake that happened on my watch.

"Can I have my shower, now?"

Her voice is like a sharpened knife, and fuck me if I don't deserve it.

"It's early." I resist the urge to smooth down her hair. It's just another excuse to touch her. "You can go back to bed."

"I'm awake now."

Hell, so am I. We have issues to deal with, but they can wait. My body is still pumping adrenaline from the shock, anger, and a gnawing hunger that has nothing to do with food. I need that run more than ever.

"Go ahead. I'll have my shower after my run."

She's not quick enough to hide her relief, or maybe she doesn't care that I see it. I make her suffer a bit longer by brushing my teeth. Noticing her cosmetics are still packed in the bag as if she wants to be ready to run at any given moment, I remove every item and stack them meticulously in the cabinet and on the vanity, where they belong. The point I'm making comes through clearly. All the while, she watches me like a cornered animal. All the while, I think about her naked pussy under that nightdress. When I can't take it any longer, I give her privacy. Pulling on my tracksuit pants and T-shirt in the dressing room, I try not to think about the only thing I can think about, how naked she is in my shower without her nightdress.

Lina

DAMIAN LEFT the bathroom door ajar. I can't bring myself to close it, not without freaking out, but when he doesn't come back for several seconds, I dare get into the shower. I'm not sure how I feel about him coming on my underwear while I was wearing it. What am I thinking? I'm not sure about him coming on my underwear, period. Yet, when I conjure the mental image of Damian stroking his erection, I don't feel the condemnation I should, not even with *my underwear* in the picture. Not even with *me* in the picture. I get wet. I imagine myself watching, and I get wetter. It's wrong, but I'm slick, and I've never felt like this before. I'm swollen and aching, and when my hand travels through the soapsuds on my belly down between my legs, it's not because I'm bored or lonely. It's because I'm turned on. Incredibly so. Enough to chase my release in Damian's shower with the door ajar and my ruined panties in the trashcan. No washing can save them. Not when the thought of what soiled those panties makes me come so hard my thighs quiver.

I got the bandage wet. Now that I know where Damian keeps them, I help myself to a dry one. I don't meet my eyes in the mirror while I'm dressing, but I do look at the scars. I count them out of habit. My body is mutilated, nothing short of belonging in a Frankenstein movie, and it hurts to look, but also helps to ground me. It kills the post-orgasm buzz. My guilt vanishes.

On my way to the kitchen, I run into Zane on the stairs. He's dressed in tight shorts and a headband with an exercise towel thrown over his shoulder. Russell is at the door, within sight and earshot. Zane's gaze slips to the bandage on my wrist, but he says nothing. His warning is a silent one as he shoulders me in the passing.

"Good morning, Russell," I say when I reach the bottom of the stairs.

"Good morning, Mrs. Hart."

"Lina, please."

"Mr. Hart will put a bullet in me if I call you by your first name, but thanks all the same."

The sad thing is I believe him.

In the kitchen, I find breakfast waiting. There's toast, boiled eggs, ham, and cheese. It's too early for Jana to be in, and Zane would rather let me starve than serve me a morsel of bread, which leaves Damian. Is this his way of apologizing for last night? No. If he wanted to, he would've done so. I can't fathom why he'd prepare me breakfast, but I'm not one to waste food. I eat until the waistband of my dress feels too tight before putting the leftovers in the fridge and tidying the kitchen. I slip two rolls into my pockets—hot cross buns, today—to dry on the windowsill.

Irony can be cruel. I'm one of the wealthiest women in the country, but I've been starving for most of my adult life. Jack found it the most effective way of keeping me in check. A hungry person will do almost anything for food. At first, withholding meals was punishment for mistakes. He made me go to bed without dinner or skip breakfast and lunch. Then it became a way of feeding his sickness, the pleasure he derived of watching me suffer. In the end, it became a bargaining chip, my body for bread. Zane was right. I am a whore. I whored myself out for food when the beatings and isolation didn't break me, and that's when Jack's torturing truly started to bloom. I rub my hands over the sleeves of my dress, testing the pull of the scar tissue when I flex my muscles, but it's not what I want to think about. I bury those memories deep down where they're inaccessible to even myself.

I pass the morning reveling in the freedom of having the upstairs rooms to myself, a big deal for someone who'd been locked up, but there's something even more tempting. The sun is shining outside. At first, I go hesitantly, but when Russell doesn't stop me, I go down the front steps and into the garden with Russell on my heels. There's enough work to warrant the garden service that, according to Russell, comes in weekly, but I spot an old man hunched over a spade by the rose bushes. He looks to be in his sixties, much too old for this kind of work. Maybe he came with the house, like Jana.

"Good morning."

He looks up, a cigarette hanging askew in his mouth. "There's nothing good about it."

"I'm Lina."

"Mrs. Hart," Russell says.

The old man ignores him. "I know who you are."

"Oh."

"Zane told me."

"Have you been working here for long?"

Folding his hands over the handle of the spade, he laughs softly, mockingly, as if he knows something I don't. "As long as Damian owns this place."

"Which is—"

"Six days."

We look at each other, me feeling like I'm trespassing and him with his cigarette smoke curling in the air.

Finally, he mumbles, "Some of us has work to do," before digging his spade into the soil, dismissing me.

I continue toward the blue water of a swimming pool, glancing back at the old man and finding his eyes on me. It's not a friendly stare.

"Who *is* that?" I ask Russell.

"That's Andries. Don't mind him. He's always cranky."

"How old is he?"

"Around sixty, I'd say."

"He's too old to be gardening in the heat of the day."

"Nah." Russell utters a wry chuckle. "He's tougher than you think."

"Why would Damian employ a sixty-year-old man?"

"He needs the job." He stops, making me look at him. "Andries is Zane's grandfather."

There's something about the way he says it, like a message he wants me to get. I do. If Zane isn't my friend, neither is Andries, but

Andries is just an old man. Even if he's grumpy, I worry about letting an old man weed the soil.

"Can't he do something else?"

Russell shrugs. "It's not my place to ask."

"Does he stay on the property?"

He points at a cottage behind the house. "In the granny flat."

By the time we reach the pool, Russell is walking next to me instead of following. He shows me the summerhouse, greenhouse, and tennis courts. For the life of me, I can't imagine why Damian needs all of this, and I can. It's a statement. It's what people ask first in certain conversations. "So, where you do live?" It's a casual question, and it's loaded. Location is everything. I, of all people, should know.

"We better head back," Russell says. "You're burning."

I touch my cheek. "Am I?" I haven't been outside for too long.

When Harold fetched me from the mental institution where he had me locked up for the better part of a year, drugged and kept on the brink of starvation, he decided isolation and starvation were effective ways of control. It was easier to handle me if I left the table always a little hungry, and never left the house at all. He didn't lock the interior doors, didn't even force me to close them, but he locked me in, nevertheless. As long as he's hiding my child's body from me, he knows I'll never escape. He knows I'll put my life on the line to find that piece of evidence. If Damian hadn't returned to his study after his run, I would've been going through his drawers already. Not having realized how tight my stomach muscles are pulled, I make a conscious effort to relax them. Impatience is like an ever-present, distant ache that gnaws at my gut. I just have to bide my time.

Russell's concerned voice pulls me back to the present. "Are you all right?"

"I think you're right. I'm not used to so much sun."

He still walks beside me as we go back to the house, making a point of showing me the high walls, electrified barbwire, and guarded gate. He's in the middle of telling me how hard it would be to break in when I stop. He pauses to look at me.

"I know I can't get out. You don't have to convince me it's impossible."

His expression turns aghast. "I was only trying to make you feel safe."

"The only place I'll feel safe is as far away from here as possible."

He doesn't reply, and I continue my stroll. After two beats, Russell falls in a step behind me. Our friendly banter is over.

After much pleading, Jana lets me help with the lunch. I have to do something. When I suggest we eat together, she refuses, explaining it would be crossing a line Mr. Hart won't appreciate, and I end up eating my salad alone. I'm packing the dishwasher when a movement at the window draws my attention. A bat almost flies into the glass before diverting at the last minute and heading into the herb garden. Rushing to the window, I duck for a better view. I've seen some bats when I was a child. We had an abandoned, detached garage where they nested. With their furry faces and tilted snouts, they look like a miniature cross between a wolf and a pig. They're insanely cute.

"There you are," Zane says too cheerfully behind me. "Dami wants you upstairs."

I don't ask where. I don't have to. When I enter the foyer, voices float down from the open door of Damian's study. One belongs to my husband, and the other I don't know.

Damian meets me at the door before I have a chance to knock. For a moment, he looks at me like a man who knows my secrets, but he can't possibly know. The longer I look into his eyes, the worse it gets, because he's a man with a goal set on unraveling me, on taking my secrets apart.

"Lina."

He's not the shivering young man I met on a cold night in June. He's hardened, and he's very much a man. He lets me know in the way he says my name and holds my eyes with something that borders on indecency. His voice is darker and deeper. There's a gravity to it that comes with experience and confidence. The sound is masculine and strong. It scares me, because it makes me yearn for something I can only find at the profoundness of his maleness. It makes me long to feel safe. To feel safe, I have to submit to his protection, but to protect me he needs to love me, and he's lost his ability to love because of Harold and me. He'll substitute love with what equals it in his twisted mind. He'll try to possess me. All of me.

When he finally steps aside, I'm the fly who enters the spider's parlor. A man with a sharp face and pointed chin waits inside. He sits behind a card table with his hands splayed out in a crow-like fashion over a black case, as if he's not keen on parting with the case. He has too thin, too light hair, and his fingernails are cut too short.

Damian skips the introductions. When he says, "Show her," the man flips back the lid of the case, revealing five rows of brilliant, sparkling stones on black velvet.

I've been surrounded by people in the business for all my life, long enough to know what a flawless diamond looks like. There are princess, teardrop, and classical cuts, all bigger than four carats. They catch the sunlight and throw rainbows over the velvet while the man behind the case looks like he's losing a year of his life for every second he keeps that box full of rainbows open. I don't even want to guess how much the box is worth.

"Pick one," Damian says.

I tear my gaze from the diamonds to look at him. He's not smiling. He's insisting.

The man starts bouncing his knee in a nervous tick. The diamond Damian is offering isn't a token of love, not to Damian. It's a token of status.

"No, thanks."

The man regards me as if I've just shot him in his jittery leg.

Damian narrows his eyes. "You need a ring."

"I have a ring." Which was forced on me. I don't need another.

"You're my *wife*. Diamonds are my *business*. Do you have any idea how humiliating it will look for you if I don't offer you an engagement ring?"

"It's a bit like offering me the mustard after the meal, don't you think?"

"Lina, pick a fucking diamond." His voice drops to a dangerously low level. "I'm giving you the choice."

"Like the choice to marry you?"

"Um." The scrawny man licks his lips. His scrawny vocal cords suit him. "The princess cut is rather nice."

"These are my best diamonds," Damian says, ignoring the man. "If you don't choose one, I'll pick for you."

"Wouldn't that make for a difference?"

He's on me so fast Scrawny yelps. One hand is in my hair and other around my neck. He's not hurting me, just holding me like an animal forcing his dominance.

"Go ahead," he says. "Spite yourself. Tell yourself you hate those stones for everything they represent. Tell yourself whatever is going through your pretty little head, but don't expect me to publicly disgrace you by leaving your finger bare."

My Adam's apple bobs against his palm when I swallow. "It's not bare."

"By a diamond magnate's standards, it is."

He lets go. I stumble, but he's ready, catching me before I fall.

This is as much as Scrawny can take. He snaps the case shut and is on his feet, heading for the door.

"She'll take the teardrop," Damian says, holding my gaze. "It seems most fitting."

The man is gone before I've found my bearings.

"Russell," Damian calls down, "tell security Tony's good to go."

"Yes, sir."

Downstairs, men are lining up with firearms. No wonder Tony is so antsy.

Damian walks to the door and kicks it shut, cutting off my view of the commotion in the foyer. I breathe faster. I pushed him. I'm still to discover his limits. The closed door doesn't help. It's not locked. *It's not locked.*

"We have unfinished business," he says as he advances on me. "You broke the most important rule I gave you. What did I say about visits with your father?"

"He never set foot on your property."

"So, you broke *two* rules. You visited with your low-life father *and* left the property without Russell."

"Russell wasn't far. He was just outside the gate."

"Number three, you hurt yourself, and that won't happen again. Not on my shift, and my shift lasts for as long as you're my wife."

"I didn't hurt myself."

"You cut your wrist raw on the handcuff. Number four, you took a pill you clearly know is too strong for you. Number five, you threw my gift and consideration back into my face."

"I don't need your consideration."

"I beg to differ, but if it's a point you wish to push, I can play your game."

"The last thing I need is you turning me into a showpiece with a big, fat diamond on my finger."

His expression darkens. "Marrying me turned you into a showpiece, has it?"

"Yes," I hiss. "And a whore." I could call *him* a whore for marrying me for my late husband's money.

"You have no idea what it's like to be treated like a whore, angel."

"Do your best. This time, try to be a man about it and do it while I'm awake."

He snaps. Nothing in his stance changes, but I feel it. It crackles on the air. This is the breaking point. This is his limit.

"Go to the desk," he says. "Bend over and pull up your skirt."

He'll have to drag me there. I'll never go out of my own will.

"Ten lashes," he says, "two for every rule you broke and every destructive thing you did to yourself. I'll add another five if I have to make you walk to the desk."

I don't move. I can't give in.

"Very well, Lina."

He walks to the fireplace. My stomach is tight with tension. I follow him with my gaze and gasp as I take in the wall. Distracted by Tony and his diamonds, I haven't noticed how the wall above the mantelpiece has been transformed. An array of whips and paddles hang on hooks, neatly spaced. My mouth dries up. I attempt a futile effort at swallowing away the dryness. He stares at the collection for a moment, seemingly deep in thought, and finally removes the paddle, which he places on the corner of the desk. In a few strides, he's in front of me, taking my arm and forcing my feet to move to his desk. With a hand around my nape, he pushes my upper body down while throwing my long skirt up around my waist. I struggle, but he easily grabs my wrists and pins them behind my back. He's not careful of my injury. My skin burns under the bandage where he applies pressure. He transfers both wrists to one hand while the other moves to my underwear. With a single yank, he pulls down my panties. I stop squirming. I pinch my thighs together, hiding what I can, but his palm caresses my globes and scorches my heart with shame.

"Count, Lina."

"Go to hell."

"Sixteen lashes. I'll keep on adding one until you learn to count."

He picks up the paddle and lets me feel the cool wood on my lower back. Slowly, he drags it over the crevice of my buttocks. I start squirming anew when he reaches my sex. Flames leak over my cheeks because in this position he sees everything.

He warns me, not with words, but by removing the paddle. He brings it back down diagonally over my globes with a smack. Reflexively, my ass clenches. It stings, but it doesn't hurt.

"Count, Lina."

I grind my teeth and lock my jaw. If there's one thing I know how to do, it's taking pain. He underestimates me if he thinks I'll break under his paddle.

"Count, Lina."

"No."

"Are you sure about that?"

I only gnash my teeth harder, preparing for the second blow, which will no doubt hurt, but I'm the one who's underestimating. Instead of hitting me, he drags the thin edge of the wood through my slit, parting my folds as if I'm an object that needs closer inspection. I jerk when he reaches my clit. The sensations from the shower return.

I'm swelling and turning slick. This can't be happening. Not while he's looking. The touch on my sex disappears, and then he slaps my left globe. Again, the smack is playful. It makes me hotter. It makes me ashamed. My nape turns damp with sweat.

His voice is hoarser. "Count, Lina."

I can't give in. I won't. This time, I know what to expect. I think of icebergs and how much I hate him, but when he touches my slit with the knob-end of the paddle handle, I realize with a shock how wrong I've been again. I underestimated him again. Dragging the thick knob down my slit, he parts me wider. My struggles are meaningless. He's too strong. When he reaches my clit, he runs circles over the nub with the wooden knob. To my horror, I turn wetter, my slickness easing the movement of the instrument. The only thing worse than my reaction is the knowledge that he's watching.

Smack. My right globe comes alive with heat. I wish he'd make it hurt so I wouldn't get aroused, but as long as he's hitting just hard enough to jiggle my ass, I feel it deep in my core. My inner muscles clench.

"Three. Count, Lina."

If he brings the paddle back to my sex, I'll come. I don't have a choice but to count.

"Three." How I hate him for making me speak when my voice quivers.

There's victory in his tone. "That's my girl." He's the master of the situation, fully in control while I'm falling apart.

Smack. Right on the crack of my ass. Too soft. Too hot.

"F-four."

The knob is back between my legs. It's wet from my arousal. He rubs it over my slit again before starting to massage my clit.

"W-what are you doing?" Why isn't he going on to five and six and seven so I can lower my dress and hide from his eyes?

"Count, Lina."

"Five."

Then he does worse. He twists the handle from left to right, wiggling it deeper. As I gasp, he applies pressure, stretching and entering me. I still in surprise at the sudden intrusion. Shock and embarrassment course through me. I want to hate it with all my being, but the sad and unfair truth is that the feeling isn't unpleasant.

I can't stop a moan from escaping as he pushes deeper. I bite back a whimper as he pulls out until the knob is barely lodged inside, stretching my opening. It's dirty and good. I've never been this needy, not even in the shower with my secret thoughts. I must be a closet pervert. I can't think when he's teasing me with a few shallow thrusts. I'm fast moving beyond the ability to reason logically. What is he doing to me?

"Count, Lina."

"S-six."

He gives me my reward, fucking me with the paddle handle. Not gently, but not hard, either. Just enough to make my wetness gush around the intrusion.

"Seven, Lina."

"Seven," I gasp as he moves the object inside me again.

His rhythm turns harder, quicker, softer, quicker, and everything inside me clenches. My senses go haywire. I'm not resisting any longer. He knows it. He lets go of my wrists to spank me with his hand while he keeps on doing his wicked work with the paddle handle. I'm breathing hard, but so is he, and I forget to count.

"Count."

"Nine. T-ten."

I don't know where we are any longer. He's careful and rough at the same time.

"Eleven," he says, urging me on.

"Eleven. Twelve!"

He changes the angle of the paddle so that the thin side presses on my clit. I gasp again, speechless, but he rolls the handle, hitting not only my clit, but also a sensitive spot inside. My nails scrape over the wood of his desk. My body goes taut. I'm going to come if he doesn't stop. I'm going to come right in front of his eyes.

"Count, Lina. Thirteen."

I'm a blabbering mess, mixing up numbers and signals. He spanks me harder, but what's supposed to hurt feels good.

"Thirteen," he repeats, relentless. "Count with me, Lina."

He leads, and I follow.

"Fourteen."

We speak in tandem. "Fifteen."

"Come for me, Lina."

It hurts. The last smack draws my tears. I don't come, I explode. My back arches, my upper body lifting off the desk. Shockwaves ripple through me. He makes me ride the orgasm so hard I go on tiptoes to escape, but there's no escaping Damian. He manipulates my body until my thighs quiver, and my knees buckle. Only then does he gently pull the invasive object out. The paddle hits the floor with a thud. If I weren't braced on the desk, I would've fallen to my knees. Unable to move in the aftermath of the violent climax, I lie still while he drags his palms over my globes, spreading them a little, and plants a kiss at the top of my crevice. His fingers dig into my bottom as he splays and kneads me, pulling me apart and pushing my flesh back together as if I'm clay in his hands.

Turning my head sideways, I look at him while perspiration trickles down my temple. The concentration on his face as he studies my body makes my cheeks heat. How quickly and hard I came makes my whole body burn with humiliation, but he doesn't rub my weakness in with victorious words or knowing smirks. He only pulls my panties up and my skirt down before gripping my hips to help me stand. With my legs still wobbly, I have to lean my back against his chest. I'm overly aware of his erection pressing against my lower back. I want to pull away, but he's holding me too tightly. His study smells like sex and me, a one-sided victory.

Running his nose over the arch of my neck, he inhales deeply. "Your punishment is over."

This was punishment? "You didn't hurt me."

"I know."

"Why not?" I ask snappily. I hate that I came. I hate the suspense. I prefer to get the unsavory parts of my new life out of the way. The quicker I know what he has planned for me, the better. I'll deal with it because it won't be forever. I'll find the evidence that will set me free. "I know you wanted to."

I can *hear* him smile, so calm and collected, nothing like the mess he made out of me, when he says, "Not today."

The answer is mild, but the meaning sets a tornado off in my head. He's the cruelest of cruel. He's giving me what I dread more than pain —the awful suspense. I suck in a breath. I want to ask when, how, where, but before I can construct a meaningful sentence, a knock falls on the door. With my nerves are already shattered, the sound makes me jerk. Damian's body tenses against mine. Before he can give his permission, the door flings open. At the same moment I register the beautiful woman on the threshold, Damian pushes me away.

CHAPTER 5

Damian

*O*f all the timing in the world, Annemarie chooses now. I'm trying to get around why I made Lina come instead of cry, and it doesn't help that I'm fighting a raging hard-on. What just happened is private. It's intimate, however warped our intimacy may have been. Lina didn't come for me by choice. I manipulated her body into climaxing. I don't want to humiliate Lina by allowing another woman to witness the aftermath of this twisted lust, which is why I put a little distance between us. It's what any gentleman would do.

When I step aside, Lina's face turns blank. With the way she folds her hands and draws back into herself, the small distance may as well be a gorge. It's as if I didn't watch her orgasm a moment ago or tell her I most definitely want to hurt her, only not today. I've just admitted to being a sick son of a bitch, and now my wife's attention is fixed on the woman standing in the doorframe. Anne's gaze settles on Lina before it shifts to the paddle on the floor.

"What are you doing here?" I ask.

Anne's green eyes shimmer with hurt. "I came for some of my things."

Goddammit. "You were supposed to do it before." Before I brought home my bride.

"I have no place to keep my clothes."

"My conditions were clear."

"Damian, please." She runs across the floor and throws herself at my feet. "Please don't kick me out. I beg you."

Letting her stay, even for one night, was a mistake. I shouldn't have given in. Housing a single, beautiful woman with revealing clothes who easily goes down on her knees is the kind of tabloid news that will make a public spectacle out of any new wife. I took responsibility for Lina when I married her, and I take my responsibilities seriously. Hurting Lina to feed my lust behind closed doors is one thing. Publically dishonoring her is another. There's enough of the crazy gossip going around as it is.

"Damian." Anne blinks up at me. "Please."

Lina's cheeks are losing their after-orgasm glow. Despite her poker face, she's unsettled. I can read it in her eyes. To her credit, she doesn't flee the awkward situation.

Anne is nothing if not insisting. She folds her arms around my legs, creasing my pants in her fists. "Damian."

I try to pry her free, but she only clings to me harder. Zane saves me by charging into the room. His face goes red as he takes in the scene. Hooking his hands under Anne's armpits, he hauls her to her feet.

"What are you doing?" he exclaims.

Lina looks between us, her blank expression finally slipping to make space for something that looks like hurt or embarrassment, maybe both.

Beyond irritated with Anne for her intrusion, I don't spare her my wrath. "I gave you more than enough money to find your own place."

"I had bills to pay."

Zane starts pulling her to the door. "Let's go."

"I don't have a job," she says. "You know how high the unemployment rate is. I've got nowhere to go."

"You shouldn't have come here," Zane says under his breath.

Lina's voice rings through the space, clear and beautiful. "Wait."

Zane stops to look at her.

"You can't throw her out on the street," my wife says. "You heard what she said. She has nowhere to go."

Both Zane and Anne stare at her in surprise. Instead of gratitude, something else flashes in Anne's eyes, something ugly. It's a nasty trait. It shows when you realize someone is a better person than you. It's called jealousy.

"It won't look good for you if she stays here," Zane offers meekly.

Lina steps forward, emanating authority as if her ass isn't still smarting—just a little—from my hand. "I don't care."

"You don't know what you're saying." She *will* care when it's head-line news. Besides, my mother used to say two women in one kitchen can only lead to trouble.

"Since my money will no doubt pay for some of the living expenses in this monstrosity of a house," Lina says, "I should have a say, even if the property belongs to you."

Oh, but she's wrong on so many levels. One, I won't use a cent of her dead husband's money to provide for her living expenses. No, the roof over her head, the food she eats, and the clothes I intend for her to wear are all paid for by *my* money. Whatever money she brought into this union is destined for two purposes only—to get back my mine and destroy her father. Two, by court ruling she's incompetent and unfit to manage her own affairs. She has no say in anything. The only say she'll have is the permission I'll give her when and how I see fit. Three, we're married within community of property. The house belongs to both of us. She would've known that if she'd paid attention to what she was signing in church, not that I blame her for being distracted on the day I married her. I don't believe in going halfway. It's all or nothing, and when it comes to Lina and me, it's all. I'm not worried she'll divorce me for half of my fortune, because I'm not letting her go.

Zane looks ready to flee. Anne is suddenly grateful, offering Lina a belated smile.

"You will *not* put her in the street when we have five spare bedrooms," Lina insists.

There's fire in her blue eyes and determination in the set of her small body. If I didn't know better, I would've thought Lina knew what it was like to be homeless, which is, of course, the furthest thing from the truth. She was born into wealth and that's all she's known. She's so strong, so convinced of her principles, and so goddamn beautiful as she stands there, dressed in black, underwear soaked, that I can't deny her. That's why she's so loveable, why I fell for her the first time we met. She'll offer a cold man a shawl and a homeless woman— a woman who for all she knows is my mistress—a room, no matter the consequences. Her compassion is her strength, and that's why I'm weak. I don't have compassion. I only have vengeance.

I cross my arms. "It will be temporarily until you're back on your feet." I shift my gaze to Zane. "This better not become a front-page tabloid story."

"Of course not," he says quickly.

Anne grips my hand in both of hers. "Thank you, Damian,"

I pull free. "Thank Lina."

Anne looks between Zane and me. "Which room can I take?"

"Lina will decide." Walking to the door, I address my wife. "A moment, please."

Outside in the hallway, I back Lina up to the wall. Zane and Anne can exit at any moment, but I need this. I need to pin her weight against me. I need to remind her how she submitted not moments ago. I need to remind myself that I have the power, even when I give in to her.

"What?" she asks, a little breathless.

Taking perverse pleasure from her reaction, I don't back up. She's been kind to me from day one, but there was no telling if she'd want me. I breathe easier, knowing it's doable. Call it a test, but after what she showed me in the study, I can teach her to want me.

"What?" she repeats, flattening her back against the wall, but it doesn't stop her nipples from brushing my chest.

As Anne barged in uninvited, there was no need for introductions. Since she'll be staying, I need to clarify the nature of our relationship.

"Anne is Zane's sister," I say. "She boarded with me for a night. That's all."

"His sister?"

"She's not my mistress."

"You don't owe me an explanation."

"As your husband, I do."

"That's what you wanted to tell me?" she asks, as if telling her I'm not fucking the guest she invited isn't important.

"We have a party on Saturday. Zane will take you dress shopping. Whatever you need, he has a credit card for your expenses."

Something in her gaze shifts. "Zane?"

"I'll be tied up with urgent business for most of the week." Such as voting Dalton off the board.

"I didn't mean it like that."

"Like what?"

"That I prefer you to take me."

"Pity." I smile like I imagine a snake would grimace at a mouse. "How did you mean it?"

"I don't need Zane to take me shopping."

"Your safety isn't up for discussion."

"I'm not talking about my safety. I don't need a dress."

"You do."

"I have enough."

Five. I've counted. All black. "Not for our wedding reception."

"Our what?"

"You didn't think I'd let our marriage pass without a celebration, did you?"

"Actually, yes."

"No such luck, angel." I push away from the wall before I'm tempted to make her come against it. I can get addicted to her orgasms. When she comes, I can tell it's overwhelming. I like to know I have the power to do that to her. "Get a dress." I walk away. Resisting her is too damn hard.

"No," she says to my back.

"Get one," I call over my shoulder.

Of course she's going to defy me.

Lina

WHAT HAPPENED? I feel like the mouse in the cat's claws. Damian has gone easy on me, but he's not done playing. Of that, I'm sure. Strung out by his game, I search Jana out in the kitchen. Her kindness is soothing. She tells me everything I don't know about my own wedding reception. I sit at the kitchen table, sipping the tea she insists I drink, while she fills me in. The party will take place at the house. An event coordinator is making the arrangements. From what she's seen of the planning, it's going to be the event of the year. My only job is to look pretty, says Jana. Over a hundred people have been invited, including the mine magnates and diamond brokers. The only person not on the list is Harold. Damian's orders.

Jana gives me a probing look from where she's scooping butternut into a blender. "May I ask why your father isn't invited?" She's finally accepted to call me Lina, but only when Damian isn't around. "It's none of my business, but I hate to see you looking so down."

I lift my head quickly. "I'm not down."

"Are you kidding? It's written all over your face. Why don't you talk to Mr. Hart? Sometimes, family has fallouts. It can always be fixed."

"It's nothing like that." I'm glad Harold won't be here, but I can't expect Jana to understand.

She rinses her hands and dries them on a kitchen towel. "I think I know why you're upset." Crossing the floor, she stops on the opposite side of the table. "You're sad because Mr. Hart didn't involve you in the planning. I'm sure he's only trying to make it easy for you. Knowing he's not around often to help, he probably wanted as little stress and work for you as possible."

"Yes. Of course."

There's no way of explaining our complicated situation to someone as sweet and uncomplicated as Jana, who's been married to a nice, stable guy with a great sense of humor—her words—for the past twelve years.

"Good." She pats my hand. "Talking of not being around often, Mr. Hart said he'd be late for dinner. I'll leave everything in the warming drawer if you want to eat earlier."

"That'll be kind."

I'm about to ask if she needs help with dinner when Anne walks into the kitchen.

"Oh, hi, Jana," Anne says, barely sparing her a glance.

Jana nods. "Anne." Turning her back to us, she continues with the meal preparations.

"You didn't say which room I should take," Anne says.

"Any one you want."

"Are you sure? I don't want to impose or anything, but my clothes are already in the room next to yours."

"Then leave them there."

"Great." She bounces on the balls of her feet. "Zane just told me about Saturday. He's taking me shopping for a dress. Want to come?"

"I'm good, thanks."

"Okay." She finger waves and skips out of the room.

"Lina."

"Mm?"

Jana leans on the counter, her expression concerned. "Tell me she's not moving in."

"She's short of money."

"Not so short she can't afford a new dress."

"Maybe Zane gave her money."

"Maybe he should've given her money for rent."

"What are you saying?"

"Be careful of that one. You may want to keep a close eye on your husband with her around."

"Don't you like her?"

"Just saying. When you're staff, people think you're invisible, but I see things when I'm working, and I saw the way she looks at Mr. Hart."

What would a wife in normal circumstances say? "I'll keep it in mind."

Maybe Anne is the distraction Damian needs. If she's willing and eager, perhaps he'll lose interest in playing cat and mouse games with me.

Damian

IT'S BARELY dinnertime when I park in front of the house. I'm home earlier than expected. I rushed the meeting for one reason only. Lina is alone. Zane called to let me know he's having dinner in town with Anne, wisely staying away from me tonight. I'm still upset about Anne's move. I'm even more impatient to get inside. Damn, the things I want to do to my wife.

"Everything fine?" I ask Russell on my way in.

"Perfect, sir. Mrs. Hart is having dinner."

"Good. Take a break."

"Yes, sir."

He leaves promptly.

Loosening my tie, I go straight to the dining room. In jail, I wanted nothing more than to dress in a power suit and tie, as if I had to prove with clothes who I could be. Now, the tie feels like a noose. I dump it on a chair in the hallway and unfasten the top two buttons of my shirt. Who the hell puts chairs in hallways, anyway? Who's going to sit on them? In the doorframe of the dining room, I pause.

Lina is sitting at the place I chose for her, immediately to the left of the head of the table. Her head is bowed over a bowl. She's spooning soup down her throat so fast she doesn't notice me.

"Slow down." I chuckle. "The soup isn't going to run away."

Pausing with the spoon halfway in the air, she averts her eyes before leaving the spoon in her side plate and dabbing a napkin to her mouth. "Sorry."

Immediately, I want to bite my tongue. With her history, I want her to eat. Badly. "Please, don't stop on my behalf. Pretend I'm not here."

Her look is cutting. I don't like where this is going. I don't want her to think she needs permission to eat, or God forbid, to stop eating all together. Hunger strikes aren't beyond her and force-feeding isn't beneath me. I just prefer not to go there. Her back sets in a rigid posture, but I'm quietly relieved when she picks up the spoon again.

The clinking of her cutlery follows me into the kitchen where I serve myself a bowl of butternut soup before carrying it to the table.

As the meal progresses in silence, I use the opportunity to study her. She doesn't strike me as someone scared of eating. On the contrary, she's eating with gusto, fast, as if she's worried the food will disappear.

"There's a bat in the garden," she says out of the blue.

Taken aback not as much by the remark than the fact that she spoke to me, it takes me a moment to formulate a reply. "I'll have it removed."

"No! They're endangered."

"I said removed, as in moved to a colony, not killed."

"You shouldn't move it. It may have a family here."

That makes me smile. My wife is concerned about a bat family. "What do you propose I do?"

"You need bat boxes."

"You happen to know about bat boxes," I tease.

"I did some research today."

"How?"

"I browsed some sites."

Not having access to a computer, she must've used her phone. "Do you need a laptop?"

"The phone is enough." As an afterthought, she adds half-heartedly, "Thanks."

"Go ahead then. Get the boxes."

"It's going to cost five thousand for the boxes, and nine hundred for the installation."

She really did do her research.

She toys with her napkin. "Will you give me permission to withdraw the money from my account?"

Absolutely not, but I'll give her the money. "Tell the company to send me the bill."

"Thanks," she huffs.

It's a sore point for her, the fact that she has to ask permission to use her money. How does it feel to be filthy rich, but unable to buy even an apple? I like to pay for everything she needs. It goes deeper than my desire to control her. I want to take care of her. I fucking love knowing I can provide her with whatever she requires. After drowning in poverty during my childhood, this is my obsession, my own private *issue*.

When she excuses herself to clear the soup bowls, I fetch the main meal. I carve the pork roast and serve us each a helping of vegetables. She attacks the food like a vulture, every now and again remembering to slow down. When she does, she shoots me a sidelong glance, but I pretend not to notice this oddity of a lady who's been schooled in table manners at the most elitist of establishments. It doesn't matter to me how she eats. For all I care, she can eat with her hands and slurp her soup, but I know where she attended school, and I know what they teach young ladies.

In many ways, Lina is a mystery. According to her medical reports, she suffered from anorexia and bouts of bulimia, but since she's been eating at my table, she eats as if every meal is her last. She has an angelic face, but she never smiles. It's not just when she's with me. She doesn't smile in her yearbook or newspaper photos. A young woman of twenty-four, she only wears black, not in a gothic or alternative fashion, but in a genuinely morbid, depressing way. She covers herself from head to toes like a goddam nun, even in the heat of summer. Russell told me he showed her the pool. She doesn't own a bathing suit. I went through her belongings when her suitcase arrived. What am I supposed to make of all this? I doubt she's crazy. Not crazy enough to be locked up for a year. Eccentric, perhaps. Spoiled, maybe. Incompetent? I have my doubts.

She pushes her empty plate away. "May I please be excused? I'm rather tired."

The question pops out before I can stop myself. "Why did you marry Clarke?"

We stare at each other, her eyes round and my heart thumping with a dead beat. The night she offered me her shawl, when I'd found her in the corridor before going to Dalton's office, I'd walked right up to her and said, "It was nice to meet you, Angelina Dalton. One day, you're going to be Mrs. Hart." There wasn't a trace of a smile on her face when she replied, "I know."

She gapes. "W-what?"

"You heard me."

"I don't want to talk about it."

When she pushes back from the table, I grab her wrist. It's out in the open, the big, fat elephant, and ignoring it will only make it bigger.

"You said you'd be mine." Not in so many words, but on the night I told her I was going to make her Mrs. Hart, she said, "I know."

I know.

She doesn't fight the hold of my fingers, maybe instinctively sensing pushing me now is dangerous.

"I was eighteen," she says in a quiet voice.

"Yet, you married Clarke."

"He asked."

"Did he, now?"

"What's that supposed to mean?"

"Your father needed mining rights for my discovery. Clarke was the only one who could grant them. It seems convenient that you suddenly became his wife."

Anger flashes in her eyes. "I didn't marry him for mining rights."

"Just for money?"

"Like you married me for money?"

I chuckle. "I told you it's not just about the money. Don't change the subject. You could've waited."

"For what?" she exclaims softly. "For a man I saw once? You were in jail for theft."

I can't believe my fucking ears. "You believe I stole that diamond?"

"What was I supposed to think? I didn't know you." Her tone is pleading. "I still don't know you."

Not good enough. She said *she knew*. She should've known. She should've waited. This is the moment I blow it. This is the moment my carefully crafted composure cracks.

"You're right, Lina. You don't know me. Not yet." I stand, pulling her with me. "But you're going to learn, starting right now."

Her calmness slips. She tries to hold back. "What are you doing?"

"I'm going to show you who I am."

CHAPTER 6

Damian

*N*o amount of kicking and fighting can stop me, not that Lina is fighting. She knows she's too small, too light. She knows we're alone. She stumbles behind me in her effort to keep up. I don't slow down. I'm not the younger version of me who told her I was going to make her mine. Back then, I meant it in a good way. Now, I'm a man stripped from everything that's good. That's all right, or so I tell myself, because she's not the girl who bewitched me. Neither is she the woman who's going to save me. I'm long since beyond saving.

With her unstable history, she's ten different shades of problems, which is why I'm walking a tightrope with no safety net by dragging her into my study, into my anger. I fling her into the room, letting go the moment I'm sure she won't fall, because the longer I touch her the more I want to hurt her, and the more I want to hurt her the harder I get. She watches me warily, like she should, rubbing at her arm where I've gripped her. Holding her gaze with all the intentions bubbling up inside me, I reach behind me and close the door.

Her throat bobs as she swallows. She's too brave, lifting her chin and standing her ground when I advance. My mind screams at me to calm down, but my heart knows no mercy. Stopping short of her, I grab at the last straws of reason. She's an incompetent woman. Her mind is fragile. So is her body. Yet, she's not insane. If there's a classical rich girl dysfunctional cliché, I can pin it on her. Attention seeking, weight obsessive, egoistic, and spoiled. The crazy label is just an excuse to hide her personality defects and justify the sympathy she doesn't deserve.

"On your knees."

"No."

"*On your knees.*"

"I'll take it standing."

She won't last, not even on her knees. She'll be facedown, smothering in the carpet before I've had time to take a calming breath. I'm seething. I'm furious. I'm a mess, all because of six years ago. All because of Dalton. All because of their betrayal. All because she fucking said, "I know," and then gave away what wasn't hers to give.

She gave away what was mine.

"It's never been yours."

Did I say that out loud? My feet seem to move of their own accord to the wall. With every nail I hammered into the fancy wallpaper, I thought about her. With every implement of torture I hanged on the wall, I thought about pain and pleasure. It's an out-of-body experience, watching my hand reach for the whip. The wooden handle presses into my palm as I tighten my fingers. My logic calls to me, tells me this is the point where I can still turn around. Yet, she's not a fantasy on a jail cot in a cell. She's here, and she's not as crazy as she should be.

I let the leather thong unfurl. It lashes the floor with a thwack. "On your knees."

"No."

My hands start shaking with both pent-up and new anger. I fling the whip again, this time closer to her feet. "Kneel."

Her heart beats like a beast under her bodice, but her voice is steady. "No."

I know how to swing a whip. The next lash flies past her face, sizzling in the air. She flinches, but she doesn't move. It's off. It's as if she's done this before, only, I can't imagine anyone posing her on a Persian rug and swinging a whip around her pretty face. That kind of cruelty is saved for men like me.

"It'll be easier if you do as you're told."

"No."

"Fine." I graze her shoulder with the wooden handle. "I was going to go easy on you, but you may as well get the full ugly of who I am."

"This isn't you."

The words are spoken with conviction. Her faith in her analysis makes her bold, but she doesn't know me. She said so herself. She could've known me, and who knows what kind of man I would've been for her? But ifs are feeble, and reality is cruel. This is what we are.

I circle her once, twice. Her eyes follow me. When I'm behind her again, I strike. The leather catches the back of her legs. Hampered by the folds of her ridiculously thick skirt, the lash doesn't do damage to her skin, but it's forceful enough to make her legs buckle. She falls down on her knees. Before she has time to get up, I cup her neck and push her upper body down until her back hits the floor. She fights me, but it's hard to struggle when your legs are folded underneath you and you can't breathe. She knows when to give up. She knows to stop clawing at me and lie still. When she does, I slacken my hold, allowing her air, but I don't remove my touch.

"Straighten your legs."

She obeys. I give her enough space until she's managed the maneuver. I don't tell her to close her eyes, because that's not the point. I let her look at me, ignoring the hatred that darkens her irises to galaxy blue.

"Take off your panties."

Those blues widen, the green and gold dots contracting like satellite debris polluting space.

"Take them off, Lina, or I'll remove them for you."

She knows this much about me. I'm not bluffing.

If looks could cut you up, I'd be strips small enough to feed a blender. Her hands dip under her skirt. She lifts her ass and fiddles a bit, getting her panties down to her thighs. I'm still pinning her neck to the ground. That's as far as she can get those panties without lifting her upper body.

"Now pull up your dress."

"No."

She really has to learn to obey. Straightening, I fold the whip double and spank her pussy once through the fabric of her dress. It's a gentle smack, but she arches off the ground.

"Either you pull up the dress, or I tear it off."

She must really not want her dress removed or her pussy spanked. She grabs a fistful of fabric on either side of the skirt. There's a short hesitation, as if she's hoping I'd change my mind.

"You should've just kneeled," I taunt. "If you obeyed, it would've been under your skirt."

She frowns. She doesn't catch my drift, but she will soon.

"Up." I hook the whip handle under the hem and lift it a good few inches to demonstrate what I need.

Her nostrils flare as she lifts her skirt to her thighs.

I tap her stomach with the handle. "All the way to here."

She shoots me another hateful look but complies. When she's lying exposed with the lower half of her body naked, except for those black panties constricting her thighs, I smile down at her reddening face before turning my attention to the juncture of her legs. She doesn't shave, but she trims. Her pussy is covered with a dusting of golden hair. I want to see her slit and arousal. Snaring the elastic of her panties with the whip handle, I pull them slowly down her legs and free from her ankles. She doesn't break eye contact or ask questions. Good. She's here to follow instructions.

"Open your legs."

Her lips purse together.

"There's no fabric to protect your vagina, this time." I show her the whip. "It's going to sting."

Everything flares—her eyes, her nostrils, her fingers—but she spreads her legs like an obedient girl.

"Bend your knees."

Her eyes go even rounder. Her silence says no.

I drag the whip up the inside of her thigh. "If you follow instructions, I'll keep my hands to myself. If I have to make you, my fingers will most definitely end up buried inside you."

"You said you wouldn't."

"I said I wouldn't stick my dick in you. However, I'm not opposed to using other things, such as my tongue." I tap her thigh. "Bend."

The threat of my tongue does the trick. She obeys reluctantly, stretching her pussy wide and almost giving me the view I want. Stepping between her legs, I enjoy that almost-view. I like to look at my most prized possessions, and her pretty cunt qualifies for both categories. Most prized, with the emphasis on possession.

The trimmed curls don't hide much. Using the whip handle, I part those pink lips. I'm still to kiss them, but I know they will be soft under my teeth and musky in my mouth. I stretch her open to see her slit and the nub hidden between her folds. She's no longer shooting daggers at me with her eyes. She's got them fixed on the ceiling.

"Look at me," I command. I want her to watch me while I study her. I want her to see me.

When she complies, I flay her open to the right, then the left, taking my time to imprint the image in my mind. Her inner labia unfold like a flower opening its petals to the night. She's not a sunflower. She's a night lily. It's not in daylight that she thrives, but in the dark hours of the night.

She may not know it yet, but she's my kind of crazy. We fit together like a pussy and a whip. I trace her slit with the handle as if I'm a scientist and she's an experiment, but there's nothing clinical about the hard-on in my pants. She's biting her lip, embarrassed at my unabashed dissection of her arousal. Yes, there's no end to my perverse gratification when the folds I'm so diligently inspecting start to glisten. They turn redder, more swollen.

Pressing the stick at the top of her slit, I pull up the skin to reveal the little hidden pearl. Her clit swells and throbs under my stare. I've seen everything when she was bent over my desk, but not from this angle. This is new. I have a feeling Lina will always be new.

The urge to touch her is severe. It's real. It's not a power game where only one of us gets to play with a whip. It's a game where I'll easily ejaculate from visual stimulation alone. Just because I like torturing myself, I flick the stick over her clit to test her reaction. She bites her lip harder. Her pussy clenches around nothing.

I drag the whip handle up and down over the nub. She whimpers, but it's when I use a circular motion that her back lifts off the floor. All the while, I inspect the button that's causing her to shiver with pleasure as if it's a million dollar-painting I'm invested in buying.

"This is sick," she whispers as she lies there with her legs spread and me probing and watching, learning what she likes.

I don't care what she thinks. She belongs to me. I can do with her as I please. I earned the right. She deserves the consequences. As long as she comes, it's not wrong. Not in my eyes. It's not how she gets there. It's that *I* get her there, even if I have to use paddles, whips, and her own fingers.

"Touch yourself."

"What?" She looks at me as if I asked her to fuck the doorknob.

"You heard me."

"No."

"We're going to work on your vocabulary." I press the stick at the bottom of her slit, applying steady pressure but not enough to penetrate her. "I'll give you a choice. You can fuck yourself here." I move down to her asshole, teasing her rosebud entrance. "Or maybe you prefer here." Lastly, I give her a soft smack on her clit. "Or here."

She gasps, her shoulders lifting off the floor.

"Choose, Lina. Cunt, clit, or asshole."

"I-I can't."

"In this house, *no* and *I can't* aren't part of your vocabulary."

She's so flustered, so wet. Red blotches mar her cheeks, and her pussy quivers. If I unfasten the ten little buttons of her bodice, will I find her nipples hard? It's difficult to say with the thick fabric covering her. Where does she buy these ugly, old-fashioned dresses? I don't know if she's wet because I'm standing over her like a school-teacher with an erection I'm not trying to hide, watching her getting wetter, or because I'm touching her in such a dirty way with an object designed to torture.

"Pick, Lina, unless you want me to pick for you. Trust me, if I do, I'll fuck your clit, pussy, or ass—maybe all three—with the stick-end of this whip until you give me what I want."

"W-what do you want?"

"Your orgasm. You have until three. One."

Her fingers flitter to her clit. She rubs in a circular motion, like I'd done with the stick. She's slick. Her movements are fast and the sounds wet. Crouching down for a closer look, I inhale her scent. She smells of sweet poison and sex. Her head is thrown back and her brow pleated in concentration. She goes faster. The sound of her fingers rubbing over her slick flesh makes me harder. She works herself up to a crescendo, her neck muscles pulling from the strain, and then she collapses.

"I can't." She shakes her head. "I can't make myself come if you watch."

The leather strip comes down so fast she doesn't know what's hit her. It falls between her legs, covering her clit and slit. It wasn't hard enough to hurt, but she squeezes her legs together and cries out in fright. At least she didn't fake an orgasm. For that, I cut her some slack.

"What did I say about your vocabulary?"

"I can't come like—"

Smack.

"Ow!"

"That was for *I can't.*"

She's angry now. "What do you want from me?"

"Try harder."

"Why?"

"I had my turn. Now it's yours." *Smack.* "Show me."

She cries out again, covering her pussy with her hands.

"Two, Lina. When I get to three, I'm fucking you with the whip, and I choose which hole."

Her chest rises and falls with fast breaths. In direct contrast, she opens her legs in slow motion, her fingers going tentatively back to her clit.

"Tell you what. Since you didn't try to fake it, I'm going to help you out."

She doesn't ask. She watches me as she fingers her clit while I push the stick end inside, fucking her lightly as she plays with herself. It's hot to watch. If my dick rubs up against her, I'll blow. Before she knows it, she's going to let me stick my dick in every hole in her body. Her outer labia clenches around the thin intrusion, telling me what I want to know. I already know from the paddle incident how to rub her up inside, and it doesn't take long. Her globes pull together. Her ass lifts off the floor. Every muscle in her lower region pulls tight. She comes with a silent gasp, refusing to give me sounds. That's all right, because I have her pleasure.

Her hips collapse. She looks spent. Gently, I remove the handle, wiping it clean on the inside of her leg. I straighten without covering her, because I'm not done looking. Our gazes are locked. There are questions in hers, so I give her the answer.

"*This* is who I am."

Lina

WHO IS MY HUSBAND? Who is the man carrying me to his bedroom in warm, strong arms, so careful with me, as if I could break, when he's just broken me on his study floor? I was right. I don't know him. I do know I'm not immune to his hands or the way his eyes turn dark with lust when I orgasm. No, I don't know much about him, but I do know he's not the boy-man who told me he was going to marry me. He's a grown man, manipulative enough to force me into marriage and perverse enough to take what he wants, no matter how shameful.

Most of all, he's a dangerous man. He not only survives the battles of life, he thrives on them. He loves the fight. I see it in his brooding eyes every time he forces me to resist, only to keep me hovering on the brink of pleasure before pushing me over ever so slowly.

Every time he spars with me on his desk or floor, I see the sinister satisfaction in his eyes when I lose the battle, when my body gives in and comes. It's not that I'm not fighting the climaxes. I do. I fight giving him what he wants with every ounce I've got, but he's clever at dissecting me, at reading the signals and figuring out which buttons to push. The one I'll never let him get close to is my heart. I take comfort in this notion as he carries me into the bathroom and lowers me to the rug. He can have my pleasure, hurt me until it feels good, and make me peak with paddles and whips, but he can't touch what's not physical. He can't touch my feelings.

The violent lust has left his eyes, but he's still hard. If he hadn't promised he wouldn't force me, not with his cock, I would've been scared. He smooths his hands down my arms. An involuntary shiver runs over me when his fingers brush the scars. I can't stand any caresses on the mutilations. The urge to pull away is so severe my skin breaks out in a cold sweat. It takes all my self-control to stay put.

His look is almost tender. "Cold?"

"No." I'm surprised my voice is steady.

The tenderness evaporates, making space for hardness. "I see."

As if sensing my revulsion, he drops his hands, but his eyes tighten and his lips thin. "Need help with the dress?"

I fold my arms over my stomach. "What?"

He trails a finger over the buttons of the bodice. "The dress. Do you need help removing it? There must be ten buttons the size of a raven's pupil."

"I'm fine." As an after-thought, I throw in, "Thank you."

He nods. The gesture is like a small kindness in exchange for what I gave him in the study.

His gaze flicks to the shower as he speaks. "I'll leave you to it."

By exiting the bathroom, he gives me another reward for letting him watch. He gives me privacy. He leaves the door open a crack, and for all my apprehension of what he's capable of, I can't bring myself to close it completely. The fear of being locked in is bigger than any other, even having my arms touched. The click of the bedroom door tells me he left the room. I peer around the door. Sure enough, the bedroom is empty. The sight of the closed door makes my throat constrict.

It's not locked. It's only closed.

I tell myself this over and over, until I feel calm enough to brave it into the shower. I only take a few minutes to clean up and pull on my nightdress. By the time I step out of the bathroom, Damian is back. He acknowledges me with his eyes from across the room. Throwing back the bed covers, he wordlessly commands me to get in. Seething on the inside, I do as I'm ordered. When I'm lying flat on my back, he grips my uninjured wrist and pulls up my arm.

"You don't have to do that," I say, already starting to silently freak out.

"I need a shower. It's either the handcuffs or Russell stands guard at your side."

My anger ignites. "Where am I going to go?"

He trails his thumb lazily over my arm. "You tell me."

I grit my teeth to bite back the repulsion as his fingers closes around the scars. "I'm not going to kill myself."

He considers the statement. "I don't believe you are."

"Then there's no need for the constraints."

Slowly, he lowers my wrist to my side. "I'll give you the benefit of the doubt, but prove me wrong..."

He doesn't have to finish the threat. It's in the unspoken promise of his unsettling eyes. He'll chain me to the wall if he has to.

"Good," he says with self-assured confidence.

I don't have a choice but to obey, not that I've ever had suicidal tendencies. I have too much to live for.

He covers my body with the sheet. The act is both careful and possessive, as if he's covering an expensive piece of art to protect it from dust and curious eyes. It's too hot for the comforter, which he leaves at my feet. Without sparing me another glance, he makes his way to the bathroom. As before, he leaves the door open, only wider. His back is turned to me as he starts stripping. I should turn on my side, or at the very least close my eyes, but I'm frozen in place. Does he know I'm looking? Does he care? Or maybe that's the objective.

His shirt comes off first. His back is riddled with hard, lean grooves. His arms flex as he goes for his belt. Every movement puts the cut of his muscles on display. He stands tall and confident as he unbuttons his pants and pulls down the zipper. When he unexpectedly turns, he catches me staring. Too late, I turn my face to the wall. I've already seen his belt and fly hanging open. I've already seen the male hardness under his black briefs. Heat burns in my cheeks.

From the corner of my eye, I continue to watch him. It's compulsive, a magnetism I can't control. He sits down on the toilet seat to remove his shoes and socks. When he straightens again, his pants and briefs follow. His erection is huge, the bulbous head and thick shaft jutting out proudly, but I can't bring myself to stare so unabashedly, not while he's watching me.

There's a smirk on his face as he finally gives me his back again to run the water in the shower. I close my eyes, willing myself not to give in, but it's fruitless. My gaze is pulled to his sculptured ass and powerful legs as he steps into the shower and closes the door. The glass is clear, allowing me an unobscured view of Damian leaning one hand on the wall while grabbing his erection in his other. I know what he's going to do before he starts pumping his fist.

The only reason I don't look away is he's not acknowledging my invasive stare. He's fully immersed in the act of masturbating. His head is lowered, the water running in rivulets through his ebony hair. His gaze is fixed on the manipulations of his hand. I imagine his breathing turning faster, the sound drowned out by the running water. I watch for no other reason than he's a magnificent specimen, a perfect exhibition of male power. My body reacts mechanically to the erotic sight, my folds swelling and my entrance lubricating for penetration.

What I feel emotionally is far from arousal. I fear the power the man who calls himself my husband holds. I feel the darkness he's holding back. A day will come when he won't be strong enough to keep that depraved darkness on a leash. I sense with instinctive knowledge my time is short. Damian's patience is thin and his lust strong. One day soon, he's going to unleash all of that darkness on me.

My breathing spikes in acknowledgement of the truth as his ass clenches and his hips jerk forward. In tandem, his body and my heartbeat peak as I fall into the devastating realization while he ejaculates behind a thin veil of steam that starts filling the cubicle. Mercifully, the choice to watch is taken from my hands as the fog thickens and hides everything in the shower from view. Damian finishes in a cloud of humidity while I'm left with an unwanted slickness between my legs.

He comes to bed wearing a fresh pair of boxers. I tense. Will he punish me now? I know it's coming, and the wait is agonizing. When he settles down and pulls me to his side, confusion consumes me. I don't understand the small acts of comfort he offers. What does he really want from me? No matter what he says, it's not only my money or pleasure. It's revenge for what Harold did to him. Maybe he wants to drive me truly insane. Maybe he wants me as crazy as the world believes I am. I'm scared he may succeed. I'm not immune to his hands or lustful intentions. I hate him with a deep-sated intensity, but he knows how to make my body come alive when my heart has been dead for so long.

"Go to sleep," he breathes against my neck.

His arm is heavy across my stomach, anchoring me to the bed. How does he expect me to sleep like this?

"Damian?"

"Lina?" he drawls.

"When are you going to do it?"

"Do what?"

"Punish me."

A second passes. "Do you deserve punishment?"

"I know you want to for the wedding dress."

"Mm." The sound is a dark statement, a validation.

"Just do it."

His lips skim my shoulder. "You'll learn."

"Learn what?"

"Everything happens on my terms." He draws a circle around my navel with his thumb. "Close your eyes. I have a long day ahead."

The surprising thing is when I do, I sleep better than I ever remember.

~

Damian

I WATCH my wife's sleeping form when I get up at dawn. The black garb isn't deserving of her fair skin and flushed cheeks. She needs soft pinks and vibrant reds. But that's not the real reason it irks me. The real reason is she still mourns for a husband she possibly loves and cares enough about to honor his departure from this world with black. The bastard might be dead, but it lights a flame of jealousy in my chest hot enough to incinerate my heart.

I consider her closet, her ugly dresses, prim nightdresses, and black ballerina flats. Zane told me she refused to go shopping for a wedding reception dress. I anticipated it. Her refusal gives me the answer to how I'll deal with that punishment she brought up last night. I'll hit her where it'll affect her the hardest, and it won't be spanking her glorious bottom.

With a last look at her peaceful form, I get dressed, closing the bathroom door to not wake her. Then I set off to conduct the business of the day, starting with seeing my father-in-law.

We meet at the Irene Country Club for breakfast. He's already there when I arrive, reading a newspaper like he's got no care in the world. Unbuttoning my jacket, I sit down at the table.

He puts the newspaper aside. His tone is sarcastic. "Married life seems to agree with you."

"If you ever come near my house again, I'll cut off your ear."

He gives a little start. "She's my daughter. I have a right to see for myself that you're not abusing her."

I smirk. "Make it both ears."

All pretense of superior calmness vanishes from his demeanor. "What do you want? I have work to do."

"I'm afraid you don't."

A waiter approaches with a pot of coffee and pours two cups.

"What the hell are you talking about?" he asks when the waiter is gone.

I take tremendous joy in sliding the contract toward him that proves I am, as of today, the major shareholder of Dalton Diamonds, soon to become Hart Diamonds.

It takes him a while to find his words after he's scanned over the content. "You've got to be kidding me."

The look on his face is a moment I've anticipated for a long time, and I'm not disappointed. His deathly pale skin and furious, helpless expression are extremely gratifying.

"You son of a bitch."

Taking a sip of my coffee, I lean back in the comfort of the luxurious chair. "You messed with the wrong man, Dalton."

He slams the contract down on the table. "I'm still a shareholder."

"Thirty percent. You're outvoted."

His lips curve in a nasty way. "You just dug your own hole. That dump is worthless. It's depleted." He turns smug. "Seems like you bought yourself into bankruptcy."

I'm not putting my cards on the table. Not yet. I shrug. "Your daughter's money is paying for it. What do I care?"

He fists his hands on the table. "I contest the buy-out. They had no right selling their shares without giving me a chance to better your offer."

"You'll be too busy filing appeals." I hand him the letter from my lawyer.

As he reads, his hand goes to his chest. "Mis-fucking-management?" He shoots me a hateful glare. "You can't do this."

"You ran the operations." I smooth a hand down my tie. "You gave the go-ahead to excavate, despite the geological reports advising against it. You knew the investment wouldn't warrant the diamond deposits from the riverbed gravel, yet, you were too greedy to let the opportunity pass. You withheld those reports from the investors, got your buddy, Jack Clarke, to issue a new report, and sold the mine to them as inexhaustible for twenty years. Six years are up, and I give it one more. You're every bit as accountable for the foreseen losses as what that forecast claims. I will sue you for every penny you've got and make sure it's a nice, big scandal all over the news. When I'm done with you, no one in the mining industry will want to touch you with a ten-foot pole."

He jumps to his feet. "You're out of your fucking mind."

I regard him calmly. "Never been saner."

"I won't go down, Hart." He points a fat finger at me. "Mark my words." With that he storms off, making the heads of the other diners turn.

He's going down. For what he did to me, death is too easy for him. I want him to live the last years of his life in utter misery. His old-man heart better not stop beating on me, because his ruination has just begun.

Damn, I'm starving. I'm so elated I can eat two full-course breakfasts.

Lina

WHEN I WAKE UP, I'm alone. Damian must've already left for work, or that's what I'm bargaining on. I dress quickly and go downstairs. Russell greets me cheerfully. Is the man ever grumpy?

"Do you know where Damian is?"

"Out on business. He'll be back tonight, but if you need him, I can call."

"No." I add quickly, "I don't want to bother him while he's working."

"Anything I can help with?"

"Nothing, but thanks."

There's no time to waste. I rush to the study. My anxiety about being locked in won't allow me to close the door. Leaving it open a crack is a risk. It's asking to be caught, but I want to work quickly, and I can't focus when I have to vent off a panic attack.

I start with the desk, going through every drawer, not that I expect Damian to leave the evidence he's blackmailing Harold with lying around. It's probably in a safe or locked away, but my meticulous side demands I eliminate the unlocked and obvious hiding places. Checking for hidden keys, I go through the desk like I'd gone through Harold's so many fruitless times, looking for clues to the whereabouts of my child, and like those times I come up empty-handed. Not in his desk. I look around the room at the paintings. Once I've established there are no safes behinds any of them, I lift the carpets. I tap my feet on the floorboards, listening for a change in sound that may indicate a hollow space or loosened board. Running out of hiding places, I check the folders on his desk. They're all branded with a Dalton Diamonds logo. I'm flipping through the top one on the pile when the door suddenly opens all the way and Zane strides in.

He jerks to a stop when he sees me. "What the fuck are you doing?"

Straightening quickly, I try to keep the guilt from my face. "Looking for something."

"I can see that. What exactly are you looking for in Dami's files?"

I think fast. "A cheque. He was going to give me money for bat boxes."

Zane crosses his arms. "Why would the cheque be in a file?"

"I don't know. I was just looking around the desk."

He lifts a finger while extracting his phone from his pocket. "Stay right there."

I already know who he's calling before he hits dial.

"Zane, please. I don't want you to bother him at work for a cheque. I can wait."

"Shut up." He turns his back on me. "Dami? Just caught your wife snooping around in your study. What would you like me to do about it?"

My heart beats cold as he listens to Damian's response. If Damian gives him permission to hurt me, Zane will make it matter. He hates me enough to put everything into it. My heart trips over a beat as Zane looks back at me from over his shoulder.

"She says she's looking for a cheque for bat boxes."

Another small silence passes as Damian replies.

Animosity contorts Zane's features. "I'll tell her." He pockets the phone. "Get the company to send him the invoice."

"I'll do that."

He tilts his head toward the door. "Get out."

Zane scares me because he's stronger and bigger, but I'm less intimidated knowing why he hates me. "Does that mean the study is off-limits? This is, after all, my home."

His face turns so red it shows through his bronze skin. "Get the fuck out before I throw you out."

Russell appears in the door. "Is there a problem?"

"It's solved," Zane replies. "Your presence is unneeded."

"Mrs. Hart." Russell holds the door for me, offering his unspoken protection.

I take it gladly, sailing past Zane and feeling his stare burn on my back all the way into the hallway.

"The way I've been taught," Russell says in a lowered voice, "men don't swear at ladies."

There's arrogance in Zane's tone. "I'm not doing anything her husband isn't."

No, he's not. What does that say about me? I'm not high on either's list when it comes to respect.

THE DAY EVOLVES with me eating as if it's going out of fashion. I steal bread rolls from the table and add them to my stash. Between meals, I search room after room on a pretense of getting familiar with the house. I start with Damian's closet, looking in every drawer and going as far as searching his jacket pockets.

When I'm too despondent to carry on, I get Damian's email address from Russell and send him the quotes from the bat box companies before venturing outside to find out where the bats are nesting. There's nothing under the gutters or in the trees. I contemplate asking the gardener, Andries, but he looks at me so sourly I decide against it. Russell, who's following me around at a respectable distance, finally asks what I'm looking for. He says he's never spotted any bats, and that it was probably just a bird.

Deciding to take a look under the summerhouse awning, I make my way to the pool, but stop short when I spot Anne drifting on a float. I'm standing behind the ornamental scrubs where she can't see me. She's wearing a red bikini that shows off her curves. She's rounded everywhere I'm not, and her skin has a healthy, tanned color. Drifting in the inviting blue water with only her fingers submerged, she's a sight to behold. Lovely. Womanly.

I both envy and resent her for her freedom. It's over thirty degrees. The sweat trickling down my back reminds me how overdressed I am for this heat. No one is stopping me from going to the pool. It's *what's* stopping me, the horrible scars and their meaning, the shame of anyone knowing.

"Why don't you take a dip?" Russell suddenly asks next to me.

Not having heard him coming up, I jump a little. "I'm good."

"This *is* your home." His gaze trails to Anne as if she's an intruder.

"Is it?"

Immediately, I want to bite my tongue. I shouldn't have said that. Not to him. I already went too far with my honesty yesterday. His look is understanding, and it only makes the situation worse. My cheeks heat with embarrassment at what I've just admitted, and to Damian's employee, no less.

I turn back for the house. "Do you stay on the property?"

"I go home. Clock off at eight or nine."

"Who's standing guard at night?"

"There's a regular shift that comes in."

"Do you know Damian personally?"

"I only work for the security company he employs."

"When you clock off, do you go home to a family?"

He stops to look at me. Oh, no. That didn't come out right. I gave him the wrong idea.

I quickly add, "I'm just curious to know if you have children."

"We don't discuss our private lives. Protocol."

"I understand."

I hurry to the house, feeling like an idiot for trying to make a friend. What the hell am I thinking? Damian's guards are not my friends.

As I'm stepping through the door, he says, "I don't have children."

Offering him no more than a polite smile, I dash up the stairs and wash up for dinner. I'm hungry again. Jana left early, but there's a casserole on the hot tray in the dining room. As I sit down at the table, I swallow a sigh of disappointment when Zane walks through the door. Anne follows, wearing a wrap around her bikini.

"What's for dinner?" she asks. "I'm starving."

Zane gives me a hostile look while his sister piles her plate high with rice and meat. After we've served ourselves, we eat in a strained silence. We're halfway through the meal when the front door flings open. Damian walks through it with big, angry strides. His face is dark, his anger barely contained.

Two men drag a third over the step. Damian doesn't stop to acknowledge us through the open door. He heads straight down the hall toward the kitchen, the men following. Russell shuts the door with a stoic face, staring straight ahead.

What's going on? I push back my chair, but Zane grabs my wrist.

"It's not your business," he says.

"Let go."

For once, he obliges. His smile is sardonic. "Suit yourself."

As I stand, Anne follows. Rushing through the house with Anne on my heels, a terrible urge to get to Damian drives me. Something bad is happening. I have to stop it.

The kitchen is empty, but the backdoor stands open. A light comes on in the storage room across the courtyard. The room is windowless, but a sliver of light seeps underneath the door. I hurry toward it, vaguely aware of Anne telling me not to go there. My hand is on the doorknob even as Anne jerks at my arm. Shaking her off, I turn the knob. The corrugated iron door swings open with a squeak. I don't know what I expected, but it wasn't the man Damian's guards dragged into the house bent over a worktable with his wrist clamped in a vice. The world seems to stop turning at the same time it falls away from under my feet. Damian is holding a meat axe, and contrary to earlier, his demeanor is disturbingly calm.

CHAPTER 7

Lina

"No," I scream at the same time as Damian brings down the axe.

His eyes widen in alarm when he notices me, but it's too late. The momentum carries his action forward. Various sounds mix in a terrible orchestra of horror. A dull thud falls on the wood. The man's howl tears through the room. Blood spurts from his knuckle. His finger rolls to the edge of the table, and my scream continues silently in my chest.

"Close the fucking door," Damian barks.

I'm shaking in the frame, my gaze frozen on the scene. One of the guards steps forward and slams the door in my face. I can't move. It takes tremendous effort to shift my feet, to lift my hand back to the door to help the poor man my husband is torturing.

"No." A hand locks around my arm.

I look up at the owner to see Russell at my side.

"You can't change what's happening."

Panic squeezes the breath from my chest. "I have to."

"He deserves it."

Terrible screams come from inside.

I'm lightheaded, as if I can't drag in enough air. Resisting the urge to press my palms over my ears, I say, "Nobody deserves that." I should know.

"It's over," he says in a placating tone. "Go back into the house."

I free my arm. "I don't take orders from you."

Coldness settles in his eyes. "Whatever you say, Mrs. Hart."

Anne shakes her head when he's gone. "You should listen to him."

Stress makes me snap at her. "To do what? Finish dinner while a man is losing his fingers?"

She cocks a shoulder. "Damian will be upset about your interference."

I can't believe how blasé she is about this. "We need to help that man." I go for the door again, but her words stop me.

"You're only making it worse for the guy."

"What?"

"The more you plead his case, the more Damian will make him suffer. He's jealous that way."

"Jealous of what?" I exclaim.

"Of a woman's concern."

"If that's true, he's a monster."

Another scream. Am I the only damn person in this house who wants to stop this?

"You can't handle Damian, Lina, but don't worry, not many women can."

Leaving me with the insinuation of that statement, she saunters back to the house. Russell's form is visible through the kitchen window. She stops in front of him. I can't make out what they say to each other, but they're both tense. It takes me one second to decide on a course of action. I grip the knob firmly. Before I can turn it, the door swings open and none other than my husband stands before me. Spots of blood cover his white shirt and a lock falls over his forehead, but other than that not a strand of hair is out of place. His face is composed.

"Damian—"

107

"Lock her in my room."

He steps aside to let one of his men exit.

"No," I cry as the man drags me away. "Damian, don't do this."

Damian doesn't even look at me. He turns away, allowing the bulk of a man to burn me with his touch on my arms, shoving me past Russell and Anne, and up the stairs.

"Please," I beg when we reach the bedroom, "don't lock the door. I'll stay. I swear."

My plea falls on deaf ears. Once he's left me in the room, he shuts the door. Through the closed door, I hear the man call to Zane for the keys. Rushing to the door, I jerk on the handle, but the guard is blocking it.

"Let me out!"

More footsteps fall outside, followed by the turn of a key. A flick of the door handle confirms my worst fear. I'm locked in.

No, no, no.

My chest closes up.

It's nothing.

It's not.

I can't breathe. I can't think. It's as if I'm trapped under water, and my only urge is to fight my way to the surface. Shamelessly, I bang on the door, a vague corner of my mind aware of the fact that everyone in the house can hear the noise I'm making, but I can't bring myself to care.

When my fists hurt too much to carry on, I rush to the window and throw it open. I already know it's two stories down with no ledge, but I search for something I might have missed, like a gutter pipe running down the wall. There's nothing but smooth brick. My dress suddenly feels to tight. I claw at the high neck, ripping off a button. Forcing myself to take deep, steady breaths, I unbutton the bodice. My hands are shaking, and the buttons are so tiny it turns out to be a daunting task.

Sitting down on the window seat, I inhale as much of the night air as I can drag into my uncooperative lungs. Sheer willpower allows me to focus on my breathing until I can let my mind drift. I'm back in time, living the happier moments of my life before my mother died, until I fall into a trancelike state that allows me to escape the reality of the situation.

By the time the door opens, I'm covered in a cold sweat. Damian stands on the threshold, shirtless, carrying a tray. Kicking the door shut, he walks to the table by the fireplace. I can't help but look at his hands when he deposits the tray. They're clean, his nails free of dirt or blood.

I tense when he walks to me, flattening my back against the cold glass of the windowpane. He towers over me, all muscles and man, and now that I've seen what this man is capable of, his dominating presence is scarier.

Eyebrows furrowed, he studies me. "I'm sorry you had to see that. It won't happen here again."

Here. He didn't say it wouldn't happen again. He just won't do it here.

My mouth is so dry it's difficult to speak. "Why?"

"He stole from me."

My voice is hoarse. "How many fingers?"

"Three."

"Was that really necessary?"

His eyes darken until the black almost consumes the brown. "This will be the fate of anyone who dares to take something that belongs to me."

I swallow, remembering he accused my family of stealing from him more than once. "Harold?"

"I have something different in mind for him. He deserves losing more than his fingers."

My heartbeat turns erratic. I don't ask what he has in mind for me. I don't want to know. When he reaches out, I flinch, but I don't move. I'm backed up against the window. There's nowhere to go.

He wipes a thumb over my cheek. "I scare you."

I don't deny the truth.

He continues to stroke my cheek as he speaks. "I can't promise to never hurt you."

Everything inside me constricts at the confession. I didn't expect anything less, but hearing him say it makes the fear more tangible, rising to lie shallower in my chest.

"I can promise you, though," he carries on, "that I won't let anyone else hurt you."

Lies. He broke that promise even before he made it, and if it depends on Zane, he'll break it many times over.

Dropping his hand, he walks to the table and picks up a glass and plate, which he carries back to me.

"You haven't finished dinner."

I take the plate on autopilot, grimacing at the lemon pie. My appetite has vanished, and the thick layer of meringue makes me want to vomit.

"I'm sorry." I shake my head. "I can't."

He hesitates but exchanges the pie for the glass. The whisky, I drink. I need the burn that opens my throat and dulls my senses.

"Tea?" he asks, still standing over me like a doctor scrutinizing a patient.

"What?"

His fingers brush mine when he takes the glass. "Would you like a cup of tea?"

Would I? I'm in no state to think, never mind analyze my dietary cravings.

"Have a warm shower," he says. "I'll bring you some Rooibos to help you sleep."

He's already at the door when I find my tongue. "Damian."

He turns and waits, watching me with those intense eyes.

"Where is he?"

Irritation plays over his face. "I presume at a hospital."

"Your men took him?"

"Of course not. They dropped him at his car." He flexes his hand, fingers splayed. "Why are you so concerned about him?"

"You just chopped off a man's fingers, and you ask me this?"

"Have your shower." He turns away from me, animosity written in the tight set of his broad shoulders.

"Damian."

He pauses. "What?"

"Please don't lock me in."

There's something in his gaze as he looks at me from over his shoulder. Suspicion. A question. He doesn't say anything but humors me by leaving the door open when he goes.

Not wanting to be caught naked, I rush through the shower and pull on a nightdress. When I step out of the bathroom, a cup of tea is standing on the nightstand, still steaming. Feeling cold to my bones, I take a sip. It's sweet, just like my mother made it that time when the car knocked me off my bicycle.

Damian

THE EVENING HAS TURNED into a nightmare. I shouldn't have brought that thieving scumbag to our home, but we snared him unexpectedly when he exited the Minerals Council, and I couldn't drag him into the streets or behind the nearest dump where the city has crime surveillance cameras.

Since my evening is already ruined, I go in search of Zane, and find him and Anne in front of the television, laughing at a slapstick comedy.

Anne looks up when I enter. "Damian, you poor baby. What an awful day you had." She gets to her feet, lithe like a cat, and grips my shoulders from behind. "Sit down. You can do with a massage. Zane, pour him a drink."

Zane shoots her a dirty look.

I shake off her touch. "We'll have that drink in my study."

I don't wait for Zane's reply. He knows better than to argue. In my study, I pour two whiskies over ice.

Zane enters slowly, his step cautious. "What's going on?"

"Sit." I point at the chair facing my desk, not the armchairs by the fireplace.

He eyes the chair uncertainly but doesn't question my motive. When he's sat down, I place a glass in front of him before rounding the desk and taking my seat.

"Jeez, Dami." He laughs nervously. "Why so formal?"

"You know I'll always be obliged to you for having my back."

"But?" he asks, more caution slipping into his tone.

"But hurt my wife, and you hurt me."

"Whoa." He raises his hands. "I didn't hurt Lina. She hurt herself. She's crazy. You do know that, right?"

"She has no skin left on her wrist."

"I told her not to struggle."

"You should've used padded cuffs."

"Metal is all I could find on short notice."

"Not good enough. I can almost forgive you for your ignorance on that one, but not for letting her take a sleeping pill strong enough to send her into a goddamn coma."

"Dami, the woman—"

"I'm not finished. You disappointed me tonight. I fucking counted on you to keep her out of it."

"I can't tell her what to do. She's your *wife*. She won't listen to me."

"Next time, try harder, or I won't be as forgiving."

"Are you for real?" He gets to his feet. "Are you blaming the fact that she gatecrashed your torturing party on me?"

"I trust you to have my back. Tonight, you didn't."

"Keeping your wife innocent doesn't count as having your back. Not in my book."

"It does in mine. Is that clear enough, or do you need a memo?"

"Dami."

"Don't test me. Not on this."

"Fine. I'm sorry about her wrist and for letting her trip on a pill, and I'm sorry if I was supposed to detain her tonight."

"Distract, not detain."

"Distract," he agrees feebly.

"I accept your apology." I lift my glass. "Are we good?"

Reluctantly, he picks up his. "We're good."

He downs the drink and slams the glass down on the desk. "Is she going to become an issue?"

Anger pulls at my patience. "Explain what you mean with *issue*."

"Is she going to come between us?"

I pin him with a stare. "Between what exactly, Zane? What are you assuming is between us?"

He swallows. "Friendship. Is she going to come between our friendship?"

"Not unless you make the fact that I married her a problem."

He lifts his hands again. "No problem." His smile turns wry. "I'm only watching out for you." Walking to the door, he throws in, "As I've always done."

He doesn't slam the door, but he doesn't close it quietly, either.

I'm going to have to keep an eye on Zane. It'll hurt me to kick him out, but I meant what I said. Lina comes first. She may hate me as much as Zane is loyal, but she is my wife.

Lina

AFTER THE INCIDENT, I avoid Damian. It's not difficult. He's gone for business every day, returning late at night. He doesn't cuff me to the bed, but I often wake with his heavy arm draped over my stomach, tying me to the heat of his body. Afraid to wake him, or more accurately, his sinister lust, I never stir. I endure the discomfort and the itch to change positions. I listen to his breathing, inhale his male scent, and remember what he's done. When I think about how intimately his hands have touched me and what those hands are capable of, a shiver always finds its way from my cold insides to the over-heated surface of my skin.

Like I'm avoiding my husband, Zane avoids me. Russell pretends I don't exist. Except for a formal greeting or a stiff reply to a question, he doesn't speak to me. He does nothing but follow me around with a small distance in physical space and a growing distance on an intangible level. I don't see much of Anne, either, who is too busy going to make-up and hairdressing trials for Saturday's wedding reception.

As the house is slowly being transformed into a gala venue, I grow more nervous. Facing a room full of people for hours on end with a poker face is not on the top of my list of enjoyable experiences. The media will be here. Photos will be taken. I'll have to play the role of someone I'm not and wear a mask among people who believe the worst of me. I'll have to pretend I don't hear the whispers, the allegations, and the musings about how crazy I am. In a room full of enemies, my husband being the greatest, I won't be able to let my guard down for a second.

In the build-up to the unwanted event, I search the house from top to bottom, but the evidence is nowhere to be found. Since Damian made a point of not inviting Harold to the party, sending a strong message to the speculating media, I don't have to deal with Harold yet, but I prefer to get my hands on those documents sooner than later. I'm prepared to make the sacrifice for the prize they'll buy me. What are three fingers in exchange for freedom?

SATURDAY ARRIVES TOO SOON. Caterers, waiters, and cleaners mill around the house. I seek refuge in the kitchen where Jana prepares a pot of chamomile tea, as if it'll soothe me.

"I know you're nervous," she says, winking.

I am, but not for the reason she presumes. I'm not a blushing bride worried about what can go wrong at her wedding party.

"Everything will be perfect." She checks her watch. "You better get ready if you don't want to be late."

"Are you staying?" I hold my breath, praying she'll say yes.

"No can do. It's pizza night with the kids."

"Of course." I offer her a meek smile. "Have fun."

A selfish part of me wants her to stay so that I have a friendly face to anchor me, but Jana has her own family to take care of.

Pouring another cup of tea, I carry it upstairs and get ready like

Jana suggested. It's a lot like our wedding ritual, with me emptying my stomach in the toilet before pulling on a black dress. It's a simple cut with a long skirt and high neck, the silk more charcoal than black. Harold bought it for me to wear to Jack's funeral when I was too drugged to get out of bed and take care of such a simple task.

The ringing of the doorbell makes my stomach tighten. The stomping of steps on the stairs makes my skin clammy.

Zane puts his head around the open door. Dressed in a tux and bowtie, he would've been handsome if not for the personality that taints his exterior looks. His gaze flickers disapprovingly over me. "The first guests have arrived."

I don't skip a beat, fitting an earring as if I'm not fazed. "They're early." And Damian is late.

"The waiters are offering them drinks. I suggest you move your ass. Dami will be here in five."

When he leaves, I notice Russell in the corridor, guarding the bedroom door. He's staring straight ahead, as if he'll turn into a pillar of salt if he glances into the room.

Ignoring the increasing amount of voices coming from down-stairs, I twist my hair into a tight bun and apply light make-up. The cosmetics aren't to look pretty, but to mask the paleness of my lips and cheeks. I'm applying lipstick when I hear my husband offer Russell a greeting.

Automatically, my hand holding the lipstick stills. Three heart-beats later, Damian's image appears in the reflection of the mirror. He stops on the threshold of the dressing room, taking me in. With one hand in his pocket and a finger hooked into the hanger of a dry-cleaning bag that hangs over his shoulder, his stance is casual, but there's nothing laid-back about his stare that seems to peel off my very skin. Like Zane, he's dressed in a tux. The fact that his thick hair is still damp means he recently had a shower. Where did he get changed? At the office?

"Sorry I'm late."

He owes me no apologies, and I don't miss this one is lacking an excuse.

"Your guests are already here." I say *your* like an accusation. I never wanted any part in this.

His lips tilt in a corner, mocking my spitefulness. "It couldn't be helped. I was occupied."

"Cutting off fingers?" I ask drily.

"If I was, would you want to know?"

I'm not going to answer that.

"I don't own a tux," he says. "I needed to rent one, but an alteration had me running late. I showered at the office."

The admission makes me a little less angry with him. I can't help but feel a sliver of sympathy for the wealthy man who doesn't own a tux. It says so much about his past.

Feeling the heat of his stare on my back, I finish applying my lipstick and rub my lips together. "I'm ready."

It's a lie. I'll never be ready, but the quicker we get this over with, the better.

For two seconds we're frozen in our staring, evaluating each other and finding one another short, and then he breaks the moment of unspoken accusations with a single step and word.

"No." His voice is overbearing, dominating.

"Excuse me?"

He advances on me. "You're not going like this."

I turn to face him, bracing my hands on the vanity counter behind me. You don't give your back to a lion. "Like what?"

His brow shoots up. His smile is indulgent. "You'll wear this." He holds the dry-cleaning bag out to me.

He came prepared. He knew how I'd be dressing, and he wasn't going to make the same mistake as with our wedding. I should've expected his course of action, but it still comes as a surprise, so much so that when he pushes the bag into my limp hand, I fold my fingers reflexively around it. I can't let go of his eyes. I'm holding them in disbelief but most of all in fear.

His gaze dips to where I clutch the plastic. "Open it."

When I don't move, he takes back the bag and pulls down the zipper. The dress he extracts is worse than I could've ever imagined.

116

Red silk overlaid with chiffon drapes low in both the front and back. Thin straps hold up the shoulders, and a slit almost reaches the hip. It's a whore dress. There's no other word for it.

I look from the dress to him in horror. He can't be serious. But he is. There's a glint of malice in his eyes as he gauges my reaction.

I can't wear that. Blood zings through my veins, shooting up from my feet to my fingers to tingle like pinpricks. I feel the heat in my cheeks and hear the gush like a drumbeat in my ears. Panic envelopes me, sending a rush of cold sweat to my skin and nausea to my stomach. As if on cue, the scarred flesh of my arms starts itching. It burns without the prompt of a touch. The mere imagination of a hundred people's eyes on a part of me I've never shown to the world is enough.

"I—" I lick my dry lips, battling to summon my voice. "I can't wear this."

He narrows his eyes with intent and addresses me with a soft, dangerous voice. "You will, or I swear to God I'll make you walk downstairs in nothing but your underwear."

I start at his words, the urge to back up instinctive, but I'm pinned between him and the vanity counter.

"You better believe I'm not bluffing, Lina."

No, he's not. It's beneath Damian to bluff. I start shaking, the blood dropping from my head to my feet, reversing its earlier course so absolutely I suffer from a sudden bout of vertigo. My body sways, only my grip on the counter keeping me up. This is my breaking point. This is my limit. This is where I start begging.

"Please, Damian. Not this dress. Don't make me do this. Anything, anything but this."

I'm ready to slide to my knees, to clutch his pants in my clammy hands and promise him anything he wants, and he knows it. Satisfaction pulls at his lips, yet, his eyes remain unrelenting. Hard. Then it hits me. Oh, my God. This is his revenge. My mouth drops open as comprehension dawns.

"Damian." I want to die of shame.

Instead of mercy, he gives me silence. Confirmation. He wants to humiliate me in front of his guests. He wants me to feel like he did when I married him in a black dress.

Straightening my back, I fight my voice not to tremble. "This is my punishment, isn't it?"

He cups my cheek. It's a tender gesture, but his smile is hard. "In all fairness, you do have the body for this dress."

The body of a whore. He has no idea how right he is.

"I recall a night," he continues, "when you had no problem putting your tits and ass on display for all the men in your father's house to see."

It's a lie. Harold bought the dress. I tried to cover most of it with my shawl.

"I have something else for you."

He walks back to the room and returns with a parcel. First, he takes out a red thong. No bra. The cut of the dress is too low to allow for a bra. Then he removes a pair of shoes from a boutique box. The clear color gives the impression that the heels are made of glass. Just like Cinderella. But this is no fairytale, and Damian is no prince.

"I expect to see you coming down those stairs in exactly ten minutes. Don't make me drag you out of this room in your thong."

Beyond saving, I stare at his retreating form. In ten minutes, I'll be beyond grace.

He turns in the door. "Oh, and take down your hair."

I try one last time. "You don't know what you're doing."

His smile says otherwise. "This round, *wife*, is mine."

With those words, he disappears, letting his victory sink in, forcing me to do a walk of shame in front of my enemies.

CHAPTER 8

Damian

On my way downstairs, I motion for Russell to follow. I trust him, but the bedroom door was open when I arrived, and he's just a man. With a woman like Lina, any man will find it hard to resist a peek at her naked body. Zane will make sure our bedroom stays off limits. I told him as much when I entered. I want Russell at the reception. His job is keeping Lina safe. I doubt one of the wedding party guests will launch an attack on her in my house, but you never know. I have too many enemies. She has enough. Maybe Lina doesn't deserve those enemies. She's not capable of hurting a fly, besides herself that is, but she's the product of her father's legacy and my name. Having been born to the one and married to the other, there is no bigger threat a person can face in the world. Our enemies combined are enough to make hardened criminals shiver.

If not for the grave mistake she made in marrying Clarke, she would've been innocent in the war for money and power. If not for her choice of attire that baptized our union as *the black wedding* in the media, I wouldn't have entered into tonight's private war with her. Let's face it, the dress I picked isn't slutty. It's revealing, but not beyond what's considered socially acceptable. The only person who'll be punished is my conservative wife and maybe my dick. I doubt I'll stay soft at the sight of her in that silk.

I look forward to seeing her in red far more than the actual reception, which sole purpose is to rub my ownership of Lina and her fortune in my advisories' noses. The arrival of my wife will definitely be the highlight of my night. She has four minutes before I go get her. Even the pleasure of excluding Dalton from the event, which is nothing short of a dishonor, comes second.

A hoard of scavengers descends on me downstairs. I drown in a mob of men wearing black ties and false smiles who want to know what my plans are for Dalton Diamonds, or more accurately, how they can bribe their way into my favor. Women too eager to suffocate me with insincere compliments hang on their arms. I accept a glass of champagne from a passing waiter, reveling in tonight's victory. Based on the mismanagement charges I slapped Dalton with and the messy investigation it set it motion, Ellis and I voted him off the board. I bought up his shares, which makes me the owner of seventy percent. The end of Dalton is a foregone conclusion. I'm yet to tell my wife I've ruined her father, but I'll save it for after the reception. I want to take my time to savor her reaction. For now, I want to gloat and let these motherfuckers grovel in my glory.

I'm good at taking in facts while directing my attention elsewhere. While I give the appropriate responses at the right times to mindless chatter about kids, exotic holidays, and so-called interesting business opportunities, I watch the time and the top of the stairs.

Exactly ten minutes after I've left Lina, she appears in a drowsing ball of chandelier light on the landing. Inwardly, I smile. It's so much like her to rebel in any way she can, even in pushing her appearance to the end of the time limit. One hand on the balustrade, she faces forward, her chin lifted proudly and her back straight. When she takes the first step out of the light, the sight I've been anticipating so eagerly hits me straight in the balls.

Fucking hell. She's a vision. The red silk clings to her figure, hinting at what lies underneath, but the chiffon makes it whimsical, softening and hiding what would otherwise have been the obvious tips of her nipples, the dip of her navel, and the swell of her mound. Like a graceful apparition, she glides to the top of the stairs, every step revealing a slender, creamy-toned leg through the slit. The valley between her breasts is deep, but not so much that the curves risk spilling out. I'm way too possessive to allow that. Her hair cascades in waves down her back. From where I'm standing, we're facing each other, me looking up and her looking down. For a moment, my breath catches. For once, I lose track of a conversation and miss the question directed at me.

She was ravishing six years ago. The woman she is today is nothing compared to that. She's ten times more desirable. And she's mine. My cock grows hard at the knowledge. My blackened heart revels at the conquest, and something in my chest jerks as a notion stabs me in the heart. It's a foreign feeling that Lina is my greatest triumph, even greater than acquiring Dalton Diamonds.

Whoever spoke to me repeats his question, but I'm only aware of the primitive sensation of ownership and exhilaration running wild through my body. I see nothing but the unwilling woman in revealing red.

I'm not the only one who's noticed. The room has gone quiet. Lina holds all the attention as she makes her descend, walking like a queen. She may fool everyone else into believing she's the epitome of confidence, but not me. I see the slight shake of her hand where it rests on the balustrade. I see the battle in her midnight blue eyes to not succumb to her embarrassment when all she should be feeling is pride.

Yes, she can do with a few more kilos on her flesh, but even too slender she's perfectly proportioned, so perfect she looks like a doll. If her eyes burn with hate for me, the moment will still be worth it. Knowing her, that's exactly what she'll give me. Hatred. I'm waiting for her to rain the fire in that glare down on me as she gets closer to my eye level, but when she takes the step that puts her at my height, a jolt runs through me. Her eyes are not burning. They're vacant. She was never looking at me. She's looking *through* me. She's not seeing me at all. She's not seeing anyone. There's something wrong about this.

My muscles tighten in anticipation for a reason I can't name. All I know is whatever is about to happen is bad. Real fucking bad. The wheel has been set in motion, and it's too late to stop it. The clogs of time keep on turning, pushing her farther one step at a time. And then she takes the turn in the staircase.

Jesus fucking Christ.

The breath she'd knocked from me earlier gets stuck in my throat. Around me, people gasp, much like at our wedding. If she hears it, she doesn't react. She continues on her downward path with her glassy eyes and proud posture. My heart rate goes into overdrive. The champagne glass shatters in my hand, golden liquid spilling on my shoes and glass cutting into my palm, but nobody notices. They're too busy staring at my wife as if she belongs in a freak show.

The marks on her arms are like nothing I've seen. Not even in prison. Thick, ragged, and embossed, only a blunt breadknife could've caused such scars. Badly healed, they speak of careless treatment. *What the fuck?* The same question is going through the heads of everyone in the crowd, because the whispered answers drift on the shocked silence.

"Self-mutilation."

"There's a term for that."

"Cutter."

All the while, Lina bears the judgment in words as well as in stares, but I see what her lifted chin and straight back are meant to disguise. I see her shame. I see her hiding inside herself, holding the room hostage to uncertainty as no one moves, everyone shocked to a standstill.

Next to me, Russell comes to his senses first. Pulling off his jacket, he takes a step toward the staircase, but when I realize his intention, I catch his wrist. He gives me a heated look, his face twisted into an expression that says not even I can be this cruel.

"No," I say under my breath. Covering her up will only make it worse.

Instead, I hurry to the bottom of the stairs so she doesn't have to venture into the gawking mob alone.

She reaches me, unsmiling. The minute she's within my grasp, I wrap my arm around her shoulders and pull her against my side. From the slight sway of her body, the act has thrown her off balance, but I don't let up. I tighten my hold. When that doesn't pull her completely back to the present, I grip her chin firmly and plant my lips on hers in a kiss that doesn't involve my tongue but lasts too long. Another second, and I achieve my aim. She stiffens. Her eyes clear. A frown pulls her eyebrows together. Her body goes rigid, her muscles tensing in preparation for action.

Before she pushes me away, I set her mouth free. Her pupils are dilated, her eyes wide in shock and anger. Good. She's back where I want her, right here with me. Her cutting look tells me she doesn't appreciate that I'm pulling her from the trance in which she's been hiding. Her bad. These fuckers won't enjoy the hot piece of gossip I've unknowingly thrown at their feet at her expense. I won't allow her to feed their vulture-like hunger for sensationalism with her shame.

Her pretty eyes narrow with the tiniest twitch. Her little nostrils quiver as if she's about to hiss at me like an angry kitten, but her threat is silent. She won't settle for pity. I don't give her any. I give her my pride and as much comfort as circumstances allow, sheltering her under my arm while we say our greetings to the people who compete for our attention, curiosity sparking their eagerness. Speculating glances always find their way back to Lina's arms, but she does a hell of a job pretending she doesn't notice. I function on autopilot, saying what is expected while questions spin through my mind.

A Minerals Council executive walks up to us. "Congratulations, Damian. I'll be honest. I didn't see that one coming."

Motherfucker. Congrats are not in order until the official announcement is made, and the bastard knows it. He's rolling on the balls of his feet, basking in expectation, watching Lina like a hawk.

A journalist who sees an opportunity interrupts. "Mr. Hart, what is your intention for Dalton Diamonds?"

To break everything Harold Dalton has built down to the ground. "I'll release an official statement tomorrow."

I start steering Lina away, but the man blocks our way. "Mrs. Hart, how do you feel about your husband's hostile takeover of your father's corporation?"

She goes so rigid against my side, I swear her frail body is about to snap. I feel her surprise in the way her ribs stop expanding with breaths where my palm rests on her side. I feel the beat of her heart increase where her body is pressed against mine. Before I can throw the fucker out for launching an attack on Lina when said attack failed on me, she inhales deeply and silently, only the expansion of her ribs giving me a clue that she's going to answer the prick. I'm about to hush her, not because I'm frightened that she'd tell the world how she feels about me, but because I'm frightened for her already bruised image and how her hatred of me will make the public spectacle I've created worse.

"Lina—"

"No comment," she says.

The cocky bastard grins as he throws more bait. "Really? That's your answer? That's all you have to say?"

She regards him coolly, as if he's a bad-mannered minion. "You heard my husband. He'll make a statement tomorrow."

Underneath her pretended loyalty, I can almost feel her emotions churning.

"You'll be wise to stay respectful of the fact that this event is a celebration," I say, "not a press conference."

Making a mental note to have the fucker's name removed from our future invitation list, I finally manage to guide Lina to a quieter corner. The minute we're away from the journalist's scrutinizing gaze, her body sags against mine. I rub her arm in a soothing gesture. My fingers brush over the horizontal lines embossed on her skin, the pads reading them like brail, as if they're a roadmap to the subject dominating my thoughts. What the hell happened to her?

At the touch, her back snaps into a rigid posture. A shiver runs over her body. If she could've pulled away without making a scene, she would've, but she'd have to fight me in front of the crowd. Slowly, I piece the puzzle together. She's only shivered like that when I've touched her arms. It's not my touch in general, because I know only too well how certain prods make her back arch and her body bow. She doesn't like her *arms* to be touched. I don't remove my arm from around her shoulder, but I lift my fingers from her upper arm. She rewards me by relaxing marginally.

When a waiter comes past, I grab a glass of champagne and hand it to her. "Drink."

She obeys mechanically, downing half of it in one go.

"More," I urge. "It'll help you relax."

She drinks the rest and hands me the empty glass. Leaving it on a nearby table, I use the opportunity to snatch a linen napkin that I twist around my bleeding palm.

Her gaze fixes on the action. "What happened?"

Exactly the question that's on my mind. "The glasses are thin."

She regards me with mistrust but doesn't ask more.

There are so many things I want to ask, facts I need to know, but we're surrounded by people who are circling us like sharks, waiting for a weakness they can exploit, which is why I'm not allowing Lina to break down. As far as everyone here is concerned, showing her scars was planned. Tonight is the night Lina decided to come out of the closet. That's the lie my eyes and smile are telling when I look down at my wife. I'm pushing her to be strong, to keep up the charade, and for the most part it's working, until Anne appears in front of us.

She's wearing an off-shoulder dress in midnight blue. The color and style become her. Her hair is twisted in fancy curls on top of her head, baring smooth shoulders and flawless arms. The comparison as she stands in front of Lina is inevitable. If I hadn't made it my business to make a study of Lina's expressions, I would've missed how her eyes scrunch with the minutest movement in the corners, as if a knife is twisting in her stomach.

Anne grabs Lina's hands. "You poor, poor thing."

Even as Lina keeps a straight face, her gaze drops to the floor.

"There's nothing poor about Lina," I say with a pointed look.

"Don't be an idiot, Damian. Look at her."

"I *am* looking at her." My tone is cool, but if Anne were wise enough to have looked into my eyes, she would've been frightened.

"Let me go get you a wrap, Lina," Anne offers, already taking a step toward the stairs.

"Lina doesn't want a wrap."

Anne stops dead. "You're not serious."

"Are you cold, Lina?"

Her voice is flat. "No."

I address Anne. "No wrap."

"You're an asshole," Anne spits out.

Amused at her outburst, I cock a brow. "What for?"

"For letting her walk around like this."

Next to me, Lina stands as still as a mannequin.

My amusement fizzles into anger. "Like what?" When she doesn't answer immediately, I repeat, "Like *what*, Anne?"

"Like this," she says, waving a hand at Lina's arm.

"Say it," I challenge.

Anne stares at me with spite. She knows it's a chess mate move. If she says my wife is disfigured, I'll throw her out of my house in front of all these guests.

It's Lina who speaks. "Scars. They're called scars, and they're ugly. It's okay. You can say it."

Zane appears as if from nowhere, his face flushed when he takes in our exchange. Our non-verbal language must say it all.

He grips his sister's arm. "Come on, Anne."

Shooting Lina another pitying look from over her shoulder, Anne walks away with swaying hips. The walk is understated, just suggestive enough to exude sexual confidence without seeming obvious, but I see it for what it is. It's a show-off. It's a walk of feminine victory.

THE REST of the evening is a nightmare to get through. I don't let go of Lina once. We drink together. We eat together. If I have to speak to someone, she listens. She doesn't participate in any of the conversations, but she replies to all the questions my guests direct at her. The few journalists I've allowed, take pictures. I wanted this event to be all over the newspapers, but I haven't anticipated the angle the articles are going to take. If Lina is to survive this, she's going to have to face the music and dance like she doesn't give a fuck.

I make sure she eats enough and drinks lots of water, even if I have to force it on her. It's close to three in the morning when the bitter-enders leave. The first thing Lina does when the front door closes on the last person's back, is kick off her new shoes, right there in the entrance. It's an act I find strangely endearing. It's homely in a normal kind of way, as if we're just another couple who've thrown a party. When she heads straight upstairs, I don't stop her. I follow.

All the tenseness is back in her body the minute we walk over the threshold. Crossing her arms over her chest, she walks to the window, staring out at the night.

"Lina."

She doesn't acknowledge me.

I move until I stand close enough to feel the warmth radiating from her skin. I'm not going to pretend the scars aren't there. Just like covering them up, ignoring them will only make the matter worse. "What happened?"

She turns her head a fraction to the side, but doesn't look at me.

Sweeping her hair over her shoulder, I run my hand along the curve of her neck, repeating the question that has been tormenting me all night. "What happened, Lina?"

A sigh pops like a fragile soap bubble from her lips. *No comment.* It's the only answer she's prepared to give me.

How deep does her self-destructive tendencies go? I can't afford to let her off the hook. "Did you cut yourself?"

Her shoulders droop in a gesture that looks a lot like disappointment. "You heard what they said."

Tightening my hold on her shoulder, I turn her around. "I don't give a fuck about what *they* said."

She blinks up at me. She's pulled so deep into herself again not even the unexpected movement brought on by my outrage against everyone who'd judged her invites a response.

Desperate for a reaction, any reaction, I give her a gentle shake. "It doesn't define you."

Her chosen reaction is compassion. She looks at me with fucking pity, as if I'm the one who's been done in. "It's who I am."

"Damn right. You own those scars. Do you hear me?" Never mind *how* she earned them. I won't allow her to hide them again. "You *own* them. There's no need to be ashamed."

"Have you taken a good look?" She holds out her arm. "They make me sick. They make everyone sick."

"Not me."

She looks away, avoiding my words and any possible meaning they could carry. The power game of punishment I was playing with the red dress wasn't supposed to turn out like this. "You should've told me, Lina."

"Would it have changed anything?"

I don't hesitate. "No." But I would've known, and I would've mentally prepared her. I would've walked down those steps with her.

She nods in understanding, but her smile is bitter.

Gripping her chin, I force her to meet my eyes. "You're beautiful."

She flinches. My words hurt her despite their truth. She tries to pull away, but I hold fast. "That dress." I drag my gaze over her slender form. "You're a goddamn sight to behold."

"Don't." It's a whispered plea.

"Don't what?" I counter-challenge.

A pained frown pinches her brows together. "Don't do this."

Determination won't let me ease up. "What are you accusing me of?"

"Reverse psychology won't work on me."

"You think I'm lying?" Turning her around, I march her to the dressing room and place her in front of the mirror. "Look."

Her gaze moves toward the glass, but it's me she looks at.

I brush my lips over the shell of her ear. "Look at you."

"Damian." Her torment is a deep, keening pain that makes her eyelashes flutter.

A shiver runs over me from the way she says my name, as if she's on her knees, begging. If I don't let go, I'm going to touch her, and she's not ready for that, not after tonight. Setting her aside brusquely, I walk to her side of the closet and yank the dresses from their hangers.

"What are you doing?" she asks in a small voice when I give her drawers the same treatment, throwing everything on the floor. She has her answer when I start tearing fabric apart.

"Damian!"

Her small fingers lock around my wrist, trying to pry my hand away, but she's no match for my strength. The black garb groans and gives with a tear. One by one, I destroy her dresses, nightdresses, and underwear until the mangled clothing lie in a heap on the floor. No more long sleeves. No more black. No more hiding. No more mourning.

Taking one of my T-shirts from a drawer, I throw it at her. She catches it mid-air, her lips parted in shock.

"Put that on." She doesn't move. I arch a brow. "Unless you prefer to sleep naked?"

Those are the magic words that make her hurry to the bathroom. A smile works its way over my face. Tonight might have been a disaster, but it worked out in a different way. I'm nowhere near understanding the complexity of the woman I claimed as my wife, but I've peeled back one more layer and took another part of her for myself. That makes me deliriously happy, because I want all of her. I won't stop until she gives me everything.

Lina

DESPITE LAST NIGHT'S DRAMA, I feel lighter when I wake up in Damian's arms. The first sensation that crashes over me is the silky brush of the sheets against my bare arms. Shame heats the pit of my stomach, but there's also something else, something that leaves a strange weightlessness in my chest. Relief. It's out there now. People will think what they will about me, but I don't have to hide it any longer. I don't have to sweat in long sleeves to protect what's left of my pride. My reputation may be trampled, my craziness upped a notch in the public's perception, but the potency of the poison can only diminish from today. The fear of having my scars discovered has been made redundant with one skimpy red dress. Harold can't use it to blackmail me any longer.

Damian is breathing evenly next to me, his face turned toward mine. The sun is up. It's light in the room. I study the stubble that darkens his jaw. How will that scruff feel on the tender skin of my inside thigh? When the lower half of my body clenches at the thought, I quickly reject the notion.

Damian stirs. His arm is heavy on my full bladder. When he doesn't open his eyes, I nudge him gently. He groans, pulling me tighter. His erection presses against my hip. I go stiff. Nothing but his boxer briefs prevent our skins from touching. He doesn't act on the hard-on applying such persistent pressure on my flesh but draws lazy circles with his thumb on my side.

"Damian?"

His voice is sleep-rough and scratchy like his jaw scruff. "Lina?"

Hearing him say my name like this, as if he'll grant me any wish, makes me want to believe it's true. It opens an ache in my chest for something I can't have. This, right here, is the crux of our war. We want very different things. I want my freedom, and he wants to chain me to him forever. He wants to keep me where he's free to punish me at his whim for the sins we committed against him. If there ever comes a day he could look me in the eye and say my name like he said it a few seconds ago, he'd tell me to ask him for anything. I'd ask for my freedom, and he'd say no. No matter how kindly he treated me last night, seeing my scars and reacting like they don't matter, I can never forget he's my enemy.

I can never ask him for what I really want, so I say instead, "I need the bathroom."

"Mm." A devilish smile tugs on his lips, and his touch becomes ticklish.

"You're crushing my bladder."

With another groan, he lets up, but not before he opens his eyes to stare at me with those pools of bitter chocolate.

Skittering from the bed, I pretend I don't see the questions or the lust as his gaze follows me to the bathroom. I rush through my morning grooming, glancing from time to time through the crack in the door toward the bed to make sure he stays there. It's when I brush my teeth that my reflection in my mirror catches me off-guard. Seeing the scars while I'm clothed is new. Grotesque and unsightly, they jar me so much I don't notice Damian has left the bed until he walks into the bathroom. The toothbrush jerks in my hand. He comes up from behind, plants a kiss on my shoulder, and pulls off his boxers. I swallow a glob of toothpaste. His erection juts out from a nest of dark hair and heavy testicles, and Damian shows it off proudly. The sharp mint flavor stings my throat, making my eyes water. I cough around the toothbrush, looking anywhere but in the mirror.

He brushes up against me, letting me feel his hardness through the T-shirt on my lower back.

"Sleep well?" he murmurs against my neck.

I blink the tears from my eyes, and mumble something incomprehensible through a gargle of bubbles.

He has the audacity to slap my ass, making me jump, before he casually gets into the shower. The water comes on, and I can't help myself. I dare another glance at the cubicle in the mirror, expecting him in the same pose from the night before, one hand braced on the wall and the other stroking himself, but he's got his back turned to me, running his fingers through the thick, dark locks of his hair as water cascades down his broad back.

Rinsing out my mouth only once, I dash through the door, but then stop as my new dilemma hits me. I have nothing to wear. Going through his cupboards, I pull on a pair of his exercise shorts before padding barefoot down the hallway to knock on Anne's door.

She opens it wide, wearing boy shorts and a crop top. I'm not sure who she expected, but the corners of her mouth drop when she sees me, and then it turns into a full-blown scowl when she takes in my attire.

"I hope I didn't wake you."

She opens the door wider. "Come in."

Stepping over the threshold, I take in the décor, and at the same time I realize I've never set foot in this room, the knowledge of who the room is intended for hits me between the eyes. It's a mirror image of Damian's room, but feminine in design. This is the bedroom meant for the lady of the house. Why did Damian put me in his room and not here? Was it because Anne's clothes were already here, or because I'm not the woman of the house and will never be? More importantly, I haven't searched this room because we have a guest staying in here. Could the evidence be hidden in here?

Her gaze runs over me. "I see last night was an icebreaker."

I look down at Damian's T-shirt, and when I catch her drift, my cheeks heat. "I came to ask if I may please borrow a dress." I iron out the T-shirt with my palms. "I, um, ran out of clothes."

Her mouth puckers. "You'll drown in my dresses." She marches to the closet and returns with a pair of jeans and T-shirt. "Take these." She motions at the T-shirt. "It has long sleeves."

"Oh. Thank you." I'll drown more in her jeans than her dresses. My ass will never be able to fill them out like hers, but I take the garments from her without pointing out my obvious flaws. "I'll wash and return these tomorrow."

"No rush." She holds the door open, my cue to leave, but speaks again when I'm crossing the threshold. "How was it?"

I grip the clothes against my chest, hiding my naked breasts underneath. "How was what?"

"You know." She wags her eyebrows.

The early morning sun that filters in from the windows catches the ruby highlights in her chestnut hair. Green eyes watch me with vivid interest. A sense of expectation expands in the air, and envy becomes a tangible thing. Does she notice she's holding her breath? She's trying to downplay it, keeping her tone light and disinterested, but it's there in the hesitation, in the way she couldn't stop herself from blurting the question out before I'd walked from the room. It's there in the way her gaze keeps on flittering back to Damian's T-shirt. She wants him. She wants him badly enough to hate me for wearing his clothes. I want to tell her that her hate is wasted, that she can have him on a silver platter with a pretty bow, and that I'll even say thank you for diverting his attention, anything to turn his interest away from my body, but Russell's voice sounds from below.

"Mrs. Hart. Miss Anne."

My gaze is drawn to where he stands in the open front door. His stance is tense, as if he's on the verge of breaking up a fight. Like Anne, he takes in my attire, but does a better job of keeping his face blank.

"Thanks again for the clothes," I say before hurrying away.

Back in the room, Damian regards the bundle in my arms, but he doesn't ask questions. When I step from the bathroom, dressed and my hair brushed, he's waiting for me.

"Oh," I say, surprised. "I thought you'd be gone."

His lips twitch. "No such luck." He picks up his car keys and jingles them on his way to the door as a gesture for me to follow. When I don't move, he says, "Come on."

"Where to?"

"We have an appointment."

He doesn't pause to offer an explanation. He simply walks from the room, knowing I have no choice but to go along. I could throw a temper tantrum and refuse to budge until he tells me where we're going, but he'll only carry me to the car in full view of Anne, Zane, and the guards. I don't mind them so much seeing, but I don't want to disillusion sweet, normal, perfectly nice Jana. I don't want to give the only person in this house who treats me normally a reason to start treating me otherwise.

Hastily pulling on a pair of flats and grabbing my bag, I follow

Damian outside to his car. He holds the door for me and fits my seat-belt as if he doesn't trust me with the simple task.

Once we clear the gates, I try again. "Where are we going?"

He shifts gears and shoots me a glance. "Shopping."

His hand, big and masculine on the gearshift, is the same hand that brought down the axe on an alleged thief's fingers. It's the same hand that curls around my throat when he holds me with frightening tenderness and a promise of dominance. It's the same hand that uses paddles and whips to make me come. I bite my lip hard, willing my thoughts away from the shameful images of me bent over his desk and with legs spread wide on his study floor.

His gaze slips over my attire in another once-over. "You don't like shopping?"

"No."

His grin is unapologetic. "Too bad."

He parks in the Brooklyn Center and comes around to open my door. With his hand firmly on my arm, he steers me to a restaurant with a terrace.

"I thought you were going shopping," I say.

He indulges my little verbal rebellion, pulling out my chair. "Breakfast first."

Like during our wedding dinner, he orders for both of us, a mush-room and sweet pepper omelet for me, and poached eggs for him. While we wait to be served, he works on his phone, and I'm secre-tively relieved for the reprieve of his attention, but the moment our food arrives, he pins me with a stare.

Leaning back in his chair, he straightens his tie. "I bought out the shareholders of Dalton Diamonds. Ellis and I are the only ones left."

I cut into the omelet. It's thick and fluffy with gooey cheese on the inside. "I've gathered."

"I'm suing Dalton for damages based on mismanagement and fraud."

Delicious. I fight not to close my eyes. "Mm."

"The plan wasn't for you to find out like you did."

Oh, my God. This omelet is so good. "Are you offering me an apology?"

"No."

I shrug. "Then it doesn't matter."

"You know what's going to happen to Dalton." It's both a statement and a question.

"He'll be sued for every last penny he owns and his reputation ruined."

"This doesn't bother you?"

I stop eating to look at him. "Do you want me to be bothered?"

"It's not the reaction I expected from daddy's little girl."

"I'm not daddy's little girl."

"Could've fooled me."

"I guess you've been fooled."

He stares at me as if he can't make up his mind about whether I'm telling the truth, but finally picks up his fork and takes a bite of egg. We're like war opponents, watching each other eat. He wanted to punish me through Harold. I could've pretended to be upset, but it's simply too much energy, plus I doubt I can fake an ounce of care. I let him stew in his thoughts until he pushes his plate with half-eaten food away.

I wave my fork at the eggs. "Aren't you going to eat that?"

"I'm saving space for the fruit salad."

It will be a sin to waste something looking so perfectly delicious. I pull the plate closer. "Do you mind?"

He seems amused. "Knock yourself out."

I clean the food off his plate and then tackle the fruit salad.

The rest of our meal takes place in silence, except for two telephone calls he answers while we're sipping our coffee. While he speaks, I rearrange the sugar packets in the glass container. Then I spread them out like cards on the table, absorbed in the task and no longer aware of the man ignoring me. I look up when I realize he's spoken my name twice.

"Do you need to use the bathroom before we go?" he asks.

If it's so that he can stand in the door and watch me pee, "No, thanks."

His lips curve around a grin, as if he's recalling a funny memory.

I can't help myself. With everything that's happened since yesterday, this is the one, tiny straw that breaks me. "Fuck you."

He brushes a thumb over his bottom lip as if he's trying to wipe away his smirk. "Is that all I get for breakfast?"

"What did you expect?"

"Thank you?"

"Thank you," I say like a bitch.

He puts a wad of bills on the table. "Let's go."

Gathering the sugar packets, I shove them in my back pocket.

"What are you doing?"

I frown. "You said let's go."

"What are you doing with the sugar?"

It takes me a moment to catch on. It's been such an automatic reaction for me, I haven't been conscious of stealing the restaurant's sugar. A stolen packet of sugar had saved my life—literally—more than once. My cheeks flame with embarrassment as I put the packets back in their container.

He catches my hand. "Keep them if you have an addiction to cane sugar."

I pull away from his touch. "I don't."

This time, I'm the one who starts walking, and he has to follow. I have no idea where I'm going, just that I need to get away from his puzzled stare.

He catches up, falling into step beside me. "I'm not judging you. I just didn't expect it from you."

I bet he didn't. People like me eat in Michelin Star restaurants without looking at the price on the menu. People like me are drilled in table etiquette. People like me don't go hungry. They don't look twice at useful sugar packets or wasted bread.

"Hey." He catches my elbow and brings me to a halt. "Lina, it's nothing."

"It's not fucking nothing."

His eyes go wide, alert.

Damn it. The last thing I want is to draw his attention to my food stealing habits. I opt for changing the subject. "What are you shopping for?"

The awareness in his eyes doesn't diminish. If anything, it sharpens, but he doesn't push me on the subject. "For you."

"Let me guess." A bruise starts spreading in my chest. "Clothes."

"There's no way you're living in Anne's clothes."

"I didn't know you disapprove of her style."

"It's my job to put clothes on your back."

"What else is your job?" I snap.

He cups my nape, pulling me closer. His voice is soft, dangerous again. "Are you sure you want me to answer that here?"

I can only shake my head.

As abruptly as he's touched me, he lets me go. "We have an hour to fit you out. We better get moving."

AN HOUR LATER, Damian is armed with enough shopping bags to fill his trunk. Obstinately, I've chosen nothing, given him no input as he gathered armfuls of shoes, sandals, underwear, and clothes in my size. Dresses, T-shirts, blouses, they're all sleeveless or short-sleeved. No jackets to cover them up. It's as if he's making a point. I hate the point he's trying to make, and I hate that I don't have a say over my own body. Yes, I'm lighter after last night. Yes, I'm relieved my ugly arms are out in the open. That doesn't mean I want to rub my scars in people's faces. I'm not that insensitive or naive. I know they're hard to look at. They're even harder to ignore.

"Stop brooding," he says, closing the trunk. "The clothes are pretty. You'll look pretty."

"Does my opinion matter?"

"No," he admits bluntly. As an afterthought, he adds, "At least, not where your body is concerned."

"You're crazy."

"That's *your* designation."

137

Every muscle in my body draws tight. I've been fighting so hard to get my financial independence back, to take the control that has been stolen from me. Reminding me about this part of my history, the part Jack used to declare me incompetent, isn't something I enjoy.

"Lina." His voice takes an autocratic edge. "I'm only fooling with you. It was a joke."

"Bad joke, Damian."

"You're right. I'm sorry."

Why do I find that hard to believe? Without letting me say more, he pushes me into the passenger seat and secures my safety belt, something he seems to have taken responsibility for.

Since we started out early, it's only mid-morning when he pulls up in front of a white complex. I glance at the medical building, suspicion and fear mixing into a poisonous cocktail in my chest. "What are we doing here?"

He doesn't answer. He comes around the car, opens the door, and pulls me out.

Arranging the strap of my bag to cross over my chest, I hug it tightly. "Damian?"

This is where I kick in my heels. The last time Harold dropped me off at a clinic, the doctors pumped me full of drugs and kept me on the verge of sanity and starvation.

"Damian, please."

Tears build in my eyes. I hate them but I can't stop them. I can't stop myself from taking two steps back, trying to escape the arms reaching for me.

His voice is soothing. "Lina, it's okay." He keeps his arms outstretched, but he doesn't grab me. "Come here."

I shake my head. My blood runs cold. Under the long sleeves, in the heat of the sun, I shiver. This is because of the scars. Last night, he pretended they were nothing. I should've known better. I should've known he'd use the knowledge of them against me.

"Lina."

The way in which he says my name is a command, but it's an order I can't obey.

Damian slowly takes a step, as if he's stalking an injured animal. "It's for your own good."

That's what Harold said. That's what the doctors who tortured me said. That's what the nurses who looked away as it was happening said.

"None of this is for my good," I whisper.

"Come to me, Lina. Now."

Why does he sound scared? That's not right. Damian is never scared. Me, I'm terrified.

"I'm counting to three," he says in that tone he used in the study.

There's nothing he can do to make me walk willingly into his arms. All the spankings and humiliations in the world are not enough to make me hand myself over to a fate that paralyses my body and dulls my mind but doesn't let me ignore the leather straps that fasten my arms and legs to a cot while hunger ravishes me and my thirst-cracked lips mumble useless pleas while the man in the overcoat sticks another needle in my arm.

Chills run over me. "No," I say, like I've said so many times in my life. Never willingly.

I roll on the balls of my feet, already feeling the flight in my veins. This isn't a game. This isn't a small rebellion of words he'll let me get away with.

His hands, the strong ones that can chop off fingers or throw a car into gear with the confidence of a man who knows where's he's going, a man with secret destinations, those hands ball into fists. "Angelina."

Everything inside me screams *no* as I take off, heading straight into the oncoming traffic.

CHAPTER 9

Damian

*F*ear is a foreign sentiment. That foreignness hits me head-on in the gut with no preamble or gradual introduction as my wife tears away from the pavement, throwing her body into the flow of traffic, double lanes, bus in the farthest one.

The first car swerves, barely missing Lina as she dodges a second and continues toward the lane where the bus is approaching too fast. Facts blur in my mind, the speed of the bus, the driver who's checking his phone, the distance to the pavement. Terror cripples me. It's like in my childhood nightmares. My feet won't move fast enough.

Tires screech. Horns blare. Shouting. Swearing.

I fly through the air, tackling the fleeing woman with the full weight of my body. We go down to the tarmac. I try to soften her fall with my arms, but they're not enough to absorb all the shock. Her bones rattle, her hip hitting the hard surface with a clack. Using the momentum of our fall, I roll us to the curb. The bus slows but doesn't stop. It rolls by, the driver gaping at us through the window. Another flick of our bodies, a roll, and we're on the pavement. Only then do I breathe again.

Lina lies underneath me on her back, her bag pressing into my stomach. Her eyes are wide, her pupils shot. It only takes a second before she starts fighting me like a rabid lioness. Pedestrians flow around us, parting like the sea for Moses. They look, but nobody reacts. In a city of violence, no one is brave enough to get involved. The chances of getting killed are too high.

Sitting up, I straddle her hips and pin her wrists above her head. "Lina." She kicks and screams, thrusting her hips. "Lina," I say louder. "Look at me."

At my stern tone, she stills. "Look into my eyes." She obliges, appearing high on shock. "Do I lie?" When she doesn't answer, I squeeze her wrists. "Do I bluff?"

"No," she croaks.

"I won't let anyone hurt you." I wait for the words to sink in. "Isn't that what I promised?"

She gives a meek shake of her head. "Not the clinic."

I repeat the assurance slowly. "I'm not going to let anyone hurt you."

Defeat brims with the tears in her eyes.

"We're going inside together." I loosen my grip marginally. "Are you going to behave?"

She looks on the verge of sobbing but nods once.

"Good." Slowly, I let go of her arms, but I don't lift my weight off her hips.

The minute her hands are free, she fists them into the lapels of my jacket. "Please, Damian." Her tears start flowing freely. "Don't make me stay here."

Her begging shakes me more than what I already am. It's not like her to plead.

"Shh." I wipe my thumbs over her cheeks, catching her tears. "I'm not going to leave you."

I give it another couple of seconds for her to calm, but also for my heartbeat to stabilize. When I'm sure my heart is no longer in danger of stopping, I stand, bringing her with me. I lock my arms around her, holding her tightly, not only for comfort, but also in case she gets it into her head to run again. I let her soak up the hug before pulling away to look down at her tear-stricken face.

"We're going to see a doctor," I say gently.

At the word doctor, her face contorts with fear again.

"Listen to me, Lina."

My authoritative tone has the desired effect. Her gaze locks onto mine. She waits and listens.

"We're going to see a psychiatrist. He's going to chat to you, make sure you're fine, and that's it. Nothing else. All right?"

"I don't need a psychiatrist."

"Your medical report says you're supposed to be on medication." Anti-depressants and appetite stimulants. More accurately, after seeing her scars, I want to be sure she's stable enough not to harm herself.

"I don't want pills."

"Your health is my responsibility. We're just going to talk to the doctor." I don't wait for her consent. "Relax."

Not an easy task, given what has just happened, but she tries, drawing in a few deep breaths.

"That's it. You're doing good."

Sure that her body is slacker and not wired for another sprint, I release my death grip to check for damage from the fall. I push up her sleeves. Her arms sport nasty tar burns. Gravel is lodged in her elbow where the fabric has torn. Going down on one knee, I roll up the jeans and find scrapes on her shins and knees. At least nothing is broken.

"We have to disinfect these."

I fold my fingers around hers and lead her to the traffic light. When it changes, we cross at the crossing. I feel her reluctance in the weight of her body. I'm almost pulling her to the building. She digs in her heels at the door, but after I give her another stern look and repeat my promise not to leave her, she follows me inside with a bowed head and slumped shoulders. As we climb the stairs to Reyno's office, she grows smaller. It's only in front of his door that she picks her fighting spirit up from the floor.

"Damian, please. May I have a moment?"

"Yes." I smooth down her hair. "Of course."

She rummages through her bag and pulls out a tissue. Wiping mascara from under her eyes, she makes the most endearing creature I've seen.

"Ready?" I ask when she's blown her nose and cleaned her hands with a disinfectant wipe she fished from her bag.

She doesn't answer, probably knowing a reply is redundant.

Reyno has a shady reputation and the fees to go with it. There's no waiting room or receptionist. It's more discreet.

I knock and enter, dragging Lina behind me.

A small man gets up from behind his desk. He's not much taller than Lina. With his over-sized, round-rimmed glasses and ash-colored hair, he looks like a character from a fantasy comic book. He greets us by surname but doesn't offer a handshake or comment on the fact that we're fifteen minutes late.

"I'm going to call you Lina," he says, cutting straight through formalities. "I'm Reyno." He indicates a chair facing a coffee table. "Please, have a seat. You can pick her up in an hour, Damian."

She jerks her head toward me.

I give her hand a reassuring squeeze. "I'm staying."

Reyno tilts his head. "I'm not sure that'll be constructive."

"She doesn't want to stay alone."

He looks at her. "Is this true?"

She gives a small nod.

"In that case, take the sofa."

I push Lina down with a hand on her shoulder, not aggressively but firmly. What she needs right now is a strong hand, someone to take charge until she feels like herself again.

"Do you have a first-aid kit?" I ask the doctor.

He glances at her elbows and below the rolled-up jeans. "What happened?"

I look at Lina to see if she wants to answer.

"I tried to run away," she says. "I didn't want to see you."

He rubs his chin. "Why?"

"I don't like being—" She bites her lip.

"Being what?" he prompts.

"Being drugged," she replies.

I get the feeling she was going to say something else.

"Mm. Let's see about that first-aid kit."

Reyno disappears into an en suite bathroom and returns with a kit he hands me. Sitting down next to Lina, I start cleaning her bleeding elbows while Reyno takes the seat opposite us.

He presses his hands together. "Why don't we start with how you feel?"

Hurting, from the way she clenches her jaw as I scrape the gravel from her skin with a pair of tweezers. My girl keeps perfectly still without complaining.

"Lina?" Reyno says. "Did you hear me?"

She hisses as the disinfectant makes contact with her broken skin. "How I feel is a rather broad question."

He chuckles at her sarcasm. "Are you sleeping?"

"When Damian doesn't handcuff me to the bed."

He doesn't as much as blink. I've briefed him on our situation. If he disapproves, I don't know, and I don't give a fuck. I pay him to turn a blind eye to everything except giving my wife a prescription if her health warrants it.

"Do you have an appetite?"

"Yes."

I can't help but tease. "For sugar."

She gives me a fuck-you look that's as hot as hell.

"Do you empty your stomach after you've eaten?" he continues.

"Not unless Damian chops off someone's fingers."

I suppress a smirk, applying too much pressure on the gauze I press on her knee. She jerks at what must be a bite of pain.

"I see." He cuts me a look before turning his attention back to my little fire-spitting wife. "How about your general mood? Do you feel sad? Depressed?"

"Not more than what my situation merits."

Another swipe of cotton makes her bite her lip.

"Are you on any medication?"

"I occasionally take anti-nausea pills."

"And sleeping pills," I add.

"I told you Zane forced it on me."

Zane knows how valuable she is to me. He won't risk it.

"Who's Zane?"

We speak simultaneously.

"A friend."

"His housekeeper."

"Does he stay with you?"

"Yes." I carefully apply a plaster to her kneecap.

"They were in jail together," she says, putting emphasis on *jail*.

Giving her a smile, I cup her nape and drag my thumb over her soft skin. "Reyno knows who I am, Lina. He knows where I've been and why I married you. He's not going to save you."

Her expression falls. "That's unethical."

"Taking bribes for prescribing Schedule II medication is unethical, too."

She looks at the shady shrink quickly, disapproval etched on her face.

Reyno remains emotionless. "A man's got to live. No suicide attempts?"

"Apart from earlier, no," I say.

"I was saying *no*, not trying to kill myself."

"You have a strong way of saying no."

Reyno gets to his feet. "That's all for today."

Lina gapes at him. "Really?"

He adjusts his glasses. "What did you expect?"

"Psychoanalysis. Hypnosis. Drugs."

"Is that how you were treated before?"

She goes stiff next to me. "I'm only using bad generalizations."

"No generalizations here," Reyno says. "I want to see you next week, same time. Let's see if you can manage a session alone. Damian has my number. Call me if you have mood swings or trouble sleeping before then."

We rise together, arm in arm, like a happy couple. I nod my thanks. She says nothing as I lead her back to the car.

I start the engine and drive home, maneuvering through the traffic like a calm person, not showing that she shook me to my damn core. I've never seen a person react like that over a doctor's visit. I don't know what to make of it, but I'm hell-bent on finding out.

~

Lina

EMOTIONALLY EXHAUSTED, I fall down in a chair in the bedroom when we get home.

Damian dumps the parcels with the new clothes on the bed, watching me from under his eyebrows. "That's what I call an eventful morning."

"Don't you have somewhere to be?" My tone is scathing, but I can't help myself.

His voice drops an octave. "Careful, Lina. I'm being patient with you."

I kick off my shoes. "You owe me nothing."

"Lina."

The way he says my name makes me shut my mouth. I know his limits and to what pushing them leads.

Shaking his head, he walks to the bed, empties the bags, and selects a pink sundress that he holds out to me. "Put this on."

It has thin straps and a low-cut back. It's too pretty for someone like me. "No, thanks."

A calculated look invades his eyes. "Why? Because I chose it, or because it'll show off your arms?"

I flinch as he drops the subject I've been tiptoeing around since last night. "Both."

Stalking me with the dress in his outstretched hand, he says, "Woman up and wear it."

Who the hell is he, the very man submitting me to this torture, to

146

tell me to woman up? Does he enjoy my suffering? Probably. No, definitely, which is why I don't argue when he drapes the dress with exaggerated care over the arm of the chair and reaches for the hem of my T-shirt. I won't give him more reason to bask in my discomfort.

He yanks on the fabric, pulling it over my breasts, and I lift my arms at the silent prompt. Since he destroyed all my underwear, I'm naked underneath. When his gaze moves from my face to my breasts, it's as if a switch flicks in him. He goes from angry to lustful in a second. This was a mistake. What I feared, happens. He circles my waist with his large hands and yanks me forward until my ass hits the edge of the seat. His eyes cut a heated trail over my midsection, coming to a stop on the button of the jeans. Crouching down, he unbuttons the jeans and pulls the zipper down slowly. I cooperate, lifting my ass, making it easy for him to push the fabric over my hips and down my thighs. Maybe, if I don't delay the undressing, he'll just pull the dress over my head and let me be. Wishful thinking. There won't be any such mercy. I know it even before he pushes my thighs apart. My abdomen tightens involuntarily.

Holding my gaze, he leans forward and nuzzles my slit with his nose. He doesn't look at the exposed patch between my legs, even if his fingers are caressing the insides of my thighs lightly, working their way closer to my sex.

His voice is scruff, like the stubble on his jaw. "I want to taste you."

I only manage a small shake of my head. No man has ever put his tongue there.

"Lina." He takes a ragged breath. "Let me eat you out."

"I don't want you to," I whisper.

What if I come? His touch does sinful things to me, things I never thought I'd be able to feel at the hands of a man. What will his tongue do? I hated Jack's hands on my body, but he never probed and prodded and pushed, exploring my tipping points to elicit my pleasure. My late husband never touched me with his mouth, and he never used his hands to hold me down. He didn't need to, because he had my permission. I traded it for food. My nudity didn't invite his lustful look. My pain did. This look, the one Damian gets in his eyes as he lightly rubs his chin over my sex, Jack only got when he carved his victory notch into my arm. One line for every time I sold my body. One line for every time I allowed him to fuck me in exchange for a meal.

"Lina." Damian's breath feathers over my clit, pulling me back to him. "Let me fuck you with my tongue. I promise you'll like it."

I'm scared of this man and the black magic of lust he uses on me. Lust is cruel. Lust is selfish. Lust chews away your defenses.

At my silent denial, he sits back on his heels. I'm about to let out a breath of relieve when he takes my hand from the armrest and places it on my sex.

"Touch yourself," he rasps. "For me."

"Damian."

It's a protest and a plea, even if I know it won't help. He may not put his hands or lips on me, but he won't settle for nothing.

Cupping my hand, he manipulates my fingers, rubbing them in circles. The friction touches a nerve of pleasure. My hips arch involuntarily.

"Slowly," he says. "Make it last."

I tense when he straightens to sweep his hands over my shoulders and down my back, but it's only to brush back my hair. The touch is so gentle, I forget what I'm supposed to be doing. My hand slips from my pussy to my thigh where it lays tentatively. I have a sudden urge to touch him, to feel the hard muscles of his abdomen, but he grips my hand and pushes it back between my legs while he towers over me, watching.

I'm used to the watching, but this is different. It's not my pain getting him off. It's my pleasure. As much as I try to remain immune to it, the pleasure starts building in my core. It spreads through my lower body in a languid fire, heating my clit and swelling my folds.

"Put your fingers inside and show me how wet you are."

My gaze snaps to his.

"Two fingers."

The instruction leaves no room for argument. There is a choice, though. My fingers or an object of his choosing. That's how his game works.

Slowly, as he demanded, I sink a fore and middle finger into my center. I'm slick and hot, signs of arousal that should shame me, but physical sensations override the guilt of my logical mind, hardening my nipples and pulling my abdominal muscles tight under his observation. The pads of my fingers rub over a sensitive spot. I can't stop myself from stroking deeper.

Gripping my wrist, he stills my movement. "Show me."

I'm so wet it makes an embarrassing noise when he pulls my fingers free.

His cheeks turn dark and his eyes wild as he inspects my glistening fingers. "You're even more beautiful when you're horny." Satisfaction mars his features. He puts my hand back in place, his middle finger lying on top of mine. Applying steady pressure, he makes me take my finger. "Show me how you come."

He sets the pace, pumping until my channel clenches, and then he pushes another one of my digits inside. "Don't hold back. Ride your fingers."

The friction is delicious, but it's not enough. As if reading my body, he pulls my wrist forward, changing the angle of penetration. The new position gives him access to my clit. The pad of his thumb presses down gently, massaging in a slow circle.

"Like this?" he asks huskily.

Yes, oh, my God, yes. My pleasure gathers from somewhere deep in my core, consuming me with a slow burn rather than devastating me with an immediate explosion. He watches my eyes as I rise gently for him, at long last reaching the crescendo he wants. My hips rock and my globes lock. It's the sweetest of agonies, helplessly coming undone with his body keeping my legs apart and his gaze bearing down on me. It's only when the aftershocks dissipate that I realize he's still rubbing my clit with lazy circles, and something other than lust shines in the possessive depths of his chocolate colored eyes. Victory.

I allowed him to touch me.

Applying steady pressure with his thumb, he lowers his body until his maleness envelopes me and his lips ghost over mine. "Put on the dress and come down for lunch."

Only then does he let go, dragging the pad of his thumb from my clit down my slit in a gentle caress before stepping back. I'm finally free to close my legs, but the knowledge of how cleverly he manipulated me holds me hostage in a trans-like state. Wide-eyed and wide open, I stare at him in both fear and shock. His gaze locks on mine before raking down my body. A bolt of self-conscious awareness zaps me back to the present. Hurriedly, I press my knees together.

His lips pull up in one corner as he takes in the belated gesture. "No underwear."

"Seriously?" How old is he? Sixteen?

"No wiping away your arousal."

I dig my nails into the armrests. "What?"

"Ten minutes. Downstairs."

With those cryptic instructions, he leaves me naked, soaked, and defeated.

~

Damian

HOLY FUCK. I knew Lina would be gorgeous, but seeing her naked body almost pushed me over the edge. I've never been at the verge of my control, but one look at her tits and spread legs almost had me burying my dick in every hole of her body, right there, on the spot. I ached to touch her so much I forced my hand. Damn. I drag a hand over my face. Her scent still clings to me, making it hard to think about anything other than what waits between her legs. I couldn't have guessed how responsive her body would be. I'm all but floating into the dining room, feeling like I'm high. Anne and Zane are seated at the table, their plates loaded.

"Dami." Zane puts down his fork. "I was looking for you."

"Checking up on me?" I'm only half-joking. I hate being crowded.

His fallen expression softens my heart. "I took Lina shopping," I say, taking my seat.

Anne, who is sitting on my right, cups my hand. "I'm sorry about last night. I can't even begin to imagine how hard that must've been for you."

"Me?" I pull my hand away. Not nearly as hard as for Lina. "I made her wear that dress."

Approval lights up her face. She thinks I humiliated my wife on purpose. Worse, she takes pleasure from the knowledge. I like her less and less. If she weren't Zane's sister and Lina didn't invite her to stay, I wouldn't have thought twice about dumping her back on the street.

Zane hands me a newspaper lying next to his plate. "I take it you haven't seen today's news."

It's not front-page news, but it's on the inside left page, which makes it just as bad. A color photo of Lina in that sexy-as-sin red dress takes up three columns. It shows her from the side, displaying a badly torn-up and healed-over arm with maximum impact.

"It's ugly," Zane says.

My voice hardens. "Are you saying my wife is ugly?"

"I was referring to the article."

"What article?" a soft voice asks from the door.

Lina stands in the frame, dressed in the pink dress that hugs her breasts and flares out around her tiny waist. I don't miss how Anne and Zane's gazes immediately fix on Lina's arms.

Folding the newspaper in half, I say, "Nothing."

She walks to me with confident steps, each one reminding me she's naked underneath that skirt. Her gait is stubborn, as is the tilt of her chin when she takes the paper from my hand.

I don't fight her. It's not that I don't want to spare her more humiliation, not that I think her scars are something to be humiliated about, but she'll have to learn to stand her ground. These types of articles aren't going away. After what I'm about to do to Dalton Diamonds, it'll only get worse.

She turns to the offensive page. Her expression gives nothing away as she reads. She takes her time before folding the paper neatly and handing it back to me.

"Lina," Anne says. "I'm sorry."

Lina takes her seat. "You didn't do anything wrong."

"I feel bad for you." Anne shoots me a look. "For you, too, Damian."

"Maybe we shouldn't talk about it," Zane says with a stern look at his sister.

Acting unaffected, Lina attacks the salad on her plate like a locust who landed in a crop of lettuce during drought season.

"Damian." Anne covers my hand again. "I have to talk to you."

Lina's gaze shifts to our hands for the briefest of moments.

"Talk," I say rudely around a forkful of salad.

She squeezes my fingers. "In private."

I pull away. "I don't keep secrets from Lina." Not much.

Anne clears her throat. "I can't talk about it in front of everyone." At *everyone*, her eyes dart toward Lina.

"Then I don't want to hear it."

She purses her lips but doesn't argue.

"I ordered the bat boxes," I tell Lina to change the subject.

She sits up straighter. "You did? Thank you."

"Installation will take place tomorrow. Think you can oversee it?"

She beams. "Of course."

"Leave it to Andries," Zane says. "The garden is his responsibility."

Lina doesn't reply, but there's something in her silence that says more than words. It bugs me. Why isn't she giving Zane the obstinacy she thrives on giving me? I study my wife closely as she finishes her salad and reaches for the serving tray of fish.

"By the way," Zane continues, "I have meal plans from Jana to sign off. I need you to have a look at the budget."

"Give it to Lina."

She looks at me quickly, surprise flaring in her deepest of blue eyes.

"You can handle that, can't you?" I ask her.

The softness that settles over her features is a bigger reward I could've hoped for.

"I don't think—" Zane starts.

"That's settled, then," I say, not looking away from Lina.

She breaks eye contact first. "Anne, about your clothes." She clears her throat. "I'm afraid I damaged them. I'll replace them." She seems to catch herself. "I'm sure Damian will replace them."

"Gladly," I say.

Anne waves a hand. "Forgot about it. I didn't expect them back, anyway."

The rest of the meal progresses with a quietly brooding Zane and Anne who talks too much to compensate for the uncomfortable silence. I'll have to have a word with Zane about Lina's responsibilities in the house. No matter how it happened, she *is* my wife. I'm not sure how she sees that forced role, but it won't hurt to try out a few duties that'll occupy her mind and keep her from unhealthy boredom. Boredom is the devil's breeding ground. Boredom is too conducive to dangerous thoughts and self-harming actions.

Lina

As soon as lunch is over, Damian announces he wants to see me in the study. My stomach lurches. The study has become an uncertain place for me, a place where he pushes my boundaries and kicks my feet out from under me.

I walk ahead of him, dreading each step that brings me closer to the door. Even Russell shoots me a sympathetic look as we pass. It's the first shred of kindness he's shown me since the torturing incident.

My whole body jerks when Damian closes the study door. Panic starts to rush in, but he hasn't locked the door. If I turn the handle, it'll open. I'm still repeating the calming notion in my mind when he dumps a pillow from the sofa on the floor.

Walking around me, he stops at my back. "Kneel."

Kneel means too many things. To kneel will put me on eyelevel with his erection. To kneel means to submit. When I don't move, he doesn't tell me a second time. He pushes me down with a warm hand on my shoulder until my knees hit the cushion. I glance over my shoulder to read his facial expression so I know what to expect. The tender encouragement I find on his hard, handsome face scares me. It makes heat travel over my skin and sweat break out under my armpits. Whatever he's planning is going to be bad.

There's a rough edge to his deep voice. "On your hands and knees."

I hear his darkness and see his tight control in the way he focuses on me with exclusive concentration. Punishment. This is what it is. It's going to be worse than bad. He's hard, and men like Damian get harder from a woman's pain than her pleasure. Despite the command, I don't move. I can't. I'm frozen in fear. This time, he's really going to hurt me. I sense it in the way the air thickens until it's hard to drag in a breath.

At my disobedience, he places the toe of his shoe on my upper back, applying soft but steady force until my body bends forward, and I have to extend my arms to catch my weight. He keeps his foot there for a moment, a silent message to stay. When he lets up the pressure between my shoulder blades, I'm not self-destructive enough to defy him.

His fist finds purchase in my hair, twisting it around his fingers before arranging it forward over my shoulder. He smooths a palm down my back and stops just before my crack. Holding my breath, I wait for the worst. It comes soon enough.

Bunching the fabric of my skirt into his hands, he pulls it up, exposing my naked lower body. A flush coming from deep within my abdomen burns my skin. The heat crawls over me, inch by inch, igniting goose bumps in its wake. He's seen me like this before, but I still feel vulnerable. Will he spank me? Will he make me touch myself again? Both thoughts make my folds swell and turn slick. What an easy, twisted slut I am. Embarrassment crashes through me, but the sound of his footsteps cut off my train of thought.

Lifting my head, I watch him through a veil of hair. He walks to the mantelpiece where his whips are displayed and takes one from the wall. The leather strap is flat and thick. He watches me as he rounds my body. Our eyes remained locked for as long as I have him in my peripheral view. Unlike earlier, I don't crane my neck to look behind me. I prefer not to witness him studying my nakedness.

The silence that follows tells me this is exactly what he's doing—looking at where I'm exposed. The creaking of the leather chair tells me he's taken a seat. Close. His fingers slip around my ankle. Gently, he removes my sandals. The tip of his shoe touches my naked heel, and then he wiggles it between my feet, forcing them apart.

"Spread your legs."

No point in arguing. It'll only drag this out. I widen my stance. Cool air brushes over my folds. I resist the urge to clench my globes in an effort to hide at least some of my intimate parts. A calloused finger runs down the crevice between my globes, whispering over my dark hole. Despite how hard I clench my teeth, I can't contain my shiver. His touch is soft, barely there, reminding me of the unspoken permission I granted him earlier. His fingers now have access to me in ways I don't care to think about, not in this position.

His voice is dangerous, that raspy quality saturated in one hundred percent maleness. "You put your life in danger today." The path of his finger continues south, feathering over my clit.

Biting my lip, I swallow back a whimper.

"Say it," he commands.

"I put my life in danger."

"You'll never do it again."

"It wasn't on purpose."

"You'll never do it again," he says a little more forceful.

"I'll never do it purposefully."

"No, you won't, because you belong to me. What does that make you?"

"Property."

A white-hot flash of pain rips over my left globe. Yelping, I arch my back to pull away from the source of the ache.

"Try again," he says.

"Yours?"

"Mine. No one endangers what's mine. Anyone fucks with this," he cups my sex roughly, "and I'll fucking cut off his hand." His fingers clenches in the swollen flesh of my folds, giving my pubic hair a soft yank that sends moisture between my legs. "Anyone who lays a finger on you will lose it. Anyone who puts you in harm's way is dead. Understand?" He pulls again, creating a painfully delicious sensation.

"Y-yes," I cry on a gasp.

"I'm going to punish you for today so that you know how goddamn serious I am about keeping you alive."

"Don't." Even as the words whispers past my lips, I know it's futile.

"Sorry, angel," he replies, not sounding one bit sorry. "You know you deserve this."

I'm about to say I don't when the next lash falls across my whole ass, covering it from left to right. It's not a knife. A blade cuts with cold pain that sets into pulsing spurts of agony when the adrenaline from the physical shock wears off. The strap burns under my skin as if every molecule has been set on fire.

"Two," he says. "Four more to go."

I draw in a shaky breath, steeling myself, but no amount of mental preparation is enough for what follows. The next lash almost cripples me. My knees wobble under my weight. Before I have time to recover, another strip of fire bursts over my skin.

"D-Damian!"

"Almost there, angel. Only two more."

He gives them to me consecutively and with no repose in between, heating the skin under the curve of my ass and the line that follows my crack. The tip of the strap curls between my legs, the clack it makes as it covers my folds and clit reverberating through my flesh in sparks of agonizing torture. My elbows cave. My upper body hits the rug. My thighs shake uncontrollably. That I manage to stay on my knees is a miracle. I won't go down, damn him. I won't give him the satisfaction of falling all the way.

I haven't shed a tear. I haven't screamed. I hold onto the knowledge while I gasp for air and will my strength to return so I can peel myself off the floor. Before I can execute either action, something presses on my dark entrance. Too weak to fight, I fling my face to the side with my cheek resting on the rug. Damian is pressing the thumb of one hand between my ass cheeks while sucking the other into his mouth. When the pressure lifts, I almost find that breath I'm chasing, but then he puts his wet, hot pad against the protesting ring of muscle.

"Breathe, Lina."

I can't, but my heart demands I do. The minute my lungs clear and oxygen expands in my chest, he sinks the whole length of his thumb into me. Two pumps, and more fingers join his thumb. I can't tell how many he's slipping inside me, but it burns and fires up sensitive tissue all at once.

"D-Damian." His name is a garbled cry.

Keeping still, he gives me a small moment of mercy to adjust to the stretch. "Let me put my tongue in you. You'll feel more pleasure."

Manipulation. Again. It's just a way of stealing more permissions from me.

My teeth chatter around my rejection of his wicked proposal. "N-no."

Twisting his fingers from side to side, he increases my discomfort but somehow decreases the burn. Then he pumps. He takes me in the only virgin hole I have left in my body with fierce thrusts, the heel of his free hand slapping hard against my folds.

"I'm going to take your ass, Lina."

I clench around him in fear, my muscles involuntarily drawing his digits deeper.

"But not today," he continues. "One day, I'm going to sink my cock balls-deep into your tight little hole, and you're going to love it."

From the bottom of my almost-empty soul, I scrape together enough strength to keep my voice even. "Never."

He chuckles cruelly, and the pace in my rear picks up with a grueling rhythm. Every thrust forces a groan from my throat. The grunts he beats out of me are raw and dirty. My fingers curl into the rug, my nails scraping over the woven thread. The rough wool is abrasive against my distended nipples through the thin fabric of my dress. I'm a slut on my knees uttering shameful sounds that give away my dirtiest secret. Despite the discomfort, despite the lingering pain, an ache grows in the empty spot between my legs. My need throbs fiercely, demanding little extra than the humiliating pummeling of my ass. A few flicks over my clit is all it takes. When he grants me the reprieve, I come with a wail. My hips give out, and my arms fall uselessly beside me. Sweating and shaking, I'm a quivering mess. Tremors run over me from head to toes. A shadow extends over me and hides me in blissful somberness. The electricity of another body bending over mine sends static sparks down my spine.

A warm breath fans my cheek. Full lips whisper in my ear. "If that's how hard you come on my fingers, imagine what I'll do to you with my cock."

I lift my lashes to look at him. Our eyes connect. Knowledge and satisfaction blend in his at the foregone conclusion as he wipes his hand on a paper napkin. That's what I am. A foregone conclusion. He knew from the day we met, before I'd even turned eighteen, he'd take me, have me, and reduce me to a woman on her knees. I can't let him break me further. Struggling, I force myself back onto my knees. I ignore the swaying of my body and the places that hurt.

His palm smooths over my sore bottom, rubbing warmth into the ache. "You'll carry these marks for a couple of days. Every time you feel them when you move, I want you think about what you promised me. Say it."

"I…" My mouth is too dry. I swallow and try again. "I won't put my life in danger."

"That's my girl."

Gathering me into his arms, he stands. I'm too weak from the physical toll to fight him. There's not a stitch of energy left in my body. He goes to the sofa and lowers us onto the plush leather. I let myself sink deeper into his warmth as he arranges my body until I'm cradled against his chest. He picks up a leather folder from the coffee table with one hand and caresses my hair with the other.

"Rest," he says in his autocratic tone.

I hate him, but bite back the words. It's as if my body recognizes the truth in his command. I'm more tired than I've been since sleeping without handcuffs. It doesn't take long for me to doze off on his lap.

He only wakes me when the shadows in the room are long and Zane knocks on the door to tell us dinner is ready.

~

THE ANNOUNCEMENT of Dalton Diamonds becoming Hart Diamonds comes a day later. Damian doesn't let me read about Harold's downfall in the newspapers or see it on television. He tells me in detail what to expect and briefs me on what to say to the media, should someone manage to get through the gatekeepers holding those calls away from me. No comment.

I'm surprised Harold hasn't called. I expect him to put more pressure on me to find the documents, but maybe he knows it's too late, at least for saving his business. I continue to look for the evidence, but a search of Anne's room produces nothing. The only room I have left is Zane's.

Since our shopping spree, Damian has worked mostly from his study, but I haven't seen much of him. The bat boxes are installed, and I've taken over the menu planning. The simple tasks bring a measure of relief from the daily stress of being my husband's captive. I had plans to study art history after high school, but when Harold married me off to Jack shortly after I turned of legal age, all chances of studying flew through the window. I've never been granted any duty other than being a sex object, and it's soothing to keep busy with actions instead of nothing but my thoughts.

In the afternoon, I push my comfort zone by pulling on the white bikini Damian had bought. I study my body in the mirror of his dressing room. My ribs are less pronounced, and my breasts are filling out, plus I have a newfound level of energy. Eating well agrees with my health.

Twisting my hair into a bun on my head, I tie a wrap around my waist and grab a towel. I'm taking a bottle of water from the fridge when a small gasp startles me.

Jana stands in the middle of the kitchen, a shopping bag in one hand and the other on her heart. She pulls her gaze from my arms to my face, her cheeks flushing red. "Lina, I'm sorry. I didn't mean to stare."

"It's a lot to take in, huh?"

"That's not what I meant."

"It's all right. It's hard not to look."

"I saw the newspaper article, but..." She bites her lip.

"It's worse seeing them in real life, right?"

"Right," she agrees meekly.

"At least everyone has seen them. Now I can get on with my life."

She regards my attire. "And wear short sleeves."

I don't say Damian destroyed all my clothes with long sleeves. "Exactly."

"Don't let me keep you." She drops the bag and all but pushes me to the door. "Go on, then. It's a nice day for a swim."

She's eager to get rid of me, but I don't blame her. The situation can't be comfortable. Granting her the space she wants, I venture to the inviting blue water. I haven't been in a pool since my eighteenth birthday. As usual, Russell follows a few steps behind. It's sweltering hot, and he's wearing a suit.

"Why don't you get out of that suit?" I ask. "You must be dying of heat."

He shrugs. "Uniform."

"I'm sure Damian won't mind if you take a dive."

"Thanks, but no thanks. It's against protocol."

We don't speak for the rest of the way. Anne is already there, as usual drifting on a float. When she spots me, she lifts her sunglasses and assesses me with unmasked curiosity.

I walk to the deep end. "Do you mind?"

She looks annoyed, as if I'm disturbing her peace. "It's your pool."

In that case...I dive in, creating enough of a wave to splash her. Just because I'm hoping she'll divert my husband's attention doesn't mean I have to put up with her sarcasm.

The water is heaven. The coolness ripples over my skin. Chlorine tickles my nose. When I surface, Anne is gasping, holding her dripping sunglasses in the air and patting her ruined hair. Smiling to myself, I swim a length. My muscles are weak from lack of exercise for too many years, but I slip effortlessly through the water, feeling weightless.

I swim only one more lap before I tire. Leaning my arms on the edge of the deep side, I stop to catch my breath. Disturbed by my splashing, Anne stretched out on one of the deck chairs. She makes no secret of her irritation, giving me a pouty look. I'm about to push myself out of the water when a pair of polished shoes appears in my line of vision, Italian shoes, shoes I felt against my naked heel, between my legs. I lift my gaze to the face of the owner. Damian is staring down at me, his hands shoved into the pockets of his suit pants. His shirtsleeves are rolled up, revealing a hint of his manly forearms.

He gives me a peculiar smile. "Having fun?"

"The water is nice," I say carefully, keeping on neutral ground. With Damian, I never know how the conversation is going to turn.

Crouching down, he pushes a wet tendril of hair behind my ear. "You invited Russell to join you."

His words are as gentle as his touch, but his eyes are probing, piercing, searching for something that isn't there.

I swallow. "How do you know?" Is he spying on me?

He doesn't answer, but at the edge of the pool Russell stands as stiff as a stick, Zane a short distance to the side. I bet Zane was following us, listening to what I was saying.

Damian's voice is tender, but there's an edge to it. "Lina?"

"It's hot. I was only being polite."

He traces a drop of water that runs down my neck with his finger before withdrawing his touch. "Are you going to invite me?"

"You're busy."

He narrows his eyes a fraction. "Am I?"

I motion to his clothes. "You're dressed for work."

His smile is all forced patience. "I suppose that means I don't qualify for *politeness*."

I can only look at him. Any answer I give will be the wrong one.

He straightens. "Don't burn." With another look that seems to *burn* right through me, he walks away.

Goosebumps break out over my body. The water suddenly feels too cold. I watch his retreating form with a nervousness building in the pit of my stomach. Zane gives me a cold look before he turns and follows Damian. I'm not the only one watching. Anne looks at Damian with lowered lashes and her lip caught between her teeth. She eats him up with her eyes from top to bottom, a sinful grin curving her lips.

There's a small movement in Russell's stance when I push myself out of the water, as if he's about to move forward and extend a hand. He must think the better of it, because he settles back into standing on attention.

I'm not going to let Damian spoil my fun. I've taken the big step. I may as well enjoy it. Following Anne's example, I stretch out in the sun, feeling the warm rays on my body for the first time in as long as I can remember.

When I get back to the house later, Jana tells me Zane is out jogging, and Damian is having dinner in town. Is that what he came to tell me at the pool? Who is he sharing his dinner with? He doesn't owe me explanations, but I can't help but wonder. Russell and Jana say their goodbyes shortly after, and I'm left with Anne and the guards patrolling the door and gate.

A quick walk through the house tells me Anne is reading on the terrace. My wet hair leaves a trail of drops on the floor as I hurry in nothing but my bikini and wrap down the hallway, but I don't take the time to change. Quietly, I slip into Zane's room. Leaving the door open a crack, I lean against the wall, taking a steadying breath. I look under the mattress and behind the paintings. I go through his drawers and closet. I even check for false drawers in the writing desk. Documents of such tremendous importance would be locked in a fireproof safe. A safe like that could be hidden under the floorboards, in the walls, or behind a false panel. The only place left is the bathroom. It's an unlikely location, but I've exhausted all other options. With a last glance through the crack in the door, I tiptoe to the en suite bathroom. It's smaller than Damian's and the one in Anne's bedroom. There's only one cupboard with towels and toiletries to search. I knock on the backboard, listening for hollow sounds, but it seems sturdy everywhere. Moving bottles aside, I check the sides. Nothing. I'm about to turn back to the room when Zane's voice speaks from the door.

"What the fuck do you think you're doing?"

CHAPTER 10

Lina

*B*ottles fall over as I back into the cupboard.

Zane's T-shirt is soaked with sweat from his run. He advances with menace edged on his face. "I asked you a question."

Ignoring the impulse to flee, I stand up straight. "In case you forgot, this is my house."

He clicks his tongue. "You were doing such a good job of steering clear of me."

"Was I?" I arch a brow. "I thought you were the one avoiding me."

He grabs me so fast I don't see it coming. His fingers dig into the scars on my upper arms. Repulsion ripples through me.

"Nothing is yours. Not this house and certainly not Dami."

The anger of where and how he's touching me squashes any sense of self-preservation and fear. "Are you sure about that? From where I'm standing, you're a guest overstepping your boundaries."

His nostrils flare. The scent of his sweat intensifies. The feeling of it as he rubs his slick body against mine makes me gag.

"You're such an ignorant bitch." He presses closer, his drenched T-

164

shirt sliding over my stomach. "You have no idea, do you? Has he hurt you yet?"

I flinch.

He smirks. "The walls are thin."

I can't stop the heat that creeps into my face.

"You like it," he says, pressing me flat against the shelves with his weight. "Is that why you're here, flaunting your half-naked body?" He pulls on the string of the bikini bottom that ties on my hip.

It's a battle not to show my panic. Focusing on my anger to disguise my weakness, I swat his hand away. "Get your hands off me or Damian will hear about this."

"It's only a matter of time before it's my turn, darling. Rest assured, when Dami gives you to me, your screams won't be in ecstasy."

He hurls me away from him with enough force to knock my body against the basin. A bone-deep pain shoots through my hip.

"Dami and I," he says, "we share everything."

Shaking with rage, I barely hold myself back from attacking him like a savage feline. "You're wrong." I wipe his disgusting sweat from my stomach with a palm. "I'm the one thing you'll never share." Damian said so himself, and he always means what he says.

"We'll see," Zane says on a snicker. "I know what you're looking for, whore. You'll never find those documents. Now get the fuck out of my bathroom."

I stretch myself taller, ignoring the ache that spreads from my hip to my leg. Maybe the small responsibilities Damian tasked me with gave me a new sense of self-worth and a chunk of courage. "You get out. Until Damian divorces me, this is *my* house as much as his, and it's *my* hospitality you're abusing."

He turns redder than a dragon on the verge of spitting fire. The backhand that connects with my cheek doesn't come as a surprise. Neither does the blood that runs in a trickle from my nose. I'm familiar with this particular pain and its symptoms.

He pales a little, as if he knows he's gone too far. There will be bruises.

He pushes his finger in my face. "A word about this to Dami, and I'll tear you apart at every chance I get, do you hear me?"

Wiping the blood away with the back of my hand, I give him the coldest look I can muster. "Hit me again, and I won't ask Damian to cut off your finger. I'll do it myself."

I limp past him, physically bruised but feeling mentally strong.

"You talk," he says to my back, "and I'll tell Dami what you're searching for. You've seen for yourself what he does to thieves and traitors."

I don't stop to deny or acknowledge the words. He's right. If Damian knows I'm looking for the evidence, he'll be furious. The day I find it, he may just chop off more than my fingers.

AFTER TAKING TWO PAINKILLERS, I shower to wash away the chlorine and blood, and pull on one of the new nightdresses Damian bought. The silk is tight around my breasts and hips, making me feel exposed, but at least it reaches all the way to my toes. Covering myself with a robe, I venture downstairs when I'm certain there's no one in the kitchen to prepare a tray I take back to Damian's room. I'm not hiding from Zane or Anne, but the splitting headache and ache in my hip demand I lie down.

I must've dozed off. When I wake, it's dark. The space next to me in bed is empty. I flick on the bed lamp and check the time on my phone. It's after midnight. For an insane moment, my reflex reaction is to worry. I chuck the sentiment as quickly as it forms. Damian doesn't deserve my concern. Concern would mean I care. A noise coming from downstairs jolts me from my thoughts. The old pipes creak as the water in the guest bathroom turns on.

Getting to my feet, I pad to the top of the stairs. Light from the bathroom in the hall falls across the floor. The grandfather clock in the dining room strikes an hour at which gilded couches would've already turned into pumpkins. The stairs don't creak under my feet. The bristle hairs of the carpet runner in the hallway tickle the under-side of my toes. The water turns off. I stop at the open door.

Damian stands over the basin, his hands gripping the edges and his head hanging between his shoulders. His back is turned to me, but I have a good view of him in the waist-high mirror. He's shirtless, only wearing the dress pants and shoes from earlier. A deep line defines his triceps. His big arms bulge. His abdomen is a hard slab of six-pack muscle. Even his sides are perfectly cut, like an athlete's. The line of his spine is an indent that runs between broad shoulders and toughened flesh. A lock of dark hair falls over his face, obscuring his expression, but his jaw is clenched, and his grip on the porcelain hard. Whatever he's battling is weighing heavily on him.

Unaware of my presence, he stands perfectly still in this bowed position, giving me time to study him. Is this what Anne sees when she looks at him? Hard, male perfection. Strength and domination. Hands with bruised knuckles that know how to cradle a body gently and pin hips down hard. Lips that know when to ambush and when to whisper kisses over forbidden places. My breathing picks up and that forbidden place Damian has so skillfully mastered starts to tingle. For the first time, I see him like other women see him. I imagine those hands and lips on them, loving their bodies for the joy of pleasure instead of the satisfaction of revenge, and a hurtful flutter tightens my ribs. It's the first time I feel jealousy. The sensation catches me so off-guard I impulsively place a hand on my diaphragm where it aches.

The action draws Damian's attention. He turns his head a fraction. His face is mostly basked in shadows, but I can make out the intensity in his eyes. He seems both savage and gentle as he regards me in silence. A strange, new awareness passes between us. It feels like a jumbled mixture of physical attraction and emotions. The pieces are broken and scattered. For the life of me, I can't fit them together to form a clear picture. What's happening to us?

He's the one who breaks the silence. "What are you doing up? It's late."

"I can ask you the same thing."

He watches me with unsettling attention, looking right into the confusion of my heart.

Eager for a distraction, I turn my attention back to his state. "What happened?"

I really want to know. Whatever it was, wherever he's been, it was dangerous. I sense it. Something other than jealousy gnaws at the back of my mind. Fear. I jerk inwardly at the recognition. *No.* I don't care. I don't want to care. I want to hate him. I *need* to hate him. Caring for a man who'll never love me will be the worst betrayal my heart can muster. I'm going to find my freedom, and I'm not leaving my heart behind.

"Go back to bed," he says softly.

I don't let him invite me twice. Hurrying up the stairs, I run from the reactions he stirs in me. I run from the boy who'd turned into too much of a man, a man who is harder than what he should be because of one fatal night. We destroyed him. We turned a perfectly normal, young man who would've grown into a good husband and father into a criminal monster who feeds on pain. I might have played my part unknowingly, but I played it. Harold might have pulled the strings, but I danced to that tune.

The knowledge breaks me with heart-wrenching regret. When I looked into Damian's eyes tonight, I saw what could have been. Inside the hardened shell, I saw a man who could've been capable of tenderness and devotion. The bad things that happened to me were out of my control. I hated that they happened, but I wasn't responsible. For how Damian had turned out, I am, and this kind of regret is the worst.

Stopping in front of the cold fireplace, as far as possible from the bed, I wait for the inevitable. A moment later, Damian enters, still shirtless. Evenings in the Highveld are cool. He didn't take off his shirt because he was hot.

Unfiltered, the question tumbles from my lips. "What happened to your shirt?"

He walks to the bed and sits down on the edge, legs spread. "Come here."

His voice is soft and beckoning. It makes me want to obey, but I cling to my better judgment and shake my head.

"I'm not going to hurt you."

The vulnerability in the slump of his shoulders calls to my compassion. A sudden urge to soothe him makes me take one step. Then another, and another. He watches me as I walk to the cradle of his legs as if I'm being pulled by a delicate string that may snap at any moment. He looks at me with hope and tension, as if he's worried I'd change my mind, even if the freedom of changing my mind is a false notion. He can make me do whatever he wishes with a small amount of force. We've already established that. But with the emotions wrestling in my chest, I'm weaker, unable to resist.

When I stop between his legs, he looks up at me, drinking me in with such concentration I feel like a fly trapped in a web. I can't move or look away. Wanton need reflects in his bitter-brown eyes as he bunches my nightdress in his fists and moves it slowly up over my hips. His broad hand dips underneath, finding the elastic of my thong. One rip, and my underwear falls between my feet. It's not a violent action, but I jump a little, nonetheless.

"I'm not going to hurt you," he says softly, reassuring me of his earlier promise.

Lifting my nightdress higher, he drops his gaze to my exposed sex. He moves his hands to my ass and fills each palm with a cheek. With a soft yank, he pulls me closer, putting my pussy in his face. I have to brace myself with my hands on his shoulders to keep my balance. Touching his warm, hard body doesn't work in my favor. The contact ignites awareness of his maleness, and a feminine part answers from deep inside. Moisture gathers between my legs and arousal throbs in my clit. My whole body tenses when he runs his nose up the length of my slit.

His tone is commanding, but when he lifts his eyes back to mine, they hold a plea. "Let me taste you."

If I allow his tongue, where will this end? I'm tumbling down the hole of seduction he's digging way too fast. If I'm not careful, I'll soon be buried, left to suffocate. Is that what he wants? The ultimate submission? My final downfall? Is this his revenge?

Chewing my lip, I consider him. "If I give you what you want, will you let me go?"

He doesn't hesitate for a second. "No."

"Why not?"

"You're my wife."

"You married me for money and sex. If you have both, why not let me go? What more could you possibly want?"

"For you to need me like food and water."

Something inside my chest twists. He won't settle for anything less than ruining me completely.

His breath feathers over my folds. "Let me taste you."

The whisper is a devil's temptation. It turns me inside out. My flesh arches toward him even as my heart screams in protest.

"Lina." He closes his eyes and sighs like a tormented man. "Let me put my tongue on you."

His fingers are digging into my ass, holding me where he wants me —ready for his mouth. I should fight, but I'm just a woman. My knees buckle a little. I'm not going to lose this round with nothing to show for it.

"What happened to your shirt?" I ask.

"Destroyed."

"How?"

He hesitates for a moment, and so do I. If he tells me, I have to allow him oral. That's how our unspoken exchange works. A part of me prays he'll reject the deal, but it's as if melting hot wax fills my stomach when he says, "I got into a fight."

I take a small, steadying breath. "What kind of fight?"

His lips lift in one corner. "You're a nosy little thing."

"What kind of fight, Damian?"

"Fists."

"Who did you beat?"

"Do you really want to know?"

"Who did you beat?"

"Sarel Visage."

One of the men who dined with Harold the night Damian and I met. "Is he dead?"

"No."

"Why did you beat him?"

"He deserved it."

"What did he do?"

"You know what he did."

"What did he do?"

"He was there."

"That's it?" That's his sin? He was present the night Harold destroyed Damian's dreams?

"He knew what Dalton was planning," he says. "They all did."

I let my mind wander back to that night. "Harold gave you a jacket when he saw you out."

"I was naïve enough to mistake the gesture for kindness." His laugh is bitter. "I didn't discover the diamond until I got home. It dropped from the inside pocket when I threw the jacket over a chair."

"Why didn't you return it?"

"There was no point. I knew I was screwed. Who was going to believe me over Dalton? Anyway, the cops he sent after me were bought."

"Why didn't you run?"

"I had no money. I hid out for a while, but it didn't take them long to smoke me out by threatening my family."

Oh, Damian. How much Harold made him suffer. "You're going for all of them."

"Yes," he replies without blinking. "Does it bother you?"

"No." None of them are good men.

"What about your father?"

"What about him?"

"Are you upset about what I did to him?"

"About which part? Taking away his money or his dignity?"

"Both."

"Do you want me to be?"

"No."

"I'm not upset."

"Why not? He's your father."

"He deserved it."

"What about you, Lina?" His gaze pierces me, drilling through the bricks of the wall I've built around myself. "What shall I do with you?"

"You're about to do it," I whisper, my voice breaking on the last word, because my destruction is imminent. He's going to chew me up and spit me out. When I escape, there'll be nothing left of me.

"I'll make it sweet." As if to emphasize the promise, he places a soft kiss on my clit, and he does.

He makes it sweeter than anything I've experienced. He gazes up at me with ravenous hunger but traces the seam of my slit ever so lightly with his tongue. It's hot. It's wet. Too soft and too much. The sensation is so good, I go up on tiptoes, lifting slightly out of his reach, but he grips my ass harder and pulls me right back into his mouth. He starts eating me out with the gentlest of strokes. I can't stop the whimpers falling from my lips. His tongue is wicked, stroking inside and igniting new, foreign fires. His lips are all over me, sucking softly. He grazes and nips my folds gently with his teeth.

"Damian." I suck in a breath when he licks me again from top to bottom. "Please."

I'm a puddle of desire, leaning into his face as he finally clamps down on my clit and grants me mercy. The climb to the top isn't explosive. It's a torturously slow crawl to the summit, wrenching every ounce of pleasure from me in a buildup that can only blow me to pieces.

I come so hard my vision blurs. The light from the bed lamp splinters into golden shards. On and on it goes, higher still. I dig my nails into his shoulders and grit my teeth to bear the torture as he continues eating me, savagely sweet. Spreading my globes, he holds me in place like a possessive lover while biting down softly. He delivers on his promise until I can't take more. My clit is too sensitive. My folds burn from the abrasion of his stubble. Pushing on his shoulders, I fight to get away from the overwhelming sensations, but he's too strong. I try to twist out of his hold, earning a slap on my ass and his bruising fingers on my injured hip. I choke on a cry. He freezes. The hurt makes my eyes tear up. The unexpected ache cuts the aftershocks from the orgasm short and kills the buzz of insupportable pleasure.

Lifting my nightdress higher, he tilts his head to examine my side. His expression turns from lustful to thunderous in less than a heartbeat.

"Who did this to you?" he asks in a voice so cold it sends a chill down my spine.

If I tell him what Zane did, Zane will tell him I'm looking for the documents, and there can be no mistaking why I'm hunting for those pieces of paper. Damian will know I'm planning to escape. I can't let him have the upper hand of that knowledge. Not until I'm long gone.

"I asked you a question, Lina."

"I bumped into the basin."

"Don't lie to me. Don't you ever, fucking dare."

It takes everything I've got not to falter under his stare. "It's the truth." I did bump into the basin. After Zane slammed me against it.

His eyes scrunch in the corners as he runs an examining gaze over me. Gripping my chin, he tilts my head. I've applied concealer to my nose. It's only slightly swollen, but he misses nothing.

"Did you bump your nose, too?"

"I was barefoot and wet from the pool. The tiles were slippery."

His nostrils flare. His chest rises with rapid breaths as violence builds in him like a storm. He's going to question every person in this house until he has a confession. Zane won't keep my secret when Damian's ire rains down on him in brutal blows.

I do the only thing I can to stop him. Gripping his hard thighs, I sink down to my knees. "Please, Damian. Let me taste you, too."

CHAPTER 11

Damian

I only realize I'm gripping Lina's hands too hard when she utters a small cry. I'm cupping them over my thighs, both stilling and willing her exploration. My intention is to push her away, but fuck it to hell and back, she's on her knees between my legs. What I should be doing—finding out why she has bruises—flies out the window. I go dumb as the little blood I have left in my brain joins the rest of my body's supply in my cock. Instead of chasing answers, I lock my fingers in an involuntary action around her wrists, preventing her from escaping.

Damn, her body is small. My fingers largely overwrap her wrists. She pulls on my hold, not hard enough to fight me, but enough to drive me back to my senses. One by one, I lift my fingers. When her hands are free, she doesn't run as she should. She reaches for the buckle of my belt. Her fingers tremble trying to undo it. She struggles for a while before I push her hands away and make quick work of unfastening the buckle and my pants. I watch her as I pull down the zipper and let my fly fall open over my erection.

She stares at the bulge under my briefs as if it's a frightening object. Surely, she's given head? The flash of uncertainty I see in her eyes makes me doubt.

"Done this before?"

She gives a small shake of her head. Holy hell. How in fuck's name can any man live with Lina, sleep with Lina, fuck Lina, and not sink his cock between those luscious lips? Unless oral wasn't Clarke's thing, which would make him the biggest dead fool ever to be buried.

"Has anyone gone down on you before?" I ask as the suspicion grows in my mind.

"You were the first," she answers softly.

Well, fuck me. I'm too far gone to contemplate the reasons, and way too satisfied in a primitive way that I got to be her first to regret not initiating her more slowly. The only thing holding me back from shoving my cock up to the hilt into her pretty mouth is the significance of the moment.

I force the words from my mouth before I lose whatever reason I have left. "It's not too late to change your mind." Maybe Clarke wasn't the problem. Maybe giving blowjobs isn't her thing.

Again, a small shake of her head. Bracing herself with her hands on my thighs, she waits, and I'm too eager to oblige. I've given her a chance to back out. She didn't run. Her mouth is mine.

I free my cock from the last layer of constraint, literally waving my hardness in her face. I want her to take it all in, to remember every single detail of what's about to happen. She stares at the first drop of pre-cum as if hypnotized, but she doesn't reach out to touch me. That's all right. I can touch for the both of us. Cupping her neck, I bring her face closer. I grip my shaft with the other hand to drag the head over her lips, coating them with that drop of arousal. She doesn't flick out her tongue to taste it, but that's all right, too. I'm going to teach her how to please me.

My voice is raw, the instruction crude. "Lick it."

Her tongue darts out, tracing her lower lip. Seeing her lapping up my seed nearly makes me combust.

Gently massaging her scalp, I reward her for her good behavior. "Now lick my cock."

The heat of her tongue is like a branding iron. She licks the head like an obedient girl before tentatively dragging her tongue down the underside of my shaft. Fuck. I nearly explode. I have to grit my teeth hard not to prematurely ejaculate. After years and nights of lusting after her, another gentle suck and it'll be over, but I want to make this last.

Gripping her face between my hands, I push my dick between her lips. She parts them without hesitation. My cock slides over her wet, hot tongue. A shiver works its way to the base of my spine. Pinpricks of pleasure pierce my balls as her tongue wraps around the agonizing hardness of my cock. Her cheeks hollow as she sucks me deeper. That's all it takes to shatter my control.

I push all the way in, until my balls hit her chin and her throat convulses around my shaft. Her eyes go wide. She gags. She fights me. Her nails scratch over the fabric of my pants, trying to find purchase. Me, I'm beyond saving. I'm fucking her throat like a savage, counting the breaths I'm stealing from her so I can time my pace. After every suffocating stretch, I pull out just enough to give her air. When she's filled her lungs, I fuck her hot mouth like it's the last mouth I'll fuck. The only gentleness left is in my hands. I hold her tenderly, reverently wiping the tears running from her eyes away with my thumbs as I ram my cock down her throat enough times to create a stunning mess of her face. I choke and make her gag until convulsions ripple her throat and spit runs down her chin. Not once does she look away from me. She stares into my eyes as she fights for her air and heaves when I grant her a breath. She lets me see her panic and tears as my cock cuts her oxygen. She lets me hear the sloppy noises she makes as my dick pulls out before sinking deep. I'm fucking her mouth too roughly, but goddamn I can't stop. She's an angel on her knees with a devil debasing her. I'm a bastard, but the power of owning her like this, of being her first, turns my cock harder. When she gags again, her throat clenches around my shaft. A rush of heat bursts through my dick, damn well near paralyzing me. Before I can warn her, my cum shoots down her throat. Her eyes grow wider and her arms flail, but the devil in me won't ease up.

"Look at me."

She fights harder.

"Lina."

At my hard tone, her eyes lift to mine.

"Swallow."

Obedience comes with reward. She knows this well enough to work her throat around me. My cock swells even more as her throat milks it. Like a good girl, she swallows my seed. She deserves her air. Her teeth scrape over my sensitized skin when I pull out, inviting another spurt of cum. She drags in noisy breaths as I spill the last of my release on her lips.

Boneless, I brace my hands on the bed to support my weight. Tears run from the corners of her eyes. Her lips are swollen, and a dribble of cum runs over her reddened chin. When we've both somewhat caught our breaths, I kiss her softly, like my lack of control wouldn't allow me to fuck her mouth. I put every ounce of gentleness I possess into the caress. I lick my taste from her lips and stroke my tongue over hers, rewarding her in the only way I know. When her breathing grows shallow again, I rest our foreheads together.

"You did well, angel."

She says nothing while I put my dick back in my pants and zip it up. I need to pick her up from the floor and take care of her knees and throat, but I take another moment to appreciate her like this, deep-throated and well-tussled.

She swallows with visible effort. Her neck is so goddamn delicate. No one should be as crude with her as I've just been. I frame her face and kiss her again. No tongues, this time. Just lips on lips, her and me.

Stroking the arch of her throat with my thumb, I ask, "Sore?"

She nods.

I almost feel remorse. Almost. But I can't regret what just happened. "I was rough."

Her voice is croaky, sensory evidence of how raw it must be on the inside. "If I married you instead of Jack, is this how you would've showed me to give head?"

I consider the question. No, without a doubt. I would've been gentle and kind. "This is who I am now."

She bows her head.

I wait for her to say more, but she's quiet for so long I lift her face with a finger under her chin. Tears stream in rivulets over her cheeks. They're not tears caused by choking, but by emotional distress. She tries to turn away, but when I won't let her hide this sorrow from me, she lowers her lashes in a feeble attempt of keeping her pain private.

Hooking my arms under her armpits, I hoist her to her feet and pull her into my lap. She doesn't fight me when I push her face against my chest. She lets me hold her through her silent tears, asking nothing but not denying the little I'm offering, either. It's only when she starts to shiver that I lie her down. Before covering her with a blanket, I tend to her knees. The scabs from the fall have reopened from the rough carpet. They require fresh plasters.

Downstairs, I prepare a warm drink with two teaspoons of honey for the ache in her throat. I make her drink everything, and when I undress and pull her against my body, my woman falls quickly into a restless sleep. I'm too high on the adrenaline of the fight and the knowledge that she opened her body to my tongue to succumb so easily to dreams. Instead, I enjoy the sound of her breathing, feeling her heart beat under my palm where I cup her breast. She stirs and makes a distressed sound.

"No, please," she whimpers, tossing her head on the pillow.

I shake her gently. "Lina, wake up."

"No, no."

"Lina."

She jackknifes into a sitting position, gulping in a wheezy breath. For a moment, she seems disorientated, looking around her with a panicked expression.

"It's all right, angel." I pull her back down to me. "I'm here." She shivers. "Shh." I kiss her temple.

Her body relaxes marginally.

"It was a dream." Or more likely a nightmare.

She doesn't reply.

"What did you dream about?"

"I don't remember," she says too quickly.

I doubt that very much. She's hiding something. I want to force it from her with every cell in my body, just like I want to force the issue of how she got her bruises, but for once I tamp my selfish need down to put her distress first. In time, I'll know everything there is to know about her. In time, even her nightmares will be mine. Rolling over her, I take her mouth before moving down her body to make her forget. In time, she'll see I'm both her torture and remedy.

~

Lina

IT'S like I've been tossed in a tumble dryer all night. I wake with pain in my throat and a bruised body. My hip and nose throb. After waking up twice more during the night with Damian's tongue in my pussy and his stubble between my legs, my labia feel as if they've been scraped with sandpaper. As usual, Damian's side of the bed is empty. I squint at the alarm clock. It's after eight.

Grunting, I roll from the bed and limp to the bathroom to have a quick shower. I'm meeting with a landscaper at nine. It was the bat box installer's idea, information I haven't shared with Damian yet.

Standing naked in front of the mirror after my shower, I study my body. My years in isolation with too little nourishment and no exercise weakened me. I tired too quickly during yesterday's swim. I want my strength back. I need my strength not only to escape, but also to survive. I've seen Zane jogging on the property, but I have no desire to run into him on an isolated path at the back of the house where Russell may not jog along in his black suit. If I'm going to get fit and strong, I'll need money.

After pulling on a red sundress and sandals, I go downstairs in search of Damian. He's not in the kitchen, but Anne is.

One look at my face, and she grins. "Damian is that rough, huh?"

Taken aback at her unwelcome insight, I blurt out, "Why would you say that?"

"Tell-tale signs, honey. Swollen lips, scraped chin, blood-shot eyes. Did he strangle you? Yep, I guess he's *that* rough."

"*That* is none of your business," I say, keeping my tone friendly.

She pours coffee from the percolator. "Come on. Not even you can be that naïve. Surely, you knew how it was going to be in the bedroom before you married him?"

Did I? I wish I could say I was unprepared for last night, but she's right. I knew how it was going to be the day his breath feathered warm and frightening down my neck, the day he announced my fate in Harold's library. What I couldn't know was how I'd react to his perverse advances or how wet I'd get when he all but chokes me with his cock. Heat pushes up my neck and into my face at the memory.

"You're too innocent for him," Anne says, no doubt taking in the change in my skin tone. "As I said, not every woman can handle a man like Damian."

"I'm many things, but I'm not innocent." I lost that a long time ago, even before I got my scars.

She regards me from over the rim of her mug. "Maybe you should get out while you still can."

"It's not that simple."

"Where there's a will, there's always a way." She winks.

"What's that about a will and a way?" a deep, familiar voice asks from the door.

I school my features before I turn. Damian stands in the frame, dressed in his habitual suit and tie. He looks fresh and well rested, not at all aching in places he shouldn't be aching.

"Breakfast?" Anne asks him sweetly.

He doesn't look away from me as he answers. "I've already eaten."

"Too bad," she says. "I was going to make pancakes. Are you sure I can't change your mind?"

There are questions in his eyes as they roam over my body and pause at my hip, an unspoken demand for explanations, but in front of Anne he only says, "I have a meeting in ten."

With a last evaluation of my face, he turns in the frame.

"Um, Damian."

He looks back at me. "Yes?"

"May I please talk to you? It won't take long."

His answer is to step aside, letting me exit in front of him. Zane walks through the front door just as we reach the steps, dripping with sweat from his run.

"Dami." His face lights up. "I need to talk to you about the quotes for the new irrigation system."

"Not now." Damian walks past him with long strides. "Lina's beaten you to it."

Zane shoots me an ugly glare. "Later, then?"

"Give the quote to Lina," Damian says without looking back.

"But—"

"Save me the buts, Zane. You heard me."

I follow him up the stairs while Zane remains at the bottom, staring at me with hatred. Does he know how thinly masked his jealousy is? I can't say I don't understand. Didn't I have an inkling of that sickening feeling last night?

Damian stands aside for me to enter his study. Once he's behind his desk and I'm in front, I feel more uncomfortable than I thought I would. I barely stop myself from wringing my hands together.

"How do you feel?" he asks, sitting down in his chair.

I clear my throat. "I'm good."

He narrows his eyes as if he sees the lie. "You sure?"

"I'll be fine."

"If you need to see a doctor—"

"I don't need to see a doctor for my throat."

He steeps his fingers together. "We didn't finish our discussion about the accident that knocked your hip seven shades of purple."

"That's not why I'm here." I finally give in to the urge to clutch my hands together.

His gaze follows the movement. "Why don't you sit down?"

"I'm fine, thank you."

His voice turns soft, almost encouraging. "What do you want to talk about?"

I clear my throat again. Damn, this is hard. I hate asking for money. I hate that my hands are so tied, I can't even buy myself a box of tampons. "I, um, I was wondering if I could have a monthly allowance."

He considers my request for a while before replying. "Why?"

"I need things."

"*Things?*"

"Things I don't want to ask from Jana or Zane."

"Tell me. I'll get it for you."

"Personal things."

"Lina, nothing between us is a secret any longer."

"Tampons," I spit out, fisting my hands. "There. Think you can manage?"

"Sure." He doesn't as much as blink. "Size small, I presume? A specific brand you prefer?"

Doing what I promised myself I wouldn't, I lose my cool. "Why make such an issue out of letting me shop for myself?"

"I don't trust you."

"To do my own shopping? I don't need to be certified mentally healthy to buy my own damn toiletries."

As much as my voice steadily rises in anger, his remains calm. "It's got nothing to do with your mental health."

"What then?" I exclaim in frustration.

"I don't trust you not to use the funds in a feeble attempt at running." His tone drops an octave. "And feeble it'll be, because I'll always find you, no matter where you hide."

Chills rake over my body, not only because he doesn't bluff, but also because there'll come I day I *will* run. I don't have a choice.

"My apologies for the shortsighted provisions," he says in an oddly respectful way. "I should've thought about it sooner. I'll pick up your tampons after lunch. Anything else you need?"

I swallow, mauling the words in my mind. No matter how I say it, Damian will take it as a sure victory. "Birth control."

"You don't."

"Excuse me?"

"You don't need birth control."

"Why? Did you have a vasectomy?"

"No."

"You can't be serious."

"I'll take my chances."

I start shaking. "You want a child with me?"

"Let's not get ahead of ourselves. Tell me what you came to ask."

"I want to talk about it *now*."

"I know how to count days."

"Seriously?" I exclaim. "You're going to rely on the calendar method?"

His answer says it all.

"Why don't you use condoms?"

"I want to fuck you bare."

"We can't, not without protection."

"Calm down. We're a long way from worrying over that." He raises a brow. "Or aren't we?"

I can't answer that.

His words are both teasing and challenging. "Shall I remind you again why you're here?"

"Damian." It's a huffed expression of shock. It's a plea.

"Focus, Lina. What else do you need? Money isn't an issue."

"As long as I don't have access to said money."

"Yes."

Just like that. Bluntly. I blink. "I see."

He gets up and comes around the desk. "It doesn't have to be like this. I'll take care of you. It's my job."

I pull away when he tries to touch me.

He shoves his hands into his pockets. "You're the wealthiest woman in the country. Say the word, and I'll get you whatever you want."

"I don't want Jack's money. You can keep all of it."

"I didn't mean his money. His money secured the mining shares.

You know that. When it comes to taking care of you, it's *my* money that pays."

"How *did* you make your money?"

"I made connections in jail. They needed someone to do jobs on the inside, and as it turned out, I was their man."

"Killing people?"

"Whatever the job required."

It can only mean one thing. "So, it's mafia money."

"Does it matter? Money is money. You can have all you need."

I look away. "I don't want your money, either."

He cups my face, this time not letting me escape the touch. "Don't make it so hard on yourself."

Shuddering with anger, I jerk my face away.

He only smiles. "Tell me what else you need, or do I have to drag it out of you?"

I swallow. Yes, it's hard to grovel, and I hate taking his money, but this is more important than my pride. "I want to go to a gym."

"Gym?"

"Yes," I bite out, "gym." This is part of why I hate asking. It's having to justify everything, not having the freedom any other human being has to earn and spend money. Besides having been locked up in a room and my food privileges taken away, this is perhaps the cruelest part of being declared mentally incompetent.

"Why?" he asks. "You have a beautiful body."

"It's got nothing to do with vanity. I want to get fit."

"Fit?"

"And healthy."

He rubs a thumb over his chin, studying me as if he can't figure me out.

"Forget about it." I turn for the door. "I'll go jogging with Russell."

"Lina." He grabs my arm. "You can be such a wildcat when you want to be."

"Let go."

Of course he doesn't. He smooths his palms down my arms, inviting shivers. "Don't be so feisty. You surprised me, that's all."

"By wanting to take care of myself?" I suppose a reputation for being self-destructive doesn't allow for a need to become fit and strong.

"When you do want to start?"

"Today?"

"Tomorrow. Sorry, I'm tied up all day."

"Russell can—"

"I'll take you. Tomorrow."

I blow a strand of hair from my eyes. "Thank you."

"You're welcome."

I duck to escape his hold. "I'll let you get to work."

A half-smile creeps onto his face. "That's most considerate of you."

As I turn, he intercepts me for a second time with one hand on my uninjured hip and the other on my nape. He turns me and slowly drags me closer, his attention focused on my lips. I try to resist, but I'm no match for his strength. With that knowing half-smile, he pulls my body flush to his and presses his lips tenderly to mine before planting a trail of butterfly kisses over the column of my throat. The caresses are soft and confusing. It makes me forget my anger and recall memories of last night. I stumble a little when he releases me, but he's quick to catch me.

"Have a nice day, Lina."

When he finally frees me, I flee from his office, bumping into Anne on the landing.

"Sorry," she says, flushing a little.

"Did you eavesdrop?"

"I couldn't help but overhear. You guys should really learn to close the doors."

I would if I could, and Damian is appeasing me without once having said anything about my phobia of being locked in.

"I don't get you," Anne says. "Damian will buy you anything your heart desires, and you carry on about not having spending rights."

"You won't understand until you're in my position."

"All I understand is that you're one lucky lady."

I'll let her think that.

"Mrs. Hart," Russell says from downstairs. "There's someone here to see you."

"Excuse me." I push past Anne and make my way downstairs to where the landscaper is waiting, but Zane gets there before me.

"Who's this?" Zane asks, blocking my way.

The landscaper looks between us.

"None of your business, Zane."

He doesn't budge. "Dami will want to know."

"He will. Now move."

"You heard her," Russell says.

In that moment, I forgive Russell for his lingering coldness toward me.

Zane steps aside with sparks flashing from his eyes.

"Shall I show you the garden?" I don't wait for the baffled landscaper's reply. I shove him out of the door, eager to escape the tension in the house.

He scratches the back of his neck and takes in the well-maintained garden. "What exactly is it you want?"

"We have a colony of bats."

"I'm aware. My friend installed the boxes. I'm still not sure why you think you need me."

"They'll need an ecosystem to survive."

He looks at me with surprise. "In the long term, yes."

"That's why you're here. I want you to turn the garden into an ecosystem."

"Whoa. That's going to cost a small fortune."

"Does it look like I can't afford it?" Technically, Damian's money will pay for it. I don't like it, but I don't have a choice. Some of those ill-accumulated funds may as well be put to good use.

The landscaper's gaze flitters to the house and back to me. I know what he sees—huge mansion, expensive cars, personal guards.

"Before you get too excited," I say, "I'll need a quote." I don't say my husband will have to approve it. Hasn't Damian just told me I only have to ask?

"Right." He turns in a full circle, taking in the vast, green lawn that stretches to the fences in the distance. "That goes without saying."

"Good. When can I have it?"

He chuckles. "You don't beat around the bush."

I'm aware of Russell's eyes burning on me when I say, "Life's too short."

"If you want a self-sustained environment, the non-indigenous shrubs and ornamental trees will have to be replaced with Highveld grass and a rock garden."

"I assumed as much."

"It'll be green in summer, but dry in winter."

"I know."

"I'm just saying you won't always have a green garden."

"As you said, that goes without saying."

"Okay, then. Let's take the tour."

We walk around the property with him naming plants and me nodding. If he finds it odd that Russell follows, he doesn't say anything.

After the full tour and having taken notes on his smartphone, he leaves with a promise to have a proposal and quotation in a week's time. It's fast for the amount of work involved, but money always gets you to the top of the priority list. The project is big enough to guarantee a huge profit.

It's afternoon when I venture back into the garden to take pictures with my phone for the visual board I'm planning. Despite my situation, I'm becoming excited about the project. I've even told Russell, who tags along, a little about it. I'm next to the rose garden when Zane intercepts us.

Propping his hands on his hips, he blocks my path. "What was the meeting this morning about?"

"Nothing that concerns you."

He presses a thumb on his breastbone. "*I* run these grounds."

"Less work for you then, I guess."

"Spit it out, Lina. Now."

"It's Mrs. Hart," Russell says, "and you're in her way."

Zane turns to Russell. "What did you say to me?"

Zane is a big, muscled man. A hunch tells me he knows how to fight dirty. I don't want a fight between Russell and Zane because of me. From the corner of my eye, I see Andries pausing with his foot on the garden fork where he's overturning the soil to glare at us.

"It's all right, Russell," I say.

Russell is only doing his job, which I assume is protecting as well as guarding me from running away, but Zane won't see it like this. Zane will hate me more for what he'll perceive as Russell's loyalty.

"What are you hiding?" Zane asks. "Why the secret meeting?"

I keep my voice placating. "It was hardly secret."

The reason I don't want Zane to know until I've already convinced Damian is because he'll oppose anything I suggest out of principle.

Andries shuffles closer, the fork clutched in his hand. "Then you won't mind telling us."

I sigh. It looks as if I have more than just Damian to convince. "There are bats on the property."

"I'll take care of them," the old man says. "Burn the nest."

"No," I cry in horror. "They're protected."

Zane gives me a suspicious look. "Is that why the man was here? To rehabilitate them?"

"There are also owls and hawks close-by."

"I've spotted some owls on the east side of the property," Russell says.

"Get to the point," the old man says with a scowl.

"I want to give them back their natural habitat."

Zane stares at me as if I deserve my crazy label. "What?"

"I want to convert the garden into a self-sustained ecosystem."

"You're out of your mind," Zane exclaims.

"Why? A natural garden can also be pretty."

"I have quotes for a new fucking irrigation system," Zane hisses, "and this is what you do? Sneak behind my back with your animal activist ideas?"

"It's not an animal activist idea."

Russell raises his hand in warning. "Calm down and watch your mouth, Zane."

"Zane is right," Andries says, pointing a finger in my face. "You'll take the food out of my mouth."

"I'm not trying to chase you away," I say. "The garden will still require work."

"Not a fucking self-sustained, ecosystem," Zane shouts.

"I won't tell you again—" Russell starts, but before he can finish his sentence, Andries charges.

He shoves me hard, making me lose my balance. I fall down on my ass, catching myself on my hands. Russell jumps toward the old man, and Anne screams something as she comes charging from the house, but I tune them out. All I'm aware of is the sharp teeth of the garden fork Andries presses on my chest.

CHAPTER 12

Damian

There's a commotion in the garden when I get back to the house from buying Lina's tampons. Andries, Zane, Russell, and Lina are all outside. It looks as if Andries is about to attack Lina. The old man is waving his finger in her face while everyone speaks at once, everyone except Lina. She stands quietly in the center of the fight.

I'm out of the car and almost there when the crazy old man jumps. With a shove, he pushes Lina to the ground. Fuck. I drop my parcel and sprint. He lifts the garden fork he's clutching in one hand over Lina's chest. Anne screams from somewhere behind me. Before I can make it to them, Andries pins the spikes of the fork to Lina's body, right on her heart. I scream for Russell, but he's already drawn his gun. As the barrel indents Andries' temple, the old man freezes. I push Anne, who arrives at the same time as me, out of the way in my rush to reach them.

Zane lifts his hands. "Dami, don't."

I'm shaking. I should order the fucker shot. The threat on Lina's

190

life warrants it. Zane knows that. It's having Andries' brains blown all over Lina that prevents me.

"Dami, please. Nothing happened."

"Put down the fork, Andries," I say in a steady but don't-fuck-with-me voice.

His fingers tighten around the shaft.

"Andries." I edge closer, slowly. "Put down the fork and no one will get hurt."

Russell is ready to pull the trigger.

"Pops," Zane says. "Do as Dami says."

"Pops, please," Anne adds in a tremulous voice.

Andries is half-senile, but he must've realized what his actions would cost him. After another tense second, he relaxes his grip on the fork. I waste no time in disarming him. Only when the fork is securely in Zane's hands do I dare to speak again.

"Get him out of my sight," I say through clenched teeth. God knows what I'll do to him if he lingers in my presence.

"Dami—"

"I said out of my goddamn sight!"

Zane jumps.

Anne takes Andries' arm. "Come on, Pops."

I address Zane. Andries doesn't exist to me any longer. "I want him and his things off my property. You have an hour."

This time, Zane knows better than to argue. He follows Anne quietly toward the garden cottage where Andries lives. Russell flips back the safety and holsters his gun.

Too shaken to speak, I hold out a hand for Lina. She allows me to pull her to her feet, trembling under my palms. Her face is whiter than the clouds in the sky. Gripping her shoulders, I drag my gaze over her. She's covered in dust, but there's no blood. Andries didn't break skin.

Wordlessly, I steer her away. I retrieve the parcel where I dropped it before bringing her to my study where I pour us each a drink. After she's downed her whisky, I pull her into my arms.

"Fuck, Lina."

"I'm sorry," she whispers.

She's sorry? "What the hell happened?"

"I want to change the garden."

"*That* caused Andries' reaction?" I ask in disbelief.

"I want to change it to an ecosystem."

"Why?"

"For the bats."

"For the bats." The fucking bats could've cost her life.

"Andries thought he'd lose his job if we do away with the cultured garden."

I take a swallow of the liquor in my glass. Not all the alcohol in the world is enough to calm my nerves. "He's lost it now."

"Where will he go?"

"Not my problem."

"How will he live?"

"Not your problem."

"Damian," she says with reprimand.

"Stop worrying. Zane earns enough to take care of him. After what happened, I don't want him on the property." I leave my empty glass on the liquor tray and catch her shoulders between my hands. "You're still trembling."

"I've had a fright."

I bloody well bet. "Why didn't you tell me about your plans?"

She steps away from my touch. "I just met someone for a quote this morning. I didn't want to tell you until I had costs."

"You should've told me."

"Are you angry?"

Am I angry? I'm fucking livid. I saw her life being threatened and felt mine cyphering away at the terrifying notion of losing her. She makes me weak, and she doesn't even know it. "Not with you."

She bites her lip as she studies me for a moment before asking, "May I go, then?"

Never. I want to make her straddle my face and eat her out just to feel how alive she is. Then I want to make her take my cock in her mouth again, but her throat must still be raw. Besides, she's as badly shaken as what I am, even if she's not showing it. My girl is strong, much stronger than I ever imagined, and it doesn't make sense. She's not the weak, crazy person Dalton's doctors made her out to be. The more I get to know Lina, the less the medical reports make sense.

It's not a subject I'd normally breach unprepared and without warning, but maybe because I could've lost her so easily, I throw it at her. "Tell me about your time at Willowbrook."

Her face goes blank. It's like a portrait that changes from reserved to closed-off right in front of me.

Her voice is steady and strong. Nothing in her tone gives away any tension, but the sudden dullness of her eyes, as if she's disconnected herself from the moment, betrays her. "I don't talk about that."

"Why not?"

"It's in the past. There's nothing to say."

She jumped from a window. She went on a hunger strike. There must be plenty to say. From what's been written in the media, Dalton and Clarke doted on her. The men in her life treated her like a princess. Why would a princess lock herself up in a tower, only to mutilate herself and try to take her own life?

"I'd like to go now," she whispers.

I prefer to hold her, to smother her until I feel calmer, but she's suffered enough for one day. With a small nod, I hand her the parcel. She grabs it and all but flees from the room. She's barely gone when Zane enters.

"He's gone," he says. "Anne is driving him to a hotel."

For the first time, my tone is hostile with Zane. "That was quick."

"There wasn't much to pack."

"He belongs in a retirement home where he can be watched twenty-four seven, not in a hotel."

"We're looking into it."

"I hope for his sake Anne is staying with him." Not that Andries is my concern any longer.

"About what happened—"

"If it happens again, you're as dead as the person threatening Lina. I'm holding you responsible."

"You said you wouldn't allow this."

"Allow what?"

"For her to come between us."

"She's my wife. I've asked you before, and I'm going to ask you again. This time think carefully before you answer. Do you have a problem with Lina being my wife?"

"You're pussy-whacked."

Choosing to ignore that, I repeat, "Do you have a problem with Lina being my wife?"

"Everything I do, I do out of respect for you. Friendship. Loyalty. The fresh flowers in the entrance every day… Do you ever thank me? Do you ever notice? Do you see the hours I'm putting into running this house, the effort I'm making with the garden? Do you? No. All you notice is your new toy, your *wife*, and she's making you blind, because you don't see what's right in front of you."

Swinging back my arm, I take a punch at his face. The blow falls on his cheek, making him stumble a step. He's good with his fists. I want him to give me a fight. I need this to blow off steam, but he only stands there, knowing I won't fight a man who doesn't fight back.

"Come on, Zane. Give it to me."

"Fine, Dami. You want me to give it to you? How about a nice slice of truth? How about the fact that Lina tried to seduce me?"

The fight leaves my body. A different kind of anger-infused adrenaline rushes through my veins. She wouldn't. She knows he's gay. *That doesn't mean she didn't try*, the devil whispers in my ear.

"That's right," he continues, giving me a snide smile. "She came into my bathroom, half naked, offering me her body in exchange for the evidence against Harold."

Rage threatens to consume me. I can't speak under the weight of it.

"She threw herself at me, so much so I had to push her away. She slipped and hit her hip against the basin. Ask her to show you the bruise if you don't believe me."

"Enough," I grit out, unable to bear the mental images tormenting my mind.

"I didn't tell you, because I didn't want you to hurt her."

Carefully, I bottle my rage, pushing it underneath the polished veneer of fake calm. I'll let it explode later, when I have every single gritty detail of the facts. "Why tell me now?"

"Because I care more about our friendship than what happens to her."

Getting into his personal space, I lower my voice. "One more mark on her body, no matter what she did, and you move into that hotel with your pops. Got it?"

A pained look comes over his face. He doesn't answer, but backtracks to the door, watching me like I've done him an injustice. Maybe I'm wrong in this. Maybe I'm wrong in hurting Zane's feelings, but Lina comes first. Always. If anyone's to put a mark on her body, it's me. I should keep away from her until I've got a handle on my emotions, especially after what happened with Andries, but my anger burns too high.

Before Zane steps through the door, I give him a command I probably shouldn't. "Tell Russell to take the afternoon off. Rest of the staff, too. That includes you."

A sliver of a smile reaches his lips. I recognize it for what it is. Satisfaction. He gets what he wants, after all. He gets his revenge on Lina, trusting my uncontrollable jealousy and possessiveness where she's concerned to take care of it. He nods as he hurries to execute my order.

Standing at the top of the stairs, I watch them go. When the door closes behind Zane, I go in search of Lina and find her in our bedroom. The door is open. She doesn't hear me enter. She stands in front of the window like a statue, staring through it with no telling what's going on in her mind.

"Lina." She jumps. "Undress."

She gives me a startled look. "What?"

"You heard me."

"Why?"

"It will be unwise to make me tell you again."

She knows I'll tear the flimsy dress off if I have to. Holding my eyes with questions in hers, questions I'll soon answer while demanding some answers of my own, she steps out her sandals, unzips the dress, and lets it fall at her feet.

"Underwear too."

Her gaze drops to my groin. "Do you want me to...?"

"You can't say it, can you?" I taunt. "No, I don't want you to swallow my cock. It's too soon."

"Then what?" she whispers. "If you're thinking of doing that to me—"

"Say it."

Defiance sets her shoulders straight. "If you're thinking of *going down on me*, I'll remind you I'm having my period."

Fuck. Hearing her say it makes me hard. "No threat of that either." I flick my fingers. "Underwear. Now."

She regards me curiously while discarding her bra and thong, no doubt wondering what I have planned for her. I don't make her wait to find out.

"Go to my study."

The color vanishes from her cheeks.

"Now, Lina."

She glances beyond me at the open door.

"I gave the staff the afternoon off. No one will see you."

She swallows. "Why? What did I do wrong?"

Stepping aside, I indicate she should go ahead of me. Her tread is light, cautious, her naked body a tableau of perfection marred with a purple stain that blooms like a flower on her hip. The meaning of that stain seeps under my skin, reminding me of Zane's accusation. *She tried to seduce me.*

Looking over her shoulder at me, she asks, "Why did you send everyone away?"

"You know why."

"Damian."

She hesitates on the threshold to the study, but I'm flush against her back. There's no way but forward. Inside, she hugs herself, watching me as I close the space between us. I'm not sure if it's a gesture of comforting herself or hiding her breasts from me.

Gently, I swipe her hair over her shoulders. Her skin is smooth and soft under my palms. Perfect. "Did you trespass in Zane's bathroom?"

She sucks in a breath. "He told you."

"What were you doing in his bathroom?"

"What did he tell you?"

"I'm asking you."

"Yes."

I drag my thumb along her shoulder, tracing the arch of her neck. "Speak in full sentences."

Goosebumps break out over her skin. "Yes, I was in his bathroom."

Slowly, I caress the line of her jaw. "That's not what I asked."

Fear sparks in her eyes, eyes the color of a sinful night, even as she holds my gaze bravely. "I was looking for something."

"What were you looking for?"

"It's not important."

"Mm." I cup her jaw, letting her warmth sink into my palm. "Let's try a different question. What were you wearing?"

"I just got back from the pool."

"What were you wearing, Lina?"

Her voice turns a little hoarse. Uncertain. Fearful. "My bikini."

I rub a strand of her hair between my fingers. Soft like silk. "Your bikini."

"And a wrap."

"Now we're getting somewhere." I stroke her hair gently. "Let's try this one again. What were you looking for?"

"Nothing."

"Nothing." Running my fingers down her back, I caress each fragile vertebra. "How did you get the bruise on your hip?"

She watches me unfalteringly, her huge eyes trained on mine. "Zane shoved me. I hit my hip on the basin."

It takes an extra big effort to tamp down the fury the mental image conjures. "Why did he shove you?"

"I shouldn't have been there."

I continue my exploration until I reach her buttocks. Cupping her globes, I trace the bruise on her hip with my thumb. "What trade did you suggest for the *nothing* you were looking for?"

"Nothing!"

"You offered *nothing* for *nothing*. Is that what you expect me to believe?"

"What do you want me to say?"

Letting go of her, I walk to the desk, retrieve the brown envelope from the false bottom of the drawer, and drop it on the corner in her line of sight. "Is this what you were looking for?"

Her pretty eyes go wide as she fixes them on the envelope.

"You must love your father very much if you're willing to pay for his freedom with your body."

She swallows but doesn't look away from that envelope. It's only when I round the desk that her gaze snaps back to me.

"You want that *nothing*?" I ask. "Give me the price you were willing to pay Zane and it's yours."

Shaking her head, she starts to speak. "I didn't—"

I silence her with a finger on her lips. No more lies. "This is what you wanted. Now you're going to take it."

CHAPTER 13

Lina

*D*amian backs me up to the desk, to the corner where my freedom lies in a plain, brown envelope. I'm tempted to look at it again, just to be sure it's real, but the disappointment in his bitter gaze won't let me. I'm not fooled by his gentleness. He's going to punish me. That's how he works. I'm acting brave, but it's exactly that. Acting. My legs tremble at the thought of all the ways in which he can take revenge. I haven't succeeded in stealing the evidence. He won't cut off my finger. That doesn't prevent him from using one of the whipping tools on the wall to put new scars on me.

He stands too close. The heat from his body burns my naked skin through the layers of his clothes. This is my disadvantage. I'm naked. Vulnerable. This is how he planned it, why he made me undress.

Gripping my waist, he lifts me with a swift movement onto the desk. The action is not what I expected. I'm trembling from head to toe, waiting for the worst. He grips my knees and spreads my legs.

"You want it, Lina?"

Slowly, he trails a finger up the inside of my thigh, higher and higher, until he brushes the pad over my folds. I shiver. No matter how hard I bite down on my lip, my body prepares for him, turning slick and swollen.

He plays between my legs, stroking me softly, waking nerve endings.

"You want it?" he repeats, his breath warm on my face, but I'm no longer certain if he's referring to the envelope or his touch.

He kisses the shell of my ear, his caress a deceptively gentle seduction. "I asked you a question."

"W-what?"

"Do you want those papers?"

Biting my lip, I glance at the envelope. It's so close, within my reach. I breathe in deeply and let out the admittance on a rush of air. "Yes."

He rubs a finger over my clit. "This is what you offered, right?"

I stare at him as his meaning sinks in. Sex in exchange for my freedom. My heart clenches painfully. He's asking me to be a whore. Doesn't really matter, though. It won't be the first time. What's once more, right? The thought hurts, but I push it away. I keep my tears inside as I reach for his zipper.

Instead of victory, there's something else on his face, something I can't put a finger on, but he doesn't stop me when I unzip his fly. It's only when I reach for his belt that he grabs my wrist.

"No touching," he says. "Put your hands on the desk."

Not understanding his motivation, I swallow the rejection and lock my elbows to lean back on my arms. He finishes the task of freeing his cock through his fly, and that's all he does. He doesn't even unbutton his pants or push them over his hips.

"I'll need a minute to use the bathroom." My face heats as I say it. I need to clean up. My period has started, and I haven't yet had time to use anything.

He doesn't grant me the privilege of that privacy. His deft fingers feel between my legs, slipping between my folds. When he finds my channel empty, he grips his cock in one hand and lifts my thigh with the other.

The enormity of what we're about to do crashes down on me. I'm going to let him fuck me without protection. I'm clean. He's been in jail for six years. I doubt he's been fucking around after he got out. He was too busy plotting his revenge. At least I'm having my period. There's no risk of falling pregnant.

Dragging the broad head through my folds only once, he places it at my opening. "This is how you wanted it."

A burning sting sears through me as he impales me to the hilt. There's too much of him and not enough give in my body. I'm not quite ready, but he doesn't give me time to adjust. He pulls out and plunges back in, making my back arch. This is his punishment. This is the price I'm paying, letting him use me. I agreed, didn't I? Then why does the roughness with which he tears into me hurt worse in my heart than in my unused channel? He stabs inside me, again and again, stretching too much, going too fast. It's not comfortable, but not everything I feel is pain. There's pleasure, too. I gasp at the sensation. Sex has never been pleasurable for me. That he holds this kind of power over me, the power of making my body sing while wringing out my heart, scares me more than any knife or notch carved on my skin. I will the tightening of my muscles away, but the pleasure keeps on expanding with every punishing thrust.

Despite the emotional coldness with which he takes me, heat unfurls in my belly. My orgasm builds quickly. I ache to wrap my arms around his neck, to hold onto something, but my arms remain plastered at my sides, my hands gripping the edge of the desk as he lets go of my thigh to rub his fingers over my clit. The other times I paid with my body, I never came. I do now, and as the orgasm rips through me and tightens my inner muscles around his cock, I feel lonelier than all the times I didn't come.

He follows not long after with a grunt, emptying himself inside me without kisses or caresses. The only place where our bodies are touching is where we're joined. It's not for long, though. The minute his release is spent, he pulls out. His shaft is pink from his semen and my blood. The mixture gushes from me, and all I can do to salvage the little that's left of my pride is to close my legs.

Grabbing a napkin from the liquor tray, he cleans himself before tucking his cock away and adjusting his pants. A moment of silence follows as we look at each other. I wait for him to say something, but he only picks up the envelope and places it in my lap.

"Next time," he says, "if you offer what's mine to another man, you'll have his death on your conscience."

With that he walks out, leaving me in a wet puddle on his desk.

It's only when he's gone that I let my shoulders sag. A band of tension snaps in my chest as I allow myself to let down my guard. It takes more than a moment to pull myself together and gather enough strength to slide off his desk. My legs wobble. I swallow back tears that get stuck in an aching knot in my throat.

Following his example, I use a few napkins to clean myself. I leave them in the trashcan, too wrought out to worry about the cleaning staff's thoughts or reactions. Forcing myself to ignore the hurt in my heart and between my legs, I face the only thing that can make it better. I face the envelope. I look at it like I couldn't earlier. I look at it without blinking until my eyes burn. My fingers tremble when I finally reach for it. My palm is a scale of justice. I feel the weight of freedom in my hand and the price of it between my thighs. My heart throbs painfully for both ends of the scale, because there's misery in having sold my soul, and, surprisingly, in walking away. A part of me already misses Damian, but I'm guessing it's the girl who fell in love with the boy. I'm thankful to him in a warped way for fucking me like a man, for making it easier for me to hate him, for making it easier to leave.

My stomach flutters as I tear open the seal. Elation pumps through me as I extract the folded papers. Finally, I'll know where my baby is. I'll know what they did with his little body. Harold will have to tell me, but what prevents him from killing me once he has Damian's evidence? He no longer has a motive for keeping me alive. Jack's money is now Damian's to manage. Before, at the event of my death, the money would've gone into a state trust, as Harold isn't my next of kin in blood. Only we know the secret. Only we know I'm the product of my mother's affair, and only she knew who my father is. She never told. Knowing Harold would kill him, she protected his identity.

Harold never adopted me, but he raised me in his house. He told me the truth on my eighteenth birthday. By then, it didn't come as a surprise. He hated me too much, never cared for me like a father, so much so he refused to put his name on my birth certificate. If I'm to die, the secret contained on my birth certificate will be known, and Harold would've lost control of Jack's money. Now that there's no money as motivation, I need a different bargaining chip. I'll keep the originals and offer Harold a copy. That will be my ticket to safety. I know too many of Harold's crimes. I'm too big a risk.

Holding my breath, I carefully unfold the two sheets of paper that hold my future. I scan over the text, taking in the shadow in the bottom left corner. It can't be.

No!

Furiously, I rub my finger over the ink, willing it to smudge, but I already know it won't.

It's fake.

The papers I hold in my hands are copies.

CHAPTER 14

Damian

*L*ina storms into the room, her eyelashes matted with tears.

I wait quietly, having expected the reaction. This is the reason why I sent everyone away. I can't do this behind a closed door, not with Lina's phobia, and no one but me will witness her breakdown. This is sacred. Private. Between her and me. The moment I break her is mine alone.

She holds the papers out to me, as if I don't know what's printed on them. Her hand is shaking so badly the sheets are fluttering. Her lips are trembling. She's barely holding herself together. Naked, falling apart, she's ravishing. The most beautiful living being I've seen.

"You deceived me."

"I never lied to you."

Her breath catches on a hitch. "You said you'd give me the evidence."

"I said I'd give you the envelope. I never told you what was inside."

She swats at the tears on her cheek. "You tricked me."

"You didn't ask what was in that envelope."

She gnashes her teeth. "You bastard."

"Are you angry about your lost freedom or that I fucked you?"

"Both!"

"Would you have been angry at Zane if it was his cock?"

"It wouldn't have been the same."

Tilting my head, I study her. She's losing her composure with every passing second. "How's that?"

"I would never have given it to him freely. I would've fought him with everything I've got."

It doesn't sound right, not according to what Zane said, but I'm taunting her, pushing her closer to the edge of her limits. "I thought you offered."

"I snooped around in his bathroom. He caught me. He threatened to touch me. We fought, and it got physical. That's what happened, not whatever you think."

I still. I let her words sink deep into my heart where their meaning can damage me. Irrevocably. If it's true, I failed her. I said I wouldn't let anyone hurt her. If what she says is true, Zane betrayed me. If it's true, Lina was bullied, right under my nose. The sleeping pill and the marks on her wrists, why would she lie about them? She has no reason for pinning the blame on Zane.

Fuck, fuck, fuck. I want to come apart with fury, but I keep it together. Only one of us can unravel. Slowly, as I let the calm seep in, doubt nestles in the seat of trust I keep for Zane. I can't give her the benefit of the doubt. Not yet. Not with her track record. I can't do it without proof. From the way her pretty features contort, she reads the truth on my face.

"Fuck you," she snarls, tearing the papers into small pieces that flitter like confetti to the floor. "I don't care, do you hear me?"

"That I don't trust you or that you let me fuck you for nothing?"

She snaps. With a cry of rage, she flings herself at me, going into the fight with arms, fists, feet, and teeth. I've never seen a woman so feral. The fact that I easily catch her wrists and constrain her only infuriates her more. Twisting and kicking, she tries to inflict physical damage, but she only has her feet to use as weapons. She's barefoot, and she's a tiny thing. There's not much she can use to her advantage.

I could've stopped her as easily as I'm constraining her, but I let her tire herself, get it out of her system.

When her energy is spent, she sags in my hold. Her legs cave in. A big sob wracks her shoulders as she slides to the floor. I let go of her wrists to catch her in my arms. Cupping her face, I press her cheek to my chest. Warm tears soak my shirt. Quiet tears. Her full, meager weight rests against me. Folding an arm under her knees, I pick her up and carry her to our bed.

"The sheets," she says through her tears as I lay her down.

"Fuck the sheets."

I tear out of my clothes in record time. All the while, she cries. When I cover her body with mine, she doesn't protest.

I frame her face between my palms and kiss the salty taste of her tears from her lips. "Let it all out, angel."

"I hate you so much."

I kiss her again. "I know."

"I'll never forgive you."

"I'll gladly carry your blame."

"Why are you doing this?"

"You're mine." If there's one thing I hoped to get across today, it's that.

When I brush my lips over hers again and again, she doesn't stop me. Neither does she resist me when I invade her mouth with my tongue. I always want to kiss her mouth the opposite of how I want to fuck it, but this time I can't hold back. The strokes of my tongue are urgent. They mimic the movement of my hips as I choose a rhythm that will work for both of us and not just me this time. She moans into my mouth, almost making me lose it. Her back arches, pushing her breasts flat against my chest. I'm thankful for my foresight to have sent everyone away, because this is the moment I've been waiting for my whole delinquent life, ever since I saw her face. The moment is too big to have it crowded with others when the walls are thin. It's my moment, mine as much as hers, even if she won't admit it. I've waited six years to be inside her. I've had no other woman since. Fucking her in the study took off the edge. I'm going to make this round last.

She's panting when I finally let her breathe. When I feel between her legs, I find her wet for me, and it's not just her period and my cum from earlier. It's sweet, slick arousal.

Looking into her eyes, I ask the question I've been carrying in my heart for so long it's branded into my soul. "Do you want me, Lina?"

The truth makes her flinch. More tears run from her eyes as she whispers, "You know I do."

"Say it."

"Damian." A sob catches in her throat. "Please don't make me."

"Say it, Lina. Tell me the truth."

"Yes," she cries on a defeated whisper. "I want you."

"Then ask me to fuck you."

"Damian."

Her nails dig into my shoulders. I know she needs this, the physical closeness. She wants it desperately after how I've treated her in the study. She needs it after her breakdown. It's no great psychological analysis. It's just human nature.

"You only have to ask, Lina."

"Please, don't."

I nuzzle her temple with my nose. "There's no shame in asking."

She stares at me for so long I'm terrified I'm going to lose the gamble, but then she opens her sweet little mouth and gives me the words I want to hear.

"Make love to me."

"Anything you want."

Lining my cock up with her pussy, I slide in slowly, watching her face as I stretch her and her body adjusts to take me. I give her what she asked for, loving instead of fucking, slowly and gently filling her until we're buried so deep in each other our groins are grinding together.

Our lovemaking is a languid dance of give and take. This time, I let her participate. She wraps her arms around my neck and her legs around my ass, pulling me to her as close as I can get. She initiates the kiss, giving me the sweetest of bliss as she tangles her tongue with mine. Her tears make way for panting until her moans fill the room and my head. Her scent is in my nose and in my memory, the smell of sweet poison that will kill me, but what a happy death it will be. I'm sliding my hands everywhere there is skin, touching with a need born from six lonely years, but she's touching, too.

She runs her hands through my hair and down my back, over my ass. I know she needs me to touch her clit to come, but when I push up on one arm, she pulls me back, not accepting the small space I put between us. Instead, her hand moves between our bodies. I take my time with her as she plays with her clit. My strokes are too lazy to stimulate another ejaculation, especially so soon after the first, but feeling her pleasing herself is all it takes. When we come, we're looking into each other's eyes. Hers are brimming with defeat, and I know mine will be shining with raw desire and conquest. I drink in her expression, imprinting it to my memory, the moment she submitted her body to me.

~

Lina

EVERYTHING DAMIAN DIDN'T GIVE me in the study, he gives me after we've made love in his bed. He carries me to the shower and washes me, always touching, always having a point of contact. Even when he squeezes shampoo onto my head, he does it with one hand, the other securely resting on my waist. He dries me and brushes my hair. I finally escape from his lavish attention to the bathroom with the box of tampons while he strips the bed of the mess we've made. When I come back, I stare at the bare mattress with longing, wishing I could crawl back under the covers to hide from myself and my significant, not to mention humiliating, loss of our war, but it's only late afternoon.

Dressed in a pair of jeans, he watches me from the edge of the bed with crossed arms. I gingerly walk to the dressing room, pretending I don't notice his stare. He doesn't crowd me but gives me space to dress. I pull on jeans and a T-shirt before joining him in the room.

"Come here," he says.

Conscious of the ache between my legs, I cross the floor and stop in front of him.

"Give me your hand." I lift my right hand. "The other one."

My hesitation lasts only a second, but Damian's eyes darken. Quickly, I extend my left hand. He takes a ring from his pocket and slips it onto my finger to fit against the wedding band. The teardrop diamond has been beautifully set inside a cluster of black diamonds. It catches the light, giving off a sparkle that seems ironic, given the circumstances.

"There," he says, twisting the ring until it fits right.

I can't bring myself to say thank you. It would be false.

Instead of commenting on my lack of enthusiasm, he asks, "Hungry?"

"Yes," I reply softly.

Offering me his hand, he leads me through the empty house to the kitchen. It's nice with just the two of us, when there's no Zane to glare, no Anne to gloat, and no Russell to watch me.

I'm surprised at how at home he is in the kitchen, throwing together an early supper of omelets and salad. He makes me sit at the table as if I'm fragile, but I'm too mentally and physically exhausted to argue. Resting my chin in my hand, I watch him move to and fro as he works. When he dashes past me again with the pan in his hand, he stops to wipe a thumb over my lips.

"This mouth is mine," he says teasingly. His smile vanishes, and his face grows serious. "You're mine now, Lina. I own you in every way."

Before I can reply, the very people I wanted to escape file into the kitchen. Zane stops just inside of the door, his arms stiff and hands fisted as he watches Damian serve an omelet on my plate. Damian doesn't acknowledge Zane, but his body tenses. Something happened between them. Anne plants a newspaper next to me.

"Didn't want you to hear it from someone else," she says with fake sympathy.

I glance down at the open page. There's a photo of me lying on the pavement with Damian straddling me. The headline reads,

Another suicide attempt for newlywed Mrs. Hart? A passerby must've taken it.

Damian reads over my shoulder. He gives the article three seconds of his attention before taking a seat next to me. He acts nonchalant, but his knuckles turn white around his fork.

Jana and Russell come walking in, chatting and laughing. They stop when they see us.

"Are we interrupting?" Jana asks. "I can come back later to finish dinner."

Damian digs into his omelet. "We're having an early one, but don't let us stop you."

"Macaroni and cheese, everyone?" Jana asks.

Zane huffs. "Do I look like I'm ten?"

"Tell you what, Jana." Damian wipes his mouth on a napkin, giving Zane a cold look. "Zane and Anne are old enough to fix their own dinner. Why don't you go home early?"

"Are you sure? I mean, I'd love to, but I don't want to leave you in the lurch."

"I'm sure they survived before you," Russell says with a wink.

"All right, then." She gives us a bright smile. "I'll see you tomorrow."

The tension is so palpable, it's difficult to enjoy my food. I don't miss the way Anne's gaze remains fixed on Damian's naked torso. He looks succulent in those faded jeans, and now that I know what it feels like to have him inside me, I'm afraid of the other woman's attention I once considered welcome.

As Damian promised, he takes me to the gym the following morning. On the way, he stops at a sport shop to get me an appropriate outfit.

"I would've been fine in shorts and a T-shirt," I say, parading the Lycra pants and sports bra on his insistence in the small change room sitting area.

"You've yet to spend my money."

"I never said I would."

"Turn around."

I sigh and show him my ass, assessing him from over my shoulder.

"Perfect," he says, his eyes turning heated. "Too much, maybe."

I charge to the change room before he can make me try on another outfit. "I'll take these."

His chuckle follows me down the narrow corridor, but when I push on the change room door, his hand covers mine. His chest presses against my back. We're the only people in the changing area, and I become intensely aware of our isolation as he pushes the door open and walks me inside.

"What are you doing?" I whisper-cry as he locks the door. There's a wide enough gap at the bottom for a body to crawl through, enough to not make me panic.

His fingers steal under the elastic of the bra, finding my nipple. "Tell me you want me."

He's made me say it at least ten times since yesterday. The novelty of it can't seem to wear off for him. Every time, my admission has been accompanied by heavy petting, which isn't permitted in the store.

"Damian." I gasp when he pushes me against the wall. "They'll throw us out."

"Tell me."

"Will you let me go if I do?"

His grin is boyish. "Maybe."

"You're impossible."

"You're dragging this out. Maybe you're enjoying it so much, you're doing it on purpose."

"I'm not!"

"Say it."

"Fine. I want you. Happy?"

"Yes." He grabs my wrists and lifts them above my head.

"What are you doing?"

He pushes the bra over my head and up my arms, leaving it just above my elbows. In this position, the tight Lycra constrains me.

With him pressed up against me, I can't lower my arms or step away.

"Damian."

"Shh." He presses a finger on my lips. "They'll hear you."

"Please, don't—"

I swallow the rest of my words as he slides down to his knees, hooking his fingers into the elastic of the exercise pants and taking them with him. I start to protest, but he hushes me again and puts his mouth on my clit. One suck and my back hollows from the hot flush of ecstasy that shoots to my core. I bite back a moan. He watches me as only Damian can, with intense concentration, as he nips and licks. He knows how to read my expressions. He knows the nonverbal language of my body. This is what all the studying and gawking while I fall apart and come in his mouth awarded him. He knows exactly at which moment to bite, and how to suck away the hurt. He knows I'm going to moan too loudly, and he already straightens and covers my mouth with his broad palm before the sound of my climax leaves my lips. He lets me pant into his hand for all of two seconds before he pushes me to my knees.

My arms are still constrained and in the way between us, but his cock is in my mouth before I can argue. I barely have time to relax my jaw before he hits the back of my throat. He holds me down by my hair as he likes to, fucking my mouth until I'm certain my jaw will unhinge and I'll never breathe sweet air again. I only give over because I trust him in this, because he's proven he won't let anything happen to me. It's when I surrender that he comes. He thrives on this, on hurting and dominating me. He thrives on pulling me into his lap and kissing me dizzy, until the taste of our arousals is intermingled.

A loud knock on the door shocks me to my senses.

"Sir? Ma'am?" a female voice calls. "You can't be in there together. I have to ask you to step out."

Stern and judgmental, that voice makes me feel like a teenager caught in a car parked on the banks of the river. That's where the kids from my class used to make out. I never made it there, to those banks and normalcy. I made it to Willowbrook and to Damian Hart.

He smooths down my hair. "Ready?"

"Yes." I push away the untimely memories and hold out my arms for him to free me.

"Sir. Step out. Now."

"In a moment," he says. "You don't want me to come out naked, do you?"

"Oh, my God." Her groan is disgruntled. "I'm calling the police." Her footsteps hurry away.

"Come here, angel."

Damian helps me into my clothes before he takes care of himself. We're more or less respectable when we exit. My cheeks burn as we pass the shop assistant who waits accusingly at the entrance of the changing area.

"There are hotel rooms for that," she says, looking us up and down. Her evaluation pauses on my scars.

Damian shrugs. "The bedroom never seems to be enough." He shoots an appreciative look in my direction. "Not for my wife. Nope, ma'am. Can't ever get enough of her."

The woman's gaze slips to my finger. When she spots the diamond, she slightly relaxes her stance, as if the fact that we're married makes what we did less wrong. She can have us arrested for public indecency.

Taking my hand, Damian pays for my purchases and leads me to his car under the burning stares of the staff. He opens my door and helps me inside, not at all acting self-conscious. Does he have a guilty bone in his body? From the way he laughs softly, he enjoys the embarrassing situation.

When we pull off, I decide to exploit his good mood. "I'd like to get a driver's license."

He glances at me. "Of course."

"Really?" Harold denied me a license because he knew how dependent that made me on him in a city with no to very little public transportation. I don't know why I expected Damian to behave the same.

He takes my hand and squeezes my fingers. "Anything you want. I've already told you."

"Thank you."

"You're welcome."

His smile is warm, approving almost. Then he lets me get lost in my thoughts until we park in front of a popular gym franchise. It's a double-story building that stretches over the whole block.

"Here?" I expected something small and obscure.

"This is where I train. It's the closest from home."

A manager, who greets Damian by name, meets us inside. Phillip looks too young to be a gym manager. He has big muscles and tattoos on his arms and chest. His banter is friendly as he shows us the health bar, sauna, tanning beds, and collective course halls where they offer yoga and stretching.

At the end of the tour, he turns to me expectantly. "What do you think?"

"It's all very impressive, but it's not what I need."

His face drops while Damian smothers a chuckle.

"What is it you need?"

"Fitness and strength training."

Scratching his head, he takes us to the upstairs level where there's a circuit and free weights section.

"If you're new to this, you'll need a program."

"Schedule it," Damian says.

We sit down on the leather couch overlooking the weight training section to fill out the necessary paperwork while enjoying complimentary cappuccinos. A signature from Damian later, and I'm enrolled. I can't remember feeling this excited about anything since food.

Wrapping my arms around Damian in a stupidly impulsive reaction, I whisper, "Thank you," in his neck.

He squeezes me tightly. "Whatever you need."

To any outsider, we must appear as a normal, happy couple. At times like these, what Damian and I are, what defines our dynamic, is so muddled, not even I can make sense of it.

~

DURING MY NEXT appointment with Reyno, Damian waits in the hallway, and I venture inside on my own. Normally, I would never have been this brave, but I have my own agenda in overcoming my fear of doctors and closed doors.

"How are you?" he asks when I take a seat.

"Are you really interested?"

He smiles. "It's my job to ask."

"Have you ever been good at it?"

He thinks for a while. "I suppose there was a time I was worth a shit."

"What happened?"

"Greed. One wrong decision. Debt. I don't know. Sometimes it's hard to pin it on a single reason. It's not clear-cut like a turn in a road that changes our direction, but hey, I'm the one who's supposed to do the psychoanalysis, remember?"

I give a wry laugh, nervously staring at the door.

"Does that bother you?" he asks. "The closed door?"

"Yes."

"Why?'

"I have my reasons."

"We can work on that if you like."

"Finding your missing conscience, are you?" I tease.

"I'll be honest. Your husband only requires me to prescribe medicine for you when needed, but since you're here and I owe you an hour, it can't hurt to talk."

"I suppose not."

"So, let's talk about closed doors."

"Let's talk about how you can really help me."

He lifts a brow, waiting for me to continue.

"Here's the deal. I need money, and you're going to give me a job. Paying under the table. And Damian isn't going to know."

He laughs softly. "Why would I do that?"

Pulling my phone from my pocket, I play the recording I'd taken of our first meeting. I activated my phone under the pretense of looking for a tissue before Damian and I entered the room.

215

When I get to the part where he all but admits to knowing Damian forced me into marriage, I press pause. "Need to hear more? My favorite part is where you admit to taking bribes for prescribing drugs."

"No." He shakes his head as if he finds me funny. "I get it."

"Good. I start next week."

"With what?"

"I don't know. There must be tasks a psychiatrist needs help with."

"You're a piece of work, you know that?"

"Thanks." I'm glad I had the foresight to record the meeting. I was worried Damian was going to have me locked up, and I wasn't going down that road without putting up my best fight.

"Damian has no idea, does he?"

"Of what?"

"Of how cunning and strong you really are."

I shrug and cross my legs. "I don't think Damian is interested in my psyche." He's all about the physical.

The smile he gives me is disarming. It's both sympathetic and pitying. "I think you're wrong."

I don't like it. It's as if he knows something I don't. "Next week, same time?"

"If you say so."

When I leave the office, Damian waits for me at the door.

He wipes a strand of hair behind my ear. "How did it go?"

"Good. I'm coming back next week."

"You are?" He seems surprised.

"You want me to, don't you?"

"I'm not forcing you."

"Okay."

"Okay? Just like that? No fight?"

"Some things aren't worth the fight," I say over my shoulder, making my way down the hallway.

I don't miss the contemplative way he looks at me, as if he's not sure if he should trust me. He keeps on telling me he doesn't, and he's right not to. The thought hurts. I face forward so he won't see the guilt in my eyes.

Catching up with me, he takes my hand and pulls me to a stop. "You may find this hard to believe, but I do want you to be happy."

"Has anyone ever been happy without freedom?" I ask softly.

He cups my face, drawing his thumb over my cheek. "You think I hold all the control."

"You do."

"You're wrong. It's entirely up to you. You can have anything you want, or you can fight me and make it unnecessarily unpleasant for yourself."

How tempting he makes it sound. A life with no commitments, no worries, no work. That's not a real life. It's just a luxurious version of being locked up.

"What do you want, Lina? Ask me. Test me. I'll give you anything your heart desires."

There are things I desperately want, but I can't tell him, because those *things* led me to committing a murder. I'm a cold-blooded killer, and I'll do it again. I'm not sure what that makes me. I only know I can't look at myself in the mirror without hating what I see.

"What do you want?" he repeats.

"A job. I'd like to earn money like a normal person."

"You're not a normal person."

The jab hurts. What he thinks of me shouldn't bother me, but it does. I suck in a slow breath. "That was cruel."

"That's not how I meant it, and you know it. I meant our circumstances aren't normal. You don't need a job," he says with finality, letting me know the subject is closed for discussion. "Anything else?"

"Nothing."

"Lunch?" he asks, rubbing his hands over my arms.

The touch still makes me shiver, but every time the repulsion is less. There was a time when food would've made everything better, but not today. Today my belly is full, and my troubles are elsewhere. Classic case of Maslow's hierarchy of needs. Now that my physical needs are taken care of, I strive to have my emotional wants met.

"I'd like lunch."

My answer pleases him.

"Italian?"

My favorite. "How did you know?"

Instead of answering, he kisses my nose.

∾

Damian

AFTER LINA'S SUBMISSION, I fuck her at every chance I get. God knows, she's been the fantasy in my head for long enough. I deserve every rush of blood to my pelvis, every hard-on, and every climax she ignites. Leaving her to go to my office in the city is almost painful, but there's much to do at the mine. Making money takes time. Making more money takes an even longer time, and I need a lot of money to keep safe in this city. I need the means to give Lina the life I promised to make up for keeping her in a cage.

Still not sure what to make of Lina's accusations, I keep a careful eye on Zane. His behavior is exemplary. He's courteous to Lina, even if he limits their contact to mealtimes. It's his word against hers, a situation of uncertainty I can't allow. Sending him on an errand while Anne visits Andries, I have cameras installed. I don't want anyone in the house to know about the added security measure. While the installation is underway, I take care of other business with Lina. It's not something I look forward to, but she needs to understand the consequences of betrayal.

I bundle her into the car and drive to the dump in Brixton.

She gives me a wary look when we exit in front of the dilapidated apartment building. "What are we doing here?"

I know what she sees when she looks up at the brick façade marred by graffiti and broken windows. She sees me, before I met Dalton. She sees hunger, criminality, and depravity. She sees hopelessness and a futile future or, if you're strong, a will to survive and rise above the debris of human scum, of parents who don't know where

218

their kids hang out because they're too busy working their fingers to the bone to put bread on the table.

Taking her arm, I lead her up the piss-stained stairs and peeling walls. At the first door on the second level, we stop.

She hangs back, looking at the crooked numbers on the door that write sixty-six instead of ninety-six, and the section around the lock that's splintered. Hardening myself, I don't spare her the knock that falls hollow on the pressed wood.

A shuffle later, the door opens. Dalton's face appears in the crack, unshaven and hard. It's what this neighborhood does to people. They stop using razors and hate people like me who have their faces shaved in a barber chair while sipping espresso and making multi-million rand deals on their smartphones.

When she recognizes her father, she pulls back harder, straining on my hold, but I push the door wide open and bring her inside.

"Well, well." Dalton looks from her to me. "Look what the cat dragged in."

"Watch your mouth," I say, kicking the door shut.

He looks ten years older in a vest, sweatpants, and slippers. His hair is uncombed, and he smells like sour soup.

"Aren't you going to say hello?" he says to Lina. "Too good for me now?"

I shove him aside and stride into the single space that defines his life. "Disrespect her again and you'll regret it."

He follows with his smug smile. "Come to gloat, have you?"

"You said you wanted to see your daughter."

She looks at the unmade bed and the dirty dishes on the kitchenette shelf. Her gaze takes in the moldy shower curtain and the grainy image on the fat-belly television. It's satisfyingly depressing.

"Don't look so surprised," he says, addressing Lina again. "What did you expect? A five-star hotel?"

This is what he's been degraded to. When he's been stripped from his business and reputation, his true colors show. He never had a bone of dignity in his body.

"It must make you happy," he continues, "seeing me barely making ends meet while you look like this." He motions at the pretty dress and sandals I've chosen for her, the brands screaming luxury.

"I don't," she says softly.

The one thing he hasn't mentioned, has avoided looking at since we've entered, is her bare arms. It's odd, not the kind of behavior one would expect from a caring father who dotes on his only daughter.

He lifts a chipped mug from the table. "Drink?"

"No, thanks," Lina says, standing there with her arms at her sides.

"Oh, well." He shrugs and downs the dregs left in the mug. "I saw you tried to kill yourself again."

She doesn't deny or confirm it. The look she gives him is pitying, if not sad.

He assesses her from head to toe, ignoring her arms again. There's taunting in his tone. "You're getting fat."

She's seen what I wanted her to. There's no need to drag out the unpleasant disillusionment. I expected at least a warm welcome for Lina, a little bit of affection, not envy for her fortune and good health.

I address him like a child, as he deserves. "There won't be another visit until you can muster respect. At least you have time to work on it."

"Time is all I have," he says with a wry chuckle. "A moment alone with Lina?"

Not on my life. "Goodbye, Dalton."

Gripping Lina's arm, I lead her back outside where we can almost breathe again. The stench of rotting garbage clings to the streets. It's part of life in these parts, as are the dogs scavenging through tossed take-out containers, and the gang of barely adults watching us from the corner. I flip my jacket aside, showing them my gun. They don't scatter, but they look away. I signal for the two cars with armed guards waiting. You can't go anywhere in this neighborhood without a convoy. The men climb out, taking wide stances. At that, the group dissipates.

I don't get into the car just yet. There's something else I want to visit. My men follow, alert and on the lookout as we walk a block down and take a right under the bridge. The church is sandwiched between a shoe factory and a run-down school. Made of gray stone, it almost blends unnoticed into the concrete and tar environment. The clock tower is black from soot from the coal train tracks that run on the overhead bridge. I take a minute to absorb the picture. Little has changed, and yet so much. The space under the bridge posts is empty. The lively flea market with its colorful stalls of vintage clothes and reject factory shoes are gone. The arched windows of the school are encased in rusted bars, and the noise of the trains is replaced with the far-off bark of a dog. It's a half-hearted, hopeless bark, lasting no more than three seconds.

I nod at my men to guard the street as I venture across with Lina. The front door is open, which comes as a surprise. Who would've thought? Not even churches or clergymen are exempted from crime and violence.

On the step, I turn to my wife. How pink and pretty and blonde and innocent she looks in the midst of all this charcoal black. "Do you want to wait outside?"

She shakes her head.

We climb over the raised step and stop inside. The inside is darker, dirtier. It still smells of candlewax and mothballs. Most of the stained-glass windows are broken, and pigeons are shitting on the windowsills. No candles burn in the alcoves. There are fresh flowers in a vase on the altar. They must still be holding services here. God knows for who.

"Wait here," I say.

Walking down the aisle, I take a trip down memory lane to the bench where I kneeled and hoped and prayed before life made me a man, a man as hard as his diamonds. That's what the media calls me. They're wrong. I'm black like soot, unclean like years layered on concrete. I step into the row and drag my shoe over the worn wood many knees have polished, the spot where I made my vow of revenge the day before the police found me. This was my haven, my escape from family fights that got too loud and the guilt my mother loaded on my shoulders for being another mouth to feed. I don't believe. Haven't for a very long time, but the space feels sacred. Many of the

221

defining decisions of my life were taken here. The decision to become rich, to dig for diamonds, to join forces with Dalton, to damn him to hell, to destroy his empire, and to take the daughter who was meant for someone worthy of her.

The very thought of Lina makes my cells hum with awareness. At once, I miss her presence as if we've been separated for weeks, not minutes. I no longer feel her at my back. Wariness creeps over my skin in an unpleasant ripple. I turn my head a fraction, sweeping the space with a gaze from over my shoulder. She's no longer standing in the light spilling from the door. Uneasiness tightens my gut. Urgency compels me to find her, even if I know she can't escape with my men stationed outside. The worn-out runner carpet cushions my steps as I move under the high arch of the ceiling. I scan every dark alcove until I get to the one right next to the door, and then I stop. Where cooing pigeons with deformed, knobbed feet crowd the windowsill, Lina stands under the broken window, staring at the portrait of Mary holding the baby Jesus in her arms. It's a portrait I know well, the one where my mother used to light a candle every Sunday.

From where I'm standing, I have a good view of Lina's face. The expression she wears as she looks at that painting stills me. Time disappears. The moment becomes ethereal. It's just her and me observing her. Her lips are tilted *just so*. It's not even a full curve of her lips, but it's the sweetest of smiles, and she has a dimple. A fucking, beautiful dimple. It hits me like a fist in the balls. It's the first time I've seen her smile. Hands folded, face turned up and serene, she looks like a Madonna. Unguarded, her face is even lovelier than usual. The light in her eyes is soft. Her expression is hard to nail. It's that something indefinable between sorrow and joy, that something that gives you the Sunday blues, that makes you miss someone you don't know. It's slight, that perfect smile, and yet so profound. It's a breeze that lifts the ends of my hair like a phantom caress in my neck, but it's a hurricane in my heart. It's the moment a realization hits me like a divine insight. Something happened to Lina, something bad.

Lost in herself, she traps me with her in the timeless space of whatever memories that painting stirs, and I'm annoyed when one of my men appears in the door and breaks the moment.

"Everything all right in here?" he asks.

Lina jumps a little. Her mask falls back in place, and she turns away from the sacred painting and the bird shit that runs like dripping candlewax down the wall.

"Who's going to attack us?" I snap. "The devil?"

"Just checking, sir."

"We're ready to go."

"Yes, sir."

I extend a hand to Lina. She hugs herself as she walks to me but unwraps her arms to accept my hand. Walking back to the car with our fingers intertwined, she's with me, and she's not. A part of her is still wherever she'd been in the church. She's too many pieces I can't puzzle together. Too many things don't make sense. I know the weight of her breasts in my palms. I know the husky little sound she makes at the first stroke of my cock inside her. I know her triggers and her thresholds. I know how to break her with rough ecstasy and make her whole with my kisses, but I don't know everything. The value of six lost years equals the weight of a clinical file. A report written on a few meager pages.

"Why did you bring me here, Damian?"

"I wanted to see if the old church still looked the same."

"You lived here?" She looks around as if she finds the notion impossible.

"Two blocks from here."

"Where?"

I point toward the ruins of the metal factory. "Right there. Next to that building."

"Don't you want to visit it, too?"

"I don't have to. I know it doesn't look the same."

I just kind of hoped the church would be an exception, would somehow have defied the sad, downward slide of the norm. Even devils like me need to believe in miracles, sometimes.

"What about your parents?" she asks. "Where are they now?"

I clench my jaw. "Dead."

A soft gasp falls from her lips. "How long ago did they pass away?"

I contemplate not telling her, but she *is* my wife. She has a right to know my family history. "My father died during my second year in prison. Tuberculosis. My mother followed the year after. Her system was too weak to fight a bad bout of flu." That's what happens when you're worn out from a life of too much work, and you can't afford a private medical aid that ensures proper healthcare.

"Damian," she exclaims, walking faster to keep up with my quickening steps. "I'm so sorry."

"Don't be. It's not as if they gave a fuck about me or my siblings."

"You have brothers or sisters?"

"Two brothers and a sister."

"What about them? Do they still live around here?"

"Don't know. My brothers are both older. They left home when I was still in school. Never heard from them again. The last I heard, my sister met a foreigner who whisked her off to Europe."

"Don't you want to get in touch?"

"What for? They made their choices. If they wanted to know how I am, they would've kept contact."

"But—"

"Not all families are happy, Lina, and not all children are pampered. Let it go."

"I'm sorry you weren't there for your parents, you know, when they..."

"Died."

"I'm sorry you were in prison instead of with them."

The apology strikes a cord, a deep-seated regret I'll never be able to make peace with. My voice is harsher than she deserves when I ask with sardonic humor, "Seen enough of the other side of the tracks?"

Tugging on my hand, she stops. "That's not what I meant when I asked why you brought me here. I meant why did you bring me here to see Harold?"

Facing her, I cup her jaw and flick my thumb over the spot where her cheek will so prettily indent when she's happy. "To show you there are worse fates than being my prisoner."

Lina

SINCE THE GARDEN INCIDENT, Zane avoids me even more than before. Damian keeps him busy, mostly running errands in town. Anne is looking for a job, which means circling newspaper ads on a deckchair next to the pool. Getting a job is a luxury she's allowed, a freedom. Why doesn't she grab it with both hands?

Russell is being Russell, hot and cold, nice and standoffish. I never know where I stand with him, but I trust him. He takes his job seriously, and he always addresses me respectfully.

Jana is worried she'll lose her job if I interfere with the cooking. To appease her, I stick to the tasks Damian assigned to me, which are menu planning and overseeing the transformation of the garden.

My universe is limited to this creaky old house with its Victorian towers and regular inhabitants. The staff from the cleaning service keep to themselves, rejecting my attempts at conversation. I can't wait to start my exercise program, driving lessons, and secret job next week, but I first have to survive a dinner party at the house tonight. It's business, and when Damian told me he invited his operations manager, I knew I was going to hate it. Fouché Ellis knows Harold from when I was in diapers. He may not know the gritty details of my history, but he knows what the world believes, namely that I married for money, drove my husband to suicide, and was locked up in a madhouse for bulimia, anorexia, and suicide tendencies. I can't say I don't care about what the rest of the world thinks of me, but they're people I don't know or have to face. Fouché is different. He's dined at Harold's house enough times to be considered as family, and the fact that I respect him makes it worse. I don't want to stand in front of his judgment tonight, knowing I'm a disappointment.

"It'll be fine." Damian stands behind me in his dressing room, facing the mirror. He kisses my cheek and drags his hands over the silk of the evening dress, stopping on my hips. "You look beautiful."

It's a blue dress with no sleeves. Damian's choice, of course.

"What are you afraid of?" he whispers in my ear.

"You know."

He traces a finger along my arm, the pad caressing the bumpy lines. "The people who'll be here all have scars. Worse ones. You just don't see them."

The longer I put this off, the longer I'm dragging out my apprehension. I take a breath and turn with determination. "Let's get this over with."

He blocks my way. "Not so fast. I'm not done."

"Done with what?"

"Turn around and bend over."

"Damian, no. We're already running late."

"I want you to remember who you belong to when you go down there."

I show him the enormous rock on my finger. "How can I forget?"

"A ring doesn't close a hole. Turn around."

"You're crass."

Gripping my waist, he twirls me around and pushes my upper body down with a palm. I have to grab onto the vanity counter to keep steady. Before I have time to get to my senses, he flips the skirt up and tears off my thong. I brace myself at the sound of his zipper and look at his reflection in the mirror. He's not undressing, just freeing his cock through his open fly. My period's been over since yesterday, and of course, Damian knows it. He spits in his palm and rubs it over my slit. No time for foreplay. No time to make sure I'm wet, although my eager body is already preparing itself for his invasion.

He places the head of his cock at my entrance and makes eye contact. He reads my face as he slams in, too full and stretching me too fast. Too deliciously. What does he see that makes him grip my hip harder? My expression is a mixture of painful ecstasy and unbearable pleasure. My eyes are unfocussed and my grimace something straight from a porn movie. I burn under his hands. I bite my lip to keep the sounds in. There are caterers downstairs. The sound will drift through the open door.

When he pulls out slowly and pushes back roughly, I choke out a moan. His face flushes with satisfaction. He covers my mouth with a broad palm and brings the other around to the front of my body, between my legs. Pivoting his hips, he pinches my clit and catches my whimpers. I break apart, crying out my climax in his hand as he flexes his ass and comes. While emptying himself inside me, he watches me, witnessing my weakness, my body's helpless surrender. When he's done, he pulls out and cleans himself with a tissue, finally allowing me to straighten on shaky legs.

As I take a step toward the bathroom, he catches my arm. "Don't clean up."

I gape at him. "I won't be able to sit."

"Yes, you will. You just won't be able to stand up, again."

"Damian."

"When my cum dribbles between your legs and dries on your thighs, remember who owns you."

I can only stare at him.

"Fix your lipstick," he says. "I smeared it all over your face."

Looking in the mirror, I see he's right. I wipe away the red traces and apply a fresh layer before brushing out my sex-ruffled hair. I'm already uncomfortable as I move to the door. His semen is running down my leg all the way to my evening shoe and I smell like sex. I just want this dinner to be over. The guests should be arriving any minute.

"There's something else," he says. "Come."

Over-conscious of my state under the dress, I follow him to the bedroom. He stops in front of the linen chest at the foot-end of the bed and pushes it aside with his foot. Oh, my God. There, underneath the rug he rolls up, is the trapdoor I've been looking for. He lifts it to reveal a safe with an old-fashioned turning knob. I know the type. Harold had one in his home office. I can't see the number sequence, because his back blocks my view, but I listen to the grating sound of the mechanism as it turns, and count the seconds. One. Three. Two.

Four. I memorize the sequence for what it's worth. My heart is in my throat. Everything I want may be hidden in that iron vault at the foot of his bed.

He carries a flat, velvet box toward me. Flipping the lid, he reveals a necklace of black diamonds. They're the latest rage. Duller than white diamonds, they sparkle with an understated shine. They're big, well cut, and perfectly set. Whoever made the necklace knew what he was doing.

"What do you think?" he asks.

"It's beautiful." Not as expensive as their white cousins, but I have enough experience to recognize priceless when I see it. The quantity and craftsmanship alone should put it on the market for a few million.

"They're from the mine."

"I thought the mine is dry."

"Not the bedrock."

"You found a deposit of black diamonds?"

"They're colored."

If they're colored, the diamonds must have a lower grade. "It's profitable?"

"Very. The yield is high, and colored black diamonds are gaining popularity by the day. The demand will soon be higher than the offer."

Very clever. If demand continues to rise, so will the value. "How did you know the bedrock is rich in deposits?"

"Always knew they were there. I was just biding my time."

To get out of jail. "Congratulations."

"It suits you."

"Me?"

"I had it made for you."

"For me?" I cover my collarbone with a palm where the diamonds would reach if they were draped around my neck. "Why?"

"You're my wife. Turn around."

I'm his wife. A showpiece for his guests. Suddenly, I understand why I'm showing off this particular necklace tonight. Damian is creating his own market. It's more than a business dinner. It's publicity, and I'm his advertising board.

He removes the necklace and chucks the box on the bed. "Turn around, Lina."

There's no point in arguing. Giving him my back, I lift my hair so he can hang the diamonds around my neck and fit the clasp.

"There." He brushes his lips over the arch of my neck. "Perfect. Like you."

"You haven't seen what it looks like on me."

"I don't need to."

Standing like this, with my back to his chest, I feel comfortable despite the situation and myself. Safe, almost. I don't have to hide my expressions or rely on my legs to carry me. I can lean on him while the weight of the necklace and the world pull me down.

"Now you're ready," he says, sounding pleased with himself. He offers me an arm. "Shall we?"

There's nothing left to do but take his arm and descend to the lounge where Zane and Anne are already mixing with our dinner guests. A new shift of guards came on duty, and for once, I miss Russell's reassuring presence. The scrawny man who showcased the diamonds for my ring is there with a redhead at his side. Damian introduces the couple as the man who designed the necklace, Tony, and his wife, Belinda, and then excuses us to greet his mining manager.

Before we're completely out of earshot, Belinda says to a blonde woman, "She's more nuts than they say. Tony said she refused to choose a diamond for her engagement ring. Have you ever heard anything like that?"

The blonde replies, "Oh, my God. I can't look at her arms. Hasn't she heard about skin grafts?"

There's not enough skin on my body for the grafts needed to fix my scars.

Damian squeezes my hand where it rests on his arm. "As I said," he says soft enough for only me to hear, "they have much uglier scars. Theirs are etched on their souls. It's called jealousy."

"Etched on their souls?" In an effort to hide my discomfort, I laugh. "Being poetic doesn't suit you."

229

"What can I say?" He flashes me a wolfish smile. "You're very..." His eyes drop to my crotch. "Inspiring."

His jest is playful and meant to put me at ease. It would've worked if he'd said something nice about my personality instead of making it sexual. It reminds me of what we are. We're physical. What we have is as dark, cold, and hard as the diamonds around my neck. My grandfather would've died before mining black diamonds. He would've said they're a sad substitute for the real thing. That's exactly what we are. A sad substitute for the real thing.

"You need a drink," Damian says.

I quickly wipe the grim look from my face, replacing it with a plastered-on smile. People are always observing, and I'm not putting my imperfect life on display.

"You all right?" he asks, handing me a glass of Chardonnay.

"Why wouldn't I be?"

"I know that look on your face."

"What look?"

"Brooding."

"I'm not brooding."

"Then what?"

"Nothing."

"You should know by now I don't settle for *nothing*." He gives me a warning lift of his eyebrow.

From across the room, Anne watches us, whispering to Zane.

"I'm just aware of being naked," I lie, "and what's dripping between my legs."

"So am I, angel," he says in a husky voice, assessing me with those dark eyes and letting me feel the static energy of his similarly dark intentions.

A waiter with a tray of hors-d'oeuvres saves me. I pop a bite-sized ricotta tart in my mouth, chewing but tasting nothing. At least, my full mouth prevents me from having to answer.

A young couple enters the lounge. The woman pushes a stroller, and the man carries a large diaper bag. Nadia Naidoo, a social butterfly and one of the most successful fashion columnists in the country, follows in their footsteps.

My feet automatically carry me to the couple with the stroller. A baby is wrapped up in blue blankets, his tiny porcelain face perfect as he blinks up at me. An overwhelming cauldron of emotions twists in my chest. Pain flashes through my heart, sharp and unforgiving, while endearment melts it. Yearning is a palpable taste in my mouth.

"I'm so sorry," the woman gushes. "Our regular babysitter cancelled at the last minute."

"That's no problem at all." Reaching out with so much longing my fingertips tingle, I ask, "May I hold him?"

"No," the woman cries before grabbing her baby and pressing him to her chest. "I mean... He's just eaten. He may burb on you." She's flustered, trying to make excuses for her instinctive reaction.

I lower my arms. What was I thinking? Which mother would let an insane woman with self-harming tendencies hold her baby?

Her husband steps up quickly. "If we can just find a quiet room to lay him down, please? We brought the monitor, so we'll hear him if he fusses."

It's hard to hide my feelings and regain my balance. "Of course. We'll use the reading room next door. He won't be disturbed there. I'll show you."

Damian watches me from across the room as I lead the couple to the hallway. His gaze is questioning, intent, and I drop my eyes so he won't see my secrets.

"What's his name?" I ask when I show them into the reading room.

"Davie," the woman says, still clutching him to her chest as if she's afraid I'll rip him away.

"Family name?"

"Yes," the father says, seeming proud.

I don't stress the young parents further with my presence but leave them to their privacy to get their baby settled. When I return, Nadia immediately corners me.

"Oh, my." She leans closer to admire the necklace. "That *is* a piece of art."

"Tony's creation," Damian says next to me.

She takes a smartphone from her evening bag. "May I? This deserves to be splashed all over social media."

"Of course," Damian says.

As if he senses my unease at being photographed, he rests his hand on my lower back, preventing me from stepping away.

Out of sorts about the reaction the incident with Davie has stirred, I smile stiffly.

Damian rubs his thumb over my spine. "Relax, angel," he whispers in my ear, planting a kiss in my neck.

A flash goes off. I blink as Nadia takes another photo.

"Perfect," she says with a satisfied smile as she regards the screen. "May I use this in the column?"

"Anywhere you like." Damian lets me go and steers her toward Tony. "Let me introduce you to the designer."

She digs in her heels. "One moment. I was wondering if you've seen this." She flips over her telephone screen and holds it up to Damian.

His expression darkens. "False allegations."

Her gaze darts to Anne. "Is that so?" Turning the screen to me, she asks, "What do you say, Lina, being newlywed, and all?"

It's a gossip column. There's a head-and-shoulder shot of Anne and one of Damian alongside. The subtitle reads, *Is Hart having an affair? Mine magnate's honeymoon didn't last long.*

Zane is there in a heartbeat, as if he knows what the conversation is about. "My sister denies those allegations."

Damian takes Nadia's arm and steers her to where a fiddling Tony waits. "This is Tony. I'm sure you have lots of questions for him." He says under his breath to Zane, "Deal with it," before jovially calling for more wine.

I inhale deeply and let the air expand in my lungs. It's a small moment of reprieve. I don't have time to dissect my emotions or battle the onslaught of so many hurtful sensations crammed into such a short space, because soon I'm surrounded by Fouché, his wife, and Belinda who all admire the necklace. It's awkward to be a mannequin for a showpiece, and I execute the role poorly, almost relieved when we at last take our places at the table.

Seated between Damian and Fouché, I endure the curious stares at my arms, the fake compliments, and the envious glances at the diamonds around my neck and on my finger. Fouché is kind enough to refrain from mentioning my turbulent past or Harold's downfall. Instead, he tells me about his admiration for Damian's vision and management policy. I've never been interested in the mine, but the facts he shares with me make me curious about the changes Damian has made.

When it's time for cognac to be served in the lounge, some of the guests follow Damian. With a stain on my dress, I have no choice but to remain seated. Fouché and his wife trickle away with the others, eventually leaving me alone with Belinda and Tony.

Belinda scoots closer. "I feel like I already know you. You're such an easy person to talk to." Gripping my fingers, she turns my hand to the light. "Tell me, did you really refuse an engagement ring?"

I give Tony a hard look, not that I can blame him for sharing the juicy piece of gossip. "I'm sure Tony told you all about it."

He turns red and suddenly finds the bottom of his wine glass very interesting.

"Why ever would you refuse?" Belinda asks. "Is it a humanitarian thing?"

She must've seen Blood Diamonds. She should know better than to base her assumption of the business on a movie.

"Yes." Let her think that or whatever she wants. The somber details of my life are not their entertainment.

"I admire you." There's not a drop of admiration in her voice. "I can't resist bling. So, how did Damian convince you to wear the ring?"

"Incentives."

"What?"

"He has the most effective incentives."

Tony coughs. "It's getting late. I think we should go."

Belinda launches into a long explanation of the family birthday party they're attending tomorrow, who's going to be there, and what they plan for lunch. It takes her twenty minutes to say goodbye, and then I'm alone in the dining room. Laughter comes from the lounge, accompanied with a waft of cigar smoke. Someone tells another joke. More laughter. No one will miss me if I sneak off to Damian's room. If I go through the kitchen, I can make it unnoticed. I'd hate for anyone to see the evidence of what Damian and I had been doing on my dress. Getting through the stares during dinner was humiliating enough.

Keeping my back to the wall, I make it to the entrance without being spotted, but my luck runs out on the staircase. I'm halfway up when Zane comes down. I glance at the double doors of the lounge. From this angle, no one can see us. The look on his face makes me tense. He drank too much during dinner. He looked at Damian a little too much, too. Anyone clever enough to pay attention would've discovered his secret.

When we reach each other, I try to dash past, but he grabs my wrist in a painful hold. The best defense is attack.

"They shouldn't be smoking," I say. "There's a baby next door. You're the *housekeeper*. Go tell them to smoke outside."

"The parents left with their baby as soon as Fouché lit up."

"How rude of him." I pull on his grip. "If you'll excuse me."

"Where do you think you're going?"

"That's none of your business."

He squeezes harder, hurting my bones. "You're the *hostess*. Go back down and see to your guests."

"You don't get to tell me what to do."

He inches closer, invading my personal space. "Don't believe you're suddenly something because you're wearing a diamond necklace. You're still Dami's whore."

"Let go."

He does, only to fold his fingers around my neck. It's a bold move. If someone exits the lounge, he'd be caught. I consider screaming, but he's squeezing too hard, cutting off my air and pressing the sharp little corners of the diamonds into my skin.

"This is what's going to happen," he grits out. "You're going to leave." He lets go with a shove.

Grabbing the rail to steady myself, I gasp for air.

He's not done. He twists my hair around his fist and yanks me closer. "What will it take to get you to leave? Huh? Tell me."

My scalp pricks. The pain makes my eyes water. "The evidence."

He narrows his eyes. "That's it? The evidence?"

"If I have the evidence, I'll be gone." He can have Damian all to himself.

His lip curls in one corner. "No money?" His gaze trails to my neck. "No diamonds?"

"I don't want Damian's money. Help me find the evidence, and you'll be rid of me once and for all."

"I don't think so." He shakes his head, pulling me closer by my hair and whispering in my ear, "Dami will find you. Then he'll kill you."

"I guess it's a chance I'll have to take."

Laughing softly, he lets go. "Don't mistake that kind of possessiveness for attachment. You're just the new toy, but like with all his toys, Dami will grow tired of you."

"Why would he want to keep me if he'll grow tired of me?"

"Dami doesn't like for anyone to have his second-hand toys. He likes to keep them locked up safely when he throws them away."

My throat constricts at *locked up*. "How come you know so much about how Damian plays with his toys?"

"I know how he operates. I've seen him in action."

It's not possible. Damian couldn't have slept with a woman in prison. Could he?

Zane laughs again. "Did you know they allow sex in prison these days? It reduces rape among cellmates."

I swallow, unable to get rid of the tightness in my throat. "Who?"

"Guess."

I can't, and I can. Oh, my God. "Anne?"

"Good guess, Mrs. Hart. Did you honestly think he lets her stay because you insisted? He's just keeping all his toys close."

When he lets me go, I take a shaky breath. I refuse to show him how much this information affects me. I didn't want to care, thought I wouldn't, but it's as if someone is pushing a thumb into a bruise on my skin. Damian owes me nothing. He could've fucked whomever he wanted in prison, but he could've told me his ex-lover is living with us. He made a fool out of me, and I'm naive enough not to have realized. Or maybe he did try to tell me, when he told me Anne is Zane's sister the day I asked her to stay, and I just didn't want to listen.

"Now," he says, "go back downstairs like a good little whore and take care of your goddamn guests. That's what Dami expects from you until you run away."

"Fuck you."

He reaches for me, but my expression must've stopped him.

I'm hurt, and I'm beyond caring who sees the semen on my dress. "If you touch me again, I'll scream." I'll scream the roof off. It's not the kind of attention I'd like to draw to myself, especially not now, but I'll do it.

Clenching his fist, he lowers his hand.

I use the opportunity to escape upstairs. It's not until I'm on the landing that I hear the voices coming from Damian's bedroom, his and a woman's. I slow my pace, my heart sloshing around in my chest. I'm almost at the door when Anne exits, her hair messy and her cheeks red. When she sees me, she irons out the wrinkles in her dress and gives me a sweet smile before darting pass.

CHAPTER 15

Damian

*A*t the sight of my wife, I stop dead. "Lina."

She's standing on the landing just outside our bedroom door. Her face is ashen and her big eyes a fraction too wide.

"What are you doing?" I reach for her, but she pulls back.

"What are *you* doing?"

Is that an accusation in her voice? Could my unwilling little wife be jealous? She saw Anne leave our room. No doubt about that.

I lift the shawl to show her. It's a long one that would fall to her knees. "I came to get you this so you could get up from the table, but I see you managed just fine."

Yanking the shawl from my hand, she walks past me. "Too little, too late, but thanks for your concern, anyway."

I let her escape into our room. This is a conversation we're having in private. I follow and shut the door. There are too many ears around, tonight.

At the sound of the click, she flings around. Her eyes turn wider, and her chest heaves with fast, little breaths.

"It's not locked," I say in a placating tone. "The door is only closed for privacy."

"Get out."

"This is my room, too."

She grips her hair and tries to barge past me. "What am I saying? This *is* your room. Stay. I'll find another."

I take hold of her arm. "*Our* room, and like hell you'll find another."

"Let go."

"Calm down."

"I am calm."

"You're not."

She makes a visible effort to control herself, breathing in and out slowly.

"That's better. Deep breaths." I let go, ready to grab her if she tries to flee again. This isn't claustrophobia. It's something else, and it makes a huge red flag pop up in my mind. I've been ignoring this for long enough. I'm done giving her slack.

"Why are you afraid of closed doors, Lina?"

"Why didn't you tell me Anne is your mistress?"

"For the obvious reason that she's not."

"I saw her. You. Coming out of here."

"It's not what it seems like."

She huffs. "You know what? You don't owe me an explanation."

I catch her wrist when she tries to slide past me again. "Yes, I do. I'm your husband."

"Oh, come on. It's not like we married for love or promised to be faithful."

Wrong thing to say. The gentleness the situation requires vanishes as the patience I set out with snaps. Despite the inner voice of my reason, I slam her body against the wall, hearing the little humph as her breath leaves her.

"You're wrong on that one, *wife*. You promised faithful along with your obedience, body, and affection the day you said your vows in a black dress."

She stares at me with her pretty blue eyes, her anger gone and caution in its place. "Affection can't be forced."

"Obedience can." Wrapping my hand around her neck, I let my thumb rest on the frantic pulse of her jugular vein. "Maybe I haven't been clear enough. Let me spell it out for you. If you touch another man, he's dead. How's that for communication?"

"I didn't take you for a hypocrite."

"I didn't touch Anne. I came upstairs to fetch you a shawl. She followed me. She made a pass at me. Yes, she tried to kiss me. I said no. End of story."

"I don't care," she whispers, averting her eyes.

"You do."

She refuses to look at me. My wife is every bit as possessive as I am, and my chest glows warm with satisfaction, enough to calm me. Lina may not love me, but she doesn't want to share me. I stroke my thumb up and down the arch of her neck. She's so breakable, so small.

"You're the one who asked her to stay," I remind her gently. "Say the word, and she's gone."

Her gaze lifts back to mine. "You didn't tell me you fucked her."

"I never did."

Her brow wrinkles. "I thought she was your girlfriend in prison."

"Why would you think that?"

"That's what Zane said."

The muscles in my face tighten. I feel it in the pull around my eyes and the strain in my jaw. "What exactly did he say?"

"That sex is allowed in prison."

"That's true. Husbands and boyfriends get to sleep with their partners, and prostitutes are brought in for the rest. Doesn't mean I hooked up with anyone."

"Why wouldn't you? Six years is a long time."

Tracing her stubborn chin, I give her the truth. "I was waiting for someone special."

She looks away again. "I'm not special."

Gripping her chin, I force her to face me. "I waited six years for you, Lina. Six long fucking years."

239

Uncertainty plays in her eyes as she searches mine. "Why?"

"I always get what I want, especially when someone tells me I can't have it."

"Ah." She nods. "It's the chase."

"The chase and so much more."

She doesn't ask about the more. Thank God. I don't know if I can explain it, if I want to explain it. How does one put obsession in words? How do I look her in the eyes and confess that I'll hunt her to the end of her days? I'll never set her free from our vows, and maybe it's better I don't admit that, right now. Maybe it's better I don't spell out another truth. One is enough for tonight. It's not like she doesn't know this is her prison. All I can say to make it better, is, "I'll give you everything in my power to make you happy."

Biting her lip, she considers the statement. It's not new. I made it not so long ago. I meant it then and I mean it now.

"Just give me this, Lina. I'm not asking for more."

"Give you what?" she asks softly.

"Take what I'm offering. Try to be happy."

She stares at me for a long time. Just when I think she's going to turn me away, she drags her fingers through my hair and pulls me down. The kiss knocks me sideways. I anticipated more resistance, more fighting the attraction, but she takes what I offer and gives me her mouth. She hikes up her skirt and wraps her sex-drenched thighs around me, grinding her pussy on my dick and making me crazy. Bracing my palms next to her face, I hold back as much as I can. The moment is too sweet. I will not bulldoze over it with my overeager cock.

I give her space when she reaches for my belt. I let her take out my cock and pump it in her fist until I hiss. I support her ass when she slides her pussy over the length of my rock-hard shaft. I take nothing more than what she gives. I let her ride me, go with her rhythm, and let her chase her own release. I watch as she rubs her clit and obliges when she tells me to move. I drive a little deeper, a little harder, and watch her come.

It's raw and beautiful. It's fragile. It's our pact, our give and take, although I'm not sure who's on the giving or receiving end. It's entangled—our limbs, our tongues, our breaths, our pleasure. Our vows. For as long as I live, I'll strive to make her happy. All she has to do is stay. She belongs to me. It's inevitable. It has always been a given.

Spearing my fingers through the roots of her hair, I pull back her head and force her to focus. "Don't try to escape, Lina. Ever." My cock is still buried deep inside her. We haven't caught our breaths yet, but a dark force drives me to say this, to be sure she understands. "I'll always find you."

Soberly, she stares at me. "How does our story go when you find me?"

"I'll make you pay, and then I'll make you happy."

Like a vicious circle. Like an infinity sign. No beginning, no end. Just me chasing, me catching, and me pleasing. As long as it takes. I'm committed to forever.

She lowers one leg to find her footing. My cock slips from her pussy and cum runs down the inside of her thigh over the dried traces of earlier. Her hair is a mess, and her dress is stained. Mascara is smeared under her eyes. Her lips are swollen from my kisses, and her neck is red from my stubble. It'll take more than a brush and a tube of lipstick to hide what we've done.

"I have to get back to our guests," I say with more regret than she'll ever know. "Want to come?"

I already know what her answer will be, but it's important that I give her a choice. Small freedoms are integral in the absence of a big freedom. It keeps a person sane. Ask me. I know that from prison. It's the books, the laptop, the correspondence degree, and the freedom of plotting my revenge that kept me whole.

She shakes her head.

"I'll try to get rid of them quickly," I promise.

"Take your time. I'm going for a shower."

I kiss her hand, reminding her no matter how hard and dirty I fuck her, I always remember she's a lady. "I'll offer your excuse."

"What will you say?"

It matters to her. She wouldn't have asked otherwise.

"The truth," I say. "That you're tired."

She nods. "Thank you."

Cupping her breast, I steal a caress before returning to duty, to the people who drink and laugh in my house as if they're my friends.

Lina

THIS IS HARDER than I remember. My breathing is heavy, and my lungs burn as I work up a sweat on the treadmill. Phillip, or Phil as he asked me to call him, is at my side, counting down and uttering every clichéd encouragement in the book.

"Almost there. You've got this. You're your only limit. No pain, no gain."

If my collapsing lungs would let me speak, I'd tell him to shut up.

Damian is sitting on the sofa in the lounge area, reading a newspaper. He's dressed in a suit and Italian shoes. A Rolex peaks out from under his shirtsleeve. He's wearing black diamond cufflinks and his wedding ring. Despite the ring, the girls on the treadmills next to me stare. Drool is a better word. His attire screams money. In Harold's circles, men would never be seen with the shoes, watch, and cufflinks. A good suit and shoes would've been enough. Anything more and you show the world you're used to nothing. New money. Money is definitely rolling in for Damian.

Damian's black diamonds are so much in demand the mine can't keep up the supply. There's no doubt Tony's fine work with the necklace put the black diamonds on the map. From the minute the photo of the necklace went viral, the price of colored black diamonds shot up around the world. How does Harold feel about Damian's success? People who come from Old Money don't respect New Money. That's what Harold used to say. What's he saying now that he can't afford more than a bachelor flat in one of the poorest suburbs of town? It's no coincidence he ended up there, of all places. Damian sent him there when he couldn't find an affordable place elsewhere.

Zane told me. It's Damian's way of taking revenge by reversing the roles.

The brunette next to me steals another look at my husband. With his dark hair neatly combed and his face clean-shaven, he looks like a respectable businessman. He's easily the most handsome man I've seen. Nicest smelling, too. He drips of maleness and virility. Resting an ankle on his knee, he seems absorbed in the article he's reading. His casual posture may fool the girls into thinking they can gawk unnoticed, but he doesn't deceive me. He's aware of everything that happens around him.

When Phil touches my arm again, rambling about mind over muscles, Damian lifts his gaze to us. It's brooding and dark enough to make Phil retract his hand. Inwardly, I roll my eyes. Damian insisted on accompanying me. He refused to let Russell bring me. Now I know why. It's so he can wrestle Phil with killer looks.

When the hour-long training is done, I wipe my face on a towel and walk to where my husband sits innocently. He lowers the newspaper and watches me with so much sexual intent my cheeks heat.

"Do I have time for a shower?"

He's already wasted an hour of his time, plus the time it took him to drive me here. I'm sure he has better things to do.

"I'll wait," he says.

I cock my hip a little, giving him attitude just because people surround us, and I can. "Is this going to be a regular thing?"

He narrows his eyes. "You know how I feel about *nothings* and *things*. Express yourself correctly."

"Are you going to sit here every time I work out?"

"Yes."

"Why?"

"Does it bother you?"

"I hate wasting your time."

His gaze trails over me. "It's no waste of time."

"Why don't you just work out at the same time?"

"If I work out, I won't be able to watch you."

He says it darkly, deeply, and my lower region contracts at his tone. I'm not sure if he means watching as in enjoying the view or as in making sure I don't escape, but it's wicked and hot and unfair, and it tightens my nipples.

Grabbing my towel, he flicks my butt. "Ten minutes. I'll wait outside the showers."

I bet he will.

I go ahead while he gathers his newspaper. A pretty girl passes me on the stairs.

"You're so lucky," she says with a sigh, looking back toward Damian.

If only she knew.

A part of me wants to agree, though, and that scares me. I can't get attached to him. I can't settle for spoiled captive. I'd rather be poor and free.

~

Damian

IT TAKES me another day before I finally find the time to visit Willow-brook. It's just over an hour's drive southeast. The private institution is situated on an acre of land, a far enough distance from the nearest town to make running away improbable. Escaping would have to be on foot. No busses service the town that's not even mentioned on a map, and Uber is non-existent out here.

I announce myself at the modest but well-secured gate. There are cameras, barbwire, and an electrified wire warning sign. An armed guard exits a guard post on the inside of the property after checking the appointment schedule. He uses a pedestrian gate to meet me. After he searches the car and pats me down, he opens the gates and waves me through.

The house is a three-story, modern building with narrow windows. They're not barred, but a body can't fit through them. Precaution against suicide and escape, I assume.

I park in the guest lot at the front and ring the bell at the entrance.

The double doors open to reveal a short woman in a white uniform with a broad smile.

"Mr. Botha," she says, shaking my hand. "What a pleasure. Please follow me."

When I made an enquiry, there was a questionnaire as well as a list of required documents, one of those being a salary slip. I guess my monthly income is the reason for the warm welcome.

The nurse doesn't introduce herself but walks me through an entrance resembling an art gallery. It's contemporary, colorful, and acoustic. Our steps echo up a marble staircase. Expensive. Cold. The space smells like toilet flowers, the kind that comes from a canister.

"The dining room, laundry, and kitchen are downstairs," the nurse explains. She stops in front of the first door. "This is Dr. Dickenson's office. Tea? Coffee?"

"No, thanks."

"Something stronger?"

It's ten in the morning. "I'm good."

Her nod is no-nonsense and professional. She opens the door and walks away.

Dr. Dickenson gets to his feet when I enter. His gaze is attentive and his handshake strong. "Please, sit down."

When we've taken a velvet sofa facing a chrome coffee table, Dr. Dickenson gets straight to business. "Tell me more about your wife."

"Privacy is my priority."

"We're all about integrity at Willowbrook, Mr. Botha. Our staff signs confidentiality agreements. How did you say you heard about us, again?"

I didn't. I left that part of the questionnaire blank. They operate strictly by word-of-mouth. There's nothing about Willowbrook in the media or online.

"Harold Dalton," I say. "He submitted his daughter for a year."

I couldn't risk them calling Dalton and asking questions about my false persona. They would've checked me out before our appointment —credit history, criminal records, and the like—and found the history one of my old cellmates created for Ben Botha. Wealthy, ruthless. All true, down to unscrupulous. A wife with a big inheritance. A business in trouble. The last part is untrue, but one quickly gets the picture.

Dickenson rubs his chin. "Ah, yes. Lina Dalton-Clarke. She was indeed a patient." He puts on a polite act of interest. "How is she doing?"

"I wouldn't know. I haven't met her. Dalton and I were business partners. We didn't socialize outside of work."

"Terrible what happened to Harold," he says.

"Mismanagement and fraud."

"Indeed."

He seems to say *indeed* a lot. "Dalton was happy with your service."

"That's always good to hear." He gives me a close-lipped smile. "You said on your questionnaire your wife suffers from dementia."

I put out my first piece of bait. "That'll need to be *clinically confirmed.*"

"Of course. We have a fulltime psychiatrist on board."

My second piece of bait is more direct. "For how long can you offer treatment? I was thinking two years."

"You must understand an establishment with our reputation is in high demand."

"Can you do it or not?"

"We are fairly booked up, but anything is possible if you can afford it, Mr. Botha."

"I don't want her to suffer unnecessarily."

"That can be arranged." He crosses his legs. "If you have no objections to drugs, we can go that route." He says it like no objection is a given. "The patients tend to suffer less when they're sedated."

"What's the alternative?"

"Isolation."

"Is that really necessary?"

"Some patients get disruptive. It's in the best interest of the other patients."

"Drugged or isolated." I drum my fingers on the armrest. "What if they don't put up a fight?"

He smiles. "They all do, Mr. Botha."

He says Mr. Botha a lot, too. I already feel like breaking his neck. It takes everything I have and more to return his smile.

He stands. "Shall we take a tour?"

"Gladly."

We go through the hallway. There are doors on both sides, and each door is fitted with a window. There's an old woman in the first room. She sits on a bed and stares at a television. The second room looks the same. Its inhabitant is a teenager with his nose pressed up against the window, looking zonked out.

I stop at the third one. A man is spread-eagled and strapped to a bed. The room is bare and white. Except for that bed, there's no furniture. His eyes are closed, but he's not sleeping. He's twitching and jerking.

I barely swallow my rage. "What's wrong with him?"

"Let's just say he's not being cooperative," the doctor says behind me.

This is worse than prison. In my cell I had books, access to study materials, a laptop, music, my own private toilet, and whores once a week, if I desired. These people are innocent, their freedom not stripped by bars but by a certificate that declares them insane.

"Which one was Lina's room?"

"We move them around as their needs demand." The doctor tilts his head. "Why do you ask?"

"I was just wondering. Was she a good patient?"

"That information is confidential. As you know, we don't discuss our patients. You'll have to ask Mr. Dalton how his daughter adapted."

It was worth a try.

We follow the hallway to the end. There are more isolation rooms than the poorly furnished rooms Dickenson calls private suits. On the top level is a bathroom with a row of open showers and toilet stalls. No privacy. For security and safety reasons, the doctor says. The psychiatrist and nurses' offices are at the end.

According to the good doctor, the food is high quality, the hygiene A-plus, and the weekly exercise compulsory, except in the case of *special requests*. In other words, it's an unethical house under the disguise of mental institution where rich people can lock up and forget about the family they can't kill. Dickenson and his staff are paid not to heal, but to bury people alive.

"Don't you want to see the dining room?" Dickenson asks when I announce I'll take my leave.

"I've seen enough."

Misunderstanding, he smiles. "We look forward to seeing your wife soon."

For the amount they charge, his eagerness is understandable.

The nurse sees me out. I can't get through the gates fast enough. I imagine Lina in one of those rooms, locked up and alone. Strapped down on a bed. The mental image alone is enough to make me want to murder the lot in cold blood.

This place is going down. Not today. Not tomorrow. Soon, though. I'll need to gather ammunition, first.

In too much of a state to go to the office, I drive home. Russell is posted at the door. I give him a tight nod and tear at the knot of my tie. My jacket feels too hot. I want to get out of these clothes stained with the stench of contemporary madness and artificial flowers.

Contrary to Willowbrook, my steps are cushioned on the carpet. My house is not white and cold, but its velvet curtains and wood-paneled walls are equally depressing. It's not a home created over years with memories. Lina had no choice in it. It's just a place I'd bought in a hurry to give an unwilling bride a roof over her head. That's going to change. Starting tomorrow, Lina is house hunting. Suddenly eager to see her, I push our bedroom door wide open and freeze. The linen chest is moved to the side and the carpet rolled up. Lina kneels in front of the safe, her night-blue eyes wide and guilty.

CHAPTER 16

Lina

"What are you doing?" Damian asks.

He can see for himself, but he wants a confession.

On my knees, I give it to him. "I'm trying to open the safe."

"What are you hoping to find in there?"

"You didn't put the necklace away." It's weak and a lie, and he knows it.

Unknotting his tie, he throws it on the bed. "What are you looking for?" The line of his jaw tightens. "Don't tell me another lie and make me have to ask again."

The darkness in his eyes scares me, but I can't look away from their hypnotizing depths. Even in anger, maybe especially in anger, they're magnificent, like the black diamonds he mines.

"I'm waiting, Lina."

There's no point in denying what he already knows. "The evidence."

He removes a cufflink and puts it on the table by the fireplace. Clink. The other cufflink drops.

He rolls back first one, then the other sleeve. "What are you planning on doing with the evidence?"

His calmness of voice doesn't fool me. His anger is like the branch of a willow tree, bent so far, it's ready to snap.

Walking to me, he gently pets my hair where I kneel on the floor. He smells of citrus and man, of winter and coldness. "I asked you a question."

I tremble under the caress. "I need it." If only Zane had agreed to help me, I wouldn't be in this position. Damn Zane. Damn Damian for coming home early.

"Why do you need it?"

"I can't say."

How can I tell him the awful truth without going to pieces, without going to prison, and without ever finding closure? If I tell him, Harold will never give me what I want. Harold is an accomplice. It's our sordid, deadly secret, and for the first time I wish it never was. I wish I'd been caught and incarcerated, but I hadn't, and I still have a shot at freedom. Or maybe not.

He offers me a hand. "Get up."

Taking it is a sentence, but I don't have a choice. I place my fate in his broad palm. He's stronger. No one is going to help me. There's nowhere to run.

"Undress."

"What are you going to do?" I'll be stronger if I'm prepared for what he plans.

"Undress."

I pull off my shoes and dress and kick them away. The door is open. It's the only thing that gives me hope. If he was going to torture me, he would've closed it. He's going to punish me, but he won't cut off my finger. I haven't stolen anything. Yet. Surely, he won't treat actions and intentions the same?

He takes a coil of rope from the bedside table drawer. "Everything."

Having me naked is his way of making me vulnerable. I won't give him that. It's just a body. He's seen it enough times. This is what I repeat in my head as I take off my bra and panties.

He walks back to the foot-end of the bed and points at the space in front of him. "Come over here."

When I'm positioned, he ties my wrists together and strings me up by the top bar of the four-poster bed, facing the headboard, until my toes barely touch the floor. My arms are already aching and my leg muscles taking strain, especially after this morning's brutal workout.

"Last chance," he says behind me. "Why do you need the evidence?"

Biting my lip, I shake my head.

"Very well." He drags a finger down my spine. "I gave you a choice. Remember that."

His touch disappears. His footsteps are muffled on the carpet, only audible on the slab of marble on the step.

He gave me a choice, but there isn't one. He offered me a gilded cage and dangled all its pretty glory under my nose with a request to try and be happy. He gave me a choice to answer, but the truth is mine to hold, mine and mine alone. Damn him to hell if he's going to punish me for that.

A sound at the door alarms me of his return. I strain to look over my shoulder and freeze. Damian closes the door. Firmly and irrevocably. He doesn't turn the key, but the click is in place. In his hand, he carries a whip. It has several straps knotted at the ends. I start to tremble when he approaches, not only from the sight of the whip but also from the fear of the closed door tearing through me. The way the manly veins bulge in his forearms and the dark hair that coats his skin, these are the details that imprint on my mind. His maleness. His superior strength. But only in the physical sense. I'm stronger in spirit. I will *not* break.

He massages my shoulders gently, working his way down my spine to my lower back. He kneads and prepares me while I battle to breathe through my fear.

I'm stronger. I'm stronger.

The heat of his body is replaced with a rush of cool air. His touch disappears.

I'm stronger. I'm stronger.

A whoosh races through the air before a firework of pain explodes on my back. The agony hits me in too many places at once for my brain to process. I'm a shambled mess of cross-wired messages. My neurons go haywire. My skin is on fire, and my flesh aches, but I'm not sure which one of the many intricate pains I feel is worse.

"Why do you need the evidence, Lina?"

I'm stronger. "I can't tell."

I hear it. I feel the air move, but I'm not ready for that pain when it crashes down on me again. It's everywhere—my shoulders, back, buttocks. A flash of fire curls around my side. Another hits the curve of my breast. My thighs. It's happening too fast and too slow. My legs give out and my arms stretch painfully above me.

"Why, Lina?"

With the next lash, I give up on keeping the sounds in. A wail leaves my chest and bubbles in an ugly sound over my lips.

"I told you not to try and escape."

The swing of his arm is rhythmic now, but the many straps fall too haphazardly. I can't predict the paths of the pain. The sting penetrates my butt and thighs, and the burn lingers deep under my skin. It stays like a resonating sound, its music continuing as Damian makes new notes and different scores on my back and my legs.

"Why?"

I nearly faint with the next blow. I've forgotten my mantra. All my energy, all of my being is focused on surviving the pain, on dealing with the sensory onslaught.

"Why?"

The same question, over and over. I don't know which blows are new and which are old. New and old blurs, until there's only lasting pain. Horrible pain.

"Damn you, Lina! Why?"

"I-I can't."

I sob. I scream. I cry. I shake. I just want to die, but *I'm stronger.*

"Why?"

I can't tell. I don't *want* to tell. It's too hurtful. Too shameful. Too private. Too devastating. Who the hell is he to demand these corners of my soul? It took me a year to breathe without breaking down, a year to sleep without waking from the pain of the part that's been ripped out of me. This is a missing part of *my* body, *my* heart, *my* mind. It's not his to share.

"It's none of your fucking business," I scream at the top of my lungs, anger and agony mixing together. "Fuck you! I'm stronger."

He lets it rain down on me. It comes from everywhere. There's a fire under my skin, in my body, in my throat, and in my eyes. I'm consumed by flames. My arms are being torn from my body. I'm not so strong, after all.

"Why? Say it." He's out of breath. "Make it stop."

My head drops back. The whip flies past my cheek, barely missing. Or maybe it's just the sound. Everything sounds closer, deeper, further, darker.

"Say it." He's lost his coolness, his utter control. His voice is angrier than the whip. "Say it's to buy your no-good father's freedom. Say it's because you hate me. Say it's because you need your overrated freedom."

Isn't there a point where the pain is supposed to start feeling good? Isn't there a point where my brain is supposed to start fooling me with endorphins?

He gives himself free reign, this time not speaking, not giving me a reprieve to drag in air, not killing me to be kinder.

I'm not so strong, and I hate myself for it.

"Why?"

"For my baby!"

For my baby. I wail and sob and hurt, not for him, but for my baby. My sweet, dear, innocent baby. The pain he gives me is not enough to smother this bigger pain, the one I'd buried so well after so long. There's no physical pain in the world that can make me forget, and for the very first time in my life I truly wish I were dead.

"Lina, fuck. What did you say?"

He's on me, behind me, I don't know. I don't care. I'm not so strong.

I'm drifting.

I'm gone.

CHAPTER 17

Damian

The door crashes into the wall. Russell enters. I jerk the throw from the bed and cover Lina's body before grabbing her around the waist, taking the strain off her arms.

Russell stares.

"What the fuck do you want?"

He drags a hand through his hair without moving his eyes away from Lina's unconscious form. "I came inside for a glass of water. Heard screaming."

"Get out."

"No." He braces his hands on the doorframe as if he needs to keep up the walls, as if the room is going to collapse around us. "I didn't sign up for this."

"Hand in your resignation tomorrow morning. You're dismissed."

Fuck. She passed out. She had this. I was sure of her limits.

"I'm taking her to a hospital."

"She doesn't need a hospital." She needs *me*.

"Mr. Hart, you're not thinking rationally."

Damn wrong. I've never been more rational. "My wife is naked. I

254

need to tend to her. If you get as much as a glimpse at her body, I'll have to kill you. For the last time, get the fuck out."

He hovers, rolls on the balls of his feet, and punches the wall. "You need to take care of that." He points at a red welt on her naked shoulder. "I'm leaving for Lina, not for you."

He cares for her. I knew it. I let it carry on for too long, but he's a damn good bodyguard. I understand his reaction. He's never seen a woman whipped, but he trusts me with her life, or he wouldn't bang the door shut and let me hear his footsteps fall down the tiled strip before the carpet swallows the sounds.

As if one intrusion wasn't enough, the door opens again. This time, it's Zane.

He looks from me to Lina. "Fuck, Dami. What have you done?"

"Bring a knife. Cut her loose." It'll take too long to untie her.

"Damn you, Damian."

I know how upset he is by using my full name. He takes a utility knife from his pocket and starts sawing at the ropes. The threads come undone, one by one. When the last one snaps, her arms fall limp.

Keeping the throw around her, I lower her onto the bed.

"Fuck, Damian." Zane paces up and down. "Fuck, fuck."

"Leave us."

"I don't think that's a good idea."

"I said fucking leave us."

"Shall I get tea? Sugar water? A doctor?"

"It looks worse than it is." She had this, dammit. I wasn't pushing her beyond her limits.

"Shall I get Anne?"

"If you don't get out now, you can bring me my gun. I'll put a bullet in your kneecap. Will that help you understand?"

"Fine." He holds up his hands. "I'm going." He retreats to the door. "I'm going."

The door closes for a second time, at last giving me the privacy I need. I pull the throw from Lina's body. She's lying on her back. Not ideal, but I'll turn her soon enough. I make quick work of studying the color of her lips and nails. Blushing pink. Her breathing is even and strong.

Gently, I slap her cheek. "Come back, Lina."

Her eyelashes flutter.

Another slap. "Wake up, baby. Look at me."

She comes back with a gasp. Her eyes fly open and her mouth forms an O.

"Easy." With a hand curled around her nape, I help her sit up and give her the bottle of water from my nightstand. "Drink."

She takes a sip and flinches. She groans. She cries. "Why did you wake me up? I was good where I was."

"Drink more."

"Not thirsty."

"Try. You need to hydrate."

"Hurts."

"I know."

She manages a few more sips before I roll her onto her stomach and fetch an anesthetic cream from the bathroom. When I put a blob on my palm and reach for her, she says through gritted teeth, "Don't touch me."

"I need to rub this into you."

"Get Anne or Jana."

"It's me you're stuck with. Take it or leave it."

She winces. Her pride takes a knock, but her pain won't let her decline the promised relief of the medicine. I rub it over her back, ass, and thighs. She's a portrait of red welts, and a couple of spots where the knots have left small bruises, but no skin is broken.

"I hate you," she mumbles when I recap the tube, tears dripping from the corners of her eyes onto the pillow.

"I'm sorry you feel that way. I'd rather we get on."

"Go to hell."

I smile. Ruined, but far from broken. That's my girl. That's the woman I sensed in the library. Strong. Resilient.

"You should've just beaten me to death," she says, staring non-seeing at the far wall.

I chuckle. "It'll take a lot more to beat a person to death. Your brain cut out. It's a normal reaction to an overload of sensory stimulation."

"Pain, you mean."

"Yes, pain in this instance. You chose, Lina. I told you, it's always in your hands."

"I didn't choose *this*. I didn't choose *you*." Her voice rises steadily. "I didn't choose—" She grapples for words like a fish would grapple for air. "I didn't choose *any of this*."

"Shh." I sit down on the edge of the bed and stroke her hair. "You need to save your energy to recover. It won't help to get upset."

"I *am* upset. I'm not a doll with a button you can push to control my moods."

"I'm very aware of the fact that you're not a doll." I drag a palm up her inner thigh to the junction of her legs. She's dry. This kind of pain doesn't turn her on. Sad as it is, wrong and depraved, her pain makes me hard, and I'm not going to apologize for it. This is who I am. She made me, together with Dalton, and this is what she gets.

"Don't touch me," she says, but she doesn't push my hand away when my fingers probe and play, teasing her clit to make her slick.

"You need this, believe me."

"I need nothing from you."

"You disobeyed me. I punished you. Now I'm going to please you."

"I don't want you to please me."

I slide a finger inside, slow and easy. She's already wet. She gasps. Her back bows.

"Tell me this doesn't feel good," I challenge with a few shallow pumps.

She cries out. I go faster. Her whole body pulls tight.

"You get to choose. Tongue, fingers, or cock."

"Nothing," she moans into the pillow.

"Bad girl." I smack her ass.

She yelps.

"You know how I feel about nothing."

"Damian, please."

"Please what?"

"Just let me hate you."

"As much as you want. You have my permission. You also have my permission to come as hard as you like, whenever you're ready."

"I'm not a sex slave who comes on demand."

Enough of the defiance. "If you won't choose, I'll choose for you."

Spreading her legs, I kneel between them. She hisses when I trace a welt on her ass with my tongue.

Burying my face between her legs, I say, "Oral it'll be."

It's not that I'm worried about getting her pregnant. On the contrary, tying her to me in blood is an excellent idea. There's nothing I would've liked more than to sink my dick into her and make her come several times on my cock, but I'm too close to breaking. I don't want to be rough with her. I want to be sweet, gentle, and slow until her pussy clenches and she utters that little distressed sound when she comes.

The effect of the cream should be kicking in by now. Most of the pain should be gone, enough for her to focus on the tongue I bury deep in her pussy. She squirms, rubbing her thighs over my cheeks. I give a gently bite to remind her to keep still. Using my thumbs, I peel her soaked lips open and eat her out like a fruit, like a beautiful, bruised fruit. That's what she tastes like. Her arousal is strong, her honey plentiful. Her senses are heightened. She'll feel the orgasm all the way to her toes.

It's over quickly, but the intensity of her release leaves her heaving and panting. Bending her arm, she puts her head in the crook and hides her face from me. It's only late morning, but I undress and lie down next to her.

Gripping her hair, I turn her face to the side. She watches me with her cheek on her arm, her eyes dripping tears and her lips set in a defiant line.

"Don't try this again, Lina. It'll never end well for you."

"You're a monster."

"Even monsters can be kind if you give them reason to be."

She closes her eyes. She's exhausted, but we're not done.

"Look at me."

She lifts her honey eyelashes slowly. "You wanted me to know where the safe is. That's why you let me see when you removed the necklace." Bitterly, she adds, "It was a test."

"Now it's a lesson." I kiss her nose. "Tired?"

"Yes," she says from the cushion of her arm, so pretty and so wronged.

"We're almost done, then you can rest."

Alarm flitters into her eyes. "Are you going to cut off my finger?"

Is she joking? "I'll never mutilate you, no matter what you do."

Her torso deflates, as if she's blowing out a breath. She's a million shades of sex appeal, but right now she's the cutest woman I know.

"It still hurts," she complains.

"What baby, Lina?"

She blinks. "What?"

"You said you need those papers for your baby. What baby?"

"It's noth—I mean I don't even know what I was saying. You were whipping me so hard. I was probably hallucinating."

Right. I'll let it slide for now. "Next time you pull a stunt like that, I'll break skin. Understand?"

"Yes," she says on a broken whisper.

It hurts me, that little whisper. I'm still hard for her, but not for her pain. Not the emotional kind. It says a lot. I'm not hiding my head in my elbow. I see the truth for what it is. I've always been lusting after Lina, but my feelings for her are growing stronger, overshadowing the physical. Needing to escape my thoughts, I go to the bathroom to fetch painkillers and take enough time to get my mask back in place. I feed her two pills with more water and watch over her until she falls asleep.

I make sure the room temperature is comfortable so I don't have to cover her. After dressing, I head downstairs to tell Jana Lina is unwell and won't come down for lunch. I instruct her to prepare a tray for Zane to deliver. Then I call the agency and get a new man—their best after Russell—for Lina. When he arrives, I brief him before going in search of Zane. I find him and Anne at the pool. Anne avoids looking at me. Zane appears wounded, as if I whipped him instead of Lina.

"She's sleeping," I say. "Jana will prepare her a tray. Take it up at lunchtime. Call me the minute she wakes."

I expect him to say something lame like not being a babysitter, but he nods.

"Sure thing, Dami."

"I'll be back after lunch to check on her."

I'm about to add that I have hidden cameras in every room of the house but bite my tongue. I may not trust Lina, but she won't tell a lie without good reason. It's time to find out if Zane is still on my side.

It takes an hour to drive to Brixton. Dalton doesn't act surprised to see me. He lets me see myself in and takes the only seat. It suits me. I'd rather not sit on the greasy sofa.

"I've been to Willowbrook."

His expression gives nothing away. "Sending her back already? Is she becoming a burden?"

"Why did you send her there?"

He props a foot on the coffee table. His toenails are yellow and in need of a cut. "She needed help."

I kick his foot away. Didn't his mother teach him manners? "Help as in drugs and isolation?"

"She tried to kill herself."

"Yeah, by jumping out of a window and going on a hunger strike. I read the report. The thing is, she doesn't seem like someone who'll starve or jump. Neither does she like being locked in, as she supposedly did to herself."

"What's your point?" he asks with an oily smile.

He reminds me of an eel, slippery and hard to nail.

"There's more to the story. Tell me about her baby."

It's the magic words. He goes stiff and blanches before stretching to hide it. "I have no idea what you're talking about."

"You remember the evidence?"

"Of course I do. What kind of stupid question is that?"

"She said she needed the evidence for her baby."

"She's delusional. Her mind isn't right."

"Right."

"That's what I said."

I could whip him, but he won't be able to handle a tenth of what Lina took. He'll crumple after the second lash, piss himself, and sell me more lies. I can't trust the filth that comes out of his mouth, not even under torture. That's okay. There are other ways.

"All right," I say.

His shoulders sag. "Just like that?"

"Have a nice life."

"Tell Lina I say hi."

I slam his door, only feeling better knowing I'm condemning him to the life he deserves. I hope he suffers long and hard.

Lina

THE NOISE of the curtains being yanked open wakes me. I sit up with a jerk, blinking at the bright light. Anne stands in front of the window with her hands on her hips.

"Chill, Lina. It's only me."

Grabbing the sheet, I clutch it to my chest. My body aches everywhere. My arms are sore and my leg muscles are cramping, but it's nothing compared to the fire in my back. I must've rolled over in my sleep, and the sheet got stuck to my sweaty back. It hurt when I peeled myself away.

"What do you want?" I'm groggy and sore. I don't have time for games.

"Damian messed you up pretty badly, huh?"

"Please, go. I'd like to get dressed."

"Need help?"

"No, thanks."

"I came to see if I should call a doctor. Social services?"

"Will calling social services make a damn difference?"

"No." She sighs like it matters. "Damian already owns most of this town, and the system *is* corrupt."

"Then why bring it up?"

She shrugs. "I was thinking out loud."

Right. "What do you want?"

"For someone who invited me to stay, you're not very happy to have me here."

"Just get to the point."

She walks to the bed and sits down. "I know why you asked me to stay."

She waits, but I'm not going to give her the satisfaction of admitting anything.

Another sigh. "You were hoping I'd be a diversion. Admit it, Lina. You wished Damian would be interested in me, so you didn't have to entertain his sexual appetite."

Does she know I'm jealous? Does she know how I felt when I saw her exiting this room with her dress askew?

"Listen." She pats my hand as if we're old friends. "Here's the deal. You make space for me, I distract Damian, Zane finds you the evidence, and then you leave."

"Make space for you?"

"Give me a chance with Damian. Create opportunities for us to be alone."

The urge to push her to the floor is so big I have to fist my hands in the sheet. "He doesn't want to be with you."

Her smile is faint, yet strong. The gesture is full of self-assurance and confidence. "Once you're out of the picture, he will."

"I won't reject him just to drive him into your arms. That's wrong."

"It's your only chance at freedom. That's the price."

My mouth drops open. "Are you bribing or blackmailing me?"

"Call it whatever you want. You give me Damian, and Zane gives you freedom. It's a fair deal."

I clutch the sheet harder, feeling the cotton stretch under my fingers. "Can Zane get the combination of the safe?"

"Where there's a will, there's always a way." She winks and gets up. "I'm glad we understand each other."

Oh, I get it, loud and clear. Zane wasn't going to give me the evidence for nothing. They were playing me, both of them. Zane knows he doesn't stand a chance with Damian, who's as straight as a big, bad, mining magnate can be, so Zane brought in his sister. The scene that played out on the stairs when Zane all but assaulted me was just an opening act for the main one playing out here. It was to get me thinking, to manipulate me into asking for Zane's help. It set the ball rolling. I took the bait. Now they're revealing their price.

Astonished, I stare at her. "Why?"

"Why would I help you?"

She's not helping me. She's serving her own purpose. "Why do you want Damian so badly?"

She shakes her head, regarding me as if I'm a stupid, dirty dog that trudged mud into a clean house. "The fact that you even have to ask shows how naïve you are. He's handsome, hot, successful, wealthy, feared, and a stud in bed." She taps a finger to her chin. "That about sums it up."

I can't help but get in a jibe. "You haven't slept with him. You can't know how he is in bed."

"Rumors, darling." She wags her eyebrows. "Are you confirming them?"

"You should get out now."

"I expect you to make the first opportunity tonight. Zane is going out. Give me time alone with Damian."

"How am I supposed to arrange that?" I exclaim.

"You're creative. Fake a headache. Better yet, tell him your back is sore. He's got to believe that." She straightens her dress. "I have some beauty sleep to catch up with. Got to look my best tonight." Her smile is smug as she darts around the door, leaving it open.

My heartbeat is loud and sluggish. A mental image of Anne in Damian's arms, in this bed, invades my brain, but I expel it quickly.

Maybe Anne deserves him. I look over my shoulder at my bruised back. I sure as hell deserve better.

~

Damian

ZANE SENDS me a text to let me know Lina ate the lunch Jana prepared and has a sudden craving for jelly beans. *Jelly beans.* He's going to the supermarket to get her some. It's after lunchtime when I finally get the meeting at the office wrapped at. Traffic is a bitch. It's late afternoon when I get home. I go upstairs to check on Lina but find her nowhere.

I knock on Anne's door. She opens it a few seconds later wearing nothing but a short robe and the kind of blindfold they use in beauty salons on her forehead.

"Have you seen Lina?"

"No." She yawns. "I *was* having a nap."

Taking the stairs two by two, I run down to the kitchen and ask Jana the same question. From the way she smiles at me, Lina hasn't told her what's happened.

"She's in the garden." Jana points at the window. "There, by the bat boxes."

I turn my gaze to where Jana indicates. Lina's hair, tied in a messy ponytail, shines like yellow gold in the sun. She's drowning in one of my shirts, looking cute and sexy and like mine. I can't tell if she's wearing anything underneath. The shirttail reaches the back of her knees. Barefoot, she climbs up a ladder resting on the wall that cordons off the herb garden and peers into the wooden box fitted under the gutter.

Relief rushes through me. What did I expect? That Lina would've run after this morning's lesson? Not even Zane would've bailed if I'd whipped him like I whipped Lina, and he's a tough motherfucker.

Grabbing a bottle of water from the fridge, I make my way outside, and stop next to the ladder where I have a nice view of Lina's legs under the shirt. She's wearing a cotton exercise short. Not totally naked under my shirt, after all. My possessive side is relieved. She's mine to look at, to touch, and to punish.

The ladder rattles when she moves. I nearly have a fucking heart attack. My uncle died falling from a ladder. A broken rib punctured his lung.

I grip the ladder on both sides to secure it. "Get down from there."

She startles and presses a palm to her heart. "For the love of Adam. You scared me."

"Hold on with both hands."

Her gaze sweeps over me. Annoyed. "What are you doing here?"

The angry schoolmistress look makes me hard. "I live here."

She wants to roll her eyes, it's there in the way she glances at the heaven, but she doesn't. "You know what I mean. What are you doing home so early?"

"Checking on you and just as well."

Ignoring me, she turns her attention back to the wooden box.

"You shouldn't be out here in the heat of the day."

"What do you care?" she mumbles with her nose in that damn box.

"You know I care. Get down."

She extends a hand. "Pass me the towel."

What happened to obeying, and please? I look around. There's a towel neatly draped over the tap. "Why?"

Pulling her head out of the box, she sighs. "Never mind. I'll get it myself."

She stiffens when I wrap my hands around her waist to aid her as she climbs down. Mindful of her back, I keep my touch light. She doesn't say thank you or push me away. When her feet hit the ground, she turns in my grip and stares at me warily. Her cheeks are flushed with heat and sweat beads on her forehead. Tendrils of golden hair stick to her temples. A sudden bout of tenderness overcomes me. I want to wrap her up in more of my clothes and carry her off to a happier ending, to a place where she doesn't look at me like I'm the enemy. She's so small, so goddamn, innocently beautiful it hurts to look at her.

I raise a hand to wipe one of those tendrils from her face, but she flinches and cowers. Goddamn, I'll never hit her, not like this.

Moving slowly, I reach for her. She tenses, but she lets me frame her face between my palms. I use my thumbs to wipe the strands of hair away.

"You don't need to be afraid of me, Lina."

"I'm not." She says it too quickly, too defensively.

I feel pain, real pain. It bleeds into my heart and spills out into my veins with the steady pump of regret. Things between us could've been so different. We could've been normal. A part of me can't forgive her for not waiting. As irrational as it is, I can't forgive her for not believing in me when Dalton accused me of stealing that diamond. I needed her to have faith in me. I needed her to want me, but she married Clarke and tried to find the evidence. She still wants to be free of me. She still chooses her father. Not going to happen.

She stands perfectly still. She waits. Frightened. Her heart gallops under the shirt. I can see it in the way the collar trembles.

"I won't hurt you if you don't deserve it."

She swallows.

I take her in. Everything. "I like you in my clothes."

She looks down. "I'm sorry. It's the only loose thing I could find to wear. The other stuff hurts." She swallows the last word, almost doesn't pronounce it.

I drop my hands, and she takes a step back, colliding with the ladder.

I look up at the box. "What are you doing?"

"One of the bats is injured. A broken wing, maybe. I saw him gimping up the vine to get inside."

"You can't put your hand in there. They'll bite. They may carry rabies."

"That's what the towel is for. The vet said I should throw it over him."

I regard her with my hands on my hips. "The vet."

"Yes. There's one near Monte Casino who treats bats."

The colony of bats has grown since Lina had the boxes installed. There's even an owl that moved in. The ecosystem specialist said it keeps the mice at bay. Nature is playing out as it should, as Lina

266

intended. Some mice make it. Some become owl dinner. Some bats break their wings.

"Is it wise to interfere?" What's the point of cultivating a natural system if we keep on punching our human stamp onto it?

"We can't just leave it like that," she says, looking at me like I'm one of those bat haters who believes bats get entangled in your hair. "It's suffering. I've got to fix it."

Suddenly, I get it. Lina identifies with the bats. Her bat obsession is born from her need to be homed, to be cared for, to be fixed. She's a woman with a broken wing, and there's no one to throw the towel over her head and make it better.

Snatching the towel, I climb up the ladder.

"Careful, Damian. It's fragile."

"I know."

"It's in the left-hand corner. The wing hangs limp. Do you see it?"

There it is, the little creature with its turned-up nose and tipped ears that huddles on the floor while his buddies hang upside down from the pole at the top.

A warm hand touches my leg. "Do you see it?"

"Yeah, I see it."

The box is too small to throw a towel inside. I climb back down and look for a stick.

"What are you doing?" she exclaims when I break a dry branch from the Acacia tree.

"Stand aside. We've got to get them out."

She grabs my arm. "No. You'll hurt them."

"Trust me."

The miracle is, she does. After a heartbeat, she lets go, biting her lip. "The vet doesn't do house calls, dammit. This could've been so much easier."

"Stand over there." I point at the shady veranda.

She backs off reluctantly.

Pushing the stick through the hole in the box, I move it around. There's a whole lot of protesting, chirping, and scurrying, and finally, they fly off, all except for the one with the broken wing. When he hops out and finds purchase in the vine, I gently drop the towel and grab the edges together.

"You have him," Lina says, sounding breathless. "Here." She opens a travel cage that stands on the ground. "Don't open the towel. It may injure itself trying to escape."

I deposit our patient inside, and she secures the trapdoor.

"Right. What now, bat nurse?"

"I need Russell to drive me to the vet."

I don't miss a beat. "Russell resigned."

"What?"

Reading her carefully, I say, "Conflict of interests."

She pales a little. She knew. She's scared. She knows the depth of my possessiveness. "Are you going to punish me?"

"You didn't do anything wrong." She didn't flirt or lead him on.

"I thought you'd be angry."

I'm a fucking beast, but I'm not unfair. "I'm not angry."

A long breath leaves her chest.

"Brink is looking out for you now. You don't leave this property without him or me." I pick up the cage. "I'll get one of the guards to drop this off at the vet."

She catches my arm. "I'm going with."

"You're going back inside the house to rest."

"I'm not a child."

"You passed out under a whip this morning. You need more ointment, painkillers, and rest."

"Whose fault is that?" she says under her breath.

"Don't push me, Lina."

She sobers at my tone.

"Go inside. If I don't find you in the bedroom when I get there, you're booked for another lashing when this one has healed."

Her nostrils flare, and her eyes shimmer with angry tears, but she obeys.

After handing the injured bat over to one of the guards, I go upstairs and find Lina waiting in the room. She's staring at the cold fireplace, hugging her stomach. Gently, I unfold her arms and arrange them at her sides. Bringing my arms around her from behind, I unbutton the shirt and push it over her shoulders and down her arms to fall around her heels. Kneeling, I pick the shirt up and press it to my nose. It smells like her. Sweet poison. The good kind of toxic. She makes me crazy. She makes me drag the little cotton shorts down her legs and leave them like a constraint around her ankles.

She trembles. I want her. She knows.

I want her for two reasons. One, she gave me a shawl when no one else gave a fuck, and, two, because her father said I couldn't have her. All the wrong reasons, yes. That doesn't mean I'm not going to take care of her. On the contrary, I take excellent care of what's mine, and she's mine as sure as her forever with me is carved in diamonds. She's worth more than stone.

Trailing my hands up the insides of her legs as I straighten, I test her pussy. Wet. My finger slips right in. She goes on tiptoes. I pull out, leaving a wet trail of arousal as I trace her spine. She shivers. I curl my fingers around her nape and push her upper body down gently. She catches the ornamental ledge under the mantelpiece to keep herself steady. She's wet and open, flowering, inviting. I free my cock through my fly. Holding the base in one hand, I position my erection at her entrance. I only touch her hip as I drag the head up and down her slit, mixing my pre-cum with her arousal. I itch to stroke my palms over her back, but it'll hurt. That artwork I only caress with my eyes. This is why I have to take her like this. Today, I won't be watching her face when I come. I'll be watching the marks I left on her body, and it makes my cock twitch. I get harder. It's depraved, but I don't need excuses for what I am. We are what we are. The map on her back makes me forget about who we could've been. It's heaven to be in the moment, in the pleasure. Nothing else matters. Nothing else exists.

When I'm well lubricated, I push inside her body, stretching her slowly. I watch her cunt swallow my cock, her lips stretching to take me while her breathing quickens and her nails scrape over the marble flowers on the wall. I keep on going until I'm buried to the hilt. Keeping still inside her so she can adjust, I reach around for her clit. Her skin is slippery. She pushes back against me when I start to rub.

She moans when my other hand finds her breast, stroking and teasing her nipple until it's taut.

When she starts moving, I grab her thighs and keep her still. This is my scene. My pace. I pull out almost all the way and thrust again. She tries to widen her stance but the shorts around her ankles prevent her. It feels tighter. There's more friction. She moans. I tell her to keep perfectly still while I slide out of her tight pussy and stab the length of my erection back in with one shove. Her knees buckle. She almost collapses. I go softer because I can't keep her up and enjoy the sight of her pussy stretching around me. She ripples and clenches inside. It's too much, even at this slow pace. I'm going to blow.

"Touch yourself, Lina. Come."

Her hand moves between her legs. Her fingers curl around my dick when I pull out, squeezing, and I almost shoot. I grind my teeth and stop moving while she rubs her clit until I hear that little sound that tells me she's there.

We go over together. I grind my groin against her ass as she pushes back against me. I wish this would never end, this feeling of euphoria and connection I've only ever had with her. She's not my first, but she's my only.

I pet her while she comes down from her high, and only pull out when there are no more aftershocks running through her abdomen. Lifting her into my arms, I carry her to the shower. I adjust the water to a lukewarm setting. Even so, it's going to sting. She hisses as the spray rains down on her back. I wash her quickly, touching her welts as little as possible. I'm careful with the towel, patting her dry gently. I give her another two painkillers and rub lotion on her back. Then I tell her to lie down on the bed and rest.

Lying on her stomach, she watches me dress with her cheek on the pillow.

"Damian?"

I can't get enough of looking at her. "I'll bring you some tea. You need to keep hydrated."

"Who was your first?"

My fingers still on the buttons on my shirt. "I didn't know her name."

"Why not?"

"We met at the waterpark. Did it behind the trees. I didn't ask. She didn't offer."

"Was it good?"

I push my shirt into my pants and zip up. "It was awkward. Why do you ask?"

"I was just wondering." Her voice is soft, far-off, or sleepy, maybe. "How many after her?"

"I didn't count."

From the soft nest of her pillow, she gives a faint smile. "That many, huh?"

Walking to the bed, I look down at her, the only woman I ever really wanted. Want. Will want forever. I drag my finger down her arm, over the bumps of her scars. "Didn't you sleep with anyone before Clarke?"

She inhales and holds it, then blows the breath out slowly. "No."

"You make me wish I hadn't."

She lifts her head. "Hadn't what?"

"Slept with anyone before you."

Something in her eyes shifts. Our gazes are locked, our breaths quiet. We're both uncomfortable in the enormity of my confession.

Preventing her from having to reply, I kiss her shoulder and leave. It's the gentlemanly thing to do.

Alone in the kitchen, as I prepare Lina a cup of tea, I let the hurt of her silence sink in. Monsters have hearts, too.

I CHOOSE to work from home for the rest of the afternoon, in case Lina needs me, and check in on her every hour. She naps a little and spends the rest of the time freaking out about the bat until the guard returns and tells us the little guy will stay at the vet until his wing has mended.

When we sit down for dinner, Lina comes downstairs wearing

another one of my shirts to say she doesn't feel well and will eat in the room. She's already asked Jana for a tray.

Every protective instinct I have goes into overdrive. I'm on my feet in a flash. "What's wrong?"

"Just, um, a little headache."

I press my hand against the nape of her neck. "Do you have a fever?"

"No."

"When was the last time you urinated?"

She makes big eyes and says in a reprimanding way, "Damian."

"Upstairs."

"You're overreacting. It's just a little—"

"Now." I take her arm and lead her to the door.

She doesn't look at Zane or Anne as she excuses herself but keeps her head high and her back straight all the way to the bedroom, even when I'm her only audience.

I point at the bed. "Lie down."

"Damian."

Retrieving the medicine kit from the bathroom, I carry it back to the bed. She's still standing on her feet, looking uncomfortable and angry.

"On your stomach," I say.

She huffs but climbs onto the bed.

I remove the thermometer and pop it into the corner of her mouth. Crossing my arms, I count the seconds. She rolls her eyes when I pull it free.

"No fever," I say.

"I told you."

"Tell me where it aches."

"Just my head."

"Are you drinking enough?"

"Yes, and I urinated fifteen minutes ago."

I lift the shirt and check her back. The welts are red, some already fading. There are no new bruises indicating shallow bleeding. I inspect her soles and toenails. I feel her pulse. Everything seems normal, but my heartbeat won't calm.

"I just need to rest," she says, avoiding my eyes.

Something is off. "Does anything hurt inside?"

"Not more than usual."

"More than usual?"

"Earlier." She blushes. "You were rough in the end."

"Was there bleeding?"

"No."

Shaking two painkillers from the bottle, I hand them to her with a glass of water. I wait until she's drank everything.

"I'll eat in the room with you."

"No," she says too quickly. Seeming to catch herself, she bites her lip. "I need time alone."

I don't like it, but I can understand. "Where's your phone?"

"In my bag." She points at the sofa by the fireplace.

I retrieve it and leave it on the bedside table. "Call me if anything changes or if you need something."

"It's not necessary."

"Not up for discussion. You call me. Understand?"

"Yes," she whispers, looking guilty.

"It's my job to take care of you." Especially when I'm the reason for her pain.

"Fine."

I take her hand, enjoying the feel of her much smaller palm in mine, and kiss her fingers. "Later."

I don't like the distance I'm putting between us when I go downstairs. The only reason I trudge forward is to honor her request, but I feel uneasy. She's not going to puke or cut herself, or she'd have done so a long time ago. I'm uneasy because I have a weird notion of somehow failing her.

Back in the dining room, Anne's sultry smile greets me. For the first time, I notice the red dress that hugs her figure. Her make-up and hair are done. She's flirting throughout dinner. Not in the mood for conversation, I ignore her unless she asks me a direct question.

When Zane announces he's going out after dessert, I see the setup for what it is. How did Anne convince Lina to play along? Is my wife so eager to be rid of me, she'll sell me out to the very guest she invited? Or is this why she invited Anne to stay? Was she hoping I'd fall for Anne and forget about her? The possibility of that happening is so ridiculous, I almost laugh out loud.

I'm excusing myself when Anne grabs my arm. "Damian, we need to talk."

I look at where her red fingernails dig into the fabric of my jacket. "I disagree."

Slowly, she removes her grip. "You've been avoiding me since the last dinner when I wanted to talk to you, the night you cut off that guy's fingers."

I don't want to be reminded of that night. It was a huge mistake to bring the asshole here, and I still regret that Lina had to see that. I get up.

"It's about Lina."

I still. Anne smiles, already victorious.

"What about Lina?"

She pushes up from the table. "You need to see this."

Walking around me, she goes to the kitchen. I follow, because she's right. Anything that concerns Lina is my business.

Tugging a laundry basket from behind the door, she plops it down on the counter. It's filled to the brim with bread rolls. I pick one up and squeeze. Brittle and dry, it crumbles, flaking into pieces.

"What's this?"

Anne's look turns sympathetic. "Damian, I'm sorry, but I thought you needed to know. I found this on the bottom of Lina's closet. She really is crazy. I mean, who collects bread rolls? I'm worried about her state of mind. This isn't right."

I dust my hands. "What were you doing in Lina's closet?"

"She said I could borrow a dress."

On purpose, I let my gaze drop to her hips. She turns a little red. She'll never fit those hips in Lina's dresses.

Rubbing a finger over my mouth, I watch her intently, until she starts to squirm. "Do you know how I feel about tattletales?"

"I had to tell you," she gushes. "Don't you know what people say?"

"What do people say?"

"You married a crazy woman. She's weird. She humiliated you with a funeral dress at your wedding."

"People are fast to judge. Who's to say she's not eccentric?"

"That dress wasn't eccentric, and you know it. Everyone knows it. It was a statement. Tony says she didn't want an engagement ring, that she practically threw a four-carat diamond back in your face. Her arms are cut up. She can't close a door, never mind locking it. She builds homes for bats. She got my grandfather fired over those damn bats. Everyone says she prefers vampires to people. Then there's the newspaper articles, and that photo of her almost throwing herself under a bus."

She pauses to take a breath.

I cross my arms. "Anything else?"

Some of her enthusiasm evaporates. She deflates. "You know better than me."

"Damn right."

"This is terrible. I feel awful for you."

"You're right. It's terrible."

"What are you going to do?"

"What do you suggest?"

Pulling on my arms, she unfolds them and takes my hand between both of hers. "I understand you need her money for your mine. I'm not a fool. Everyone knows why you married her. This is going to sound terrible, but you can have the money without having to put up with her."

My insides tighten. Anger coils through my veins. "What are you proposing?"

"There are places you can send crazy people."

I narrow my eyes. "Institutions."

She nods enthusiastically. "Yes. To get better."

"Let me get this straight. You're suggesting I have her locked up."

"I prefer to see it as being cared for by people who can help her. You'll still manage her money. You'll still have your mine."

I pull my hand free. "That sounds rather selfish."

"You have to start thinking about yourself, about your image, and how you want the world to see you. Your success is growing, day by day. Do you want your international liaisons to know you as that guy who married the crazy woman, or the successful, respected businessman you are?"

"Wow, Anne. You really are a piece of work."

Her demeanor slips. "What do you mean?"

"You're vicious, self-serving, and cruel. The judgment you so persuasively chose for Lina will be yours. Pack your bags. I want you out by tomorrow morning. Be glad I'm not having you *locked up*." Not able to look at her for a minute longer, I grab the basket of bread and walk to the door.

"Wait." She runs after me. "Everything I said is true. I'm doing this for you."

"Don't say goodbye before you go."

"Where are you going?" she cries.

To interrogate my wife.

My footsteps fall hard down the hall. I'm mad with Lina for setting me up with Anne, livid with Anne, and most of all, if I'm honest, worried about my wife.

Lina is sitting up in bed, tense. Her eyes grow big when she spots the basket in my arms.

I dump it on the bed. "Explain."

She looks between the bread and me. "They're bread rolls."

"I know the *what*. I want to know the *why*."

"In case we run out of bread."

"Fuck, Lina." Frustrated, I rest my hands on my hips. "That's lame. You can do better than that."

Biting her lip, she looks toward the window.

"What happened in Willowbrook, Lina?"

She shakes her head.

I walk around the bed, into her line of vision. "I went to Willowbrook."

Her eyes turn bigger still. "Why?"

"I wanted to know what happened to you."

She only looks at me, wide-eyed and trapped.

Sitting down on the bed, I take her hand. "Tell me what they did to you."

Her voice is even, but her hand trembles in mine. "Nothing I'd like to repeat."

"I need to know."

Her eyes turn out of focus. She's tuning me out, hiding from the past.

"Look at me," I urge gently. "I'm going to shut down that hellhole. I need to know what they did to you."

Her expression is hopeful, uncertain.

"I'm going to make them pay, each and every one of them." Bringing her hand to my mouth, I rub her fingers over my lips. "I swear it to you."

"Why do you care what they did to me?"

"Nobody hurts what's mine and gets away with it."

"I wasn't yours back then."

"You were. You always were."

"Damian." She pulls her hand free. "You're insane."

I smile. "That makes two of us."

Her regard is reprimanding. "That's not funny."

She's got to stop giving me the schoolmistress act or I'll forget why I'm here. "Have I ever lied to you?"

"No," she whispers.

"Then trust me in this. They'll never work again, not one single person who's ever been connected to that place. Say the word and I'll kill them all for you."

"No," she cries with a start. "I don't want you to kill anyone."

"Then start talking."

She utters a tremulous sigh. I know the exact moment she takes the mental jump. Her hands fist and her lips part. There's a pause, and then it all comes gushing out.

"They strapped me to a bed, injected me with drugs, and starved me."

It's the conclusion I already came to, minus the starving part. Hearing her say it makes my organs boil in vengeful anger. Dickenson will be exposed. I swear.

"That's why I stole the bread. It's compulsive."

In case I take her food away. In case she goes hungry. I've suffered many wrongs, but never deliberate starvation, not even at the hands of my no-good parents. I can't begin to imagine what she went through. The pieces that didn't make sense come together. How she gobbled down her first meal in this house, how she always eats as if there won't be another meal, why she dried an emergency stack of bread, the sugar she took in the restaurant, everything now makes sense.

"You didn't steal anything. What's mine is yours. I'll never let you starve." Wrapping my arms around her, I pull her close. I hold her lightly, still mindful of her sore back. "I'll give you justice. I promise."

She buries her face in my chest and grabs a handful of my shirt.

"Why did Dalton send you there?" I ask, worried she'll stop talking.

"I was being *difficult* when he brought me home after Jack's death."

Clarke had her declared incompetent. Her right to make decisions had already been stripped. She wouldn't have been able to contest a decision Dalton had made *in her best interest*. She was locked up against her will, but why starve her? It's not the loving father image I had in my head. The more I hear, the more that image unravels and the ends don't tie up.

"Dalton knew what was happening there." I kiss the top of her head. "There's more to it. I want to know everything."

She stills. For a moment, I believe she's going to tell me, but then she says, "There are things I can't trust anyone with but myself."

Pulling away, I offer her a smile. It's soft. It's meant to put her at ease. Yes, it's manipulative, but I'll never use any information she shares with me against her. I'll never judge her.

"You and your *things*," I say, making light of the statement.

She doesn't take the bait. "There are *secrets* I can't trust anyone with."

"Haven't I earned your trust?"

She scoffs and pushes me away.

"Have I ever not done something I said I would?"

"No," she whispers, averting her eyes.

"I'll avenge you, Lina, even if you never tell me." I'll find out, though. I want to know every fucking sin ever committed against her. "I don't know what you're hiding or why, but I'm not your enemy. I'm your husband. You're mine, and I'll protect you until my dying day."

She blinks. She searches my face as she digests my words. "You forced me to marry you for your warped motivations. You're keeping me tied to you against my will, and proclaim you'll do it until your dying day. How can I trust you?"

I narrow my eyes at the truthful accusations. On any other day, I would've gladly reminded her how much she likes to be kept against her will, but not today. "Have I lied to you, ever?"

"No," she says again.

"Trust me, angel. Try, at least. No one can carry their secrets alone forever."

It's true. I see the realization in her eyes as she studies the pattern of the bedspread. I see the weight of her past in her slumped posture and the temptation to unburden herself in the way she works her lip between her teeth.

After a while, she looks up at me with big, tormented eyes. "I need time."

I accept the olive branch. "I can be patient."

"Thank you."

The words are barely audible, but she gave me something. She gave me gratitude.

"Now you can tell me about your addiction to jelly beans."

She blushes redder than raspberries.

I grin. "Zane said he cleaned out two stores. How many jelly beans can one, meager woman eat?"

"I…" She wipes a strand of hair behind her ear, not meeting my eyes. "I need jelly beans when I'm upset."

Chuckling, I grip her chin and lift her face to mine. "I'll remember that. I'll have to keep a supply."

She looks away again.

"You only have to ask. No amount of jelly beans will ever be too much."

An almost-smile tugs at her lips. It's not enough to make her dimple appear, but it warms my heart in a foreign kind of way, a good way. I want that smile more than anything, but I won't have it tonight. There's one more thing standing in the way of trust and smiles.

I peel off my jacket and walk to the bathroom. In the door, I turn. "Anne is leaving tomorrow. If you ever try to hook me up with another woman again, it won't end well for you, either."

The raspberry red drains from cheeks. "Are you going to punish me?"

"As you deserve, but only when you've healed." She needs to understand how seriously I'm taking our vows. "It'll give you something to think about until then."

I WORK from home the following day, setting myself up in the lounge while the cleaners vacuum upstairs. It's to keep an eye on Zane. He blamed Lina for Anne's hasty departure, and I don't like the expression on his face when he looks at my wife. I drew several security tapes and watched them randomly but didn't spot anything out of the ordinary.

There's an even greater distance between Zane and me, and no flowers in the entrance, today. Signs are everything. Taking the sign of the empty vase to heart, I order one of my most trusted guards, Drew, to watch every single security feed, second by second.

The next task of the day is getting a jail connection to look into Clarke's household staff records. I want names, dates, and designations. I instruct him to also get an employment record for Willowbrook. If someone had been paid under the table, I want to know. If someone had as much as licked a stamp and stuck it to an envelope in the name of that establishment, I want to have his name.

Ellis is in town to oversee the purchase of new equipment. He grudgingly comes over for a meeting in the afternoon when the annoying vacuuming finally ceases.

"Where's that lovely wife of yours?" he asks when I show him into the study.

In bed, wearing my shirt. I get hard just from the thought of it. "Busy."

"Pity. She's a good one. You'll be wise to hold onto her."

He has no idea. "Drink?"

I go over to the liquor tray and lift the decanter. Something on the bottom catches my attention. I hold it up to the light. Strike me dead. Gooey balls, some discolored, spoil my five-thousand-rand whisky.

I replace the decanter. "Or maybe not."

Ellis gives the alcohol a curious look.

"Let's get to business." I take a seat and shift.

Something hard and knobby digs into my ass. Letting out a disgruntled groan, I get up and pluck the thin cushion aside. Fuck me. The seat of my favorite chair is covered in colorful balls.

Jelly beans.

"Is everything all right?" Ellis asks, taking the visitor's chair.

I brush the candy aside, unable to hide my grin, and sit down as the little balls run in every direction over the floor.

"Perfect." I open my leather satchel and take out the file I prepared, only to have jelly beans tumble from the bag. They're everywhere, the little fuckers. In every fold, nook, and cranny of the bag.

Turning the file upside down, I shake. Another explosion of balls hops and bounce everywhere.

Ellis leans to the side, staring at the balls and raising an eyebrow.

I'll have to teach my pretty wife a thing or two about revenge. My smile is drawn-out and broad, this time. Still determined not to let Lina's stunt distract me, I flick open the file. The paper is filled with colorful stains. Pulling it from the folder, I hand Ellis the ruined contract.

He looks it over, his frown deepening. "Are those...?" He leans to the side again and scratches his head. "Jelly beans?"

I hold up a finger. "Excuse me. I'll be right back."

I march straight to our bedroom. The door is open, but Lina gives a start when I enter. She's sitting in a window seat, reading a driver's license manual.

She lowers the manual warily when my steps eat up the distance between us.

"Damian, I—"

I don't give her time to say more. I grab her face between my hands and kiss her hard. Urgently. I bite her lips and suck on her tongue. The manual drops to the floor, discarded like candy. She's one of a kind. My kind. I knew it six years ago. I know it now.

Cute, innocent, beautiful, clean, the light to my dark. I'm going to buy her a jelly bean gun so she can shower me in candy bullets. She's fucking priceless.

I love her.

I still. I pull away.

Her lips are red and swollen. Her eyes are unfocussed and lustful.

I'm hard and shocked.

"Damian?"

"In an hour, I want you naked on your hands and knees in my study."

She pales. "Why?"

The minx. She knows exactly why. "You're going to recover each and every jelly bean from the floor, and you're going to do it without interrupting my work. If you make as much as a chirp, I'll spank your ass, welts or not."

Her mouth drops open.

I backtrack to the door, shaken, imprinting her there in my shirt on the seat, messily kissed, remembering how she looked when I realized I love her.

Lina

OH, how I hate Damian.

How I hate his study floor.

The tiles are hard and cold. The rugs are rough and scratchy.

While he watches, I crawl around naked and drop the candy in the empty jar he gave me.

He nudges my thigh with his shoe when I move around his chair.

"I think you missed one under the desk."

Glaring doesn't help. He only grins at me briefly before turning his attention back to his file. Every so often he stops and criticizes, telling me to check behind the curtains and under the rugs.

When there's not a single candy astray and my knees are raw, he takes the jar and leaves it on the corner of his desk.

"Get up." He offers me a hand.

My legs are stiff from crawling. I don't have a choice but to accept. Standing naked in front of him, he looks me over. My punishment isn't finished. I can see it in his eyes. He's going to make me pay more. The question is how.

I know soon enough when he sits down in his chair and opens his fly. He releases his cock but doesn't undress more. He doesn't even unbutton his pants. He's big and hard. He curls his finger at me, calling me closer.

After the long time on all fours, walking feels weird. It takes two steps to find my balance. I stop next to his chair.

"Ride me."

I blink in shock. Except for that one time when I saw Anne leave his room, he's been doing all the taking. "I'm not sure—"

"Ride me or give me your ass. Your choice."

My breath catches. I don't want the latter.

Holding my eyes, he turns his chair so he's facing me, giving me access. He already knows what my decision will be. I glance down at his hard cock, jutting out from the expensive fabric of his pants. His legs are spread wide, taking up the entire seat. He takes up all the air in the room. It takes all I have and more to grip the armrests and put my knee on the outside of his thigh. He makes a little space for me, a small concession. I lift my other leg and he gives me the same. Just enough. He watches my face as I straddle him. I have to stretch my legs wide. Somehow, it makes it more intense that he's watching my face and not looking down between my legs. My pussy is on display. My feelings are hidden. He knows it. He wants to see the hidden, to take what's not for the taking. I lift myself over his cock and still he studies my face. My body is unclad but it's my soul he wants naked.

I bite my lip as I feel the head of his cock on the right place. I try to lock my feelings away as I lower myself onto him, but the moment he shifts his hips, the truth spills out of my mouth. I gasp as he rolls. He's not even inside me fully, and my back arches from the delicious heat.

"Show me," he grits out.

I do. I take his whole length inside me. I lift and lower myself again to feel the stretch, the pleasure. He holds onto my face with his eyes as I clamp my hands over his on the armrest and dig my nails into his flesh. I move for myself, taking for me, crossing the last line.

It doesn't take me long. Angling my body, I find the friction I need on my clit. I come before he does, crying out the truth he wanted to see. It's only then he takes over, jamming himself up until my body bounces and all my restraints fall away. I let go of his hands to snake my arms around his neck. He bites my nipple and pinches my clit. With his cum inside me, I climax again. My head rolls back as he smacks my ass and licks my other nipple.

He takes everything I have, because he's larger than me, larger than life. He's larger than my self-control. When he fucks me, he makes me forget everything. It's only now, relaxed and sated in his arms, that I realize we haven't used protection.

Cupping my head, he makes me look back at him. He starts moving again while his finger traces the seam of my ass. I squirm when he applies pressure on my dark entrance. I moan when he breaks the resistance of the tight ring of muscles. His finger sinks deep, and undiscovered nerve endings pulse to life.

"Do I need to stop, Lina?"

Yes, and no.

"Do you want this, angel?"

No, and yes.

He moves his finger. "Like this?"

Yes, and yes.

"Do you want me?"

I'm beyond words. He starts fucking me with his cock and finger like he knows this. I'm falling apart, inside and out.

"Tell me," he urges. It's the seductive words of an experienced lover who knows how to get what he wants. "Tell me you want me."

I want him, and I don't. He pushes my limits to extremes. He stretches me until my heart and mind splinter like a piece of wood axed in two, until I'm torn up inside. He pulls me until my grip slips, until I lose my hold and fall from grace. When I have no place left to go but down, he catches me and mends me.

Over and over, the pattern repeats, but like a tormented soul that dies only to reincarnate and live the suffering from scratch, I'm unable to stop. I'm unable to resist him. I come for him every time, no matter if he fucks me hard or commands me gently. He creates this weakness in me so that he can exploit it, because only in weakness is my body his. We both know this, but he wants it to be different. This is what he's looking for so hard in my face. He's looking for a fissure in my soul, the first crack he can exploit. I hold back the feelings and cry out my orgasm, collapsing in his arms. In this very weakness lies my only strength. He takes me by seduction, manipulation, and trade. Nothing I give is given freely. My love still belongs to me.

CHAPTER 18

Lina

*E*ven monsters can be kind.

Damian holds the power over my money and decisions, but he's not unaffected by my behavior. After the jelly bean incident in his study, he makes himself vulnerable by giving me power over his body, and by letting me know how much I hurt him when I helped set up Anne's failed seduction. He goes down on his knees to bring me to orgasm as often as he can, and he brings the healed bat home. He looks into my eyes with raw passion when he climaxes inside of me, and he pays for my driving lessons. He lets me hear how much I turn him on with growls and grunts, and he tells me how much he loves the little sound I make when I come. I'm a slave to his touch. I'm not counting the days between my periods and ovulation. What's the point? I'm never regular. I want the knowledge of my easy surrender to shock me, but it doesn't. Maybe, subconsciously, I want this to make up for the past. It's wrong, but what am I if not sick in the head? What is our situation if not insanely twisted?

Zane says Damian will grow tired of me now that he's gotten what he wanted, but Zane isn't there when Damian takes me several times in the middle of the night. My husband is insatiable. Sometimes, his needs leave me with an ache between my thighs and sore muscles all over my body, but I'll lie if I say I don't enjoy being used. It's a coping mechanism, an addiction, and if I tell Reyno about it he'd tell me it's sick.

We both are, Damian and me. In our own different ways, we're sinners. We're both lost and doomed, driven by needs that will never redeem us. Those needs are the axle around which our actions are spinning, and it fills this house with the deviant energy of our desires, of hunting revenge, and chasing closure.

Damian is trying to take away the pain he suffered the vengeful way. An eye for an eye. In his life, there's no turning the other cheek. Harold took from him. He took that back and more. He took me. He took my freedom and my most basic human right, the right to make decisions. As for me, my soul won't rest until I stand over the remains of the baby I never held in my arms. My heart won't find peace until I put an angel on his grave to watch over him. Only then will I be free to mourn and let go. Our destructive ways run from days into weeks. Like planets bound to orbits, we're stuck to our paths, unable to break free.

I find my own routine in our unhealthy environment. A warped kind of stability dawns, giving me time to think. True to his word, Damian gives me patience. He never asks about my baby or Willowbrook again. He waits for me to tell him I'm ready, and many times I'm tempted. Many times, I get close to giving up, to forsaking my oath of a white angel tombstone on a black heap of sand, but then I wake up in a cold sweat and shame, and I go back to the mundane tasks of living.

Physically, I'm thriving. I picked up weight and filled out. Besides going to the gym three times a week with Damian, I swim every morning. I have a driver's license test booked for the end of the summer, and I see my shrink every Wednesday. I work secretly for Reyno, transcribing his recorded notes. We make progress. I can close a door behind me without completely freaking out, and I'm not collecting bread rolls any longer. The walls still get too much sometimes, but a walk in the new natural garden is always the right remedy.

I don't bring up the issue about money again, because I'm earning mine under the table. While Damian gives me vulnerability and truth, working hard on building trust, I give him lies and my body. Every day, it gets harder. Every day, my reasons muddle more, until the day Zane corners me at the pool after his run.

He wipes his face on a towel, regarding me with open hostility. He still hasn't forgiven me for driving his grandfather and Anne away. "Looks like you're settling in to stay."

I get out at the shallow end and wrap myself up in a towel. Brink isn't far away. Zane can't hurt me, but I don't like the way he looks at me.

Zane drops his voice so Brink can't hear. "Do you still want the evidence?"

I don't trust him. My answer is wary. "What do you want in return?"

"Disappear from Dami's life. Forever."

The offer works in the favor of my own plans to get Reyno to restore my mental status, and to save up a bit of money so I can escape when I finally have the evidence. I'll give copies to Harold, and he'll tell me what I want to know. The only price I have to pay is Damian.

A few weeks ago, I wouldn't have hesitated, but now he's shown me that monsters can be kind. He's fighting for me, for my trust, and it gets tougher to imagine a life of fleeing from him. Damian is my solid rock. My captor is the only man I believe. He says what he means, and he means what he says. I know exactly where I stand with him. He told me he would punish me for the move I pulled with Anne, and even if he risked our newfound peace, he kept his word. He made me kneel on the jelly beans I'd collected in the jar and suck him off while the candy dug into my knees and the color rubbed off on my skin. He took his time to come, until I was crying around his cock from the pain the little candy pebbles caused.

I can have a lifetime of punished pleasure and truthful captivity, or a lifetime of running alone in fear, constantly looking over my shoulder. Or I can let the past go. I can grieve without a gravestone and carve the eulogy in my heart. I can give up and let Damian take care of me. I can even take the last leap of faith and tell Damian what he wants to know. I can believe he'd give me the *anything* he promised and ask him to find the grave. The only price will be my freedom.

Two very different lives. Two very different gains. Two very different sacrifices. In one, I remain a pampered captive at the price of my freedom. In the other, I gain freedom at the price of loneliness and unequalled fear.

Either way, the price seems too high.

"Lina?" Zane frowns. "Maybe you should sit down in the shade."

I hate that everyone thinks I'm as fragile as when I arrived here. "I'll give you an answer tomorrow."

"What's with the hesitation? Getting used to a life of luxury?"

I don't bother to answer.

When I get back to the house, I change and ask Brink to drive me to the church in Brixton.

While Brink and the other guards wait outside, I walk into the depressing darkness. In front of the painting, I stop. I stare at her face, the doting face of a mother. How did she feel when Jesus was arrested in the Garden of Gethsemane? How much pain did she suffer when they nailed him to a cross? I'm not religious, but I kneel on the hard floor, folding my hands together.

"Please tell me what to do."

I stay for nearly an hour, and when I leave, I still don't have an answer.

Hesitant, I pause on the sidewalk. What now? Big, fat raindrops start plopping down on the concrete. They hiss when they hit the warm tar road. The smell of rain mixed with soot fills the air. Brink unfolds an umbrella and holds it over my head, but I push it away. The rain feels good. Clean. It runs in rivulets down my back and arms, washing away the stickiness of my sweaty skin. I look down the street, toward the sad apartment block, and it's as if my feet carry me there of their own accord.

My bodyguards follow. Their order is to protect me, not to pose questions. In front of Harold's building, I stop to look up at his window. The drops sting my eyes and tickle my nostrils. Visiting Harold is against the rules, but surely Damian won't punish me if I explain my reasons.

My footsteps echo on the stairs. Away from the rain, the dirty smells assault my nose and cling to my wet clothes.

I don't have to wait long after knocking. The door opens, revealing Harold in surprisingly clean clothes.

"Well." He looks over my shoulder at the guards. "Where's Damian?"

I push past him. "I need to talk to you." Turning to Brink, I say, "I'll just be a few minutes."

"Sorry, ma'am, I can't let you go in alone."

"I'll leave the door open. I only need a word."

I move toward the far end of the room. The place isn't tidy, but it's cleaner. Harold seems to be getting his act together.

"Where is it?" he whispers.

"I don't have it."

"Then why are you here?"

That's when I know my answer. "To tell you I'm not doing it. I'm not getting you the evidence."

He sneers. "Don't you want to know? Not so long ago, it was all you lived for."

"Damian will find it. He'll do it for me. You may as well save yourself the torture and tell me now what you did with his body."

He scoffs. "What about your freedom?"

"It's not important anymore," I lie.

"What about the murder? If I talk, you'll be locked up, again."

"I'll tell Damian everything. He'll get me a good lawyer."

He shoves his hands into his pockets and smiles. "No, you won't."

"You don't know me. I'm not the starved, weakened woman you fetched from Willowbrook."

His gaze slips over me. "You're making a big mistake, Angelina."

"Goodbye, Harold."

"It's not goodbye," he says to my back as I walk through the door. "I'll have the last word yet."

Damian

WORK TAKES ITS TOLL. There's always too much of it and too little time, but when my guard, Drew, calls to say he's found something on the security recording, I drop everything and go home.

Drew waits in my study as instructed. He stands on attention when I enter.

"Sir."

I go around the desk and push the play button on the laptop. It's the night of the business dinner. Lina is dressed in her diamonds and cum-stained gown. She walks to the stairs like a crab with her back to the wall. She's halfway up when Zane comes down. He stands in front of her, blocking her face from the camera, but when she takes another step up, it's obvious she's upset. They're having words. She bends backwards over the rail as far as she can, but he reaches out, fast like a snake, and fastens his hand around her neck. My vision washes out until everything goes white. Static noise crackles in my ears.

I can't formulate more than a clipped question. "Sound?"

"I can get it, sir."

"Do it. Now. Anything else?"

"Not so far, sir, but I still have a couple of weeks' worth of watching left."

"Watch everything, every second."

"Yes, sir."

"Where's my wife?"

"Out, sir."

"Out where?"

"Brixton."

I still. "What is she doing in Brixton?"

"I don't know, sir."

Disappointment stretches ugly, black wings in my chest. "How many guards?"

"Five, including Brink."

I nod. "You're dismissed."

He's scarcely gone when I dial Brink. I bark out my question when he answers. "Where's my wife?"

"Brixton. She's safe, sir."

"Doing what?"

"Visiting her father."

Anger burns through my veins. Why does she insist on defying me? Just when I thought we're making progress she takes us right back to square one.

"Sir?"

"Bring her home."

Hanging up, I throw the phone down on the desk and drag my hands over my face. I don't look forward to what I have to do, but I've never shied away from making good on my promises. My priority is Zane.

Going through the house, I find him in the kitchen, preparing a sandwich.

"Dami," he says when I enter, clearly surprised.

"Where's Jana?"

"Picking up supplies. Want me to fix you a bite? I didn't expect you home for lunch."

With a swipe of my arm, I clear the counter. The half-made sandwich and utensils crash to the floor. The plate cracks in two. Mayonnaise splatters the tiles.

Zane doesn't move as I advance on him. His expression is sober. He took a risk and knows he's been caught. He's not going to deny it.

"Why?" I ask, my voice not betraying the violence sweeping through me.

"How?" he deflects.

I bang a fist on the counter. "Does it fucking matter?"

"You spied on me." His tone is bitter. "Of course it matters."

"I trusted you."

"She's playing you."

"What are *you* doing, Zane? Playing me, too?"

His Adam's apple bobs. "I love you, Dami."

"I've been clear from the start."

"I hoped you'd..." He looks away.

"You hoped I'd what? Turn bisexual?"

He bends to pick up the mess, but I kick the plate away.

"Is that why you hate Lina? You're jealous?"

He straightens. "I don't hate her." Anger flickers in his gaze. "You're losing your shit over her. You're turning weak. I'm doing you a favor."

Lina didn't lie. The one person I trusted did. "Is that why you cuffed her and fed her a sleeping pill?"

"I cuffed her to prevent her from jumping out the window. Her screaming kept me up. That's why I gave her the pill."

"She screamed because she can't be tied up or locked in." I get into his face. "Do you know what they did to her in the institution where she spent one whole fucking year? They strapped her to a bed and isolated her after pumping her full of drugs. I think you can cut her some slack for freaking out."

He blinks. His face is blank. No remorse.

"What happened to her hip, Zane?"

"I told you. I found her snooping."

"You hurt her on purpose."

"It was an accident. She provoked me."

"Why did you strangle her on the night of the dinner party?"

He gives a cynical laugh. "Is that what she told you?"

"That's what I saw. She hasn't told me anything. Lina is no tattle-tale. Unlike you, she has some honor in her."

"Honor?" His lip curls. "You're so smitten with her you only see what you want to see. You so badly want to believe she's a good person, that she cares."

My patience is running out. I fold my fingers around his neck, just like he did with Lina. "Say what you mean and make it fast."

"She didn't tell you, because we have a deal."

My composure dents. I give a fraction, but I don't remove my grip.

I shouldn't ask something that will destroy the fragile relationship growing between my unwilling wife and my obsessive self, but I can't stop. "What deal?"

"I get her the evidence. She disappears."

The fight leaves me. I let him go. It was an idle dream. She'll never come to me freely. My love is tainted and one-sided.

More pieces come together. That's why she went to see Dalton, to share the news. "Did you give it to her?"

"Not yet."

"When were you going to?"

"I've almost cracked the code."

"Why tell me?"

"This is the end, isn't it?" His eyes beg me to deny it.

My tone is cold and dead, like my heart. "I gave you the benefit of the doubt over Lina. You made a fool of me. You betrayed me."

"I did it for you."

"You did it for yourself. I gave you friendship, but it wasn't enough. You hurt an innocent woman for something she didn't choose, just because you couldn't have it."

"Dami, please."

"You saved my life." I take my cheque book and pen from my inside jacket pocket. Scribbling a figure, enough to set him up comfortably, I sign it with a flourish and finality. "I won't forget you saved me from being raped. It's the only reason I'm not bashing your head in and breaking every bone in your body." The cheque tears smoothly on the perforated line, a clean break. I push it over the counter toward him. "We're even."

His eyelashes stick together with the wetness of his unshed tears. He takes the check without looking at the amount. "We're not even."

I don't give a damn about his difference of opinion. "You're out of get-out-of-jail cards. If you fuck with me or my family again, I'll treat you like anyone else."

His lips quiver. "You don't mean that."

"I'll cut your throat myself."

"Dami, you said she wouldn't get between us. You said—"

"Clean up this mess and get out of my house. I want you gone before Lina gets home."

He stares at me, body trembling, but he's already dead to me.

After sending Jana a text to tell her to take the day off, I lock myself in my study. The sound of a suitcase being rolled down the hallway filters through the walls. The front door opens and shuts. A vehicle starts up. Silence descends. The dark house reeks of squashed hope and loneliness, of meaningless lives and unfamiliar ghosts.

It's just me and my frazzled thoughts.

Lina betrayed me.

I lost the war for her affection.

Lina

THE HOUSE IS quiet and cold when I enter. Even in the heat of summer, it's always cold inside. I thank Brink for driving me, who nods and takes up his post by the front entrance. I close the door, shutting him out with the sun, and shiver in my rain-drenched clothes. There's something ominous about the silence today. Where are Zane and Jana?

Dropping my handbag on a chair in the entrance, I kick off my wet shoes and pad to the kitchen. I'm about to enter when someone grabs me from behind. I'm yanked against a hard chest. A big hand covers my mouth. Citrus fill my nostrils. Muscles bunch in the arm circling my waist. Damian is holding me too tightly. Despite recognizing him, I struggle in reflex, but he easily lifts me off my feet. I kick and tear at his arms, which only makes him squeeze harder. It feels as if he's pressing the air out of my lungs.

Carrying me like this, he climbs the stairs. My efforts have no effect on him. In his bedroom, he kicks the door shut and drops me to my feet. I fling around to face him.

He doesn't look at me. His jaw is set in a hard line, and his brown eyes are turbulent. He knows I've been to see Harold.

"Damian, please let me—"

He holds up a finger. "Do not speak."

Turning a laptop on the coffee table toward me, he presses play on a video clip. It's footage of Zane and me on the stairs. Shit. He has hidden cameras. I should've known.

He moves to another clip of Anne and me in the bedroom, when she stated her terms.

Looking at him with big eyes, I gauge his reaction, but his face is blank. Cold. I can't read him.

"Did you accept Anne's terms?" he asks.

He knows I did. I remain quiet.

"Did you accept Zane's terms?"

"No," I whisper.

He glances at the laptop where the scene with Anne is still playing out. "That's not what it looks like."

"I said I'd answer him tomorrow, and my answer was going to be no."

"You expect me to believe that after the lies you've been hiding?"

Imploring him with my eyes, I say, "Yes."

"I gave you truth." He slams the table. The laptop rattles. "I gave you *love*."

I stare at him, my lips parting, not sure I heard right.

Stalking to the window, he grips the sill so hard his knuckles turn white. "I gave you affection. I gave you everything that's mine." He turns his head to look at me, disappointment engraved in the beautiful lines of his face. "After everything, this is what you choose."

His words ignite a spark of anger. I will not stand here and let him accuse me of ungratefulness when he forced the *everything* he so eloquently quoted upon me. "You forced me to marry you. You forced me to lie when you forced me to stay."

"I didn't force you to fuck me, and yet you do, often and with enthusiasm. Is that a lie, too? Every time you cry out your orgasm, do you fake it?"

"No!" How dare he degrade the only pure memories I have? Suddenly,

I'm shivering with rage. "Don't you dare judge me when your own hands are stained black. Yes, I took the bait when Zane threw it at me. What did you expect, Damian? I'm not a wife. I'm a goddamn prisoner."

He straightens too slowly, with too much calculation. "I made you a promise I have to keep."

I remember only too well, and too late. I should've kicked him in the balls when he was angrier. Now, he's too controlled. Observant, he watches my every move, predicting my intentions. I glance at the door. His gaze follows. He believes I'll try to bolt.

I move. He jumps. Instead of fleeing toward the only exit, I grab the paperweight from the table and fling back my arm. Before I can throw it, he grabs my wrist. I whimper in pain and frustration as he squeezes until my fingers open, and the heavy weight drops with a plop on the carpet.

"Cooperate," he hisses, "and I'll take it easy on you."

I believe him, because he never lies. Fighting will only make it worse.

He undresses me slowly, tenderly almost. He caresses my breasts and stomach. He trails his hands over my back and buttocks and tells me how beautiful I am. He brushes my hair over my shoulder and kisses my neck.

"I hate you for making me do this," he presses against my ear.

Trembling in his arms, I rest my cheek against his chest. "You don't have to."

He lifts first one then the other arm, stretching them out horizontally. "I never break my promises."

He fetches rope and secures me to the bed frame like the last time, but instead of stringing me up, he ties each arm to a bedpost, making me kneel with my upper body on the bed and my ass in the air. Unlike the last time, I know what to expect. It makes the anticipation worse. When he pushes a ball of socks into my mouth and secures it with his tie, my fear skyrockets.

I shouldn't have gone to see Harold. I should've asked Damian to take me, but I never wanted him to find out what I was planning.

Whatever he was so painstakingly building, whatever love he mentioned, is wiped away by this one, impulsive act.

Turning my head sideways, I watch him pick up a cane from the chair. My heart stammers. He didn't have to fetch it from the study. He had it waiting, because he made a promise.

My courage fails. I protest around the fabric in my mouth. I want to beg him to believe me, but he won't, not after the damning evidence he's seen. He's going to punish me for accepting a deal with Zane. He's going to punish me for running to Harold, and for plotting my escape. Whatever I tell him now won't matter.

"Ten," he says behind me.

He runs the thin, smooth wood over my globes, letting me feel the potential viciousness of his instrument of choice. I pinch my eyes shut.

When the first lash falls, my upper body bows off the bed. I suck in a breath, but gag on the ball in my mouth. It's excruciating. I thought the whip was bad, but this pain is thinner, deeper. It burns to the bone. The second has me writhering, trying to make myself flatter on the mattress. Tears steam from my eyes. I bite into the ball in my mouth, but it doesn't help. He hits me again before I have time to catch my breath. I wail around the fabric that muffles my sounds. It feels as if I'm suffocating. Spots dance in front of my eyes. I wish it was from a deprivation of oxygen, but it's from pain. I can't stand it. I won't survive it. Every muscle in my body clenches. Cramps pull my calves and feet tight. I scream into the ball of socks, the cotton sucking up my saliva and leaving my throat dry and burning. I try to block it out, pray to faint, but I'm awake and sensitive, feeling every lash that whooshes through the air and turns my skin into a canvas of fire.

There is a point of relief, after all. My vision starts swimming and something else pushes through the pain. Arousal. The lower half of my body is glowing. Heat devours my globes. My clit throbs. Grinding my hips on the edge of the bed, I seek distraction for the ache. Damian lets me, and just as well, because when he cries, "Ten," the lash that follows cripples me. It hurts a thousand times worse than all the others. I don't have to look to know this is the one that broke skin. Shaking, I half-choke and half-sob. The magic word is ten, but the hurt is far from over. It's too deep under my skin. It's traveled all the way to my heart and nestled in my soul.

I'm clenching my knees and rubbing my thighs together when his hand comes between my legs. He touches me where it aches with pleasure until a new kind of burn starts to build. My sensory impressions are cross-wired. Raw need overtakes the pain until my lower body throbs with desire. I'm high on it, relaxing my muscles and giving over to the touch.

Damian says pretty words of how good I'm doing, but they're nothing but white noise. I home in on the rough timbre of his voice, letting it stroke my senses as the calloused pad of his finger strokes inside me. He enters me with another finger in my dark entrance. I'm hot with fever, burning up. I push back against his palm and make disgusting noises around the gag. I'm submersed in a fire where climaxing will be my only release. He stokes it higher, raining kisses over my back and in my neck, beckoning me to look at him.

I try, but my eyes won't focus. He's got something in his hands. Lube. He tells me to tell him no and squirts cold, slick liquid around my anus. I pinch my eyes shut again, because I can't cope with more than processing the different sensations I'm feeling. It's already an overload, the way he puts pressure on my dark entrance with his cock, and how the muscles stretch to accommodate the large head.

I can't tell pain from pleasure any longer. It hurts when he pushes in, and it feels good in other places. It feels unbearably good where his fingers are pumping inside my pussy. He's going too slowly. I can't take it anymore. It hurts too much. I just need him deeper, to go from torture to pleasure. I push back, but he holds me down with his hands on my hips, keeping me still.

"Shh. You'll tear."

Everything is already torn. My heart is bleeding, and my skin is mourning the loss of what we could've had even as the burn twists into pleasure.

I heave and remember I can't swallow.

He pumps, going shallow. It takes a long time, so long I start to drift in a sea of happiness. Just when I'm about to go under, he presses a finger on my clit. I start to contract around him, too full, too filled with Damian. He's in my pain and under my skin. A band of pleasure pulls my womb tight, and my vision splinters into spears of light. He moves faster, igniting fresh pain and pleasure. The sound of my scream is lost as he releases himself in my body. He stabs his hips into my burning buttocks. His muscles lock. He grunts and pushes me deeper into the mattress. Just when I think my ribs are going to crack, he lets up and pulls out.

It's over.

My senses separate. The fleeting pleasure flees. Pain returns. It leaves tears in its wake, and agony in my heart. Wetness dribbles from my ass, between my legs. Kneeling, I'm an epitome of punished humiliation. I wish for the floor to open and swallow the bed with me tied to it.

Damian works fast to free me. First my hands, then my mouth. My tongue is thick. My mouth is too dry to swallow. I look at him as he throws the ropes aside. He didn't even undress. He took me like this, fully clothed. He's already zipped himself up. When he disappears into the bathroom, I collapse to my knees. I roll onto my side, huddling on the floor, facing the wall. I can't look at him.

"Lina."

He's standing close, speaking softly.

"No," I manage to croak out, "don't."

He crouches next to me, a wet rag in his hand. "Let me take care of you."

"Get out," I say through clenched teeth.

"Lina." He reaches for me.

"Don't you dare touch me."

"You're not yourself."

Anger floods me, white and bright. It clears my vision and eats up my pain. My body pulls tight and straight. My nails cut into my palms. I'm screaming at the top of my lungs. "Get away from me. Leave me alone."

He straightens abruptly, hovering next to me.

"Go away. Get out. Leave." I choke on a sob, barely able to catch it on time. He can't see me break down. I won't give him that, too. "Now, you son of a bitch. I hate you."

Soft footsteps retreat to the far side of the room. The door opens, then closes. I lie dead still in the silence that follows. I've never felt lonelier. I'm shaking with sobs and pain.

What he did to me, I can never forgive him. I didn't think there could be anything worse than a whipping. How wrong I was. How much worse can he do? What comes after the cane? He's just shown me how dangerous it is to trust a monster, how stupid to forget a monster is not made of kindness.

Rolling onto my stomach, I push to my knees. I have to use the bed to pull myself up. My legs are quaking so much I can't make it to the bathroom without the aid of the wall. For the first time since I married Jack, I lock a door behind me. I turn the key and feel the welcoming safety enveloping me. Gripping the edge of the vanity, I heave as a wave of nausea sets in. Aftershock. Adrenaline. I wait for it to pass before I open the faucet and wet my face. I cup my hand and take a sip of water. Turning, I look at my backside in the mirror. Nine red welts run across my ass. The tenth is bleeding. At least he only broke skin once. I study the new marks and imprint them in my mind.

With a shaking hand, I turn on the water in the shower and wait for it to run warm. I wash myself as much as I can endure, everywhere I can. I force my legs to comply until I've stepped out of the shower, and then I sink down on the rug. I take the time I need, enough to feel emotionally more stable, before I dress and put on my shoes. I take a bag from the closet and throw in a few changes of clothes. Draping the sling over my shoulder, I open the door.

Silence greets me.

The grandfather clock strikes. It's five in the afternoon.

I walk down the stairs, softly. I pass every room. Empty. He left.

In the entrance, I retrieve my handbag. I take out my phone and leave it on the table with the keys. The phone will be tracked.

Brink doesn't bat an eyelash when I open the door. He didn't hear what happened upstairs. He goes to the car and opens the door. I get into the back, wincing at the pain as I sit.

"Where to, Mrs. Hart?" he asks when he takes the driver's seat.

"To the supermarket, please." I don't have a plan. I'll figure things out from there.

His eyes find mine in the rearview mirror. "You have a bag."

"I'm going to the gym afterward," I lie.

"Yes, ma'am."

We pull off slowly. The car rolls by the bat boxes and the new Acacia trees. We pass the gates and take the off-ramp to the highway. As we hit the traffic, I make myself a promise.

No one will ever hurt me like this again.

CHAPTER 19

Damian

*S*lamming the steering wheel, I turn the car around. Everything inside me protests at the distance I put between Lina and me. I don't even know where the fuck I was heading. There's an urgency in my gut to be with her, something gnawing, something disturbing. Everything feels wrong. Upside down. I'm a fucking mess. My head screams I shouldn't be near her right now, but my heart doesn't want to listen. If I hadn't left the house, I wouldn't have been able to respect her wish for time alone. Fuck time alone. Fuck the fact that right now I'm emotionally about as stable as a ticking bomb.

Cars honk as I skip lanes and force myself between a minivan and a truck. I don't know what's driving me so hard. I only know I need to get back to her. Maybe it's the little voice in my head that tells me I fucked up. Couldn't I for once not deliver on a promise? I clench the wheel harder. I can't make exceptions. It's the shortest way to losing credibility. Why the hell did she have to force my hand? Lina's pain makes me hard, but what I had to do today didn't turn me on. I didn't enjoy breaking her perfect skin. I desired her like always, but it wasn't the sadism. It was the need to possess her. It was an all-consuming burn to own her in every way and hole possible, so she knows to who she belongs, where she belongs. I didn't fool around. I took her hard. I should've ignored her request for space, damn it. She needs me.

Cold sweat breaks out on my forehead for no explainable reason. Exceeding the speed limit, I try to make it back to the house before peak hour traffic hits, but it's too late. It takes over an hour before I get home.

Brink isn't at the door. It's a different guard.

"Where's my wife?"

"Out, sir."

Fuck. "Out where?"

"Supermarket, sir."

I hope with all my soul it's to buy jelly beans, but my gut already knows otherwise. Goddamn. I shouldn't have left her. Not like that.

Charging through the door and up the stairs, I dial Brink. "Where are you?"

"At the strip mall, sir."

"Where's Lina?"

"In the pharmacy."

I stop on the landing, my heart slamming to a standstill. "Tell me you're with her."

He clears his throat. "She said she needed tampons."

Of course that's what she fucking said. The idiot. She doesn't have a cent in her purse. "Can you see her?"

"Yes. Uh, no. She must be behind the shelf."

"Go the fuck inside. Now."

"Yes, sir."

A car door slams and footsteps fall. A bell chimes.

The wait is too long. Five, ten seconds, but I hold onto hope.

A curse. A shuffle. Another bell.

"She's gone, sir. Backdoor."

"Find her."

"Yes, sir."

I cut the call and dial Lina. The phone rings from downstairs. Peering over the rail, I see it on the table in the foyer. Fuck. She's alone, without money or a phone. So fucking vulnerable. Raking my hand through my hair, pulling at the strands, I try to think like Lina.

She ran. After what I did to her, she fucking ran.

I kick the wall. I dial my security company and get the manager, Maze, on the line. I tell him I want my wife back, unharmed. He puts ten men on the case, pronto. There's nothing money can't buy. Except my wife. I call a jail buddy and get word out. The reward is big enough to get anyone interested. Then I dial the guardhouse and summon one from the entourage who accompanied Lina to Brixton.

A short while later, a guard with a pistol and rose tattooed on his bald head enters the study.

He shifts his weight. "You wanted to see me, sir?"

"Tell me what happened at Dalton's place."

"Mrs. Hart went in to see him. She asked us to wait outside but left the door open so we could see them. They spoke for five minutes, and then she left."

"Did you hear what they were talking about?"

"Only bits and pieces of the conversation. They kept their voices down."

"Tell me what you heard."

He swallows. "Brink was at the front of our group, sir. He would've been in better earshot."

"I'm asking you."

He glances behind me at the whips on the wall.

"I suggest you start talking. You don't want me to make you."

He sobers. "Mrs. Hart said something about getting evidence for him. They had an argument, but I couldn't hear what about. I assumed it had something to do with the fact that she didn't have it."

"You're dismissed."

He doesn't let me invite him twice.

The guard's testimony confirmed my actions were justified. Lina lied to me. She collaborated with Anne and Zane. She knowingly broke my rule by going to Dalton. She planned her escape when she agreed to Zane's terms, not that she'll ever be able to hide from me. Now she's gone. I showed her what I'm capable of, and she couldn't handle the monster. It must've been pretty bad for her to have run, knowing what I can do to her when I catch her. Fear burns like a slow fire through my insides. My stomach twists, and my skin turns clammy. The thought of losing her makes me physically ill. This is my fault. Who I am makes me sick.

Charging to the fireplace, I rip the cane from the wall and slam it over my knee. With a clack, the wood breaks in two. I chuck the pieces into the empty fireplace. The whip follows. I do the same with the paddle and every other instrument designed to inflict pain. Then I pour firelighter liquid over the lot and light a match. The things I did to Lina go up in flames. It'll burn to ashes. The marks will vanish. Will her hatred? Will she ever give me her faith again?

There's only one thing I can do. The only thing I'll ever do. Every single time.

Bring her back.

~

Lina

PHIL OPENS the door to his townhouse and lets me enter first. It wasn't that hard to escape. Brink trusted me. I've never tried to run during his employ. I said I needed tampons and used the backdoor of the pharmacy to escape. I ran for a while, until a woman stopped and asked if I needed a lift. She dropped me at the gym, and I convinced Phil to give me shelter for the night. Not the best move, as Damian will definitely question everyone I know, which means everyone at the gym, but it'll give me time and a place to sleep until tomorrow. I don't have another alternative except for Reyno, and as I know Damian, he'll check there first.

"Sorry about the mess," Phil says. "I didn't expect company."

I dump my bags on the sofa and hug myself. "Don't stay for my sake. Do whatever you were planning on doing. I'll be out of your hair tomorrow."

He leans an arm on the wall, caging me in from the side. "There's always been a spark between us."

I back away. "There's no spark. Never was. Never will be."

He winks. "You don't need to play hard to get with me. I'm all over you, babes."

"I don't play that way."

"Fine." He shrugs. "Want something to munch?"

"I thought you were going out for drinks with your friends."

"With you here? Plans have changed."

An uneasy feeling slithers up my spine.

He walks to the kitchen and pours two glasses of wine. "Wanna talk about it?"

I take the glass he offers. "No."

He downs his wine and slams the glass down on the counter, smacking his lips. "I could never put the two of you together. I mean, you and Damian, you're like opposites."

I take a gulp of the wine. It's sour. "I said I don't want to talk about it. I'm really tired." And sore. I need painkillers. "Do you mind if I just rest for a while?"

He walks down the short hallway and braces a shoulder on the doorframe. "In here."

I follow and try to peer around him, but his body takes up half of the hallway. His chest bulges as he crosses his arms. "You look like you can do with a massage."

"I'm good."

I step around him and stop. The bed is unmade, and clothes are scattered everywhere. A baseball cap hangs on the bedpost.

"This is your room."

He gives me a crooked smile. "The other room is a study. I only have one bed."

"I can take the sofa."

He steps forward, backing me up against the wall. I hiss as my ass hits the bricks. Wine sloshes over the edge of the glass.

"Cut the chase, Lina. Admit it. That's why you're here. Why else would you look me up at the gym?"

Panic floods my system. My ears start to ring. "I looked you up because I need a place for the night. Nothing more."

He slams his palms next to my face. His breath is hot on my mouth, smelling of wine. "A girl like you must know what you do to men in your tight gym pants and exercise bras."

I push on his chest, spilling wine on his T-shirt. "Get off."

He grabs my jaw and brings his lips to mine. "If you want to play rough, I'm all in."

"You're crazy."

"You're so innocent and untouchable. That's why Damian wants you, isn't it? He's one of those bad guys who likes good girls, and you're one of those good girls who likes pain." He motions at my scars. "I can be bad, babes, as bad as you want me."

I shove him, hard. The glass drops to the carpet. "Get off me."

"Not a chance. Not now that I finally have you alone."

He crushes his lips to mine. It's a thin, wet, sickening kiss. He fumbles with the buttons of my blouse, pressing me to the wall with his weight. I ache where Damian caned and fucked me, but it's nothing compared to the revulsion that fills me. I feel sick. When he gives me breathing space, I bite down hard. He lets go with a yelp, tearing my blouse in the process.

Licking his bleeding lip, he stares at me incredulously. "You bitch."

I slap him, hard.

He grabs my wrist and tries to turn me. If he twists my arm behind my back, I'm as good as raped. I claw at his face, winning another fraction of distance, enough to lift a knee. He grunts as the blow hits him between the legs. Letting me go, he cups his crotch and whines in agony. I don't hesitate. I run for the door. I yank it open just as he recovers enough to straighten. Leaving behind my clothes and hand-bag, I run for the corner where the only streetlamp burns, yelling at the top of my lungs.

Phil's loud curse comes from a distance behind me. When I look over my shoulder, I see the neighbors peeling out of their doors. Their interest is enough to make Phil turn around and limp back to his house.

I stop running. What if he calls Damian? I feel like hitting myself on the head. It was a stupid move. Now I'm stuck alone, outside, in the dark, without my bag and purse.

Looking up and down the road, I consider my options. I have to find a way of getting to Reyno. I can bribe him for money. He doesn't have to know I left my phone with the incriminating recording behind. I'm going to have to hitchhike.

Setting off in the direction of the main road, I glance behind me again. The neighbors have gone back to their dinners and televisions. Phil's door is firmly closed.

As I blow out a sigh of relief, something hard hits me over the head. My mind cries *no* as I fall to the pavement on my hands and knees. Before I have time to look at the face of my attacker, he hits me a second time.

Pain explodes in my skull. Stars follow, and then darkness.

∼

Damian

My first stop is at Reyno's. He opens the door wearing slippers and a robe with a Holiday Inn logo.

"It's after nine," he says even as he opens the door wider.

For the fee I pay him, he'll open his door at two in the morning if I say so. I follow him to the lounge and let him pour me a drink while I weigh my words.

He hands me a whisky. "What happened?"

"Lina's gone."

He turns as white as his stolen hotel robe. "Gone how?"

Twirling the glass, I stare at the liquor. "She ran."

He flops into an armchair and downs his drink as if the shock is personal, as if Lina ran from him.

"Any idea where she might've gone?"

He looks at me accusingly. "No."

"She's not safe out in Johannesburg alone."

He slams his glass down on the side table. "Tell me something I don't know."

"You're her shrink. You must have an inkling of what her thought process will be."

Agitation filters into his tone. "She had nowhere else but *you*."

My pulse thuds in my temples. "Say what you mean."

"Why did she run?"

I take a sip of the alcohol, welcoming the burn in my throat. "I punished her."

"How?"

"Cane."

He scoffs. "And you wonder why she ran?"

"I don't wonder why. I wonder *where*."

"For her sake, I wish I could help you, but I can't."

"Is there anything I need to know?"

"You're asking me to break my patient confidentiality clause."

It's my turn to scoff. "Don't pretend to be ethical, all of a sudden."

"No," he says angrily. "There's nothing else you need to know."

"Call me if you hear from her."

"I'm sure she's just hiding out somewhere, licking her wounds. Lina is proud. She's not the kind of woman who'll enjoy being punished."

"Does anyone?"

"Some women crave the pain. I don't know the history of her self-mutilation, but I don't think Lina is a masochist. If that's what you need, you have the wrong partner."

"I didn't ask for psychological advice." I leave the glass on the table and turn for the door.

"Damian."

I turn and wait.

"She's not crazy. I don't think she's ever been."

I continue to wait, feeling there's more to come.

"You should let me declare her mentally competent," he says carefully, measuring my reaction.

"No."

Perplexed, he stares at me. "Why not?"

It's easier to keep someone against their will when their legal decisions are in your hands. Holding all power over Lina is warped. I'm not beyond admitting it. It doesn't change the fact that she's mine or that I'll never let her go. I'll use whatever means I must to keep her.

"Call me." I slam the door behind me as I go.

It starts to rain, again. Running my hands over my head, I look up at the dark sky. In no time, my jacket and shirt are soaked, but I don't feel wetness or cold. All I feel is the ice in my heart. A piece of me is missing. Without her, my heart may as well be hacked out. She's been a part of me for so long, I don't know how to exist without her. She's been a part of me from the day I first saw her, even when she belonged to another man. I won't rest until she's back where she belongs.

～

Lina

THE PAIN in my head is horrific. The hammering won't stop. I'm aching everywhere from my waist down. Opening my eyes slowly, I take in my surroundings. I'm sitting on a chair in the darkest corner of a room with a single lamplight. I try to swallow the dryness of my mouth away, but my tongue is too thick. I try to move, but my arms and legs are tied. Panic flushes through me, intensifying the throbbing in my skull. My memory returns with sharp shards of fear. Forcing calm, I try to breathe and not alarm whoever has taken me to the fact that I'm awake.

I sharpen my senses. Movement catches my eye. There are two people in the room, their outlines visible in the dark. A woman, by the shape of her body, and a man. The hammering sound is rain pelting the roof. From under my lashes, I take in the furniture to get an idea of where I am. There's a bed and television. A kettle and jar with instant coffee packets stand in the circle of lamplight.

Their whispering reaches me.

"He was never going to fall for you," the woman says. "I was our only hope."

"You ruined it," the man replies. "You shouldn't have shown him the bread rolls."

Zane? Anne?

Fear, boiling hot, fills my veins. If this is about revenge, I'm dead.

"Go check on her," Zane says.

"Why me?"

"Fuck it." He stomps to the chair and yanks my head up by my hair.

I yelp at the pain that doesn't help my headache.

He lets go with another pull. "She's awake."

Anne approaches, her expression hidden in the dark. "I need more light."

Zane carries the lamp as close as the cord allows and leaves it on the floor.

The light washes over Anne as she regards me with her hands on her hips. "Is she still bleeding?"

"It stopped."

My voice is scratchy. "What do you want?"

"You can't be *that* naïve," Anne says, her tone mocking.

Zane takes his smartphone from his pocket. "I'm calling Dami."

"Wait." Anne grabs his arm. "Let him sweat it out a bit longer. He'll be easier to outsmart if he panics."

They're doing this for money. They're going to ask for a ransom. They didn't kidnap me to kill me out of revenge. That doesn't mean they won't kill me. No, I'm not *that* naïve.

"How much?" I ask.

"How much what?" Anne snaps.

"How much is my life worth?"

She grins and looks at Zane.

He answers, "Thirty million."

He must be joking. "Damian can't just sign over thirty million. He doesn't have that kind of cash."

"No, but he can sell his mine."

"Sell it?" I choke out.

"We already have an investor lined up."

Oh, my God. They're vicious. They found a company that must've had its eye on a mine for a while, a company with enough resources.

"Who?" I force from my dry throat.

"Who do you think?" Zane asks.

It can't be, and yet, it's the obvious answer.

"Dalton Diamonds?" I whisper, fearful.

"Of course," Anne says. "Oh, and Damian will also have to hand over the evidence against your father."

My stomach drops. Harold's cronies must've gotten the funding together. How did they do it? International loans? How they managed, doesn't matter. If Damian gives in to Anne and Zane's demands, the mine will fall back into Harold's hands. That mine means everything to Damian. Every single drop of energy he spent during the last six years went into getting that mine back. It means more to him than money, or he wouldn't have taken the risk of buying a dying mine. He founded the black diamond initiative and turned a dead project into a profitable one. The mine represents the sum of his existence. If that's what they want, I'm dead for sure.

"Damian will never give up his mine."

"You underestimate your value, honey," Anne says. "He even got rid of Zane for you."

"What?"

"Shut up," Zane hisses.

Damian threw Zane out? "I didn't know."

"You must be mighty proud," Anne says bitterly. "You managed to get rid of all of us. Don't you know it's nasty not to share, darling?"

"How is this supposed to work?" I ask. "Do you get commission?"

"We'll get our cut," Anne replies, "but this alone makes it worth the while." She lifts her hand and turns it to the light.

A teardrop diamond glitters on her finger. I gasp. She took my engagement ring? How low can a person go?

Taking in my expression, she chuckles. "You didn't want it, so it shouldn't matter."

"You can't just steal someone's engagement ring."

She makes a face. "Don't tell me you're superstitious about symbols of love and all that crap."

I'm not. In all honesty, Damian didn't give the ring to me with affection or love. He gave it to me so I wouldn't be publicly humiliated if one of the world's biggest diamond magnates didn't give his wife a diamond ring. It would've been a clear message that he doesn't love me. The whole world would've known for a fact what they're only suspecting. The kindness of the act hasn't dawned on me until now. I accused him of making me a whore and showpiece, but he's never once publicized the ring or demanded something in exchange. The necklace is a different story, but he's not guilty where the ring is concerned. I said I didn't want it, but I suddenly want it back with my whole heart.

"Give it to me," I say through clenched teeth.

Anne smiles, admiring the stone. "I don't think so. It's a nice bonus."

"How much longer do you want to wait?" Zane asks, sounding irritated.

"Give it until morning. Damian will be nicely worried by then."

Despite all of Zane's shortcomings, Damian has been loyal to him. Damian deserves better than this. The more I'm submitted to Zane's nasty tactics, the more he comes across as a gold digger. It makes me wonder. Has he ever been Damian's friend?

"How long have you been planning on getting your hands on Damian's money?" I ask. "Since you got out of jail or from before?"

"Tell her," Anne says. "It's not like it matters any longer."

"Since he shared his plans with me in jail," Zane says.

It was a scam all along. That's why Zane brought Anne to live in the house. It was to seduce Damian, and when that didn't work, they settled for plan B—kidnapping me.

"How did you even find me?"

"It wasn't too hard," Zane says. "When Dami put out word to our network that he was looking for you, the information was bound to reach me. He may have thrown me out like trash, but we still share the same connections. I reckoned you only have two friends in this world

—Reyno and Phil. Anne watched Reyno's place, and I waited outside Phil's. Was no big surprise when the two of you arrived like lovebirds in heat. I have to say, you made it pretty easy for me. You practically ran into my arms."

I never liked Zane, but I thought his actions were born from jealousy. Now he fills me with nothing but disgust. "Since when have you been scheming with Harold?"

"Since you made Dami get rid of Anne."

"You mean since your backup plan when you couldn't get Damian's undivided attention failed."

"Doesn't really matter now, does it?" he says. "It's all just logistics."

Not all of it. "Did you fall in love with him before or after he made his money?"

His face twists into a mask of fury. He lifts his hands, but I don't cower. I push out my chin, waiting for the blow. I've taken worse.

Anne grabs his wrist. "Don't. If Damian asks for proof that she's alive, we don't want to show him a bruised face."

Glaring at me, he lowers his hand.

"I need water."

Zane nods at Anne. "Give her some. You're right. We need her in good shape."

"Why me?" she whines.

"Fuck it." He kicks my chair and marches to an adjoining room.

Anne smiles at me. "You better hope Damian wants you back badly."

Damian

It's after midnight when I knock on Phil's door. He opens it warily, as if he's expecting trouble. My instincts go on high alert.

"I'm looking for Lina."

"Lina?" He scratches the back of his neck.

"My wife," I grit out, suppressing the urge to knock his head against the wall.

His gaze moves to the lounge for a fraction of a second. "Why would she be here?"

Shoving him back, I walk inside and shut the door. If I need to get rough with him, I don't want witnesses.

"Hey, man." He raises his hands. "Easy. She's not here."

I scan the lounge. My travel bag and Lina's handbag lie on the sofa. Premature relief and rage mix in my veins. I lift him by the front of his T-shirt, walking him back through the house.

"Bedroom," I say.

His toes barely touch the ground. He's tripping all over himself as we move deeper into the house.

"First door left," he chirps.

The bed is empty. The second room holds only a desk and chair.

I shake him. "Where is she?"

"I don't know!"

Something crunches under my shoe. The remains of a broken wineglass lie in a red stain on the carpet.

Dragging him behind me, I go to the kitchen. There's a stack of dirty dishes in the sink and a wineglass with a red ring in the bottom on the counter.

Two wineglasses. One dropped in the hallway. I swear to God, if he put a dirty finger on her, I'll hack it off.

I smash his body into the wall. "Where is she?"

"This is not what it looks like." He cowers. "I can explain."

Fucking coward. "I'm listening."

"She came to the gym, said she needed a place to crash. Look man, I don't know what happened between the two of you, but she was pretty shaken up. I couldn't leave her there and I was anyway locking up, so I brought her home with me."

I twist his T-shirt and slam his shoulders into the bricks. "And then?"

"We got here, and she got all weird on me, attacked me and shit."

"Think carefully about what happened, because I'll find Lina. When I do, your stories better match up. If they don't, you're dead."

He starts to cry. "I knew you were bad news, man. I never should've let you into the gym."

"Man up, Phil. Start talking."

He wipes snot from his nose. "I gave her wine to chill because she was so strung out, as in really flipping, if you know what I mean. And I mean, a girl isn't at a guy's place to watch television, right? She was here for a revenge fuck."

I still at the phrase, rage clawing through me. If he put his dick in her, he's definitely dead.

"She said she was tired. I mean, she was hinting, man. When a woman says she's tired, she wants to go to bed, right? So, I showed her the bedroom, and she started getting all weird." He saws his teeth over his lip, clearly not eager to carry on.

"Then what?"

"Then I kissed her, and she fucking bit me. She slapped me and scratched me like a wildcat. I tried to calm her down, but she kneed me in the balls and took off."

That's my Lina. *My* Lina. I barely hold it together enough to finish my interrogation. "Where did she go?"

"I don't know. She ran off in the direction of the main road."

I narrow my eyes. "Leaving her bags behind."

"Like I said, she freaked out, man."

"You touched her."

He pales. "Damian, please. You're a man. You know how it is."

"Do *not* compare me to you." I grab his hair and drag him to the counter. "Let me tell you something about how it is. When a woman says she's tired, it's because she's tired. If she says she doesn't want to fuck you, it's because she doesn't want to fuck you. Get it?"

"Yes, yes!" He tries to pry my fingers from his hair.

I grab his wrist and slam it down on the fake marble surface. "Splay your fingers."

"No! No! What are you doing?"

I take a meat knife from the block. "Do as I say, or you'll lose all five."

"Oh, fuck. Fuck, fuck. No, man. I didn't do anything."

"Shut up. Let this be a valuable lesson and be glad it's only one."

He falls down, using his weight to try and pull free.

"Splay them, Phil."

He slobbers like a puppy, crying and spluttering incoherent words, hanging off the side of the counter.

"Your choice." I position the knife. "Five fingers."

"No! Wait!" He pulls himself up by his free hand, screaming and crying. Snot flies everywhere, but he splays his fingers.

"I'm going to be nice. I know you need your index and middle finger to grip weights, so I'm going to take your ring finger."

"Oh, man. Oh, man oh man oh man—"

I drop the knife.

He pisses himself.

I let go. "You'll want to call an ambulance before you bleed to death. Better explain it as a kitchen accident or I'll come back for the rest. Got it?"

He drops to his knees, clutching his arm against his chest. I find his phone in the bedroom and put it on the floor next to him.

Outside, Brink stands on attention. "The screams woke the neighbors, sir."

There's light in all the neighboring windows on both sides of the road. Just as well. I'll be interrogating every single person in this neighborhood.

I tell Brink of my intention and instruct him to start at the other end.

"Shall I wait to deal with the cops?" he asks.

I shake my head. "They won't come." Not in this neighborhood.

Lina

318

THE CURTAINS ARE CLOSED, but enough light filters through the thin fabric for me to make out we're in a cheap hotel room. Anne brings me a sandwich and a glass of milk, which she feeds me. When I've eaten, she nods at Zane.

"It's time," she says.

The bread gets stuck in my throat. Damian will never part with his mine. Everything that happened between us was because of that mine. I was a means to an end, not the end. My head still aches, and my muscles are stiff from sitting in one position all night. The bonds are tight. The chair is hard, reminding me of how sore my butt and tender my asshole are, but all of these discomforts are minor compared to the thudding of my heart as Zane presses the dial on his phone.

"If Damian agrees to your demands," which I'm dead sure he won't, "are you going to let me go or just kill me anyway?" If I had any money, I would've put it on the latter.

"You'll just have to wait and see," Anne says.

The alarm clock says it's ten in the morning. By now, Damian would be at the office. He would've had breakfast, been to the gym, and showered. Maybe he looked for me, or had his men search the streets around the pharmacy where I dodged Brink.

The strain on Zane's face is clear when he holds up a finger, indicating Damian is taking his call.

Zane's voice sounds hollow and haunted. "Hallo, Dami."

Whatever Zane tells himself, he cares about more than the money. He cares about Damian. How far will he let his greed drive him? Does he care enough to not go through with this? I hold my breath, but if I was hoping Zane would change his mind, it's squashed at his next words.

"I presume you're looking for Lina. If you want her back, you'll follow our instructions. Check your inbox."

He hangs up.

"What if he calls the police?" Anne asks.

"He won't," Zane says. "It won't help."

He's right. I'm not sure anyone can help me now.

~

Damian

I STARE AT THE EMAIL, seething with suppressed fury. Zane took Lina. He kidnapped my wife. That terrifies me. Zane hates Lina. He blames her for everything that's not her fault.

Brink enters the study, looking grim.

Zane fucked me over well. For the amount he's asking with little over a day's notice, I don't have a choice but to sell to his nominated investor. I'd be selling back to Dalton Diamonds. The evidence I have to deliver with the deal will ensure Dalton walks away a free and wealthy man, once more. Bitterness fills my chest. My mine will fall back into Dalton's hands, but it's nothing compared to the emptiness I'd feel if Lina is gone.

"Sir?" Brink reminds me he's still waiting for my instructions.

"Did our men find anything?"

"No, sir."

No trace of Zane. He knows how to wipe out his trail.

"Lina?"

"Nothing new, sir."

"Thank you."

When he leaves, I dial the head of the security company. Maze is discreet and trustworthy. His business depends on it.

"What's the situation?" he asks tersely.

"You saw the demands." I forwarded him the email in an encrypted message.

"Dalton must be in on this."

"No doubt."

"How are you dealing with him?"

"I first want Lina back safely."

"What about the demands?"

"I'm going to meet them."

There's a pause before he replies. "Have you considered all options?"

"Yes." I drag a hand over my face. "There are too many places in this city to hide." It doesn't mean I'm not trying. I'm using every connection and all the influence I've got.

"Look, I know your business dealings aren't one hundred percent clean, but the cops have a larger network and workforce. They'll gladly take on the case and turn a blind eye for a bribe."

"Too risky. You read Zane's threat."

"Will he go through with it?"

"If he must." I shudder at the thought.

"Whatever you need, my men are at your disposal."

I thank him and hang up. Then I call my attorney and set up a meeting for within the hour.

Lina

MY KIDNAPPERS untie me twice to use the bathroom. They feed me another dry sandwich and a glass of water. Thirsty, I drink every drop. They take turns to eat, sitting on the bed and watching me intently. Too late, I realize my mistake. As if on cue, my headache starts to slip and my vision splits. They drugged me.

"What did you give me?"

No answer.

Goosebumps break out over my skin. My scalp itches. A wave of nausea hits me. When it passes, my head starts to buzz. My control starts to falter. I fight it, but it's no use. My eyes draw close.

"She's gone," Zane says.

"Let's get her in the car. We can start driving to Germiston."

"Not before the money comes through."

"What difference does it make? She'll be at the bottom of the lake before noon."

"I don't want to be on the move before the deal is done. Someone may recognize us."

"We have disguises."

"Still, I don't want to take a chance."

"Damian won't let this go. I don't like just sitting here."

"Check the email. As soon as we have proof, we move."

Their voices drone on and tune out. It feels as if I'm falling into a jar full of jelly beans. Color erupts behind my eyelids, but before I can enjoy the rainbow, it turns into nothing.

CHAPTER 20

Damian

The disadvantage of being a diamond magnate is that everyone wants your money. You always risk kidnapping, or worse, having your loved ones kidnapped for ransom. The advantage is that you have power at your disposal. You have resources at your fingertips. The advantage of being an ex-con is that you have connections and loyalty.

Lucky for me, I am both. Zane is nothing. By taking my wife, he broke a code of conduct. By blackmailing me with her life, he signed his death warrant. Not one of our jail connections will protect him. The minute word has gone out, and I made sure it went out wide, our allies distanced themselves from him. Most added money to the price I put on his head. A man doesn't turn on his people. It's like killing your mother. My allies did what anyone would do for family. They dropped whatever shady dealings they had going on and started to hunt for Zane.

For the right incentive, be that money or fear, people will always talk. It just so happened that the night cleaning lady at the airport saw a man and woman carrying someone into the hotel across the highway. She took a photo with her phone. It wasn't hard to identify Zane and Anne's physiques, even if they wore wigs. Zane's solid build and vanity betrayed him. I'd recognize those made-to-measure crocodile leather boots anywhere.

I would've gladly paid the thirty million Zane is asking. There's not enough money in the world to make up Lina's worth. Not even the mine is worth her life. She's family, the future mother of my children. She's the motivation that kept me going in jail. I'm not even sure it was about the business. Yes, I wanted to take back what Dalton stole from me. Yes, I wanted revenge. Lina has always been a part of the plot to achieve those goals. Somewhere along the line, she became the plot. Standing here, outside the hotel, I suddenly know with startling clarity that's not true. She didn't gradually turn into the end-goal. She's always been the goal.

The gun in my hand shakes slightly as I internalize the insight. The moment is huge, as huge as it's about to get when I break her free. Around me, the day rolls out like any other day, as if I'm not at the biggest turning point of my life. The smell of smoke from a neighboring township hangs thick in the air. It burns my nostrils. The sky is blue with swatches of clouds on the horizon, a promise of late afternoon rain. The sound of traffic from the highway is a constant noise. People are carrying on with the business of living. The day and its extraordinary mundaneness imprints in my mind. My body hums with adrenaline and awareness.

It's an easy mistake to believe the change in my ambitions crept up on me, but they already changed the day I first walked into Dalton's house. From the moment Lina gave me her shawl, diamonds weren't my priority any longer. It was her. It *is* her. Knowing she's in room number sixteen with a man and his sister who could push a gun against her head and pull the trigger is worse than torture. It kills me. What have they done to her? What are they doing to her even now as I load and check my gun?

Pulling up her image in my mind, I imagine her scared and lonely. I remember the night I requested an audience with Dalton and how out of my depth and ashamed of my poverty I'd felt, but certain of my abilities and hopeful of my future. I sure as hell wasn't scared, but Lina was, and fuck me for not realizing it until now. When she offered me her grandmother's shawl, she said it made her feel safe. She was scared that night, but I was too occupied with my own, selfish mission, with convincing Dalton to invest in my project, to realize that in giving me her warmth and security, she left herself vulnerable. When I saw her standing in the hallway, I saw a beautiful girl dressed in a gown that cost more than what I earned in a year. Revisiting the scene in my mind, I see her wide eyes and tense shoulders. I see the way she turned into herself when Dalton wrapped his arm around her. She feared that night. Why? Because Dalton was choosing her a husband. She was dressed up like a showpiece. That was what the business dinner was about.

When I showed Dalton my discovery, I made up his mind. I sealed the deal on Lina. All he needed after getting rid of me was the mining rights. That's why he gave her to Clarke. Unknowingly, I set Lina's fate. Fuck me. I only have myself to blame for how our history turned out. The accusations I loaded on her shoulders for not waiting, for not believing in me, are unfounded. There was nothing she could've done to alter the path I paved with my naïve ambition. Dalton's greed would never have allowed it.

The knowledge shatters me. It makes me hate myself more than I already do. The insight comes too late to change how Lina and I have started, but I still have the rest of her life. I'll live to make it up to her. I'll be what she wants, who she needs. I'll forsake the reason that made her run. I swear this to myself, Lina will never have another reason to escape me. If I can have her back in one piece, I'll never crack a whip over her back again. I make the oath as I wipe the sweat from my face on my sleeve, getting ready to take down the door that stands between us.

Brink sneaks around the corner, giving me a tense nod to let me know the men are in position. The hotel is surrounded. There's no way out but through us. A few connections from jail have pitched to offer their assistance, but they're hanging back, acting on my command. The revenge is mine. It's our unwritten rule.

"I want Zane alive," I say into the mike that connects me to the men. I need answers. When I have them, I'm going to kill Dalton.

The sun burns down on my head. My shadow is a tight circle around my body. The curtains of room sixteen are closed. They're a faded yellow with a sunflower motive. Those curtains will haunt me in my sleep. Every time I close my eyes, I'll see Lina in a field of faded sunflowers. I'll remember what it felt like to feel fear, the real kind that can shatter your soul. I'll recall the pressure of my index finger on the trigger, and the foreign urge to pray. I'll see Lina's face as she stared up at the portrait of Mary and feel the ache in my soul for that missing smile. I'll see the possibility of a smile in every moment I'm yet to steal from her future.

Brink waits. Sweat beads on his forehead. His ponytail ruffles in the breeze. I give the signal. Slowly, we creep toward the door. The sounds of a news channel filters through the walls. Taking aim, I motion for Brink to kick down the door. It crashes into the room, sending dust up from the carpet. I take stock of the situation in a millisecond.

Lina is slumped in a chair, tied up. Shrieking like a hellcat, Anne jumps from the bed. Zane jerks with a start. Disbelief registers on his face. He recovers even as I charge, reaching for a gun on the nightstand. Before he can get it, I fire a warning shot into the wall. Anne's eyes are wild and feverish as she grabs the object closest to her, a stone ashtray.

For an instant, my focus is distracted. Zane uses the moment to pull a knife and leap over the bed, straight toward me. I don't think twice. I aim for his arm and pull the trigger. The knife drops to the floor. He loses his footing. Blood pumps from his bicep. Anne screams, hurling the ashtray at an unconscious Lina. It's a good aim, going for Lina's head. Projecting myself sideways, I intercept the heavy object, taking a knock under my breastbone. I hit the floor hard, shoulder first. Something cracks inside my body. I feel the fissure and hear the sound but feel no pain.

Zane has recovered the knife in his good hand and comes at me with a snarl. Rolling onto my back, I lock my elbows, point the barrel at his kneecap, and pull the trigger. He grunts as he goes down.

"Hart," Brink shouts. "Three o'clock."

I'm just in time to see Anne retrieve the gun on the nightstand.

I shift my aim. "Drop it, Anne."

She turns the gun on Lina as if she hasn't heard the deadly threat in my tone. Hatred fills her eyes. Her finger curls around the trigger. I'm vaguely aware of Zane using the bed to push himself up. Between Zane, Anne, and me, there's no choice. The choice is always Lina. Before I can eliminate the danger threatening my wife, a shot goes off. Brink. His first priority is protecting Lina. Anne collapses. At the same time, Zane lifts the knife and dives. I barely have time to fire. His body jerks from the impact. His knees hit the carpet before he falls facedown.

Brink moves to the bathroom and signals it's clear. One of the guards is already cutting Lina loose. I waste no time in getting to her, leaving Brink to check Anne and Zane's vitals.

With his finger on a jugular vein in Zane's neck, Brink gives me a negative sign. Anne took a headshot.

"We'll clean this up," Brink offers.

I lift Lina's limp body into my arms. "Leave it. It'll look like a gang shootout."

My ribs protest as I walk outside into the glaring sun, but it's the happiest pain I've felt. One of the men opens the car door for me. I lower my precious bundle into the back before taking the seat next to her. After fitting her seatbelt, I arrange her body to rest in the crook of my arm.

"Hospital?" the guard who's driving asks, shooting a wary look at Lina's unconscious form.

She'll have to be checked by a doctor, but it'll have to be a house call. I can't afford the routine questions that'll come with a hospital visit.

"Home," I say, pulling her tighter against me.

Lina

I WAKE up to a warm and comfortable dream. I'm in a boat, rocking to a soothing rhythm. Outside, a storm is brewing, but inside I'm safe. I'm lying on a soft bed, wrapped up in strong arms. A delicious weight presses me deeper into the mattress. We're rocking together, moving with the ebb and flow of the tide. Like lazy waves, we lap at the shore.

Reveling in the feeling, I snuggle deeper. From afar, the cold tendrils of consciousness reach for me, trying to pull me from my dream, but I'm not ready to let go. It feels too good here. The rocking continues as new sensations join. Hands, broad and warm, drag over my shoulders, breasts, and hips. My awareness shifts, turning from languid to sensual. Slowly, my body comes alive. The tide builds, but this time, it's inside of me. I moan.

A deep chuckle caresses my ears. The rough timbre resonates through my breastbone. The sensual rocking escalates, waking a hunger in my core. I arch my back, and am rewarded with hard, hot skin sliding over skin. The hunger becomes unbearable, the rocking insistent. The wave rolls, but the crash remains just beyond my reach. I ride it like the boat, rocking, ebbing, but forever falling behind. Panting, I chase the crescent that cruelly escapes me. I moan again, frustrated, and this time we go faster until, at last, the wave lifts and curls.

I reach out, needing something to hold on to. My fingers tangle in damp hair. A hint of winter and citrus drifts over my senses. The harsh tendrils of reality finally strip me of my comfortable dream. Opening my eyes, I stare into a pair of dark ones. Damian hovers over me. My dream and reality merge. He's inside me. He cups my face and rocks his hips with that lazy rhythm that creates beautiful dreams and frightening realities. Sucking in a breath, I tense.

"Shh." He kisses my lips, never ceasing his movement.

A part of my memory is missing. I have questions and fears, but I'm too far down the road to release to stop him. His hand moves between our bodies, finding my clit. I jerk when he applies pressure, the touch too intense and not enough.

"Come, Lina."

I convulse around him. Needing him deeper, I wrap my legs around his ass. He groans with approval, driving his hips harder.

"Please, Damian."

He gathers my slick from where we're joined and runs it over my clit with the heel of his palm. He rubs in a circular motion, holding my eyes, reading me like the open book I am. I still feel disorientated, like I'm lost at sea, but the pleasure he creates with his hand and cock outshines my fear.

"Come," he says again.

I dig my nails into his shoulders, feeling adrift and unanchored. "Where am I?" I recognize his bedroom, but I have to be sure this is real.

"Where you should be." He grips my hair and pulls lightly, bringing my focus back to him. "Come."

"Damian."

He pinches my nipple. "Come."

When he kisses me, I do. The minute I let go, so does he. We come long and violently, breathing hard and shuddering in each other's arms. He holds me until the very last aftershock has passed before turning us on our sides, keeping our bodies locked together. He winces as he does so.

Alarm tightens my chest. I should feel many things, apprehension being on the top of the list, but I'm not myself. I'm disorientated, and with my mind's rational ability suppressed, all I feel is concern for the man whose seed is still inside my body, the man who makes me feel so safe, so warm, so good. So awful.

"What's wrong, Damian?"

"Nothing important. Just a broken rib."

My emotions are all over the place. Tears well up in my eyes.

The sound he makes mirrors the chuckle from earlier. "Your concern is endearing, but it's nothing to cry over."

The languid pleasure from earlier evaporates. My fear becomes sharper, but for a different reason. "Are you going to punish me?"

"Relax, angel." He kisses my lips. "I'm not going to punish you today."

I blow out a slow breath of relief, forcing myself not to think further than today so my body can once again relax and soak up his warmth. If I don't, I'll freak out about what has happened, Zane and Anne's last conversation returning with unwelcome clarity to my mind.

"Why did you run, Lina?"

Biting my lip, I try to look away, but he grips my chin and forces me to look at him.

"Was it the cane, or because I broke skin?"

"Both." My voice cracks. "I can't handle it. I can't handle you."

I'm not crazy enough for his darkness and not strong enough for his punishment. I can't take the depth of what he needs to find his warped pleasure. I may as well admit what my actions have already confirmed.

"What about the whip? Did you want to run after that, too?"

Will my answer have repercussions?

"I want your honesty," he says as if reading my mind. "I won't hold it against you."

"Yes," I whisper. "I wanted to run then, too." I still do, but for different reasons.

"Fine." He brushes a thumb over my lips. "I'll have to find a different way of punishing you."

The vice around my heart squeezes harder. I don't want to be punished at all.

"Relax." He rubs my back. "Your spine is about to snap."

Making a conscious effort, I try to relax my muscles.

"Good," he coos. "Are you going to tell me about it?"

"About what?"

"About what happened after you ran."

He makes it sound as if I have a choice, but there isn't one. One way or another, he'll find a way of making me talk. It doesn't matter. These aren't the truths I want to keep hidden.

"What do you want to know?"

"Did they hurt you?"

"Other than hitting me on the head, no."

"I had a doctor check you out, but I want to be sure."

Automatically, my fingers find the egg at the back of my head. "It doesn't hurt any longer."

"The doctor injected you with a painkiller. You may have a mild concussion, so you need to rest."

"What happened to your rib?"

"I took a knock in the fight."

My muscles tighten again. "What fight?"

"It's not important. Rest."

For now, I concede. I look toward the window where daylight filters in. "What time is it?"

"Go back to sleep."

"How did I get here? They drugged me. I can't remember anything after."

"I fetched you."

"How did you find me?"

"Easily."

I trail my hand over his side. The familiar weight of my engagement ring pulls my attention. It shouldn't be there, but it is, as if Anne never took it. "The ransom—"

"It's over, Lina. You're safe. Forget about the rest."

"It's so much money," I whisper, miserable with guilt.

"Which I would've gladly paid."

"Would have?"

"I didn't have to."

I'm still angry with him for what he did to me, but I'm also thankful that he found and saved me. As always, my signals where Damian is concerned are crossed. It's confusing. I don't know how I should feel, so I focus on filling the missing gaps in my memory.

"Zane? Anne? What about them?"

"Lina," his voice turns strict, "close your eyes and go back to sleep. The doctor said you should rest."

A fresh rush of fear clears some of the cobwebs from my mind. "Damian, please tell me. I have a right to know."

"Let it go."

"Are they...?"

"Dead, yes," he says, suddenly cold and angry.

Oh, my God. I can't bear to ask, but I need to know. "Who killed them?"

"I shot Zane. Brink shot Anne."

"Was it...?" I swallow. "Was it really necessary?"

His dark eyes pierce mine. "It was them or us."

"This is my fault."

"No," he says sternly. "When Zane realized he was cornered, he went into the fight with the intention of not coming out alive. He knew the risks when he decided to kidnap you. He's lucky I didn't have a chance to torture him to death."

Shivers wrack my body. His arms tighten around me. I bury my face in his neck, inhaling the wintry scent of my dreams and nightmares, finding comfort in my captor, a man who killed his best friend for me. He didn't want to tell me, but I insisted. Now, I'm an accomplice. I'm as guilty as Damian. We hold each other as we sink deeper into the mud of our dark existence.

MIRACULOUSLY, Damian manages to keep my kidnapping out of the media. Except for the people involved, no one knows what happened. That includes Jana, who corners me before dinner in the kitchen when I go down to make a cup of tea.

"Lina." Her gaze sweeps over me. "Are you all right?"

"Of course." I force a smile. "Why wouldn't I be?"

"You look like you're coming down with something. There's a flu virus going around."

"It's nothing. I'm just a little tired."

"Did you sleep enough? You're so pale."

"I could do with a few more hours," I say honestly.

All I seem to want to do is sleep. Damian says it's the aftereffect of the drugs. It should be worked out of my system in forty-eight hours.

"I put last night's dinner in the freezer." She watches me curiously. "Weren't you hungry? When I got in this afternoon it was still in the oven."

"Oh." My cheeks heat as I battle to think up a lie and fail. "We, uh, didn't get around to dinner."

"Ah." She gives a knowing grin. "Still on honeymoon, I see."

Feeling horrible for letting her believe the untruth, I busy myself with filling the kettle so she won't see the conflicting emotions that must be written all over my face.

"I don't want to be nosy," she continues, "but I couldn't help but notice Zane's things are gone."

My hand starts shaking on the mug I take down from the cupboard. "No, he, um, didn't Damian tell you?"

"Tell me what?"

I swallow hard. "He left."

"Ah. If you don't mind me saying so, it's probably for the best."

From nowhere, shock slams into me. The full impact of what happened and what could've happened makes my knees weak. I grip the counter, feeling nauseous and unstable. Sweat breaks out over my body.

"Lina!" Jana rushes toward me. She takes my arm and leads me to a chair. "Here. Sit down."

"Lina?" Damian's dark voice says from the door.

"Mr. Hart." Jana gives him a concerned look. "I think Mrs. Hart is coming down with that bug that's in the air."

In two steps, Damian is at my side. He presses a hand against my forehead and peers into my eyes. "What's wrong?"

"Nothing. I just had a little dizzy spell. I'll be fine."

Ignoring my protest, Damian scoops me up in his arms. "Back to bed."

"I'll make some soup," Jana offers. "I can bring up a tray."

"That'll be kind," Damian says before carrying me back to his room.

I'm shaking so hard my teeth chatter. He lays me down on the mattress and pulls the duvet up to my chin. Not bothering to undress, he only kicks off his shoes before getting under the covers with me. I crawl into his arms, hiding in the warmth and false safety they offer.

Rubbing his hands over my arms, he soothes me with tender words. "It's all right, angel. You're having a delayed reaction from the shock."

Two more people are dead because of me. Because I ran. Because I'm a prisoner.

"I don't want to be here." I no longer want a part of this life. Everything I touch is tainted.

"You went through a traumatic experience. It'll get better."

I'm not sure it will, but I don't have the energy to debate my present or future feelings. It wasn't like this when I shot Jack. Then again, Harold immediately dragged me to Willowbrook. Before reality could set in, I was already sedated, my senses dulled, and my body numbed.

"Sleep," Damian whispers, planting a kiss on my forehead.

"Will you stay?"

He hesitates. "I have something to take care of, but I won't be long."

"What?"

"Nothing to concern yourself over."

I gasp, clutching at his shirt. "You're going after Harold."

"He put your life in danger, Lina."

"Please, Damian." He has no idea how dangerous Harold can be. "Stay with me. Don't go. Don't leave me. I beg you."

His hesitation stretches a little longer this time. Finally, he says, "I'll never leave you again when you need me."

"Thank you," I whisper on a sigh, fisting his shirt harder, as if that will prevent him from slipping away.

I drift off with the comforting knowledge that he'll stay, because he always keeps his word.

~

THE FOLLOWING MORNING, Anne and Zane's murders are all over the news. According to the police report, gang violence is suspected. No suspects have been arrested. My stomach tightens so much at the last part, I almost empty my stomach in the toilet.

True to his promise, Damian hasn't left my side. We woke together with him still fully dressed. After he made love to me in the shower, he took me outside to have breakfast on the terrace, claiming some sunlight will be good for me.

"Shall I ask Reyno to come over?" he asks, pouring me a cup of coffee.

"I'm not ready to talk about it."

He concedes with silence, watching me intently as I sip the strong brew.

"Will you stay, today?" I ask tentatively.

"Do you need me to?"

"Yes." For many reasons. I don't want him to have more blood on his hands by going after Harold. Harold still has the information I want. More importantly, I can't stomach the idea of anything happening to Damian.

"What do you want to do?"

"Maybe I'll watch a movie." Something mindless to help me forget.

"Sounds good."

"Really?" I didn't take him for the type to sit quietly on a sofa for longer than ten minutes.

His smile is indulgent. "I'll even let you choose."

I can't remember the last time I watched anything. I don't even know what kind of films I like, but I grab the offer gratefully. I'll do anything not to be alone and to keep him home.

JANA ARRIVES with grocery bags in the late morning. By the look on her face, she's seen the news. She regards me silently as I help to unpack the food.

"It's terrible what happened," she says after a while.

"Yes," I reply softly.

She doesn't ask questions, but there's suspicion in her eyes. Her former warmth makes space for distance and a tangible coolness. When we discuss the dinner menu, she's all formality and business. She politely but firmly declines my offer to help with lunch, making it clear my presence is unwanted.

What did I expect? She's not a foolish woman. After Damian threw Anne and Zane out, she must've suspected there was animosity between us. She must know Damian is a dangerous man who doesn't walk the straight and narrow. It would be naïve not to think us involved in their sudden murders.

Feeling uncomfortable and in the way, I excuse myself to take Damian up on his offer to watch a movie. I feel guilty for keeping him from work. He's always busy. More so now with the many loose ends he needs to tie up after the almost-sale of the mine.

Halfway through the film, I fall asleep on Damian's lap. I wake up with him dragging his fingers soothingly through my hair. My guilt is still a knot in the pit of my stomach. I'm on pins and needles, expecting the police to break down Damian's door at any minute, but I feel less nauseous and cold.

I don't still his hands when they start to wander. I need his touch. I don't argue when he turns me over, pulls down both our pants, and takes me hard and fast from behind. I move against him like a demon woman, taking what I want until we both collapse. I'm still tired and sore and don't protest when Damian urges me to take a nap after lunch while he works from a chair by the fireplace. He's been nothing but sweet and considerate, my kind monster, and it's hard to remember not to get used to his kindness.

WHEN I WAKE UP LATER, I'm alone. Through the window, the sun sits low on the horizon. It's a depressing time of the day, a time when you wake from a nap and realize you've wasted all the possibilities of a day away. The chill of loneliness always seems to descend with dusk.

I rub my eyes. My bladder is so full it hurts. Getting to my feet, I make my way to the bathroom. The doorbell rings. I hear voices downstairs and tense. One of them belongs to Damian and the other I don't know. I can't make out what they're saying, but the conversation seems to be pleasant. It's not the police. It must be a business associate.

After relieving myself, I have a quick shower to wash away the remains of our lovemaking. Exiting the bathroom with a towel wrapped around my body, I stop in my tracks. A strange man stands in the bedroom. He's unclipping a metal case that displays several instruments of torture. Damian is sitting in the armchair, sipping an espresso.

This is it. Much sooner than I expected. My punishment has arrived.

CHAPTER 21

Lina

"Get dressed," Damian tells me.

"Why?"

Possession flashes in his eyes. "Do you really have to ask me why?"

"What's going on, Damian?"

The man ignores me, lining up his tools.

Damian gets to his feet and walks to me. I stare up at him, fear blooming in my heart. Holding my gaze, he embraces me. My wet hair soaks his dress shirt, but he seems oblivious to the wetness. The dark intention in his eyes is in direct contrast to the tender way in which he holds me. It's confusing. My brain gives my body more conflicting signals. Anxiety mixes with the soothing feeling of his comforting hug. This is what it feels like to love a dangerous man.

My heart almost stops.

The realization bulldozes over every other sentiment except that tendril of fear. The fear and this secret, this terrifying insight, form a potent cocktail of absolute devastation.

I'm in love with my husband.

I think I've always been. I fell for him when he was hardly a man, and I never stopped falling. I tried very hard for this not to happen. Now it's too late. He's my downfall, my beautiful destruction.

Dragging his lips over the arch of my neck, he stops at my ear. His voice is soft and low. "Do as I say, angel."

My breathing spikes with a rush of adrenaline. I'm trying to cope with the knowledge that fixes with thorns and parasitic roots in my heart while getting a handle on my apprehension. I don't miss the silent threat in Damian's order. With a last glance at the stranger, I hurry to the dressing room. I'm drying myself, mindful of the marks on my bottom that still hurt, when Damian steps inside.

He looks at the yoga pants and T-shirt I've put out on the chair. "Put on the pants," he says. "Leave the T-shirt."

My mouth goes dry. "Why?"

He gives me a regretful smile. "You know why."

"You're going to punish me," I whisper.

"Yes."

My hands start to tremble as I pull on a pair of panties. "How?"

He tilts his head toward the bedroom. "Come on out when you're ready."

I fumble with the pants, pulling them on the wrong way around. Too distressed to change, I towel my hair dry and brush it out. Keeping the towel wrapped around my breasts, I step back into the bedroom.

The man has pulled on a pair of surgical gloves.

"On the bed," my husband says.

A plastic sheet has been spread out. It looks like a murder scene.

At my hesitation, Damian flicks his fingers. "I don't want to have to constrain you."

I shoot the man a pleading look, but he stares straight through me. I don't have a choice but to oblige. Damian makes me lie down on my stomach, ensuring the curves of my breasts are covered with the towel at my sides.

"Where do you want it?" the man asks.

"On her shoulder."

He's going to tat me.

"I don't want a tattoo," I say.

"Black?" the guy asks.

"Yes," Damian says. "Black seems appropriate."

The man dabs my skin with a disinfectant swatch. "You have to keep still."

While he prepares me, Damian sits down on the other side of the bed and takes my shaking hand. He rubs it reassuringly between his palms.

"Why are you doing this?" I ask.

"I gave you a ring, but you rejected what it stands for."

I get it. He gave me the status of wife, but since I ran, he's branding me like a cow. Like property. I'm being degraded.

The man starts tracing a design on my shoulder.

"Damian, please don't do this."

"Hush, angel," he says, not unkind. "This is so everyone knows to who you belong."

Meaning he's having something put on my skin in permanent ink that everyone in the city will recognize.

"Anyone who sees that," he continues, "will think twice about kidnapping you in the future."

"Why? What will be different next time?"

The hum of the machine starts up.

"One, I made an example of the ones who were stupid enough to try, and two, everyone in Johannesburg now knows nobody messes with what's mine."

Unwanted tears leak from my eyes as the first sting penetrates my skin. It's not painful enough to warrant tears, but my tears are not for the physical pain. My tears are for how far Damian will go to keep me, and that I love him, nonetheless.

Damian sits with me for the two hours it takes, not once letting go of my hand. When the tattooist finally pulls away to admire his work, my flesh feels a little bruised. He looks at Damian, who nods. I'm about to push up from the bed, but Damian clamps his hand around my nape, keeping me face down with my cheek on the mattress.

"Not done yet," he says.

I strain my eyes to look back at the man. Coldness engulfs me. He's filling a hypodermic needle from a vial.

I start to struggle. "What's he doing?"

Damian easily constrains me by pinning my arms at my sides. "Shh. Relax. It's not drugs."

My voice rises hysterically. "What are you going to do to me?"

"Calm down. It's just a local anesthetic."

"Why?"

While Damian holds me down, the man injects the needle in the fleshy part of my good shoulder. I battle to breathe as fear runs hot and cold up my spine.

After a moment, the man prods me with the needle somewhere at the base of my neck.

"Do you feel a prick?" he asks.

"N-no." Should I?

"It's all right." Damian kisses my temple. "We gave you a shot so it doesn't hurt."

"So what doesn't hurt?" I cry, nearly hysterical again.

When the man brings a thick needle to my neck, I start fighting in all earnest.

"Keep still," Damian hisses. "If he hits a nerve you can be injured."

I freeze at the proclamation, crying silently. There's more prodding, but I don't feel pain, not even when a thin trickle of blood drips down my neck onto the plastic sheet.

"Doesn't need stitches," the man says. "I only made a small incision. The glue is sufficient. Keep it disinfected, though."

When Damian lets up, I gather the man's work, whatever it was, is done.

While he sterilizes and packs away his equipment, Damian secures the towel around my breasts by folding one end over the other before helping me sit up and discarding the plastic sheet.

He brings a glass of water to my lips. "Drink. It's for the shock."

Too numb to argue, I drink it all. It tastes sweet. Why do people always give me sweet drinks when I've suffered a shock?

The man lifts his case. "I'll see you around."

Damian shakes his hand and says he'll see him out.

Swinging my legs from the bed, I try to look at what has been tattooed on my shoulder, but my neck hurts too much to turn. I clutch the towel to my breasts and walk to the dressing room for a better look in the mirror. The ink on my shoulder is the size of a coaster. A falcon's head peers back at me. In the background is a diamond, sketched three-dimensional, and at the bottom the initials, DH. Damian's business logo. It's right next to my armpit. The tattoo will be visible under any sleeveless piece of clothing, a clear statement for all to see. As I'm lifting my hair to inspect the small cut at the base of my neck, Damian enters.

I rub a finger over the bump under my skin that sits just above the cut. "What have you done to me?"

Crossing his arms, he leans against the doorframe. "It's a tracker."

I've seen it done to dogs and cats, but never to a human. Clenching my fists, I bite back fresh tears.

"I'm not losing you again, Lina. Ever."

"Which one is the punishment?" I snap, on the brink of shedding those tears I swore I wouldn't.

"Both," he replies, unflinching. "I said it before, and I'll keep on saying it. You get to choose."

A ringtone fills the room. He pulls his phone from his pocket and checks the screen. "Excuse me. I have to take this. Go back to bed. You haven't rested nearly enough."

Walking away, he leaves me in front of the mirror with my new tokens of ownership. Where the ring was a statement of kindness, designed to spare me humiliation, the tattoo seems the opposite. His words stay with me as I flop down on my stomach on the bed.

You get to choose.

There's no way around it. I chose him when I confronted Harold. The knowledge is mine. Damian doesn't know. I can pretend it didn't happen, but that won't make the truth vanish. I already sacrificed my freedom, even before Damian put his logo on my shoulder and a microchip under my skin. I may as well admit it.

Damian

A MINE DOESN'T RUN itself, as Ellis likes to remind me. There are contracts waiting to be signed, but I can't focus. I'm sitting behind my desk in the study with papers spread out in front of me, and all I can think about is how close I came to losing Lina. She's been through an ordeal. Punishing her is not what I wanted to do, but not punishing her would've been worse. She needs to know she can always trust me. I can't give her reason to doubt my word. Besides, I feel better now that she's branded as mine in every way.

Dalton needs to be dealt with. I almost lost my mine to him twice. He made a deal with Zane that put his daughter's life at risk. Taking my gun from the drawer, I check the chamber. Six bullets. I plan on using each of them. If I can't make Dalton suffer for the long years I planned, I'll make him suffer in death. No one puts Lina in danger and gets to live.

The very object of my turbulent thoughts walks through the door. Inconspicuously, I return the revolver to the drawer and close it. Business with Dalton will have to wait. Lina associates my study with punishment. I know how little she likes to be in this room. She wouldn't have come here unsummoned if she didn't have something important on her mind. Dressed in yoga pants and the shirt I removed this morning, she looks impossibly small and fragile. Impossibly mine. She pads barefoot to the fireplace, her eyes fixed on the naked wall above the mantelpiece.

The atmosphere is fragile. Her ego is still bruised from being tattooed and chipped.

"What did you do with them?"

I don't have to ask what she's referring to. "I burned them."

She turns her head quickly toward me. "Why?"

343

"You said they made you run."

Hugging herself, she says quietly, "I thought that's who you are."

Not at the price of losing her in more ways than one. She already hates me for our forced marriage. I broke something other than her skin, something inside her, when I punished her with the cane. I hurt her pride. She'll never admit it, but that's why she asked me to leave. She couldn't even stomach the aftercare I offered. I can't give her the freedom she wants, but I can at least try to give her the happiness in my control. There are other ways of feeding my dark obsessions she'll enjoy. We'll find them together.

Weighing my words carefully, I say, "I can be someone different for you if that's what you want."

Her midnight blue eyes turn wary. "You shouldn't have to change for anyone. If this is who you are—"

"It's called compromise. Isn't that what marriage is about?"

I don't like her silence, but I ignore the feelings it stirs in my chest. This isn't about me. I pat my leg. "Come here."

After a moment's hesitation, she walks to me and sits down in my lap. It's not like her to be so compliant after what just happened.

I fold my arms around her. "What's up, Lina? Got something you want to say?"

Resting her head on my shoulder, she traces the buttons of my shirt. "I'm sorry about…" Her voice almost breaks. "Anne and Zane."

My words are harsh. "I'm not."

She winces. "You were friends."

"I don't consider anyone who kidnaps my wife and tries to steal my money a friend."

She studies my face, seeming to search for the right words. "He was jealous. He was in love with you."

"If he loved me so much, he wouldn't have done what he did." If he loved me as much as he claimed, he wouldn't have hurt me by hurting the only thing that matters.

"He told me your money was his objective even in jail. I'm sorry you have to find out like this, but I thought you deserve to know, and I…"

"You what?"

"I thought it would make it a little easier to cope with the loss if you knew the truth. I'm truly sorry."

"Stop saying you're sorry. Zane's actions aren't your fault."

"I didn't want to be the one to tell you."

"I already knew."

"You did?"

"I figured when I threw him out of the house."

"Why did you take him and his family in and give them jobs? Did you owe him?"

"Yes."

She abandons the buttons and lowers her hand to my stomach, absent-mindedly brushing her palm over my abs. "What did you owe him for?"

"Saving me from rape. Zane had alliances. He threatened my attackers with food poisoning."

Her hand stills. "They believed him?"

"He wasn't bluffing. There was also a time he saved me from taking a sharpened toothbrush in the kidney."

She covers her mouth with a hand. "That's awful. You suffered all of that just because…"

"Just because Dalton accused me of stealing his diamond so he could steal my mine."

"Yes," she says softly, avoiding my eyes.

I don't tell her about all the other times, about the routine beatings and sodomies. Jail in Africa isn't for the weak. "You didn't come in here for my history with Zane."

"No."

Stroking her back, I say in my best reassuring tone, "Tell me."

"This is hard." She fumbles with my buttons again. "I don't know where to start."

"Start with how you escaped. I want to know everything."

"Why?"

So I can prevent it from happening again. So I can be sure there are no hands to chop off or people to kill. "Making conversation. Once you start talking, the rest will flow."

Inhaling deeply, she fixes her gaze in my lap. She tells me how she evaded Brink, how she ended up at the gym, and what happened at Phil's place. She tells me about running away from Phil and being knocked over the head, how she woke in a strange room, and what her kidnappers did. She confesses that she heard Zane and Anne talking about killing her as she slipped into unconsciousness. I listen to everything in silence, unable to stop the growing rage inside me for the people who'd touched my wife, even if those people have paid. She tells me she went to the church in Brixton to think about Zane's offer, and that going to Dalton wasn't planned. It was a spur-of-the-moment visit to tell him she wasn't going to get him the evidence.

Holy fuck. It comes as a surprise, but I believe her. I've already punished her for conniving to escape and for visiting Dalton. She's got no reason to lie about it. Zane is gone. Even if she still wanted to find the evidence, her only chance of doing so is dead.

I'm left with one question. "Why did you decide not to do it?"

"I had to make a choice. You or my freedom."

The statement hits me everywhere at once, right between the eyes, in the gut, and in my heart where it burns as conflicting feelings mash up inside me.

She chose me.

It's what I wanted, for her to come to me willingly, yet, I find no joy in the sacrifice. She chose me, and I fucking broke her skin with a cane because a man like me has to honor his promises. A man like me has too many enemies to break even one. A man like me can't cultivate trust by cutting anyone slack, least of all his wife.

I don't deserve her choice, but I'm not a good enough man to refuse. I let the knowledge settle, let it feed my possessive side until my soul demands to hear the words again.

"You chose me."

She looks away as if she's ashamed about her decision, about giving up the fight. A better man would let her go, but I pull her closer. I feel the weight of my ring on her finger, my logo on her skin, my tracker under her flesh, and my seed in her womb. Still, it's not enough. Her words aren't cold yet, but they don't dispel my fear. My fear of losing her is bigger than her word and my tokens of ownership. I don't own her heart. I doubt I ever will. This is why I accept her decision like the greedy monster I am, ignoring the fact that I'm not that different from her dead husband, trapping her in a loveless marriage. I bet Clarke promised kindness. My promise is punishment. He lured her with honey. I'll keep her with pain.

Kissing her neck, I inhale the sweet scent of her skin. Even now, after her shower, the seductive smell of her perfume clings to her hair. It's everywhere—in our bedroom, on our sheets, in the study, and all over my clothes.

It's too soon, but I can't resist. I slip my fingers into the elastic of her pants and pull them down her thighs and over her feet. Making her straddle me, I unzip my fly and take out my cock. I barely push her panties aside before sliding into her. The shirt that's too big for her obscures my view, but it's not our fucking I'm interested in watching. It's her face as I own her.

She gasps as I go too deep, hitting a barrier. I pace myself and take her shallower. If I can't have her love, I'll take her choice. It'll be enough. This is what I tell myself as I grip her hips and move her on top of me with easy strokes. When she gets the rhythm, I grab her ass. Her globes are full and firm. I imagine the red lines running across them and my cock twitches. I imagine her skin, whole and unmarked, and I'm as close to ejaculating as I'll ever get. I don't need marks on her body to turn harder than steel. I only need her tight little cunt. I'm not going to hurt her in any way she won't enjoy ever again, at least not in a physical way. There's plenty not to like when love isn't in the equation, but I refuse to think about it now.

Lifting her, I pull my cock free and gather some of her arousal before easing her back onto me. She moans as I spread her wetness over her clit and up her crack. She rises on her knees and sinks down over my cock while I rub her little button the way she likes. She cries out when I sink a finger into her ass, and squirms when I start to pump.

"Damian."

"Come."

I took her only a few hours ago, but we both explode as if we've been abstaining for months. Her ass and pussy clench with sporadic aftershocks as I empty myself, making sure every drop is spilled inside her. Spent, I lean back in the chair, bringing her with me. She wraps her arms around my neck and rests her head on my shoulder. I revel in the power of holding her like this, of rubbing my hands over her arms and not feeling her shiver with repulsion. I would've liked to stay like this forever, but our conversation isn't over. I need to warn her of my intention with Dalton. She knows I'm going after him, but she deserves to know what I plan. She needs to be prepared.

I start carefully. "There's no love lost between you and your father."

"He's not my father."

I freeze. What? This is news.

"I'm a result of my mother's affair."

Well, hell. That explains a lot. It certainly explains Dalton's animosity toward her. "Who's your father?"

"I don't know. My mother never said."

To protect her lover, no doubt. "I thought Dalton doted on you."

"He hates me, almost as much as I hate him."

Fuck. If she didn't accept my marriage proposal to save Dalton, then why did she? "If he's not your father, and you don't care for him, why try to get him the evidence? What hold does he have on you?"

She pulls away to look at me. The sight of her face, cheeks pale and eyes hollow, stills me. It not only scares me. It terrifies me. I've never seen her like this, not even when I tied her up, gagged, and caned her.

"I did something terrible, Damian." She exhales on a tremulous breath. "I killed a man." Her hands lie calmly on my shoulders, but it's in her twisted expression that the storm prevails. With my cock still inside her body, she makes her confession. "I shot Jack, and I'm not sorry."

I start at the divulgence. Holy damn. It's the last thing I expected. I try to picture Lina with a shotgun in her hand but fail to conjure the image.

"My arms," she continues, "Jack did this to me." A tremor runs over her body. "He locked me up and starved me until I agreed to give him my body. I gave him sex for food."

My shock explodes into a fury from hell, but I bottle it up and twist the lid on my anger to keep her talking.

"Every scar is a notch of victory, a reminder of what he won."

That son of a dead bitch. I'll have his gravestone flattened to the ground and crushed. It's a good thing Lina killed him, or I would've given him the slow death he deserved.

"I fell pregnant," she says, her voice so soft I have to strain my ears to hear.

She what? Sweet Mother of Jesus. Her baby. This is the baby she mentioned before I whipped her unconscious. I can't formulate a question. My brain won't function. It's stuck on her words. *I fell pregnant.*

"It wasn't supposed to happen. He was upset, angry enough to throw me through a window."

The self-mutilation, hunger strike, locking herself in, jumping through a window, all of it was Clarke. Her dead husband imprisoned and tortured her. I was wrong. Clarke didn't come to her with kindness. He came to her with cruelty. Dalton must've known about Clarke's sadistic tendencies. They were too close for ignorance. I can't speak for the fear of losing it.

A single tear drips from her eye and runs over her cheek. "The fall... The placenta ruptured. I lost the baby." Her lips start to quiver even as she bravely meets my gaze. "I came back from the clinic, took a gun, and shot Jack. When I came to my senses, the housekeeper was already calling Harold."

The bastard used it to his advantage to control her. "Dalton covered it up to look like a suicide and sent you to Willowbrook while taking over the management of your inheritance."

Her answer is a broken sob. "Yes."

349

That's what he's holding over her head. "He's threatening to tell the truth if you don't give him the evidence."

"He won't tell me what he did with my baby's body. That's what he'll give me in exchange for the evidence."

She's breaking down on the outside, trying bravely to conceal her shivering and hold in her tears. Me, I'm falling to pieces for her on the inside.

I grapple with the information. It's difficult to speak past the knot in my throat. "How many months?"

"Eight," she says, and then the dam wall breaks. Sobs wrack her shoulders. "He was eight months old."

"Jesus." Wrapping my arms tighter around her waist, I pull her to my chest and let her get it out.

There are so many tears, enough for all the years she carried this alone. "I told them the truth at Willowbrook, but they didn't listen."

That's why she didn't run away when Dalton brought her home from that fucked up institution. He held her hostage with a murder and her baby's remains. That son of a bitch.

Grabbing her face, I force her to meet my eyes. "Listen to me. You did the right thing to kill that bastard. He raped and tortured you."

She shakes her head. "I sold my body. I'm a whore."

"You're not a whore. He starved you. He cut you up. He killed your child. He deserved a lot worse than his fate. We'll find the remains of your baby. I promise you. I swear to God, Dalton will pay for what he did to you. He'll pay with his life." I kiss her forehead. "I'll find you what you want if it's the last thing I do. You can count on me."

My wife's sudden attachment to me is part separation anxiety due to her trauma, and part a cunning way of preventing me from committing another murder. I've given her time. It can't wait any longer.

After feeding Lina and putting her to bed, I instruct Brink to stand on duty by the bedroom door while I put five guards at the front door. I wait until my wife is in a deep sleep before I dress and holster my gun. Two cars with armed guards wait in front of the house on my instruction.

Word of my friendship with Zane got out. A television crew and several journalists are camping outside the property. I'm not worried. I don't own the police force, but I have enough connections who do. Paparazzi follow on motorbikes as our cars clear the gates, but my driver is skilled. We lose them in the busy hub of Centurion, cutting across to the R21 that will take us to Johannesburg.

The man I've put on watch in Brixton calls to say Dalton's flat is quiet. No movement. No lights. It won't do him any good to hide under the bed. He's out of resources. He's got nowhere to go, except hell.

"Coast is clear," one of the guards say when we park a block away from the flat.

"Has anyone been inside?" I ask as we make our way down the deserted sidewalk.

"No, sir, as you requested."

"Good." Dalton is mine.

We're quiet on the steps, not because I'm afraid of warning Dalton of our arrival, but for the sake of the neighbors. I know exactly where I'll finish Dalton off. I'll drag him by his hair to the train tracks. There's only one train that passes these days. It's a long time until 5am. Long enough to find a place on his body for each of my bullets before I tie him to those tracks.

Drew, my guard, takes up a position on the landing and nods. It doesn't take much effort to force the door. The first thing that hits me is the smell. The place stinks of rot and decay. Drew covers his nose and reaches for the light switch. I already know the flat is empty before the overhead bulb flickers on. From the looks of it, Dalton ran in a hurry. Clothes are strewn over the unmade bed and floor. A half-eaten plate of ham and mashed peas, the meat green and the peas black, are covered in flies. A thick crust of fungus grows on a glass of milk. Maggots crawl from the overflowing trashcan.

"Fucker," Drew says, shaking off and stamping on a maggot that climbed up his shoe.

Dalton didn't leave today or yesterday. Judging by the decomposing food, at least two weeks ago. He must've been scheming with Zane for longer than I'd thought.

Assessing for themselves that there's no threat, the men stand back, as far away from the stench as possible, while they wait for my orders.

"Clear out."

"The coward ran," Drew says.

I holster my gun. "I'll find him."

On the way back to the car, I call Maze and put word out that I'm looking for Dalton.

All the way home, I contemplate how to break the news to Lina. How do I tell her I don't have what I promised because her no-good excuse of a stepfather escaped?

To my agitation, she's not in bed when I arrive, but drilling Brink in her sleepwear. The only thing that prevents me from killing him is that she's pulled a robe over her revealing nightdress. When she sees me, she flies down the stairs and into my arms. The action takes me so much by surprise I almost bring us both to the floor.

"Easy," I say, gripping her waist.

She hisses like a cat. "Don't ever do that again."

"Study. Now. We'll talk there." The mention of the study is enough to shut her up.

My men shoot me sympathetic looks as I march my angry wife upstairs. She's the only person with so much power over me. There's only one, fragile, dainty, little female who can rake me over the coals.

When the door is firmly closed, she turns on me. "Don't you dare leave me sleeping when you're putting your life at risk."

"Calm down."

She shoves me. "Don't tell me to calm down. I was worried sick, and Brink refused to tell me anything."

Kudos for Brink. I can't help the smile that creeps onto my face. "Worried? About me?"

"It's not funny."

"No." I grab her around the waist before she can escape. "It's sweet."

She lets out a little humph when our bodies collide. With her palms on my chest, she tries to push away. "It's cruel. Inconsiderate."

I'm not going to contest the cruelty, but ask, "Inconsiderate?"

"How would you feel if you wake up in the middle of the night and I'm gone?"

Her words elicit a growl from deep within my chest.

"See? You won't like it either."

Her wiggling and feistiness make me hard. I'm trying to cushion my dick in the soft spot between her legs, but she arches away from me.

"Lina." It's a groan. It's a warning. I need her.

"No," she says, stubbornly turning her head away.

Frustrated, I concede to something I never thought I'd do. "Please."

The fire in her ceases a little. Her body relaxes marginally as she turns her head an inch back to me. "Please what?"

I fucking beg. "Please let me fuck you. Here. Right now. Against the wall."

"Not before we lay down some rules."

The minx is blackmailing me. With *sex*. Fine. I'll play along. This could be fun. "What rules?"

"If you're going on whatever mission, you don't leave this house, or wherever we may find ourselves at whatever point in time, without kissing me goodbye, even if you have to shake me awake from the deepest sleep I've ever slept. Understood?"

I grin. Fuck, she's cute. "Yes, ma'am."

"I'm serious, Damian."

"Yes, angel, I know." Nuzzling her neck with my nose, I sneak in a kiss. "I still think it's sweet that you care."

"Worry," she corrects.

Whatever. To worry she needs to care. "Worry," I agree readily because I'm eager to sink my cock balls deep into her.

"Fine," she huffs.

"Fine."

All her fire suddenly gone, she looks like the dog that caught the car. "Okay."

I pull at the tie of her robe as I back her up to the wall. "Don't you owe me something?"

She pants as I push the robe off her shoulders. She watches me warily as I move the strap of her nightdress aside. When I clamp my lips down on the soft spot between her neck and shoulder, she leans her head against the wall.

That's right, baby. I know exactly which buttons to push to make her surrender.

Cupping her hand, I place it over the erection straining in my pants. While I mark her skin with a hickey, she rubs me. It feels so fucking good, I pivot my hips into her palm. I try to go slowly as I free the other strap and let the nightdress fall around her feet, but my body has other ideas. Taking just enough time to remove my jacket and holster, I free my cock through my fly. When I align my dick with her pussy, she catches my wrist.

"No," she whispers.

No? I'm beyond myself with lust-crazed desire and a hairbreadth away from impaling her, and she tells me now?

"Everything," she says, looking at my pants. "For once, I want you naked."

Fuck, I can do that. I disrobe in record speed before crushing her body to the wall. It feels good all over, her skin against mine. I can do this forever. I want her. Forever.

Pressing our foreheads together, I grab her thigh and lift her leg around my ass. I don't slide in gently like I intended. I slam everything in with a single thrust, cramming as much of myself as I can inside her. I cover her mouth just before she screams, knowing she'll scream a hell of a lot more before I'm done. I want to drag it out, but she makes me go straight for the kill with her sweet concern and sexy blackmailing. I hammer out a rhythm that'll make me shoot before she's climaxed. With my fingers on her trigger button, I help her get there with me. We explode together. She sags in my arms, but this was just the appetizer to take off the edge. I'm not close to being done with her.

"Damian," she cries out as I twist her around and bend her over.

I can never get enough of my name on her lips.

Taking her again with her hands braced on the wall, I make her say it over and over until we're both covered in sweat, and I climax dry. I go down on her and fuck her again. By the time I carry her to bed, she's as limp as a deflated stickman balloon.

"Shower," she mumbles as I put her down on the mattress.

"Tomorrow." I lie down beside her and pull her to my side.

She nestles closer. "Where were you?"

"Looking for Dalton."

Her body tenses. "Did you find him?"

"No, but I will."

She utters a little sigh of surrender, wisely knowing she can't stop me. "Next time tell me. Please, Damian. I mean it."

I kiss her nose. "What woke you?"

"Nightmare."

"You're still having those?"

"Sometimes."

"You never told me what your dreams are about."

"Mostly what happened with Jack."

I drag her thigh over mine, getting as close as I can. "Why did you agree to marry Clarke?"

Two seconds tick past before she answers. "He seemed nice. He was kind to me before we got married. He was my ticket to freedom. I just wanted to get out of Harold's house, and I had no money or job."

"Maybe you should talk to Reyno about your nightmares." The unethical fucker actually did a good job on weaning her off her fear of closed doors.

"I will."

"You're safe with me, Lina." I hug her tighter. "I'm not going to let anyone hurt you again."

This time, her sigh is a sound between happy and sad. "I know."

I know, too. She's not entirely happy. Not all the lust in the world can change the fact that she's still my prisoner. Only, this time round, she's a willing prisoner.

Lina

DURING THE DAYS THAT FOLLOW, Damian is exceptionally tender with me, especially during our intimate moments. He takes care of my each and every need. He makes sure I eat enough healthy meals, and that I see Reyno twice a week. Telling Damian about my baby has reopened an old wound. I can't go a day without thinking about it. I start dreaming about it more frequently again. Twice already, Damian caught me paging through baby catalogues. Wherever I go, I see babies. I seem to only notice strollers, bottles, and little bundles wrapped up in blankets.

Reyno and I talk about it. We talk about the grieving process and letting go. We talk about my conflicting feelings for my husband who imprisons me by lust and marriage. Mostly, we talk about the disempowerment I felt at Damian's punishment, my escape, the kidnapping, and my tattoo, but we refrain from bringing up the murders. We pretend the terrible cost of saving my life disappeared with a part of my memory. Denial isn't a healthy way for a psychiatrist to approach treatment, but we both know who saved me. Not even client confidentiality is enough protection for Reyno. He's safer not having my confession.

The next time Damian takes me to the gym, I learn from the girls in the change room Phil lost his finger in an accident with a kitchen knife and asked to be transferred to the Germiston branch. I suppose I should be thankful he's not dead. It's the fear for his life that prevents me from asking Damian about the incident. I don't want to stir Damian's ire. Best let sleeping dogs lie.

The skin Damian broke is healing, but the bruises are far from gone. Damian tends to them morning and night, rubbing soothing lotions and tissue oil into the marks to prevent scarring, but there's no medicine for the scarring of my heart. I made my decision. I'm living with it. I came clean about Jack and my baby, baring my shame and most private grief to Damian, but there are two secrets I still keep, my job and my love for my captor. I don't tell him about working for Reyno. Without that small notion of independence, I'd genuinely go insane. It's because of the powerlessness I bring up in every session with Reyno that I keep the knowledge of my feelings to myself.

To tell Damian how I feel would lay down the last of the power I have left. I lock it away in the shadows of my soul, because my love belongs to the darker side of life. My love for Damian is like the black diamond etched on my shoulder, dark, pure, and indestructible. There are times I catch him looking at me as if he knows my secret, but if he does, he grants me the mercy of feigned ignorance. In turn, I give him my obedience, doing everything he asks of me, which includes taking over some of the food shopping and cooking duties. As if driving a point home, he tries hard to make a housewife out of me.

The house is too big for us. We don't need Jana to cook just for Damian and me. Her attitude toward me has turned from cool to quietly judgmental. How can I blame her? When you live the normal life of a law-abiding citizen, the lines between good and bad are clear-cut. It doesn't surprise me when she resigns to accept a partnership with a restaurant owner. Neither does it surprise me when Damian announces he'd like to move. He's brought it up before. Putting the responsibility on my shoulders, however, catches me off-guard.

We're having breakfast outside on the terrace when he announces the news. "I want you to start looking for a house."

I put down my coffee cup. "Me?"

"I never took to this place, and I have a feeling neither have you."

"Not really."

He grins. "It's old and stuffy, right?"

"Right."

"I want a place that's ours, a place where we can make our own memories."

The intensity of his declaration makes me shift in my seat. "What do you want?"

"Whatever will make you happy."

"Really?"

"I'll be spending an increasing amount of time at the office. You'll be at the house more than me."

Playing with my napkin, I digest the kindness of his offer. I can't say he's not trying. "Thank you."

"It's only normal." He cups my hand, stilling my fiddling. Then he smiles, trying hard for this to seem like a normal conversation. "What does your dream house look like?"

"I don't have one."

"You've never dreamt about a place where you'd like to live and grow old?"

"No."

"If you could have anything, what would you choose?"

I look at the distance where the grass polls are starting to dry. Winter will be here soon. "I always thought it's nice to live on the water."

"As in a boat?" he asks with surprise.

"As in on a shore, next to a river or dam."

"There's the Hartbeespoort Dam."

"It's far from your office."

"Only an hour's drive or so."

"You'll be stuck in peak hour traffic."

He shrugs, as if the sacrifice won't matter. "Call a few agents today. Take Brink with you if you go out to visit properties."

I know what he's doing. He's giving me the choice in all the decisions he can, from what we eat to where we live, to compensate for the loss of the decisions I'm not allowed to make, the ones that need financial freedom and legal sanity.

"Wouldn't that please you?" he asks gently.

"Of course." I force a smile. "I'll call today."

Inexplicable emotions clog up my throat. His offer makes me both happy and sad. It makes me happy because he's trying so hard, and sad because he has to try at all. If he granted me my basic human rights, he wouldn't have to work so hard at making up for taking them away.

Leaning over, he brushes my hair behind my ear. "What's wrong?"

"Nothing."

"Lina." A warning slips into his tone. "What have I said about *nothing*?"

Desperate to change the subject, I blurt out, "I'd like to visit the mine."

"You would? Why?"

"I've been curious since Fouché mentioned the changes you've made, plus I've only seen photos."

"I didn't know you were interested."

"Neither did I. I never used to be when Harold owned it."

A smile warms his face. "A visit can be arranged. How about today?"

"Now?"

"Sure."

"What about flights?"

"Anything is possible if you can charter a plane. I'll give you a personal tour." He motions at my empty plate. "Finished?"

When I nod, he starts clearing the table. In the kitchen, he loads the dishwasher while I wipe down the counters. To an outsider looking in, we'd appear like any normal married couple, but it's a dangerous illusion. Damian has been too sweet with me. He's been too gentle. He may have burned his paddles and whips, but he needs an outlet for his dark sexual cravings.

I haven't realized how hard I'm gripping the counter until his arms fold around me from behind, and he whispers in my ear, "Relax, I know what you're worried about."

"You do?"

That darkness I both fear and crave slips into his voice. "I'm not going to hurt you, not unless you deserve it."

"You want it."

"You're enough."

I turn in his hold, staring at his beautiful face. My question is doubtful. "Am I?"

He kisses my lips. "Yes."

"If I can't give you what you need…"

His tone hardens. "I'm not letting you go, Lina."

I place my palms on his chest. "That's not what I meant."

"No?" His piercing eyes hold a challenge. "Explain."

"I don't want you to…" This is hard to say. "I don't want you to start looking around."

His expression softens. The tension in his face evaporates. "You're jealous," he says as if it's a wonderful thing.

My cheeks heat. "I'm not."

He rests his forehead against mine. "That's so fucking endearing."

"I'm *not* jealous."

"There's no reason to be insecure. You're the only woman I want."

"Until you need violence."

"It's not about violence."

"What then?"

"It's about control."

"You like to hurt me."

"Only if it makes you wet."

"It doesn't."

"We've already established that."

"Well, not all of it." A flush moves up my neck as I say it.

He raises an eyebrow. "Which parts did you enjoy?"

"The spanking, when it wasn't too hard."

"Mm." He places his hands on either side of me on the counter, caging me in. "What else?"

"When you watched."

His eyes darken, and his erection grows against my stomach. "I may need a reminder."

"What, now?"

"You're the one who brought it up," he says with a devilish grin.

"The mine—"

He reaches for the buttons of my blouse. "Can wait."

I nearly go to pieces as he undresses me. I didn't know until this moment how much I craved another taste of his devious side. Pushing the edges of my blouse aside, he exposes my naked breasts. I'm still not wearing a bra. The strap irritates the healing tattoo. He weighs each breast in his palm before giving my nipples a gentle kiss. Then he unfastens my pants and pushes them over my hips. Turning me around, he pulls my panties down to my thighs. With the restriction of the fabric, I can't widen my stance. I peer at him from over my shoulder to see him open his fly and take out his cock. He pumps twice and uses the pre-cum to lubricate my slit before pushing in slowly.

The friction and stretch make me go on tiptoes. He only allows me a brief repose to get used to his size before he starts pumping. His gaze is locked onto where we're joined, and I'm watching him watching us, knowing from the way his cheekbones darken how much it turns him on. He grunts.

"Aren't you going to spank me?" I ask.

"No."

"Why not?'

He stops moving and kisses my back. "You didn't do anything that deserves punishment. On the contrary."

"Don't stop."

He starts thrusting again, faster. I'm on the brink of coming when he stops.

"What are you doing?" I utter on a frustrated moan.

He turns me around and lifts me onto the counter. "I'm going to give you what you like. I'm going to watch. Fuck your fingers."

As I start acting out the command, he pulls my pussy open, looking at the work of my hand with so much concentration I falter in my rhythm. He swats my thigh in a wordless reprimand. My inner muscles contract. Pressing the heel of my palm on my clit just like he's taught me, I rub in circles. I'm about to go over the edge when he grips my wrist and pulls my hand away.

"Damian."

"I like this kind of torture, too."

Too late, I realize what he means. "Damian, please. Let me come."

He places the broad head of his cock at my entrance and pushes in gently until he's buried to the hilt.

"I need—" My words cut off when he starts to pump. "Yes." Again, he brings me to the edge before slowing. "No," I moan, lifting my hips and trying to take him deeper.

"Shh," he taunts. "I'll make it worth it. I promise."

When I think I can't take more, he twists me around again and rubs my arousal around my anus. I grip the edges of the counter, shaking as the head of his cock breaches the tight muscles of my dark entrance. He works carefully, going slowly, and by the time I've taken all of him, he has his fingers in my pussy and on my clit.

I need just a little to get me there, and still he refuses me, keeping me in that impossible place between pleasure and pain until I'm begging. It's only then he gives me what I need, rolling my clit between his fingers. I explode with pleasure, coming so hard I feel lightheaded.

He groans. "Fuck. Can you feel me filling up your tight little asshole with my cum?"

His vulgar language makes me come harder and longer, until my upper body collapses on the counter, and I forget why we're here or where we're going.

"See?" he breathes triumphantly next to my ear. "I don't need to spank you to come the hardest of my life."

Damian

THE DAY IS cool but sunny in the Richtersveld. Autumn is setting in. I help Lina from the car and pull her jacket around her shoulders. She stops to look at the small mountains of sand in the distance and the offices in front. Sucking in a breath, she grabs my arm.

The mine has undergone a metamorphosis. The muddy pools in the office grounds are gone. A natural garden, inspired by her ecosystem, stretches from the east to the compound in the west. The area beyond has been paved and fitted with tables and umbrellas. The food truck has been replaced with a proper canteen where warm meals are served. The raised housing with its pressed wood walls has been leveled to the ground, and in its place stands a solid brick structure with decent heating and air conditioning. There's a games room at the back, and a medical office with a full-time nurse.

The heaps of excavated soil are systematically being leveled on the riverbed and planted with indigenous grass. The polls should cover the whole area by next summer.

"Damian." She looks at me in surprise. "Why didn't you tell me?"

"You didn't ask."

She glances back at the office area. "It looks…"

"New?" I tease.

She swats my arm. "Clean. It's so different from the ugly photos I saw."

"I'm glad you approve. Come on." I take her hand and lead her to the front building where Ellis' office is situated.

He comes out when he sees us, giving Lina a warm welcome.

"Wow," she says, looking toward the new transport area.

"I know." Ellis follows her gaze. "Big changes."

"The Union must be happy," she says.

"So are the miners," Ellis replies. "The other mine managers, not so much."

"There must be pressure on them now to meet the same standards."

"You bet. Better working conditions, better security measures."

Lina turns to me. "Congratulations, Damian. You must be proud."

"It's not finished. This is only the first phase. We're planning on adding visitor's accommodation and a pool."

"The excavation of the bedrock was the priority," Ellis says. "Taking the full tour?"

"Definitely."

"I'll get you a hardhat and a safety jacket, then."

Ellis is most in his element when he's playing tour guide. As he buzzes off, I study my wife's face while she takes in the transformation. She's not smiling, but her eyes twinkle with excitement. She looks happy for me, like you can only look happy for someone if you care. This new pride, the times she worries about me, her decision to come clean and to stay, all these smaller acts add up to one enormous truth. I didn't plan on bringing it up now, but the moment has presented itself, and I don't believe in wasting moments.

Gripping her chin, I turn her face to me. "Lina, do you love me?"

She goes still. Her face turns white.

The subject is more delicate than I thought. We've always been fighting a war, me for her affection and she for freedom. Acknowledging to loving me is admitting she lost. I tread gently. Bruising her ego or rubbing her nose in her losses isn't the objective.

"There's no need to hide it from me. I won't use the knowledge against you."

Her stance slackens. She averts her eyes.

"Look at me, Lina." Reluctantly, she obeys. "I've suspected for a while."

She jerks as if I've pumped a round of bullets into her. "How?"

"You're terrible at hiding your feelings."

"Am I?"

"It was there, just now, in your eyes." I bring her hand to my lips and kiss her palm. "You looked happy for me."

Pulling her hand away, she bites her nail and turns toward the distance. She's not even pretending to look at something. She's staring miserably at nothing.

"It's nothing to feel bad about. You never stood a chance, angel. I came at you with everything I've got."

She glances at me from over her shoulder. "It must be good to know you have so much power."

"Hey." I grip her shoulders and turn her back to me. "I'm going to make this good."

"If I tell you I love you, will you give me my freedom?"

I drag in a breath, playing for time. I don't want to hurt her, but I'm not going to lie to her. "You know better than to ask me that."

"I'm not asking you to set me free. I'm only asking for my right to make independent decisions back. Make me a competent human being again, Damian. Please."

Cupping her face, I brush the wind-blow hair from her cheeks. "I can't do that."

"Why?" she exclaims softly. "If I love you, why would I run? Why won't you trust me?"

Love isn't always enough. Because she'll wake up one day and realize she deserves better. I told myself if I have her heart, I'd feel safe, but I don't. I own her body and heart, and the fear of losing her won't let me go. I can't answer her. I can only stand there and look at her while her face twists into a mask of pain as I break her heart.

"Tell me, Lina."

She's carried enough secrets to bog her down for a lifetime. It's time to snip that final cord that anchors her to the little island she's created in the sea of her confusing emotions. It's time for us to go into this as one. No more islands. No more she and I. From now on, it's us.

"Tell me," I urge with a small shake when she purses her lips.

A battle passes through her eyes. She wrestles with it, fights with her last strength, but we both know it's a losing battle.

"Tell me."

The confession gushes from her lips, broken and perfect. "I love you."

As if the admittance has taken all her energy, she sags in my arms. Her breath catches on a hitch. Warm tears wet my shirt. All I can do while she cries for the last piece of herself she's lost, is hold her in my arms and tell her over and over I'll make it good for her. I won't let her sacrifice her freedom and love for nothing. I'll give her the love I've been carrying in my heart for so long. I'll give her everything money can buy, anything she wants.

"Anything at all in my power," I whisper in her ear, cradling her frail body. Anything but freedom. "Your love isn't one-sided. I feel the same."

What was supposed to be a love declaration sounded more like a weak consolation.

Ellis, who rounds the corner with a pink hardhat and safety jacket, stops in his tracks. He shoots me a panicked look.

"She's fine," I say. "Just a little weak spell."

Lina wipes her eyes with the back of her hand, fighting to regain her composure.

"Say, isn't that...?" Ellis walks closer and peers at her shoulder where her jacket has slipped away. "Holy macaroni, Lina. You take loyalty to new extremes." He whistles. "I'm impressed."

Wrong thing to say at the wrong time.

"I have to visit the ladies. Excuse me."

Lina runs off toward the sign for the toilets, not sparing either of us a glance.

Ellis scratches his head. "Was it something I said?"

"No." I watch the door close behind my wife with a burning sensation of regret. "It's me."

~

Damian

OUR MARRIAGE WILL NEVER BE normal, but we fall into the closest thing to a normal routine. Lina tends to the garden and cooking when she's not house hunting while I throw all my energy back into the business of mining. Well, almost all my energy. I'm still gathering evidence against the Willowbrook staff and looking for Dalton. The latter has disappeared from the face of the earth. I underestimated him. There is one sliver of light in the midst of my failed attempts to smoke Dalton out. The jail connection I employed to gather information on the late Jack Clarke's household staff traced Clarke's former housekeeper to an obscure little village in Switzerland. Dora Riley immigrated around the time of Clarke's death. At the age of sixty-seven, without any Swiss family, it seems off. She has no telephone number or email listed. All I have is an address.

I don't tell Lina the reason for my so-called business trip. It could be a false lead. I put more guards on duty around the house and give Brink strict orders to call me if Lina needs anything. Then I honor my feisty wife's wish by kissing her goodbye before boarding the plane.

Lina

I FIND A HOUSE. The minute I walk through the door, I know it's the right place. It's a Tudor style cottage on the banks of the Vaal River with a small jetty and a wooden deck. It's much smaller than the house in Erasmuskloof, but it's cozy. The big windows let in lots of sunlight. It's a house in which I can breathe and relax, a house made for living. I make an appointment for Damian to visit it as soon as his schedule allows and ask Brink to drive us home. We make it back with enough time to spare for grocery shopping at one of my favorite malls.

We head straight for Food Lover's Emporium, but a window display pulls my attention. Slowing my steps, I come to a stop in front of a toy store. My heart clenches painfully. A wooden train with blue and red wagons passes under a yellow bridge. The scene is static, like a snapshot. I'm hurled back in time to a different snapshot when Dora served my meal on a tray lined with an old supermarket sales brochure. It was just before Christmas. When I'd eaten like an animal with my hands tied behind my back so Jack could laugh and call me a dog, the soiled brochure was left on the floor. Later, after I'd earned my scar, I picked up the brochure. Not having had access to reading material, I read anything I could get my hands on. The train was on the second page. It was black and electric with an infinity track. There were hills and pine trees and bridges. It was so pretty. So perfect. A boy knelt next to the track, his eyes bright and his hands clasped together. I'd put my hand over the place where my baby was growing, already knowing I'd skipped two periods, but still able to conceal it from Jack. I wanted the promise in that brochure so badly, the happy train with its lucky boy. I wanted the white paper world with its snow and fairy lights. I wanted that baby. I wanted him with all my soul.

A sound escapes my lips. It's a horrible sound, one only an animal can make.

"Mrs. Hart?" Brink touches my shoulder.

I jerk at the contact. My voice is choked as I dash toward the entrance, escaping my past and postponing the future, even if only for a short while. My voice cracks on the syllables. "I'll just be a minute."

"Mrs. Hart."

He waves a credit card at me, but I shake my head, biting back uncontrollable emotions and stepping aside for an elderly lady to enter. The sliding doors close behind us. The voices and hurried steps of the passersby disappear. A smell of tinsel fills the air. I'm shut inside the world of brochures where snow is warm and children are safe while Brink looks in from a crueler reality outside.

Standing over the display, I stare at the static little train that's going nowhere in the window and everywhere in my heart.

"It's beautiful, isn't it?" a woman's voice says next to me.

I turn to the owner of the voice. She's pretty and sophisticated, old enough to have firsthand experience of the joys of toy trains.

"It's wood, not plastic," she says. "Hand-crafted. Locally manufactured. We only stock community products. Ten percent of the profit goes back to the township."

Drawn to the toy, I look back at the wagons. There are twenty-six. Each carries a letter of the alphabet.

"How old is he?" she asks.

I glance at her again. "What?"

Her smile is patient, as if we have time, as if everything else can wait. She makes me want to cling to the illusion that inside here the world is on pause.

"The boy you're shopping for," she says, "how old is he?"

"Two years and three months."

"Then this is the perfect gift. I'm sure he'll like it."

"Yes," I whisper. "He will."

"Shall I wrap it up?"

"Yes. Please."

One by one, she wraps the wagons in tissue paper. With much care, she packs them into a paper bag, and rings them up.

"Six hundred rand," she says.

Reaching inside the hidden zip compartment of my bag, I take out the money Reyno has paid me. I hold the stack of hundreds in my hand. For the first time in my life, I count out six notes, and place them reverently on the counter. The moment is sacred, and it seems fitting that it's here, in this place where smiles are patient and time stands still. It's fitting that my first purchase with money I and no one else has earned is a silent train that can spell many unsaid words. My heart floats up from the pain in my chest. What I've bought is not a piece of handcrafted wood. It's a gravestone. It's a gift for a boy who exists only in my heart.

"Thank you."

The woman hands me my receipt. "You're welcome."

Clutching the parcel to my chest, I turn back to the glass doors. Outside, Brink waits. He stares at me peculiarly. His expression is a mixture of pity and concern. The light in his eyes is hesitant, as if he's not sure what he should do. Inside, I'm safe. Answers will be demanded when I step out of here. Why did I buy a toy? Who am I going to give it to? Where did I get the money to pay cash?

Swallowing hard, I straighten my spine and ready myself to walk back into my reality. There's no escape from it. Brink already has his telephone in his hand, no doubt calling Damian. I push through the doors when his attention is on the call, using his distraction to compose my features. A cold breeze tunnels down the walkway. The smell of fried corn dog and onion mixes with the bustle on the pavement.

Someone bumps hard into me from behind. The heel of my boot twists inward. Loosing my footing, I go down. The parcel slips from my fingers as I use my hands to break my fall. The concrete scrapes the skin off my palms. The bag splits open, and the pieces spill out. No! On my hands and knees, I crawl to get to them. A black shoe falls in my vision. The sole lifts even as I scream. A crunch shatters the air. The heel lifts. The tissue paper is torn down the middle.

No.

I reach out with a trembling hand, but someone jerks me up by my arm before my fingers can make contact. More feet hurry past, people bumping and onions burning. The tissue paper parcels scatter over the concrete as anonymous feet kick them in all directions. No one stops.

"No!"

As I fight the painful hold on my arm, one hand stretched toward the ground with splayed fingers, my gaze connects with Brink's. His face is horizontal, his cheek resting on the pavement. Next to him, the red locomotive lies broken in pieces.

CHAPTER 22

Damian

The air is thin this high up. It's spring in Switzerland, but snow still covers the mountaintops. After getting off the train I took from the airport, I store my overnight bag in a locker at the station and go into the village on foot. I need the walk to clear my mind and decide on a course of action.

At a tourist shop, I buy a Swiss Army knife. Slipping it into the pocket of my summer coat, I make the steep descent to where the wooden house stands alone on a stretch of property. A cowbell rings somewhere on the hilltop. The unkempt lawn is full of yellow wild-flowers.

The gate pushes open without a squeak. There's no doorbell. I use the knocker.

A lady with white hair wearing a housecleaning overcoat opens the door. I recognize her from the photo. In real life, Dora Riley looks older than her age. No surprise registers on her face as she takes me in from head to toes.

"Come on in," she says with a Durban accent. "I've been expecting you."

She goes ahead. I close the door and follow her to the kitchen where she waits at the table with a pot of coffee.

"Sit." She motions at the only other vacant chair.

"You know who I am?"

She pours the coffee into two mugs. "No, but I know why you're here."

"Do you, now?"

"No one's come to see me in two years. There can only be one reason you're here."

"Lina."

"Lina. Ah." The words are pitiful, sad. She pulls the mug between her palms. "How is she?"

"She's my wife."

"Do you love her?"

"Yes."

She pushes the sugar my way. "Good."

"I want to know everything."

"She hasn't told you."

"She told me enough. I want to hear it from you."

"I was hoping I'd never have to tell that sad tale to a soul."

"You do, so start talking."

"Where do I begin?"

"How about with what your role was?"

"Don't look at me like that, Mister. I didn't hurt her. What her husband did to her broke me."

"Yet, you never said a word."

"My husband was on life support. Cancer. Jack paid the medical bills. My husband died nine months ago. There's no more reason for me to keep quiet."

"Start at the beginning, from when you first met Lina."

She sighs. Her gaze turns inward. "I always knew what Jack was. He brought prostitutes home, and they never left in a good way. When that young, pretty thing walked through his door, I knew what was going to happen to her, and there wasn't a thing I could do to stop it."

"Go on."

"She found out the very first night. The following morning, she called her father and begged him to fetch her, but he told her to grow up and face her responsibilities."

She adds two cubes of sugar and cream to her coffee. "Jack locked her in her room and kept her there, as naked as the day she was born. He ordered me not to serve her any food. The fridge and kitchen were locked, and only I had the key. After a couple of days of starvation, she gave up the fight. Jack got what he wanted."

"You had the key."

"I already told you, I didn't have a choice."

Like hell.

"Every time Lina gave in, Jack granted her a meal. He'd tie her up and make me serve it on a newspaper on the floor so he could watch her eat it like a dog. Sometimes, he invited friends to enjoy her humiliation. Then he'd carve a line on her arm, so she'd never forget how many times she sold her body."

My insides boil. My heart combusts. I wish with every part of my soul I could resurrect that vicious bastard to kill him all over again with the slow and torturous death he deserved.

"Jack traveled often," she continues. "His instruction was to give Lina just enough food to keep her alive. Whenever he left, I sneaked extra food to her. Especially when she realized she was pregnant."

"Clarke didn't know about the pregnancy?"

"She was so thin, you could hardly see the bump. Didn't show until she was almost seven months."

Which explains why Lina doesn't have any telltale stretch marks. "Why didn't he want his own child?"

"Lina was an object to him, something he could use and abuse. Children weren't on his agenda."

"Then why not use protection or give her birth control?"

"I'm not sure it even crossed his mind. He was away on business for long periods. Who knows how his mind worked? All I can say is that he wasn't always right in the head. When it came to sex, he had unsavory tastes."

I can't keep the accusation from my tone. "And you never tried to help her."

She gives me a levelheaded look. "On the last trip, Jack was gone for six months."

"Why so long?"

"He was overseeing the construction of a new mine somewhere in the Richtersveld, I think."

I clench my fists under the table.

Taking a deep breath, she wraps her hands around her cooling mug again. "He was furious when he came home and found Lina with her big belly. I huddled outside the door. There was a lot of screaming and begging. Then came the crash. It was horrible. Glass splintering and Lina's scream. I still hear it in my dreams."

"He threw her from the window," I hiss.

"Second story."

"It's a miracle she survived."

"She landed in soft soil. The gardener had just upturned it that morning to plant new ferns. Broken collarbone, cracked ribs, a few scrapes and cuts."

"What happened?"

"She was so still. We thought she was dead. Jack told me to call an ambulance and tell them she jumped. Suicide. Only, when they got there, she was very much alive. Jack was a mess. Lina's father took charge. He had her transferred to a private clinic."

Where her secrets could be swept under the carpet and forgotten.

"When she was discharged, Mr. Dalton loaded her into his car and brought her right back to Jack. Jack went straight back to his old habits, locking her up and starving her. I couldn't take it anymore. I slipped the key under the door." She falls silent, staring into the distance.

The woman in front of me fills me with disgust. She turned a blind eye for two years so her husband could stay hooked up to machines that did the work of his organs. That's what loves does to you. It makes you selfish and unscrupulous. It makes you dangerous.

"Finish the fucking story," I grit out.

She flinches. "I thought she would escape, but no. When she unlocked the door, she went to the study, took the hunting rifle from the mantelpiece, and blew Jack's brains out. He must've been on his way out, because he was dressed in a suit, the car keys clutched in his hand, but the face... You couldn't recognize the face."

"Then what?"

"Lina collapsed. She was weak from her injuries and malnourishment. I couldn't call the police, not with being implicated, so I called Mr. Dalton." She shrugs. "Who else did she know? He came over and staged it like a suicide."

Which he conveniently held over Lina's head.

"That's all I know," Dora says. "The house was packed up and sold. The staff was paid off."

"Enough to keep them quiet."

"Yes."

Then Dalton sent Lina to Willowbrook and took over the management of her inheritance while conveniently keeping her declared mentally ill.

"Why did you come here, to Switzerland of all places?"

"I was the only one who knew what went on behind the closed door of Lina's bedroom. The other staff believed what Jack told everyone, that Lina was self-destructive and not in her right mind. They didn't know the real crazy one was Jack. He was good at acting."

"Dalton exiled you."

"I didn't fight very hard." She chuckles. "I know when to shut up and do as I've been told."

"You said Dalton took charge of Lina's admission to a clinic when Clarke threw her out of the window."

"Yes."

I get to the crux of our talk, to what I'm really here to find out. "Where's the baby's body? What did Dalton do with it?"

She gives me a startled look. "There was no body, Mister. The baby didn't die."

My heart jerks to a standstill. "What?"

"He survived. He was in an incubator for a month, but I know he lived because I heard Mr. Dalton on the phone when he brought Lina home to Jack." Her face twists with uncertainty. "Mr. Dalton was making plans for the baby. I thought he took the little boy. Didn't he?"

Fuck, no. Lina's child is alive. He's out there, somewhere in the world. I swear to God, I'll make Dalton sing like a canary before I kill him.

"Didn't he, Mister?" Her eyes fill with panic. "Please."

I can't tell her what she wants to hear. All I can see is Lina's hollow expression and that almost-smile in the church, that perfect beauty in the broken, just like the sublime portrait of Mary hanging under a frame of shattered windowpanes and pigeon shit.

"How many times did Lina ask you for help?"

"Every day in the beginning."

"When did she stop?"

"A couple of months later."

A *couple* of months. "Give me an exact date."

"I can't." She pulls up her shoulders. "I didn't keep book."

"Don't you remember?"

"No."

Something so profound and she's can't fucking remember. She should've remembered the month, day, and time. The exact second Lina gave up hope should've been carved into her heart.

"You know what has to happen."

Her voice doesn't waver. "Yes."

Taking the knife from my pocket, I place it on the table. "I'll give you the choice."

She looks at the knife for a couple of beats before pushing herself up with her palms on the tabletop and fetching something from a cookie jar that she carries back to me. A bottle of pills. I read the label to be sure and give her a nod.

She shakes the lot into her palm and swallows them with her cold coffee. When the mug is empty, she walks to a daybed that faces a window, takes off her shoes, and lies down. The window has a nice view over the green field with the yellow flowers. Grabbing a throw from the sofa, I cover her legs. It's the most kindness as I can spare her for not doing enough.

"I slipped her the key," she says, staring at the window, talking to herself.

Too little, too late.

Exiting the warmth of the house, I close the door behind me and leave it unlocked so whoever finds her body won't have to break it down. I walk back to town slowly, trying to process the information. How do I tell Lina? Do I call her? Do I wait until I see her? Do I tell her now, or after I've found her child? Definitely after. He could've been adopted. There will be legal shit to sort out. How much dirty laundry is Lina willing to wash in public? How much is she prepared to share with the world?

I'm halfway down the hill, my thoughts heavy, when Brink calls. Unease seeps into my gut. Something's wrong. He wouldn't otherwise call me in Switzerland. Just as I swipe the button to accept the call, the line cuts.

My unease explodes into full-blown panic. I start to run even as I dial Maze.

His tone isn't reassuring. "Damian, where are you?"

"Abroad. Brink called, but we got cut off."

"I know. You've got to catch the next flight back."

I stop. My heart thuds like a bull in a matador ring. "What happened?"

"Lina's been taken."

CHAPTER 23

Lina

*T*his can't be happening. Not again.

Blindfolded, I'm lying on my stomach on a hard, cold surface. My hands and feet are tied. I'm shaking from the shock. My cheek throbs where it was smashed against the window when my kidnapper threw me into the van, and my hipbones feel bruised from being knocked around as the vehicle skid around the bends. It's cold, but I'm sweating. The perspiration makes my scraped palms burn.

Lifting my shoulders off the floor, I try again. "Where am I?"

So far, no one has replied to my question. There are two people in the room. I only saw the face of the one who grabbed me. He pulled a bag over my head before I could make out the face of the driver, and he replaced the bag with a blindfold before leading me from the van. We climbed stairs for what felt like forever, until my lungs burned from the exertion, before reaching the floor where they're keeping me. It was especially difficult with the blindfold. I still feel the toll of the effort on my legs.

"Who's there?" I ask.

I can make out my kidnappers' distinctive footsteps when they move. The man who took me wears shoes with rubber soles. They squeak when he walks. The other is a flat heel that falls hard, like a man's dress shoes.

"Can I please have some water?"

"Take off her blindfold."

I freeze. That voice. Oh, my God. A gulf of anger eradicates my fear.

Someone hauls me up by my arm. A sharp pain shoots through my hip when I put my weight on my legs. I try to find my footing and limp when he lets go. When the blindfold comes off, I'm already beyond my shock. I only have disgust left for the man facing me. Harold looks alarmingly well, a far cry from the disheveled man I saw in Brixton. He wears an expensive suit and shoes. He had a haircut, and he's freshly shaved. We're in a circular room. The view makes me gasp. We're even higher up than I thought. Yellow mine dumps stretch into the distance. Johannesburg. From the scattered and broken furniture, I gather the place is abandoned.

I glance behind me at the man who pulled me to my feet. He's the one who took me at the mall.

"Where's Brink?"

"He'll live," the man says.

"What did you do to him?"

"Stun gun."

I turn back to Harold. "Damian is going to kill you."

"If he had any intelligence," Harold says, "he would've killed me the day he got out of prison."

"That's what vengeance does to you," the man says. "It clouds your good judgment."

"Who are you?"

He drags his tongue over his teeth. "Someone who'll get a big cut of the profit pie."

"What's the meaning of this?" I ask Harold.

"Told you the last word will be mine."

"What do you want?"

"What's mine."

"What's that supposed to be?"

The man pulls a chair closer and pushes me so hard onto it my teeth clack.

"The mine and evidence in exchange for you," Harold says. "Sweet deal, no?"

"You can't be serious. The only reason Damian married me was to acquire that mine. You're dreaming if you think he'll give it up for me."

Harold grins. "Apparently, he values you more than the mine. He's already agreed to my terms."

My mouth drops open. "How's this supposed to happen?"

"Wait and see, Angelina."

Is Damian bluffing about giving up the mine and evidence? No, he never bluffs. A startling insight hits me. He could've used the evidence to clear his name and win back his mine, but he didn't. He used it to get *me*. It's never been about my inheritance. He chose me over the chance of clearing his criminal record. Hope swells with love in my chest.

He'll find me. I refuse to lose him now. I'm suddenly overwhelmed by his foresight to plant a tracker in me. What had seemed like a punishment at the time turns out to be the biggest blessing of my life. It's going to be all right. It has to be.

"When Damian finds me, you're going to die."

"We destroyed your phone," the man says. "No one is going to find you."

He doesn't know how wrong he is. The question is, will Damian find me in time?

Damian

A CAR IS WAITING for me when the plane touches down. The driver throws my bag in the trunk and holds the door. I duck to get inside and pause. Russell sits in the back.

My fingers clench on the doorframe. "What the fuck are you doing here?"

"I'm Maze's best man, and you know it."

"I can't trust your feelings not to get in the way."

"It won't. Get in. Time's not on our side."

I ignore the fact that he's just given me an order, because he's right. We only have two hours before Dalton's deadline. I needed Maze's men to hold off an attack until I arrived. I don't trust anyone but myself with Lina's safety.

Sliding into the back, I check the tracker on my phone, the small, vulnerable dot that represents Lina. Dalton isn't moving her around. She's still in the same place as twelve hours ago.

The driver has barely taken off before Russell hands me an iPad with a kaleidoscope of drone images. Dalton is keeping her in one of the top floors of the Hillbrow Tower. The tower has been closed for security reasons since 1981. It can't be too difficult to break into a dilapidated and deserted tower. No one goes there anymore. Not even the police. It's a dangerous neighborhood. The floor used to be a revolving restaurant called Heinrich's. At two hundred meters high, there's no other building on the former Heinrich's level. No place from where to launch a sniper attack. There's only one way up and one way down. It's a good place to hide a captive. Too damn good.

"Are you meeting his demands?" Russell asks in a solemn voice.

I give him a cold look. "Of course I fucking am."

He narrows his eyes to slits. "Just checking."

"I emailed the contract my lawyer drafted." A whole team worked on it through the night. "I'm waiting to hear back from Dalton. He's probably reading it as we speak."

"The minute you sign it, there's a good chance she'll end up dead anyway. We can't trust Dalton to meet his end of the bargain."

My stomach lurches, and my heart beats harder. "That's why we have to get her out before. How many men has your drone picked up?"

"Infrared shows three people. We couldn't get a visual on their faces. They'll spot our drone if it hovers in front of the windows. Those damn windows run three hundred and sixty degrees around."

I wipe a hand over my face, the strain of two sleepless nights catching up with me. "We have to assume two of the people are Dalton and Lina. The third is probably the guy who took her. Did Brink get a visual?"

"He only saw a man dragging her to a van."

Cold fury rages through me at the mental image. I should've sent more guards with Lina, a mistake I won't make again. I never expected anyone to strike after the example I made of Anne and Zane. After the failed kidnapping, I thought Dalton was on the run, knowing what I'd do to him when I find him. I never expected him to pull such a move.

Russell taps on an old photograph of Heinrich's in its former glorious days. "There's a fire exit on the east side of the room and the main one facing the escalators, which are out of order. We could take the stairs, but there's no way of breaching it from the doorway without being spotted. Plus, Dalton isn't stupid. I'm one hundred percent certain he has the stairs booby-trapped. We need an element of surprise. I say we go in air-borne and snipe Dalton and his crony."

"No."

At my harsh tone, Russell looks at me quickly.

"I need Dalton alive."

His face contorts with the emotions he'd sworn wouldn't get in the way. "He took Lina."

"He'll pay when I'm good and ready."

"What the hell is wrong with you, Hart? Do you want her to die?"

I slam a fist on the seat between us. "I'm not going to let her die."

"Then explain why you won't snipe that bastard. It's the best damn solution."

Exhaling deeply, I stare at the blue almost-winter sky through the window. "Lina has a child. Dalton is the only one who knows where he is."

"Holy Mother of God."

"Yeah."

"What do you suggest?"

I lift the iPad again, enlarging one of the drone photos. "There's a panoramic terrace at the top. Below used to be a smaller restaurant."

"The Grill."

"How's the tower structure inside?"

"Hard to say. The last time anyone's been up there was when Carte Blanche broadcast from the old Heinrich's in 2013. No safety checks have been filed with the municipality since 1980."

I search for behind the scenes images of the broadcast even as he speaks. "No engineering reports?"

"Zilch."

A few photos of the Carte Blanche studio setup prove helpful. They give a view of certain spots inside. The interior structure looks sturdy with a few places where the ceiling boards are peeling. I flick to the blueprints. Ventilation tubes run around the ceiling, but they're too small to fit a human. A trapdoor between the floors of The Grill and Heinrich's catches my attention. The blueprint shows stairs. In the earliest days, the floors must've been connected. I flip to the photos of the restaurants in the days when they were still in operation. No stairs. The interior was redone.

I point to the blueprint. "There's a trapdoor here. We get onto the terrace and enter through The Grill. Then we use the trapdoor to access Heinrich's through the ceiling."

Russell rubs his chin. "The trapdoor will make noise. It puts us at risk for a few, unprotected seconds, but it could work if we check Dalton's position on the infrared before we move."

I check the time on the screen. Still twenty minutes before we get there. We need to get to the top of that tower. Pronto. "What were your air-borne plans?"

"Helicopter."

"Too much noise."

"We don't have an alternative."

"What has radar picked up?"

"Nail bombs at the ground floor entrance, but no other explosives."

"Wired?"

"Worse. Heat sensitive. Anyone who dares it inside will end up like a voodoo doll full of needles."

"Then we climb up from the outside."

He shifts in his seat. "You're out of your mind. The ladder is metal."

"What's your point?"

"*Metal*, Damian. You're a mine magnate. You know better than anyone what that means. Rust, erosion. Need I say more?"

"We'll just have to take our chances."

"We won't have a safety rope."

"I won't. You will."

"What do you mean?"

"I climb up and attach the rope at the top. We use an electric harness to pull you up."

"It'll take too long. I won't make it up on time."

"Then I'm on my own."

"Fuck." He leans his head back on the headrest and closes his eyes, seeming to think. After some time, he regards me warily. "Can't let you do it. I'll go up. You wait at the bottom."

"She's my wife."

"Exactly. You can't be as levelheaded as you need to be."

"Neither can you."

Rubbing his temples, he blows out a long breath. "It'll be stupid for both of us to risk our lives on the ladder. I'll stay at the bottom, but if you don't make it up, I'm calling in the helicopter and the sniper."

"If I don't make it up alive, I swear to God I'll haunt you if you don't get her out, do you hear me?"

"I'll get her out."

He will. Russell is a good soldier. More importantly, he's a good man. If I don't make it, I hope he'll hang around for Lina. She'll need someone. I'm not going to jinx myself by saying it out loud, though. To hell with that. As long as I'm alive, I'm the only man she'll have.

Russell calls the waiting unit and gives them instructions before briefing me. A few armed men in civilian clothes are hanging around the tower, pretending to be beggars. I'm pretending not to be sleep-deprived and going insane. I'll happily give the mine and everything else I own if I thought I'd get her back, but Russell is right. I can't trust Dalton. This isn't something he sucked out of his thumb yesterday. It's a well thought out and premeditated plan. He must've been hiding in that tower, perfecting his scheme, for the two weeks I've been searching for him.

MAZE'S MEN wait at the bottom of the tower with the equipment I need when we park. The security company has cordoned off the area and is waving around guns big enough to scare away curious spectators.

"What did you tell them?" I ask the man who hands me a backpack with the harness and rope, a smart wristwatch, ear pod, and pistol.

"Contamination."

"Good."

There was a soil contamination issue at the gasworks not far from here a few years ago. It made a lot of noise. No doubt people still remember the scare.

My phone pings with an incoming email. Both Russell and I still. My gut churns as I open the message. It's from my lawyer. Dalton returned the contract. He's waiting for me to sign. I don't think twice. I drag my finger over the screen, signing my name at the bottom before handing the phone to Russell.

"Don't send it a minute before the agreed time."

He nods.

I strip my suit on the street and dress in the cargo pants, T-shirt, and heavy-duty boots from the security company before pulling the goggles over my face to protect my eyes against insects and wind.

Russell pats my shoulder. I give him a nod before I put a foot on the first bar of the service ladder fixed to the side of the tower. I wiggle the tip of my boot to find my footing and shift my weight onto the first step. The metal groans.

To his credit, Russell spares me the worried look. Instead, he tests the link to my watch and ear pod, making sure both are connected before giving me the thumbs up.

The ladder rattles under my weight. The steps are far apart and the space between the ladder and wall just big enough to fit the toe of my boot. The backpack is heavy and the ascent grueling. The wind doesn't help. Aside from the noise in my ears, my body is rocked every time a gush of air rushes through the skyscrapers. It's a typical autumn day with a clear blue sky. The sun reflects directly off the concrete, making it feel as if I'm mounting an oven. By the time I'm a quarter of a way up, my T-shirt is drenched with sweat despite the cooler morning temperature of fifteen degrees Celsius that my watch shows.

A long time later, I've only reached the halfway mark. I stop to catch my breath. I'd kill for a sip of water. Below, the buildings are a maze of concrete and the people mere dots of movement. Wiping my forehead on my sleeve, I carry on with my ascent. It's a damn good thing I don't suffer from vertigo. I'm not going to lie. It's fucking scary. Especially when I reach the flat bottom level of the six floors that requires horizontal climbing for a short distance. Thank God I'm in good shape. It's the one plus that came out of my imprisonment. I don't think I would've pumped iron as hard if I'd remained a free man.

I'm reaching for the step at the first-floor windows when my leg starts cramping. Motherfucker. My calf contracts into a painful ball. Catching the step above me, I flex my foot, trying to alleviate the pain. It hurts like a bitch. I'm hovering like that, all but balancing on one foot, when a gust of wind rips around the tower. It flings my body sideways. My footing slips. I'm barely holding on with one hand. My sweaty fingers slip as I try to swing myself back and find leverage on the step with my feet. Fuck, I should've worn gloves. I grunt with the effort but manage to steady myself. It takes a few breaths before I'm ready to move on.

"Everything all right?" Russell's voice asks in my ear.

"I'm at the bottom level of the floors."

"Not far to go."

I catch my first view through the glass. The floor is an open space of broken chairs and bar counters. The second is empty. The third and fourth, too. It's the next level where I have to be careful. If I make a noise or Dalton spots me, Lina is dead. When I clear the concrete foundation that forms the floor, I rise slowly. My heart hammers not only from the exertion, but also from fear. I can't screw this up for Lina. It's my fault Dalton took her. If I hadn't taken the mine, this wouldn't have happened. I'm not going to let her down.

Holding my breath, I lift myself just high enough for a visual. The floor is in less of a shamble than the others. There are sofas that Carte Blanche probably used when they broadcast their program. I scan the space until I spot them on the far side. My heart slams to a stop in my ribcage. A spell of lightheadedness threatens to overwhelm me. Lina sits on a chair, her hands and ankles tied. Dalton has his back turned to me. Another man stands next to Dalton, a gun clutched in his hand. A rush of relief replaces the lightheadedness, but the danger is far from over. In less than fifteen minutes, Russell will have no choice but to email the contract to Dalton. I have little time to make it past the windows and onto the terrace.

I pray my movement won't attract Lina's attention. I don't want her reaction to alarm Dalton. They're talking. Lina is saying something, her face too far and too much in the shadows to make out her expression. Moving as fast and quietly as I can, I climb past the windows, praying for the first time in my life, bargaining with gods and angels and demons I don't believe in.

Almost there. One more step. Thank fuck. I'm about to pull myself onto the terrace when a rusted bolt securing the ladder rips straight out of the wall. Bits of concrete flake around the hole. One of the bigger pieces hits the window with a sickening noise before it falls to the network of streets and buildings that looks like a Lego land below. The step swings on one hinge, hitting the wall with a clang.

I stand dead still, shaking in my boots, but it's too late. From directly below, a frame creaks as someone pushes open a window.

CHAPTER 24

Lina

There's a thud on the window, as if a bird hit the glass, and then a louder clank, like metal on concrete. I jerk in my bounds. Harold spins around, reaching for the gun in his belt. His partner joins him. I stretch my neck to see past Harold as he rushes to the window, but there's only blue sky. Harold grips the window handle and shakes. It's stuck. I rise awkwardly for a better view, trying not to fall over. The frame gives. The window doesn't open far, but cool air rushes into the stale interior the sun has quickly baked hot through the expansive windows.

Harold leans out and looks up. He pulls his head back into the room with a curse. "There's someone on the service ladder."

"Cop?" his accomplice asks.

"I only saw his boots." He turns, waving the gun at me. "Untie her."

"What are you going to do?" the man asks as he starts working on the knot at my wrists.

"We're going up. You stay here and secure the floor. Make sure nobody else comes up that ladder."

Life flows back into my arms with painful pinpricks when the constraints come free. I rub them to aid the blood flow while my assailant works on the rope around my ankles. My heart beats fast with fear, but also with hope. Someone came for me.

"Do you have the contract?" the man asks.

Harold takes his smartphone from his pocket and checks the screen. "Not yet." He motions for me to come closer. "Call that son of a bitch and tell him I want it now. Tell him to call off his man or she's dead." Nudging the gun between my shoulder blades, he says, "Walk."

We exit via the fire escape next to the broken elevator. My legs are shaky from being tied up for so long, but also from frightening, sickening panic. We mount one level and walk out on a rooftop terrace. Sucking in a breath, I grab the balustrade. We're so high the closest rooftops look like Monopoly pieces. The horizon is a convex with smog pollution framing the edge.

In the distance are the Ponte and Auckland Park Tower landmarks. Oh, my God. We're on the Hillbrow Tower.

"Walk," Harold says, giving me a push from behind.

I stumble a step. Putting one foot in front of the other, I inch closer to where he's forcing me—to the edge.

My whole body starts shaking when we reach the rail. It's waist-high and in bad shape. The metal is rusted and bent in places. The protective net that once covered the open space is long gone. The wind whips my hair around my face, the cold penetrating my bones. I shiver in my coat. Frantically, I search the terrace for the person Harold saw, but the more I squint into the sun, the more I think he's mistaken. There's no one. The longer I stand on the edge of the most horrific drop, the more certain I become about why we're here, but I'm not ready to face it.

I chance a look at Harold over my shoulder. The wind is loud. I have to shout to make myself heard. "What are we doing up here?"

My foolish heart hopes for a good answer, but my body knows better. My legs already go into convulsions of shock, barely carrying my weight.

Harold keeps the gun trained on me, his demeanor alert as he scans the terrace. "Quiet."

"You don't have to do this."

"This is where it ends."

This is where I die. I feel like crying, but my eyes are dry. My heart won't grant me tears. There's no space for anything but the terrifying, dry fear. To set me free from my miserable existence would be a mercy, but I'm not ready to let go of life. I cling to it with everything I've got. I don't want to die.

My voice cracks. "What have I ever done to you?"

"You know too much."

I know about his criminal business dealings. I know he traded me to a sadist in exchange for mining rights. I know he planted the diamond on Damian to get him out of the way so he could exploit Damian's discovery. I know he cheated his partners. I know he organized my abduction. Still, he knows things about me, too. He knows I shot Jack. He can use the information to make sure I keep my mouth shut. This isn't about me knowing too much. It's about something entirely different.

Pushing back my windblown hair, I turn to face him. "It's because my mother didn't love you."

The truth flashes over his face for just a second before his expression turns into a mask of disgust. Ignoring me, he looks right and left.

"Are you going to push me?" I ask in a strangely calm voice.

"You're going to jump." He offers me a fleeting smile while continuing his scanning of the surroundings. "You've always been suicidal."

"If I'm dead, Damian will come at you with everything he's got. He'll have nothing left to lose."

"He can't come at me if he's dead."

"Oh, my God. You're pure evil."

"I know you're there," he screams over the wind. "Come out wherever you are or she walks the plank."

A shadow extends from behind the staircase room. A man steps out with his hands raised. Damian. I feel sick. I feel sick and happy. My feelings are jumbled up. I can't make out my fear from my relief. I can't sacrifice him.

My gaze locks with Damian's as he pulls a pair of goggles from his eyes. The truth reflects in those dark brown depths. Harold can't shoot us both at once. He'll take out the biggest threat first. He'll shoot Damian, which will give me time to run. Oh, my God. Damian is going to sacrifice himself to save me. My soul screams no. My heart shrivels. If Damian believes I'll get away, he's not alone. He brought reinforcements. Someone must be close on his heels. I scan the terrace that stretches beyond Damian and spot the electric rope reel attached to rail at the same time Harold calls, "Stop where you are."

Damian stops. "You have what you wanted. Let her go."

"Put the backpack on the ground. Gun too. And don't bother to deny it. I know you have one."

Damian slips the straps from his shoulders and lowers the backpack to the ground. "Gun's in there."

Yanking me by my arm, Harold flings me in Damian's direction. "Open the bag, Lina."

I stare up at Damian, hoping to God I can tell him everything I need to with my eyes. There's an eternity of love in my heart, and only a second to show it.

"Now, Lina," Harold says behind me.

Damian gives me a small nod. As I crouch down, his lips lift in a reassuring gesture. Even while being held at gunpoint, he offers me comfort.

My fingers shake on the buckle of the bag. It takes a few seconds to get it open.

"Kick it over," Harold says.

Straightening, I nudge the bag with my shoe. It slides over the concrete to where Harold stands.

"Search him," Harold says. "If you find a weapon on him, you throw it my way. Don't even think about trying to use it. I'll shoot him before you have time to cock a gun."

Doing as I'm told, I pat Damian down.

"Anything?" Harold asks.

I shake my head.

"Must I come over there and check? If I find a weapon on him, I'll shoot off his kneecap. Get my drift?"

I swallow and nod.

He pulls his phone from his pocket, keeping the gun trained on Damian, and flicks over the screen.

The wind ruffles Damian's hair. He looks both eternal and destructible. The sun makes a halo around the needlepoint of the tower. If I squint a little, I can see the portrait of Mary and Jesus painted in a sudden appearance of clouds across the sky. My losses peel away as I see the face of another baby in Jesus' place, and the man-boy Damian used to be returns to me. This very moment, right here, is how we would've been if Damian had stayed on the terrace with me instead of going to Harold's study. It was love at first sight. We both knew. It was too big not to. We lost six years and forever, but when love is this great, even a moment is enough.

A satisfied smile spreads over Harold's face. "Glad to see you kept your end of the bargain, Hart." His trigger finger curls.

My shaking stops. My fear dissipates. Suddenly, it's startling clear. All the events of my life led me to this moment. To this purpose. It only takes one step to put me into the path of the bullet.

Damian's voice rings out with alarm. "Lina, no!"

The shot goes off. Pain explodes in my side. My knees give out. I fall forward, knocking Harold to the floor. The gun is sandwiched between us.

"Sniper, now!" Damian says. "Ambulance."

My blood is wet and warm, soaking our clothes. I'm dead weight. Harold struggles to roll me over. He points the gun, but Damian is already there. Bones snap from the impact of Damian's boot as he kicks the weapon from Harold's hand. The gun flies over the edge of the terrace. Harold's scream rises to the sky. Pressing a hand to my side, I try to stop the steady pump of blood that seeps through my fingers.

Damian is like a demon. Grabbing hold of Harold's feet, he drags him to the rail.

"Damian, no," I croak, reaching for him with one hand. "He's not worth it."

Damian will go back to prison, this time for murder, and they'll never let him out again. My plea is for nothing. Damian hoists Harold head-down over the rail and shakes him over the abyss.

"Where is he?" Damian screams. "Talk, you bastard."

My vision starts swimming. The scene goes in and out of focus. The noise of a helicopter rises from the distance. Another face appears above mine. Russell?

"Shit. Fuck. I've got you, Lina." He rips off his jacket and presses it on my wound. It hurts. Badly. "A helicopter is on the way. You hold on, do you hear me?"

It's Damian's voice I try to hold on to, the same phrase repeating itself.

Where is he?

I fight to remain conscious. "Don't let him kill Harold."

Russell only shakes his head, as if it's too late.

When I turn my gaze back to Damian, coldness envelopes me. He's empty-handed. His arms are stretched out over the edge, fingers splayed as if he's giving a blessing, and his eyes are trained below.

My breath catches. It hurts to swallow. It hurts to move and speak, but I grab Russell by his T-shirt, bringing him closer. "I killed him. *I* pushed Harold."

He frowns as he seems to battle with my meaning, and then his face contorts with denial. "Lina—"

"I killed him." I shake him as hard as my waning strength allows. "I killed him. Do you understand?"

His eyes brim with tears. His face dissolves and comes back into focus.

"Please, Russell. Promise me."

He wipes the hair from my face. "Don't talk." He breathes out through his nose. "Fuck. Damian! Get over here."

"Please." I beg with all my being, with everything I'm capable of. "Please, Russell."

"Yes, damn you."

His voice is breaking, or maybe it's my hearing that's slipping away with my sight.

"Tell me you understand."

He forces a smile. "I understand."

I sag back on the floor, suddenly too tired to hold myself up. "Thank you."

"Lina." Damian kneels beside me.

The hurt lifts, and for a moment I feel fine. My senses are sharper than ever. I see Damian clearly, every line on his face. I feel his breath on my lips as he cups my head. I smell his skin, sweat mixed with citrus.

"I'm sorry, Damian. I'm sorry for everything we did to you."

His lips part. They move, but he's not making a sound. His tears drip on my cheeks and run down my neck. I want to tell him it's all right. I don't need him to tell me what I already know. We don't need wasted words.

Cupping his cheek, I whisper what's on my heart. "It was perfect."

I feel it in my body and in my soul. I feel it in my smile as I let go.

CHAPTER 25

Damian

I wanted Lina's smile for so long, and now that picture will haunt me forever. Rubbing my hands over my face, I hang my head to relieve the ache between my shoulders. My eyes burn from a lack of sleep. I haven't moved from the hospital chair since they brought Lina from surgery.

It's been a day and night. The surgeon reckons she'll be fine. No organs were damaged. She was damn lucky. I wouldn't be surprised if she has a guardian angel. Angels would definitely watch over someone like her. Her words come back to haunt me.

It was perfect.

I don't deserve her. I gave her a prison. She gave me her life. She gave me her smile. Her fucking smile. I press the heels of my palms against my eyes until I see white spots.

The door opens. Russell pushes inside with two Starbucks cups and puts one on the nightstand next to me.

I still feel like strangling the motherfucker. I hope he can see it in the killer look I'm giving him. No matter what I threaten him with, he won't budge. He won't change his statement. He hard-headedly maintains Lina pushed Dalton off the tower after he'd shot her. I got the best lawyer in the country, who said Lina would've been charged with manslaughter and gotten off with self-defense under normal circumstances, but since she's officially classified as mentally unstable —a nicer term for insanity—she can't be put on trial. Did she realize that before she convinced Russell to lie for her? Is that why she took my guilt on her shoulders? I have an inkling it's got nothing to do with getting off scot-free with murder, and everything with her heart. It's just how Lina is. It's how she's always been. A physical pain lodges under my breastbone as every time I think about what I need to do.

Russell motions at the paper cup. "You going to drink that? 'Cause you look like you can do with some caffeine."

My gaze slips to Lina's pale hand that lies on the white sheet. She's hooked up to an IV line and heart rate monitor. As so many times since I planted my ass in this chair, I almost touch her. It takes enormous effort and some more to hold back. Touching her will only make what I have to do harder.

"You can do with a couple of hours of sleep," Russell continues. "Maybe shave before she wakes up. You look like a caveman." He scrunches up his nose. "Starting to smell like one, too."

Lina has regained consciousness, but she's on morphine. I doubt she'll remember I was here. Maybe it's better like this. The doctor said they're reducing her pain and sleep medication from this afternoon. She'll wake up soon. The surgeon said if she remains stable, she can go home in a couple of days.

It's time.

My palms start sweating at the thought. Wiping them on my pants, I force my legs to stand.

"Are you staying?" I ask, hating, envying, and sadly appreciating Russell right now.

"Yeah."

I slap his back. "I'll have that shower, after all." Before taking care of other business. "I'll send you a cheque."

He grabs my arm. "For what?"

I look at where his fingers dig into my skin. When he releases his grip, I say, "For services rendered."

"Fuck you. I did it for Lina, not for money."

"Doesn't matter. You did your job. You'll get paid."

"Hart."

I stop in the door.

He looks at me warily. "What's going on?"

"I'll send you instructions."

"What instructions?"

"To wrap up the job."

"It's done."

"Almost."

His expression sobers. "Don't be a selfish prick."

No, this is the one unselfish thing I'll do in my life.

His fingers tighten on the cup, denting the sides. "She loves you."

Fuck, it hurts. Before he can say more, I push through the door. I don't need a last look at my wife. She's a permanent picture in my mind.

DREW FINDS the boy where Dalton said, in the care of a nanny, living on a secluded farm north of Pretoria. When I speak to the woman on the phone, she says Dalton told her the boy's mother is mentally ill and a danger to herself and her baby. She doesn't know more. Dalton settled the bills, but he didn't visit more than once a year. It makes sense why he hid Lina's child. He wanted Clarke's fortune all to himself. In the case of an inheritance, a blood relative takes priority over a legal guardian. An heir meant the money would've gone into a trust fund until the child was of legal age.

Susan Bloem cooperates when I tell her about Dalton's death and who I am. When I bring Reyno with me for a visit, she produces the birth certificate for Lina's child on which the father was declared as Jack Clarke. Dalton or Clarke, whoever named the boy, called him Joshua, or Josh for short.

We're standing in the lounge of the shabby house when she calls the kid to come and greet us. A chubby boy with Lina's dark blue eyes and, fuck, her dimple, comes in from the backyard with a plastic horse clutched in his plump little hand. All kinds of emotions clash inside me.

I go down on my haunches. "Hey, Josh. I'm Damian and this is Reyno. We're friends of your mom."

"Mommy's sick," he says.

"Not anymore. She's gotten a whole lot better, and Reyno here is a doctor. He says you can see her. Would you like that?"

He glances uncertainly at the old woman, who smooths a hand over his hair. "He's shy. It'll take some getting used to."

She seems to be good to him. I stand to face her. "I don't know how long it will take for Lina to regain her strength, but she'll need a hand until she's back on her feet, and seeing that you're the only family Josh knows, I'd like for you to stay on until Lina makes a decision. I'll pay you well for your trouble."

"That's mighty kind of you, Mr. Hart. Josh and I are close, and, well, work is scarce these days, especially for an old woman."

"That's settled then."

I ruffle Josh's hair. "How would you like to live in a house on the river with your own fishing boat?"

His eyes grow large and his smile wide.

"I'll take that as a yes." I hope Russell knows how to fish. Otherwise, he'll have to learn fast.

The thought is a bitter pill to swallow, but I brush it aside. After leaving Susan to pack, I arrange for a driver to fetch them tomorrow. There's still the property deed and transfer of ownership to take care of, as well as Dalton's estate. My attorney assures me Lina won't be held responsible for Dalton's debts. They're not blood relatives, and Dalton never adopted her.

When I've taken care of the most pressing business, I go back to the big, empty house I won't be selling, after all. In the quietness of the study, I light a fire, pour a whisky, and turn on the television. Dalton's accomplice, a freelance mercenary called Samuel Rourke, was detained by the security company and handed over to the cops when, alerted by a body splattered on the pavement, they arrived on the scene. He took a shot at Russell as Russell was being hoisted up by the electric reel I'd fitted to the rail, but missed. Russell wounded him in the leg, ensuring he wouldn't get far climbing his way down all those stairs. Wisely, Samuel made a deal. In exchange for telling the police everything, he gets ten years for kidnapping instead of twenty-five. Won't matter much. I know people on the inside who'll take care of him. For the part he played in Lina's abduction, he deserves to die. For now, the cocksucker is doing me a favor, spewing the facts all over the news channels. He's telling how Dalton paid him to kidnap his daughter, about the ransom, and Dalton's plan to make his daughter's murder look like suicide.

I down the rest of my drink and slump in my chair. I can't face sleeping in a bed where Lina's smell lingers. I can't face tomorrow or the day after. Swinging back my arm, I hurl the glass into the fireplace. It shatters with a satisfying crash. A blue flame shoots up in the chimney. It lasts for all of a second before the flames go back to normal. Life continues quietly, making a mocking of my tantrum and laughing in my face.

Lina

When I wake up, Russell is there. It's Russell who puts a straw to my lips and offers me water. It's Russell who keeps the media away from my door and brings me a bag with my clothes, as well as a new smartphone the next day.

The fact that Damian isn't here hurts. I don't understand, but I'm not going to ask Russell for an explanation my husband owes. If Damian isn't man enough to tell me to my face we're over, so be it. We've been through more than what any couple should have to handle. Some damages are beyond repair.

When the doctor signs my discharge, I get dressed in the luxury of my private bathroom and brush my hair. Russell waits at the door. He takes my bag and leads me to his car in the parking lot. I get inside and buckle up without asking where we're going. During the ride, he's quiet. The bearers of bad news carry the kind of tenseness that sits in his shoulders, which is why I still ask nothing when we drive past Erasmuskloof and head toward the Vaal River. I'm not surprised when he pulls up at the cottage.

We sit in silence with him clenching the steering wheel and me staring at the water. After what feels like forever, he opens his mouth, but I'm not sure I can handle what he has to say. I shake my head, at which he clamps his lips together. With a sigh, he takes an envelope from the cubbyhole and places it on my lap.

It's the first time I permit myself to speak. "What's this?"

"Damian asked me to give it to you."

I don't want to open it, but I'd rather know what awaits me before I get out of the safety of the car and walk toward my future.

My fingers tremble as I break the seal and pull out a stash of documents. The first is the deed to the house, in my name. The second is a bank statement. Damian not only transferred my full inheritance, but he's also paying a ridiculously big monthly allowance. The third is divorce papers. I don't look at the other documents. A knot gets stuck in my throat. It feels as if my heart is wrenched out. This is why Damian didn't come to the hospital. He's finally done it. He set me free. I should be exuberant, but all I feel is a hollowness in my chest. Chewing my lip, I let the knowledge settle. My eyes remain dry. The shock will come later. I'm selfish about my pain. I want to suffer this in privacy. No one else deserves a part of it, not even Russell who helped to save me.

Russell's voice sounds strange after such a long silence. "You all right?"

Reaching for the door handle, I nod. The essence of the days to come is survival. I'll fill the hours with packing, moving, and unpacking. I'll buy furniture and hang curtains. I'll keep myself busy with starting a new life until I'm ready to face my losses.

"Wait." Russell grabs my arm and flicks his gaze to the stack of papers in my hand. "You missed some."

Reluctantly, I move the divorce papers to the back of the pack and look at the next document. It's a certificate signed by Reyno. I focus and refocus my eyes. My sanity. He's given me back my right to work, have a bank account, buy property, and make decisions. The emotional dry spell that's been haunting me since the kidnapping breaks. Tears build in my eyes. The saltiness stings. For the first time in my life, I'm an independent adult. I'm free to make my own choices, and no one can stop me. The beauty of the gesture dawns on me. Damian isn't giving me a clean break because he doesn't care for me. He's giving me freedom because he loves me. Clutching the papers to my chest, I inhale deeply, savoring the biggest love declaration of my life.

"There's one more," Russell says.

I'm my own woman. The house of my dreams belongs to me. Damian Hart loves me enough to let me go. I've made my peace with my past on that tower. I promised myself if I get out of there alive, I'd live every moment without regrets. What Damian and I had was perfect in its imperfection. We found beauty in our ugly worlds. I was just too damaged to see it. I have love, the deep and profound kind you sense on first sight and carry to your grave and into forever. I had Damian. I found a soul mate, and even if he never wants to see me again for the warped reasons he conjured in his mind, I'll never need a single thing more.

Russell's voice carries to me through the chirp of birds and the croak of a frog. "Lina?"

I haven't noticed he's opened the window. His eyes are warm and welcoming. I look away from the invitation in his gaze because I don't want to hurt him.

He sighs. "Maybe it's too soon."

"I love him, Russell."

He's silent for a while. When he speaks again, his voice has lost its hopeful edge. "I know."

"Are you angry?"

"I used to be, but I don't think Damian is as bad as I thought."
I laugh. "He's worse."

He joins me with a chuckle. "Damn right."

"Is that why you're here? Damian thought you're a better man?"

"It doesn't matter why I'm here. What matters is why you are." He motions at the papers I clutch against my chest. "Finish it."

This isn't just about reading a stack of papers. It's about moving on. Lifting the last document from the pile, I hold it to the light. It's a birth certificate. Joshua Clarke. My heartbeat slows to a thump that falls loud in my ears. I check the date. It can't be, and yet, deep in my soul I know the truth.

Covering my mouth with a hand, I suppress a sob. It takes a moment to regain my composure. I can only stare at the official words on the yellow piece of paper, a clinical record that reflects nothing of the devastation that shreds my heart.

Where is he? Damian's words run painfully through my mind.

"Damian found the grave," I say when I can speak again.

"Not the grave," Russell replies gently.

I look at him quickly. "What?"

"He isn't dead."

I blink fast, trying to make sense of a meaning that refuses to sink in. "What?"

"The boy. Your son. He's not dead."

"What?" I shake my head. It doesn't make sense.

"Go inside, Lina."

"But… No. I don't understand."

He gets out and comes around the car to open my door. "Come on."

"Russell."

He takes my hand when I don't move, pulling me out and turning me to face the cottage. An elderly lady and a boy stand in the door. I vaguely register her gray hair and homely face, but I can only focus on the child. He must be around two years old. He has my lips and eyes.

"It can't be," I whisper.

"They're waiting for you," Russell says behind me. "Go on."

He encourages me with a hand on my lower back, but I'm stuck in fear. What if it's a mistake? What if he's not mine? He doesn't know me. What if he doesn't understand? What if he doesn't like me? What if I screw this up?

Russell's voice is patient. "She calls him Josh."

Joshua Daniels. My maternal grandfather.

My heart leaps with a crazy beat. I take one step, and then another. That's how we'll do this. One step at a time. I walk until I'm in front of them, aware of their curious gazes.

Extending a hand, I introduce myself to the woman who I presume to be Josh's caretaker. "I'm Lina. It's a pleasure to meet you."

Her handshake is strong. "Same here, Mrs. Hart. You can call me Susan."

Going down on my haunches, I offer Josh a smile. "Hi, there."

He sticks his finger in his mouth and drills his big toe into the ground.

"I'm Lina."

"Are you better, now?"

"Yes," I say, fighting my overpowering emotions. "Much better."

"We have tea and cake waiting," Susan says.

I hold my hand out to Josh. "Shall we go inside, then?"

He hesitates for a moment, but then folds his fingers around mine. They're warm and sticky, just like I always imagined a child's to be. Gulping down a sob, I straighten my spine. We have much to work through, and many answers I'd like. I want to know everything I missed, from his first tooth to his first step. I want to know when he smiled for the first time, and what his favorite food is. Yes, there's much to learn, but we have time.

On the step, I look back to see if Russell is coming inside with us. He's leaning on the car, arms crossed. He wears a thoughtful smile, the kind that says goodbye. I give him a small nod, offering my gratitude, before stepping over the threshold of a new life.

TWO MOMENTOUS THINGS happen during the following weeks. I receive a newspaper clipping in the mail about a South African born woman who'd been found dead in her house in Switzerland. The cause of death was an overdose of sleeping pills. I don't have to look at the name. I recognize her photo. I still don't know what made her push the key under my door. Would she have done it if she'd known I'd kill Jack? The rage in me was too great. There was no other course of action I could've taken. If given another chance, I'd do it all over again. Despite the fact that Dora freed me, the torture had been going on for too long to find more than fleeting compassion in my heart for her passing. We never communicated. I never knew the woman who'd fed me an egg and slice of bread a day with a cup of water. When I've read the article, I flush the clipping down the toilet. Damian has been to Switzerland around the date of her death. You don't have to be Einstein to connect the dots.

The second big event is the arrest of Dr. Dickenson and the closing down of Willowbrook. The staff, including the ones who'd been employed during my admission, were charged with fraud, assault, and the intention to do serious bodily harm. After Carte Blanche had received an anonymous tip-off, one of their investigative reporters went in under cover with a hidden camera. The story made international news, resulting in an investigation and the uncovering of a hideous and cruel institution. It's a scandal the country won't live down for a long time.

After giving it much thought, I decide it's time for the world to know the truth or at least a part of it. In an exclusive television interview, I tell what happened at Willowbrook. I tell the truth about how Harold framed Damian and stole his discovery, and how Damian went to jail innocently while I was pawned off to Jack in exchange for the mining rights. I tell the world about my imprisonment and torture, and that I shot Jack. My lawyer advised me against it, but it was part of the weight I needed to get off my chest.

An investigation that takes several days follows. In the end, the judges and psychologist who attended my hearing decide I had indeed not been responsible for my actions at the time, and no charges are laid. Reyno testified to my treatment and recovery, stating I'm a capable mother and no threat to society or myself. What I don't talk about is Zane's kidnapping and how Damian forced me into marriage. We've done him enough harm. I'm not going to send him to jail for a second time. He did what he did because he loves me. Since I told the truth about Jack and Harold, the media speculated that Dora's suicide was due to her burden of guilt. A few weeks later, the investigation into Zane and Anne's murders are closed due to a lack of evidence.

I take my time to settle in with Josh. I take my time to enjoy my autonomy and independence. The situation is new to all of us. We need time to adapt. I spend every free moment with Josh, reveling at the wonder of him, and when he's in bed at night, I ask Susan to tell me stories about him.

Reyno offers me a contract, a real one for a real job that comes with health and retirement benefits. The day I sign it is one of the happiest of my life. It's good to earn my own money. It's good to figure out what I like, and to decorate a house that's ours. I get my driver's license and buy a car. When winter changes into spring, I plant sweet peas and daisies in the garden.

Life on the water is everything I've dreamt of. Susan, Josh, and I take our small boat out on weekends. Who would've guessed I'd enjoy fishing? I make friends with our neighbors, and Josh has plenty of play dates. People still recognize me wherever I go, but the novelty of being stared at is wearing off. I'm getting better at coping with it and diverting the curious questions.

Sometimes, I get the feeling someone is watching me. A few times, I notice men trailing me in traffic or shopping malls. I know they're Damian's men. He's become a powerful man. He has alliances in all the right places, including the law enforcement department. During all the time I'm making a home for Josh and a new life for myself, there's no news from him, not even a phone call. I keep in touch with Brink, who tells me Damian is living alone in the big house, throwing himself into work. When the longing gets too much, I call Fouché, who tells me Damian is doing fine. I can't help myself from asking if he has someone new in his life. According to Fouché, every single woman, widow, and gold digger is running after him, but he's not seeing anyone. The news warms my heart. I haven't signed the divorce papers. I still have a chance.

Three months after Russell brought me home from the hospital, a man in a blue suit knocks on my door. It's a sunny Saturday morning. Josh is playing with his new train in the backyard while I'm baking scones for breakfast. Susan gets the door and tells me a messenger wants to see me.

Wiping my hands on my apron, I meet the man at the door. "Can I help you?"

His manner is curt and professional. "I'm here on Mr. Hart's request, ma'am."

"Yes?" I say, even if I already know what the visit is about.

"He would like for you to sign the divorce papers."

"Thank you for letting me know, but you didn't have to drive all the way out here just to tell me this."

"You don't understand. I'm to wait for the papers and deliver them to him."

"I'll deliver them myself, thank you."

"When?"

I give him a hard look. "When I'm ready."

"Sorry, ma'am, but if I return empty-handed, Mr. Hart would like to know a date."

"Soon."

I close the door before he can say more. I'm being rude, but I'm not going to communicate with my husband via a messenger. Anyway, it's time I face Damian. I've healed from the gunshot, Josh is adapting well in his crèche, Susan is happy here, and I'm a working mom earning a decent salary. I've done what I set out to do. This can't be put off any longer.

After lunch, I put on a pretty dress and make-up, and tell Susan I'll be out for the rest of the afternoon. The drive to Erasmuskloof has my stomach churning and my insides twisting. Despite everything, I'm not sure what kind of a reception I'll get. I'm not even sure how Damian feels about seeing me. I'm certain he loves me, or he wouldn't have given me my freedom, my inheritance, and a house, but maybe he doesn't want to be a dad. Maybe he doesn't see himself living with a family. Maybe I come with too much baggage. Damian is wealthy and successful. His criminal record has been cleared. Like Fouché said, women are falling over themselves to be the next in line to wear his diamonds. The choice is wide with much more enticing and less complicated partners than me. Still, I'm not going to allow my fear to stop me from paying him this visit. I have to do this. If he sends me away after I've spoken my mind, I'll respect his choice and sign the papers, no matter how hard it'll be.

There's a new guard at the gate who doesn't know me. He tells me to get out of the car so he can search me. At least Damian is home. It was a gamble, but I didn't want to warn him of my visit in the fear he'd refuse me. At the sight of my arms, the guard apologizes profusely.

"I'm sorry, Mrs. Hart. I didn't recognize you."

"No problem. You're just doing your job."

He runs to the guardhouse to dial the house. I hold my breath as he speaks into the intercom. What if Damian doesn't let me in? I'm biting my nails as I wait for the verdict, but the gates swing open and the guard waves me through.

The grass has been burnt in preparation for summer. I itch to check the bat boxes but drive straight to the house and park in the circular driveway. My heart batters my ribs as I approach the door. It's both foreign and familiar. I remember coming here after our wedding like yesterday, and yet, it feels like it was years ago. That I have to knock is a bad sign. If Damian were excited to see me, he would've met me at the door. Placing a hand protectively over my stomach, I wait.

I'm taken aback when the door opens to a stranger's face.

"Good afternoon, Mrs. Hart. I'm Klara, the housekeeper. Please come inside."

Damian employed a housekeeper. That's not good. He wouldn't have done that if he weren't planning on staying indefinitely in a house he once claimed to find old and stuffy.

I follow Klara up the familiar staircase to the study, my courage failing with every step. When she leaves me in front of the door, I take a deep breath and knock.

"Come in," Damian's deep voice calls from inside.

I have an irrational urge to fling the door open and rush into his arms. I recall the day of our wedding, when he'd brought me here and offered me a drink to settle my nerves. I remember the hostility and the fear. I want to start over, with a clean slate. It's that hope that makes me behave like a teenager, yanking open the door, ready to take the biggest gamble of my life.

I realize my mistake too late. Damian isn't alone. Tony is with him. They're sitting on opposite sides of the big desk, papers spread out in front of them. Tony jerks his head toward me. His eyes flare in surprise.

Damian's face is expressionless. He looks at me like one would look at the selection of coffee in a supermarket, wondering which brand to buy. My confidence takes a knock, but I stand my ground.

Damian's gaze slips to the brown envelope I clutch in my hand. "Tony, you remember Lina."

Tony clears his throat and looks back at Damian. "That should wrap it up. I'll send you the buyer list."

He gathers his papers and stuffs them into a satchel before flitting past me and out the door. I suppose our first encounter in this room was enough for Tony. He's not sticking around to witness what will happen this time. Both Damian and I have been followed relentlessly by paparazzi. It's common knowledge we don't live together.

When the front door bangs, I'm suddenly over-conscious of the awkward silence in the study.

"Hi." I cringe inwardly at how hoarse my voice sounds.

"Hello, Lina. You look well."

"Thank you. So do you."

"Drink?"

I can do with one, but I'm not drinking alcohol. I'd rather just get to the many points I want to tick off my list, starting with, "You didn't come to see me in hospital."

He folds his hands together. "I was there."

"While I was unconscious."

"I thought it would be easier that way."

His eyes track my movement as I walk to his desk. "Easier for who?"

"Both of us."

I don't take the seat Tony has left, but sit down on the corner of the desk, so close I can touch his arm if I reach out. "There are things I wanted to say to you."

His demeanor is cold, distant. "Why are you here?"

I drop the envelope in front of him.

He doesn't as much as glance at it. "You could've given it to my messenger."

"You didn't give me a chance to say thank you."

"For what?"

"For saving my life. For the house. For my sanity. For giving me freedom." I swallow down untimely emotions that bubble to the surface. "For Josh."

"Thanks for speaking out and getting my record cleared. We're even."

"You didn't tell me you were going to Switzerland to kill Dora."

"I didn't kill Dora."

"Not technically."

"What's your point?"

"Did you hold a gun to her head so she'd swallow the pills?"

"I gave her a choice. She chose pills."

"Why did you do it?"

"To avenge you. She deserved nothing less."

"How did you find Josh?"

"I asked Dalton."

"Right before you dropped him."

His nostrils flare. "Yes, right before I sent him to the fate he had planned for you." There's a chill to his voice. "Seems fitting, no?"

"Your men are still following me."

"Are they bothering you?"

"No. I was just wondering why you'd think I still need protection."

"The world is full of threats, Lina. I'm not taking any chances."

"Is it going to be a permanent thing?"

"Yes, a permanent *thing*."

"You don't owe me anything."

"That's not the way I see it, but security stays, regardless. The mere fact that you were once connected to me will always make you a potential target."

"Were?" I bite my lip, imploring him with my eyes.

"You got what you wanted. I thought you'd moved on."

"You can say that. I've been very busy building a new life."

A muscle ticks in his jaw. "Then there's nothing left to say."

I motion at the envelope. "Open it."

He glares at me, his bitter chocolate eyes hostile. It reminds me of how it was when we first got together. This is worse, because there's no lust in his regard. There's no thirst for revenge. There's nothing. It's enough to make me want to flee, but I'm not giving up this easily.

"Open it. Please."

Pursing his lips, he pulls the envelope toward him, but he doesn't open it. He just stares at the brown paper under his palm. I can't help but notice the largeness of his hand and the veins that disappear under his sleeve shirt. I remember the feel of those hands on my skin, and I long for it with such intensity my chest hurts. There was a time, not so long ago, when touching Damian was my freedom. His house was my prison, but I had access to his body. Now I am free, and the liberties of intimacy are no longer part of my privileges. It's a crazy reversed situation, but I know what I want.

After a while, he lifts his eyes to mine. "I suppose I deserve this."

"What?"

"Revenge."

He's referring to the time he made me fuck him for a copy of the evidence, but he's got the reason I'm doing this wrong.

Finally, he reaches for the letter opener and cuts through the seal. He's all business-like as he pulls out the white sheets. It's as if he's adopted a professional persona to distance himself from me and what he expects to find inside. He looks at the bottom of the first page where my initials are missing, and then flips through the stack, coming to a halt on the last page where only his signature is signed.

There's genuine confusion on his face when he looks back at me. "What game are you playing? Aren't you happy with the terms? Do you need more money? What is it you want?"

"You."

He places the papers on his desk, meticulously square, and pushes them away. "No."

My stomach drops. "What?"

"It's not going to happen."

I have to force the word from my throat. "Why?"

He gets to his feet. "I'll see you out."

My voice rises with the anguish that's slicing through me. "I deserve a reason."

"Don't do this, Lina."

"Is it Josh? Is it because I have a child?" If it's because he doesn't want children, we're definitely over.

"Jesus, no." He drags a hand over his face. "It's got nothing to do with Josh."

"What then? I know you love me, or you wouldn't have offered me a divorce."

"Do you know how fucking wrong that sounds?"

"Yes," I whisper, "but we've never been your average couple. I love you, Damian. You know. You've always known."

"You wanted your freedom, and you deserve it."

"I wanted the freedom to be independent, to make my own choices, not to be free of our marriage."

"It was too damn hard to let you go once. I can't do it again."

A flicker of hope lifts from the ashes of my emotions. "I choose you. I choose us, if you'll have me with my baggage and child."

Pressing his hands on either side of my body, he cages me in with his arms. "You don't understand. If I take you back, I'm never letting you go. Ever. If you make this choice, you're stuck with me. Letting you go nearly killed me. I won't have the strength to do it again. If you let me back into your life, you belong to me for as long as we both shall live." His regard is fierce, angry almost. "Can you handle that?"

If his speech was supposed to put me off, it didn't work. I know what I'm letting myself in for. "I'm not letting go, either. You're mine, Damian. You can come back home with me, and we can learn to be a family, each with our space to grow, and you can tell those women running after you to back the hell off because you're taken." I flash him my wedding band and ridiculously big diamond. "This ring says so, and so does the contract we both signed on the day you married me."

He clenches his jaw as he searches my eyes. Two seconds pass. "You better be damn well sure about this."

Snaking my arms around his neck, I plant a kiss on his lips. "I wouldn't have been here if I weren't. I came to take you home."

Emotions run through his eyes. Still he doubts me, fights me. "You waited three fucking months to tell me this?"

"I had a life to sort out. I'm not coming to you broken and needing to be fixed. I'm coming to you whole, offering you everything I have, if you'll have it."

He rests his forehead against mine. "Fuck, Lina."

"That's all you have to say?"

He grins against my lips. "Fuck, yes."

"That's better."

He cups my ass, jerking me to the edge of the desk and against his hardness. "There's something else that'll be even better."

"Wait." I push on his chest. "There's more I need to say."

He growls. "Can you say it quickly? It's been a while."

"I'm pregnant."

He releases me so fast he stumbles a step back. "What?"

My hope dwindles again. Maybe he doesn't want this, but he's the one who refused me birth control. "We didn't use protection, Damian."

"I know that. Say it again."

"I'm pregnant."

He looks shell-shocked, but also something else. He looks at me as if he's seeing me for the first time, and when his gaze drops to my stomach, there's reverence in his eyes.

He lifts those dark, haunted eyes to my face. "How long?"

"Three months."

His jaw locks. "You should've told me."

"I wanted to sort out my life, first. I needed that time alone, and I knew you wouldn't grant it to me if we got together again."

He drags a hand over his face, staring at me with that stunned look.

"If this isn't what you want," I continue, "I'll understand."

"If this isn't what I want." He raises his head to the ceiling and closes his eyes. When he looks back at me, he appears upset. "I knew exactly what I was doing fucking you without a condom."

"Then we're okay?"

"No, Lina. We're not okay. We're better than okay."

"You mean you're happy?"

He lets out a long breath. "Ecstatic." Grabbing me to him, he crushes me in his arms. "But if you ever hold back information of this proportion from me again, anything that concerns you, me, or us, there'll be consequences, and you're not going to like them."

"You burnt your whips and paddles."

"There are other ways," he says in a low voice, his lips ghosting over mine.

"Denying me orgasms is a hard limit."

"Fine. We can go shopping for toys."

"Toys?"

"I'm a semi-sadist, and you enjoy the pain."

"Semi-pain," I correct.

"Semi," he agrees, "but from now on, I want to know everything. I want to know when you have a menstrual cramp and when you bump your toe." He taps my temple. "I want to know when you're sad or have a doubt. Can you do that for me?"

"Can you give me space?"

After a couple of seconds, he asks, "How much space?"

"Enough to be me."

"Yeah." He frames my face between his hands. "That's doable, because I want all of you, everything you are, and everything you're yet to become."

Biting my lip, I give him a sultry look. "I think this can work."

"I know it can." He slides me off the desk and lifts me into his arms.

"What are you doing?"

"I was going to fuck you until you pass out, but seeing you're in a delicate condition, I'm going to make love to you until the sun comes up."

My laugh is happy. Free. "I have to get home. I have to be there for Josh when he goes to bed."

"I know. That's why I'm coming with you."

I rest my head on his shoulder. "You are?"

"You're never sleeping alone again, Mrs. Hart."

"That's the best promise I've heard in a long time." When he starts moving toward the door, I press a hand on his chest. "Wait. What about the house? What about the garden and the bats?"

"Stop worrying about the bats."

"But—"

"I had a good offer for the house. The buyer is a nature conservationist. He wants to maintain things as they are."

I can't help but smirk. "*Things?*"

"Are you being condescending? I think I need to teach you a *thing* or two, put your new brave pussy back in its place."

My smile is so big it stretches my cheek muscles.

"Do that again," he commands in a husky voice.

"Do what again?"

"Smile for me."

It's easy. I have a lot to be happy about.

An answering curve pulls at his lips, and his eyes light up with a dangerous glint. "You're so fucked, Lina."

As I nestle deeper into his arms, a weight lifts off my heart. It all but floats up to heaven.

I'm no longer crazy.

I'm no longer a hostage to our past or a prisoner to my husband's revenge.

I'm no longer Harold's fake daughter or Damian's forced wife.

I'm Angelina Hart, tired mother, happy assistant, and above all the woman who loves Damian.

Always have.

Always will.

Man

Krinar World Novels
(Futuristic Romance)
The Krinar Experiment
The Krinar's Informant

ABOUT THE AUTHOR

Charmaine Pauls was born in Bloemfontein, South Africa. She obtained a degree in Communication at the University of Potchefstroom and followed a diverse career path in journalism, public relations, advertising, communications, photography, graphic design, and brand marketing. Her writing has always been an integral part of her professions.

After relocating to Chile with her French husband, she fulfilled her passion to write creatively full-time. Charmaine has published eighteen novels since 2011, as well as several short stories and articles. Two of her short stories were selected for publication in an African anthology from across the continent by the International Society of Literary Fellows in conjunction with the International Research Council on African Literature and Culture.

When she is not writing, she likes to travel, read, and rescue cats. Charmaine currently lives in Montpellier with her husband and children. Their household is a linguistic mélange of Afrikaans, English, French and Spanish.

Join Charmaine's mailing list
https://charmainepauls.com/subscribe/

Join Charmaine's readers' group on Facebook
http://bit.ly/CPaulsFBGroup

Read more about Charmaine's novels and short stories on
https://charmainepauls.com

Connect with Charmaine

Facebook
http://bit.ly/Charmaine-Pauls-Facebook

Amazon
http://bit.ly/Charmaine-Pauls-Amazon

Goodreads
http://bit.ly/Charmaine-Pauls-Goodreads

Twitter
https://twitter.com/CharmainePauls

Instagram
https://instagram.com/charmainepaulsbooks

BookBub
http://bit.ly/CPaulsBB

46466701R00258

Made in the USA
San Bernardino, CA
06 August 2019